A Distortion of Fate

A TAPESTRY NOVEL

M. J. LINDSEY

To Juniper,
Thanks for reading!
MJ Lindsey

Copyright © 2024 by M.J. Lindsey

All rights reserved.

No part of this publication may be reproduced, distributed, or transmitted in any form or by any means, including photocopying, recording, or other electronic or mechanical methods, without the prior written permission of the publisher, except as permitted by U.S. copyright law. For permission requests, contact Three Bugs Publishing.

The story, all names, characters, and incidents portrayed in this production are fictitious. No identification with actual persons (living or deceased), places, buildings, and products is intended or should be inferred.

Book Cover by Helena Elias

ISBN: 978-1-965213-03-2 (ebook)
ISBN: 978-1-965213-02-5 (paperback)

For my father
Who listened to a strange little girl.

NORTH SEA

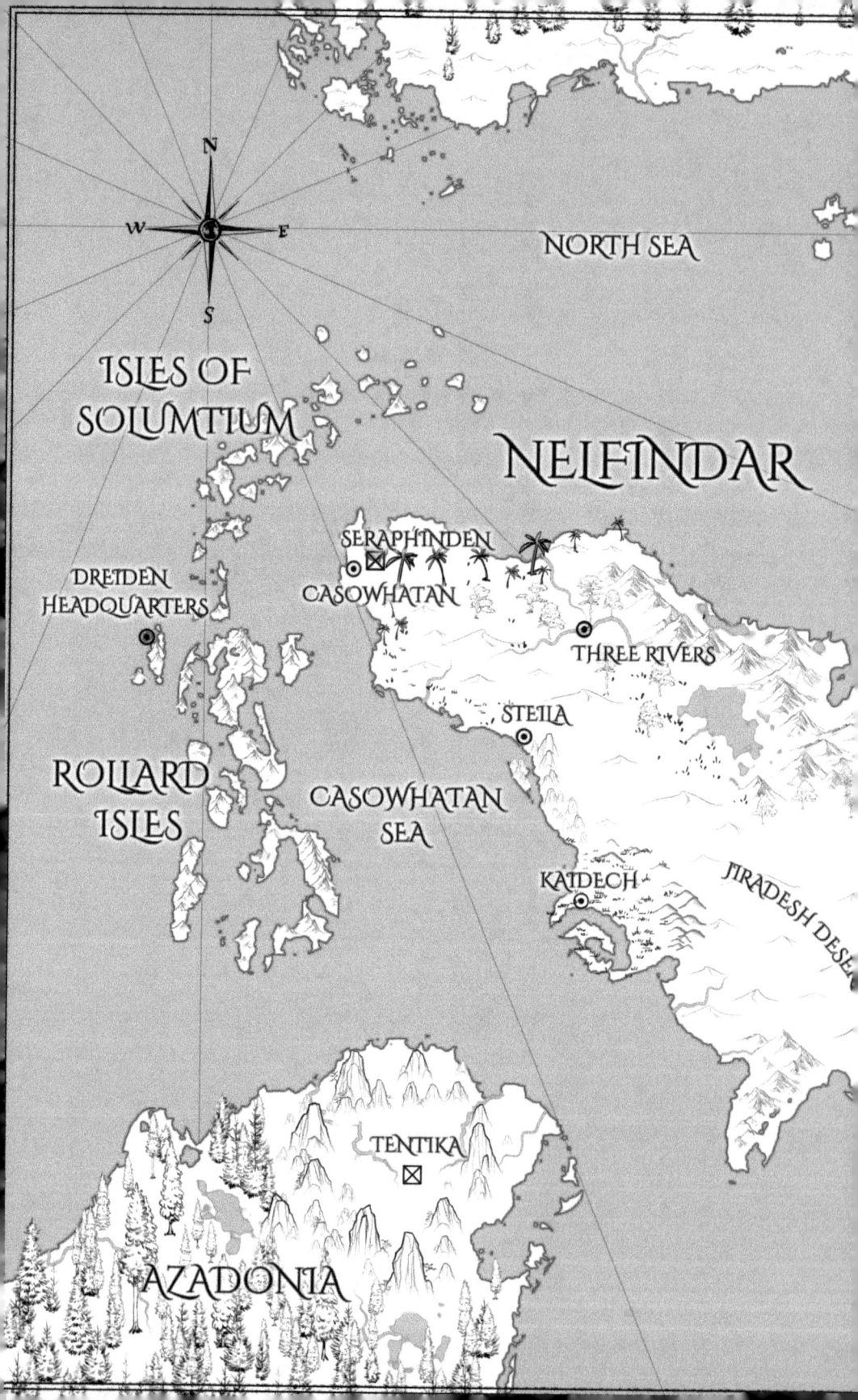

ISLES OF SOLUMTIUM

NELFINDAR

SERAPHINDEN

CASOWHATAN

DREIDEN HEADQUARTERS

THREE RIVERS

STEILA

ROLLARD ISLES

CASOWHATAN SEA

KAIDECH

JIRADESH DESERT

TENTIKA

AZADONIA

TERATHIAN NORTHLANDS

PAZIR
⊠ YALUSA

KAMIL ⊙

GEMBOITA ⊙

FENCATA ⊙

TOBOBA ⊠

TSORAP MOUNTAINS

TENINCA'PUI ⊙

CHIRANA ⊠
SHARINASH FOREST
⊙ KARVAL

CHORI

A Glossary of Names and Terms

Abiathar Methu'su — An operative in Nelfindar's Green Wing during the Nelfinden gray period.

Aetech – The colloquial abbreviation of Aethertech Mechanics, Nelfindar's flagship distortion company, founded shortly after the Nelfinden gray period.

Azadonia – Kath's oldest civilization, stemming back since pre-cataclysm times. The Azadonians moved below ground to survive the event, building out underground structures that endured for a near-millennium.

Bovak Ani – The Tera'thian Emperor.

Casowhatan — The sea bordering Nelfindar to its south and west.

Cataclysm — A catastrophic natural disaster which wiped out the majority of human civilization. Research from Tennca'Pui has attributed it to a rapid shifting of Kath's magnetic poles.

Chikoto — An Azadonian term which translates roughly to "born from an asshole."

Chira'na – Nelfindar's southernmost city. Chira'na's walls were built by temu'amic in the year 263 post-cataclysm, when Nelfindar was under Tera'thian occupation.

Chori — A nation to the east of Nelfindar, and Nelfindar's greatest threat during the gray period.

Cul'Mon — The Tera'thian Tohatu.

Distortion — The manipulation of energy from unmanifested realities into present reality.

Dowaga — A three-bladed weapon of Chori origin, favored for its versatility as both a throwing and melee weapon. The dowagian arts developed around using the dowaga as a primarily defensive tool.

Dreiden – A rival Nelfinden distortion corporation aiming to break Aetech's monopoly over distortion trade.

Gray Period — The decades spanning the hiatus of the Ruxian bloodline from Nelfindar's throne up until Prime Taranil's election as oligarchical head and the ensuing Azadonian quarantine and embargo of all foreign trade.

Groundling — A caste in Nelfinden society which resides on the ground, as opposed to on the skywalk. According to the 748 post-cataclysm Nelfinden census, the Groundling Caste constitutes 96% of the Nelfinden populus.

Hakuni — An Azadonian term of endearment translating directly to "honeyed tea".

Haloucha — Nelfinden street fare equally famed for its size and its grease. Sixteen layers of dough are bundled around the chef's choice of filling before it is deep fried in cintas oil.

Hukata — A multitiered costume worn by Azadonian dancers of the Lethoso

Jenolavia — Azadonia's queen and prime matriarch leading up to the Kovathian coup

Jiradesh — A desert spanning the majority of Nelfindar's central landscape

Kaidech — A Nelfinden port city along the Casowhatan and the major hub for Nelfinden/Azadonian trade during the Nelfinden gray period

Korshuva — An upper class Groundling district in the Nelfinden capital city of Seraphinden

Kovathians — A dissonant sect of Azadonia's legislation with strong allegiances to the Tera'thian state.

Kretch — A Nelfinden curse meaning "my ass is in front of me."

Lethoso – An Azadonian art from, primarily encompassed by a step dance conducted in subterranean pools.

Moss – Slang for brophyta arcana, a type of moss which thrives in the Azadonian underground. When used in its natural form, brophyta arcana is a mild stimulative with anti-inflammatory properties. When processed into tab form, as traded in the Nelfinden dark market, moss takes on hallucinogenic and analgesic effects. In this form, it is extremely addictive and its withdrawal can be deadly.

Nelfindar – A continent and nation in Kath.

Pazir – A large island nation in the Northern Sea. Pazir is renowned for its spices and the general wealth of its population.

Prime — In Nelfinden hierarchy, the supreme authority of a group or division, specifically in government or military.

Ratka – A tera'thian glyph meaning "survivor."

Ruxian – A race of humans with a mutation in their pineal gland which allows them extrasensory perception to see indefinite probabilities or realities and, when trained, the ability to control physical futures.

Ruxichorin – A synthetic simulation of the Ruxian hormone which allows for the distortion of energy.

Seraphinden — The Nelfinden capital city, named after its first Ruxian king, Natoluphut Seraphindo.

Skywalk — A series of buildings and residences built six stories above the ground and home to the Nelfinden elite. In high Nelfinden society, it is seen as a sign of purity for patricians to have never touched the ground.

Sharinash — Nelfindar's densest deciduous forest, west of the Tsorlap mountains.

Shrat – A Nelfinden curse meaning "gull excrement" or guano.

Shrokan - A Groundling district in the Nelfinden capital city of Seraphinden with a reputation for being the most impoverished region in all of greater Kath.

Strikapa — A deadly pathogen spread through the skin or by intake of affected fluids.

Taranil — The current Nelfinden Prime.

Temu'amic – A system of labor established by the Tera'thian state in which children are bred in slavery and "milled" before reaching adulthood.

Tennca'Pui – A sovereign, monastic colony of eunuchs stationed east of Nelfindar's Tsorlap mountains. Tennca'Pui's cenobites are dedicated to the lifelong study of natural sciences and receive regular research commissions from the Nelfinden Capital.

Tentika — The Azadonian capital.

Tera'thia — A dominant nation to the north of Nelfindar.

Tipiana — Traditional Azadonian garb. A one-size-fits-all sheet of silk, produced by Azadonia's cavern worms, is wrapped around the body six times and tied on the side. This unisex outfit is most often embroidered with religious symbols, birds, or flowers.

Tohatu — The commander of the Tera'thian military.

Chapter 1
Calverous

Four hundred and twenty-three days.

If Calver's scheme went according to design—and Fates help him, it would—he had four hundred and twenty-three days left to live.

Calver crouched outside the city of Chira'na, waiting to take the next step—a step closer to redemption, a step closer to death. The city's walls loomed high above him, their storm-colored stone stretching four stories into aether. He adhered to their shadows as his eyes fixated on the still-vacant point where the glinting metal of the train's guiderail connected with the skyline.

The distortion shipment was late.

His lips, which rarely fell into any expression, twitched downward. Believing that a single shipment demolition might fix something already lost to the lockbox of the past was stupid enough. Believing it while its likelihood for success quickly evaporated was insanity.

But sometimes, one believed for the sake of belief itself: a phantasmal thing—bright, beautiful, and with all the empty meaning that he could catch in his fist...

Calver shifted like the ground was hot beneath his feet. The grasslands outside of Chira'na were redolent with the primal echo of prowling beasts, heavy with the musk of earth and the whispers of tall grass in an endless breeze. He forced air into his chest to the slow cadence of the void mantra; ground the ball of his foot into the earth; checked the straps that holstered his steel dowaga for the tenth time—*anything* to ward off the churn of his stomach, the constriction of his lungs, and the subsequent *presence* for which panic served as harbinger.

The open air would elude him soon enough, when he bartered it for the stale rot of the city within. Fates help him, after so many years a slave, how was it that the scents of freedom and fear were one and the same? He swallowed back his nerves. The motion always came with difficulty, given that he lacked a tongue, but more so at times like this when his mouth ran dry.

Aetech's locomotives ran on automated timetables. The shipment would come. Had to come. He'd timed dozens of shipments. Practiced endlessly and for any contingency.

Except for the impossible: the fated train not showing up.

Fuck. He'd missed something. He knew it in his bones. He knew it like any dowagist knew his blades. Like a—

Calver's skin prickled in warning.

No. Nope.

He forced the intrusion down, leaning instead into the fluttering in his chest at the thought of what might await him should he succeed: Fankalo's trust. An invitation to return home, even. Finally not being alone. Calver inched forward as though the futile motion might grant him a vision of the locomotive.

Was there a word for holding on to hope, even when a person knew a thing to be hopeless? His mouth steeled into a line. Psychosis, maybe.

The horizon remained as empty as a beggar's bowl. *Fuck.* In his circumstance, who wouldn't have psychosis?

Calver's forced stoicism faltered for a heartbeat, the swell of anxiety brimming over his well of control. That was all it took. The Survivor's disembodied presence seeped forward in his skull like water trickling from the first crack in a dam. Its voice was as cold as steel in the depths of winter and, though it came as a whisper, it felt like it echoed across the Four Winds.

{You will fail in this task. Let me do it. I lack the weakness you possess.}

Calver gripped at his hair, wincing against the sudden spike of pressure.

No, nononono.

{Let me.}

A shuddering breath in. Another out. He held back the mind-djinn's ever-building surge against him with a focused wash of calm.

Just one day. Just one job without the Survivor bloodying his hands.

The presence was gone without a trace, like yesterday's dream.

Calver released his grip on his hair and leaned against the wall behind him, resting his head on its cool stone. That Fankalo had trusted him alone with this task was a small miracle. He was another accident waiting to happen. He slid his fingers across the rough surface of the wall, reassuring himself of his control over his body.

Chira'na's walls had stood through five centuries of rising and setting suns, never falling, never failing. He could only speculate at how the slow creep of time might alter the latent mentality rooted in such a structure. Walls, like man, desired to serve a purpose. And without the possibility of a threat from the outside, their purpose could only turn toward keeping something in.

That gave them solidarity.

Calver shook off his unease and crept forward again, eyes fixed on the horizon.

It was then that Aetech's distortion-powered locomotive careened into view from beyond a grassy hillside in the distance. A jolt of adrenaline spiked into him. This was his chance—his only chance—to make Fankalo's plan fall into place. Yet even as Calver made the next step, he knew he was beyond redemption—that even success today wouldn't fix things between them. The sliver of him that wasn't ready to die still hoped that Fankalo disagreed.

He broke into a run, hugging close to the wall, sights set on the port gate where he would intercept Aetech's machine. The shadow cast by the wall at mid-lowsun was narrow—half an arm's span. He glanced up to ensure none of the guardsmen on the ramparts had the unlikely thought to crane their necks beyond the wall to look down.

Of course, they did not. The plan *would* work. The plan was still without error.

He arrived at the gate, a distortion-powered barrier which only opened in tandem with the train's sensors. The locomotive slowed to a creep as it passed through the stone walls. Timing it carefully, Calver slipped into the joint between the penultimate and final carriage and braced himself with the steady press of his limbs as the machine glided into Chira'na.

When the train reached a full stop inside the walls of the isolated port compound, the glowing guideway below him deactivated. Calver dropped down into its waist-high trench, landing soundlessly in a crouch. These last six carriages held the Aetech shipment that Fankalo wanted eliminated. He only had minutes before the port's guards and employees would spill onto the platform to unload it.

He reached into his cloak to palm a small glass orb. The device was an Aetech distortion lamp, but not. He had tampered with it, and four others, in the way that only he could, shifting its ability to retain influx energy so that it would overcharge rapidly and exponentially. He'd lost more than a finger practicing the limit at which he would replace its influx retainer. Not his fingers, true, but he'd lost them nevertheless.

He crawled on knees and elbows through the metal guide rail, planting the lamps beneath every other carriage as he progressed to the front of the train. Chaos, his broad shoulders nearly brushed against the sides. Navigating the space felt horrifyingly similar to the day he'd wriggled through the black tunnels of the Tera'thian palace sewer system. When sludge had coated the fresh, bleeding wounds of the disciplinary barbs in his back.

Four hundred and twenty-three days.

It wasn't long before he would return there, to the final destiny that waited for him.

Void.

In moments like this, moments when his every nerve sat on a knife's edge, the number seemed too short. It went to show what he was at the core of things: a coward.

If he weren't, Fankalo would have never sent him away.

Void.

Calver filled his lungs again to quell the dark force shifting from the back of his mind. He would show Fankalo he could complete this task without bloodshed, for once.

He would discontinue the broken legacy of his father.

He would be dependable until the bitter end.

He—

Dozens of footsteps suddenly echoed from the base of the car directly above him, like passengers preparing to disembark. Calver's tissues turned to timber.

No one should be on this train.

The door to the carriage opened. Calver listened with bated breath to the crescendo of fast-falling footsteps against the port dock above him.

Then a man's voice spoke in Tera'thian, the language from his nightmares. "Secure the port before we unload."

Calver's eyes screwed shut. Tera'thians couldn't be in Chira'na. This couldn't be happening—Cul'Mon's agents tracking him past enemy lines. Not now... He forced himself to breathe. To keep control of his mind. His once-master had pursued him unceasingly for eight years. He should have expected this, no matter the protections of Nelfinden territory.

After several frozen heartbeats, he summoned the nerve to peer out from the gap between two carriages. Sixteen men dispersed around the platform. They wore the blue sirwal and tunic of Chira'na's guard. Imposters. It was clever—the only way foreigners could have bypassed the city's strict entry policy without instigating an invasion protocol from the guard. Clever, and oh so wrong. Calver cringed lower. Every second weighed against him.

He brushed his thumb over the lamp's metal activator in his palm. Just a small application of pressure, and there wouldn't be Tera'thians in Chira'na anymore. No more problems. No one to capture him. No one to take him to Cul'Mon.

He hesitated, like he always did when left in control of his own mind. He didn't want to kill anyone else...

But these were Tera'thians.

Time stretched thinner until it was so appallingly fragile, Calver thought he might break along with it.

Collateral damage or not, the shipment needed to be destroyed or everything would fall apart.

Even as he made the decision, the men secured the perimeter of the port, many with three-bladed dowagas in hand. Calver cursed internally. That cut off his primary line of escape. He looked at the lamp and imagined what it would be like to combust into a thousand pieces with it. He and Fankalo had prepared for his martyrdom, yes, but at the Tera'thian coronation. Not now. If he couldn't retreat into the city, this task was a failure.

Teeth in lip, Calver turned back toward the port gate in Chira'na's wall to exit as he'd come in. It sealed itself shut before his eyes.

Trapped.

The Tera'thian commander spoke again. "There's a man in the furrow."

Fucked.

Calver sensed the projectile before he heard the twang of its release, saw it reflected in the guiderail around him, felt it displace the air in its deadly path. A metal tanka bit hurled into the furrow and burst the lamp in his hand, shattering its ruxechorin core.

Even more fucked.

He gritted his teeth and scrambled onto the platform. If he stayed in the trench any longer, it would become his steel mausoleum. Another flash of insight tuned him into a second tanka bit hurling with acute accuracy toward his skull. He unlatched the dowaga from his back and spun it in a single deft motion, blocking the bit. Its three ends—claw, dagger, scythe—pirouetted with his two-handed exchange at its axis, casting a pellucid steel reflection of his dark complexion over the imminent battle in his sight.

As he deflected the projectiles, an enemy dowagist lunged toward him in his peripheral vision. A second soldier followed, bearing a staved cosalt. Together, they struck.

Calver moved with supple ferocity, flipping his weapon forward to slam against the first imposter's scythe, then stepped back, twisting the dowaga in a flowing defensive pattern. The deadly strokes he'd dedicated his life to came with the ease of walking. The twang of a tanka launch heralded the zip of another barbed bit. Again, he deflected it and the next three that followed.

He was outnumbered.

No collateral damage. No bloodshed.

But defense wouldn't free him from this. Fates, who was he kidding? He'd never had a talent for sparing lives—only taking them.

He caught the shaft of the second soldier's cosalt with the dowaga's claw, wrenched it from his grip, and jabbed it through his chest. His swiping recoil plunged into the remaining soldier's neck, splitting bone from sinew. The men's dire screams pierced the air before they slumped, still-hearted, to the cobbles. The Survivor weighed against Calver, relishing the sound like music. Skin crawling, Calver voided his mind-djinn and reset his stance in preparation for the next assault...

And stared, chest heaving, at the bodies of the fallen, like gutted fish on the port platform. Claws scraped at the back of his throat.

He'd failed.

His eyes flashed to meet with the Tera'thian commander's, which were wide with sudden recognition. Of appearance or proficiency, it was hard to tell.

"Take him alive," the man ordered, confirming Calver's fears. They knew who he was and intended to return him to his infamous master. "Or dead, given no alternative."

Run.

His capture would be far worse than his execution.

Spinning on the ball of his foot, Calver jumped to the closest junction between carriages and clambered atop the train. His eyes darted to the city's walls—deemed insurmountable—separating him from momentary safety. *Chaos curse it.* He bolted toward them.

"Aim to wound," called the Tera'thian.

The enemy launched tanka projectiles at him as he raced along the tops of the carriages, metal clanging beneath his boots. Flying bits whizzed past him, close enough for their wind to caress his overgrown beard. With whatever senses the Fates had granted him, he always knew—or perhaps felt—how to lean to evade them.

Chest hammering, he pulled a metal disc of his own invention from his cloak. With a flick of his wrist, he hurled the distortion disc upwards a few spans in front of him. It hung stationary in the air. In a feat of equal parts stability and strength, he leaped off the train to grab it and pull himself on top, balancing on its hand-wide breadth.

It was a precarious maneuver, but one he'd practiced unceasingly. In the past eighteen months of isolation, he'd focused on evasion—the one thing which guaranteed his continued freedom—over anything else. Now for the even more precarious part. He flung out a second disc, this one closer to the city's wall, and repeated the process. Stepping onto the second disc, he deactivated the first, which promptly snapped back into his hand. Calver scaled from one disc to the next, giving the illusion of walking on air. A piece of him reveled in the thrill of it. The Tera'thians would think it was magic—a man who could walk among the clouds—fueling the reputation they'd forced him to inherit. Once he had been a slave. Now he was a god.

He banished the momentary confidence. Confidence was what had taken everything from him.

When he reached the ramparts, he scrambled over their lip. After waiting for his heart to slow, he peered back into the port. They had given up shooting at him. Half of the imposters had dispersed off the platform below him, exiting its isolated compound and looking for all the world like typical Chira'na guardsmen as they entered the city. He could only expect them to regroup and pursue him another way. Cul'Mon was like the fated sun to Calver's night: he just kept coming back.

He mirrored the distortion disc routine on the way down to the ground on the wall's exterior, jumping the final span. Once he hit solid earth, he broke into a sprint, heading for the grassy hills due east of the city.

He offered a quiet prayer to the Fates that it would stay that way—that he wouldn't be followed. A prayer he knew wouldn't be received. The Fates would never believe in a man who didn't believe in them.

Chapter 2

Niklaus

Niklaus lay recumbent on the polished marble floor of his quarters and stared upward. It was the burnt end of the day when the ceiling turned orange. Among other colors, anyhow. An ornate ceiling came with an elaborate variation of hues at sunset: crimson ridges, russet valleys, marigold everywhere between. Those shades were auspicious. A proposal that the day would soon end and sink beneath the ocean.

And drown there. Lucky bastard.

Niklaus craned his neck to affirm the status of his libations. A thin film of liquor coated the bottom of the glass in his hand. The other held his morning's crumpled work. He let his head conk back into the marble. He'd forgotten the paper was even there.

He sighed, the sound pathetic as a mewling kitten. Given that he was gainfully employed as the heir to a fortune, some might argue him capable of anything. And yet sloughing through the rest of the evening seemed insurmountable. Why did he even try anymore? He'd only written a short handful of entries since the Groundling Papers. None of them had made it to publishing. Neither printer nor press had accepted his submissions in the subsequent year of slander against him. Today, the memory made him especially bitter.

But at this point in his daily routine—wake, moss, drink, wait for the ceiling to turn orange—all his thoughts were bitter.

It was not that Niklaus believed his birthday to be more significant than any other day, but this one struck a subjective nerve. The planet had made an entire journey around the sun since his discrediting and dragged him resentfully along with it—kicking and screaming, naked, and bound by a leash tied to his little toe. Metaphorically, at least.

The only empirical evidence was the year-long writer's block it had left in its wake.

Niklaus tilted his head to rise and noticed that only one foot sported a red leather loafer. The shoes drove most of Nelfindar's patricians mad just to look at, but he considered them quite boffo mostly due to the aforementioned reason. The other foot proffered a wildly patterned sock that hung flaccid from his toes, threatening to slide off entirely.

No, writer's block was an understatement. He'd had a year of life block. He had no goal for the day, or for the next year, for that matter. No objective which coerced him from one whiskey-tinted breath to the next.

Thirty-three years.

If he had been absent for those thirty-three years, there would be no difference in the world. Well, except that the oligarchy would only have a degree of its current corruption and Latouda would still be alive. Kretch. The world would actually be better off without him. None of this meant anything anymore, except for statistical proof that he was dying slowly, and far too slowly for his own tastes.

It crept up again, like a stray dog returning to a trash pile it had been dispelled from repeatedly—the thought of ending it all. But then the thought retreated, tail between its legs. His previous attempts had gone abysmally. He'd ultimately decided there was no point behind killing himself either.

Fates have mercy, he was beginning to sober.

Niklaus furrowed his brow at the empty glass. Best to end this abysmal day. He teetered to his feet and stumbled, single shoe *thunking*, toward a hearty, glass-paneled cabinet in the room's corner. After rustling through its shelves, his hand clenched around the moss tab tin, hidden in the corner behind a gin bottle. He pulled out a tab between his fingertips, broke off a third—not too much, he wasn't a fated addict—and set it on his tongue.

Five minutes. Five minutes, and he'd be floating on a cloud. He could make it.

The gin bottle he'd moved in search of the tin was still in his hand. Why not?

Niklaus poured a few thumbs' worth. Then he strode to the window to watch the sunset, lifting his glass in mock toast.

"This is for you, Roskaad Thyatira. Whatever fated game you're playing, you've won."

Leaning against the window frame, he stared apathetically into the world below. Glimmering sunlight danced across the ocean as the glowing orb that was its source sank slowly beyond the horizon. It was a sight which could only be seen by those fortunate enough to look down from a very high point, such as his chamber along the skywalk. The great green wall of Seraphinden prevented any groundling from seeing into the blissful sea beyond.

And it was wasted on him.

Would that he could cling to that orb and sink into the ocean with it. Niklaus pressed his forehead into the glass pane, ignoring the spots that formed before his eyes as the last rays faded away and the world fell prey to the darkness of night.

A soft knock came at his door.

"Kill yourself," he groaned quietly—not quietly enough.

"That seems superfluous," a velvety voice said from behind him.

Niklaus turned—a motion which nearly set him back on the floor—to see the door open. An unbearably attractive maid entered and curtsied. He pinched the bridge of his nose. She was clearly his mother's doing. In her own twisted way, the old woman probably believed she was providing him consolation.

The maid's faultless bow of a mouth droned into perfectly stilted speech. "Good evening, Niklaus. Sesu Meyernes requests your presence at the meal she has occasioned for you. The Goroviches will be in attendance."

Niklaus pressed his ruffled hair flat and removed a quill from behind his ear, vaguely aware of the fact that, in doing so, he streaked ink across his cheek. Kretch. His mother was hosting a dinner party for him? Was this some kind of game of 'how miserable can my adult son possibly get' to her?

With Hashod Gorovich brought to mind, he actually gagged. The maid wrinkled her button of a nose—a feature far too delicate to produce the perfect, snorting cackle Latouda's once had—before regaining her composure.

"Well, that was funny," he slurred. "I'm really not sure if I did that on purpose or if it was inadvertent. But honestly, I couldn't really tell you right from left right now, dear-o." He set his glass on the windowsill and smoothed the crumpled poem against his blouse. "Ah. Hello..."

He left due pause for the maid to give him her name. She chose not to, her body as stiff as the lustrous ebony plait coiled about her head.

"I... ah... no, thank you."

The maid frowned. But of course, she would respond with persistence. She was new, after all, and had yet to realize that any attempt at communication with him was like a cart's wheel, building momentum as it barreled down a hill, all edge without a point. "She insists that you are present."

"Yes, I'm sure she does."

The maid's lips parted to respond, but Niklaus beat her to it with a loud belch, unintentional but amusing. "I must regretfully decline. Have a... good night."

She opened and closed her mouth again. Worked her sculpted jaw. Unholy Chaos, she was adorable. She didn't deserve his pathological insolence. Maybe this one he would go along for. Let her get the pat on the head from his mother she probably needed.

And then he thought of Hashod again.

Niklaus studied her through squinted eyes, trying to think through squinted thoughts. The idea of a dinner party with the Gorovich family sounded about as desirable as leaping out the window, tumbling off the skywalk, and plummeting six stories into the Casowhatan. Hashod would want to discuss Aetech's military investment, no doubt. No. That was not what he was going to do this evening, Fates help him.

"Please go away."

The maid shook her head. "It's time—"

"Tell me, what time *is* it, without reference to the time of day? Is it time for sowing or a moment of silence? Is the morning whistle blowing? Is now the time for violence? Time for tea or, perhaps, your turn to boast? Do you like restitution with a side of—"

She interrupted him this time, a fast study. "It's time to move on, mesu."

"—toast."

"And move through whatever mental quagmire you've gotten yourself stuck in, or otherwise submit to it. Your pick."

Finally. Someone spoke truth.

He waggled a finger at her. "Rushing is violence."

"And so is this thing that you are doing to yourself."

Truth indeed, delivered by a blade with two edges. Preservation, he preferred a quality mind over an ephemeral face any day. Just like… Niklaus's thoughts dove head-first into the lack of fluid in his glass, snapping their necks at the bottom.

"What are you going to do in your room all by yourself on your birthday?" she tried, a hand on her delightfully proportioned hip, impatience unambiguous.

"Enjoy the sanctity." Perhaps the argument would have been convincing had his words not been stricken with sibilant slurring.

She scoffed. "Come now, I've prepared a bit of fun for you."

She disappeared into the hall and returned a moment later, pulling a wheelchair behind her. A small cart hosting a variety of liquors and glassware had been affixed to the chair's arm.

Niklaus gaped at it, swaying on his feet. "Did you build me a liquor chair so you could transport me willingly to my mother's dinner party?"

"Yes."

There went any argument he might have procured. "You're good." He narrowed his eyes. "Be careful about being too good at this job. The last maid who managed to stick around wound up in the ground because of it."

The maid without a name ushered for him to sit without an expression. "I know the story, mesu. I'll accept the risk. Now get in."

He heaved a sigh that whined like a fly. "I really don't have a choice, do I?"

"None of us really have a choice, do we, mesu?"

Fates be stayed, this woman was blunt. He sat in the chair, and she proceeded to mix him a drink.

He took a sip, and his upper lip curled. "This is hardly liquor."

"Just enough," she said.

He frowned. "I don't want to remember tonight."

"I doubt you will."

"Fates. You *are* good. Would you like to join me as a guest at my dinner tonight?"

"No thank you, mesu." Her response was flat as weathered stone.

"A wise choice." He tipped the glass back for a sip. "Let's get this over with."

Niklaus helped himself to another drink as the maid pushed him wordlessly into the distortion lift that would take them to the dinner hall. It was a trap. Her humanity toward him was a ruse—carefully followed orders wearing the guise of novelty. And he'd gone along with it. Kretch. He really didn't have any authority over his life anymore. He was the thing he most feared: another insect working for the hive mind under the foolish and false conviction that he had some sort of autonomy because he lacked the senses to see the bigger picture.

"Listen," he started. The maid hummed in a way that insinuated her entertaining his request without actually listening. He spoke regardless. Fruitless as it was, it was the only power he possessed. "Keep your chin up, eah? Even if you fail in whatever thing they hired you to do with me. It stands as no testament to your worth." Oh, Fates. He'd officially hit his bottom—doling out the advice he most needed to hear to a stranger from a liquor chair. "You're important. Believe in yourself. Even when no one else does. Because that is what worth *is*. And that... it's amazing."

The clattering of wheels across marble filled the space where the maid would have responded, were they having a conversation. And then his body lightened and expanded, emotions dulled, sensations muddled, all indicative of a moss canopy. Niklaus squinted against the brilliant reflections of distortion lamps where they blossomed across the pristine floor. This was his home, yet he'd never noticed them before. Who could possibly need so much light at lowsun?

They came to a stop in the anteroom to the dining hall.

"May I assist you, mesu?" The maid held out a hand to him and he took it, allowing her to ease him to his feet. He swayed once, twice, and then steadied himself.

"Splendid, then. Happy Birthday, mesu," she said, before wheeling the cart down the hall without looking back.

Niklaus stood bleary-eyed beneath the lintel of the dining hall entrance, his empty glass still in hand. Frowning at it, he set it in the middle of the floor. Where it didn't belong. It felt like him, there; he was one with the glass. And it was pure chaos. Pure freedom. Pure art.

Joy sparked—

Suffocated heartbeats later by his mother. "Ah, Niklaus. You've arrived. Please sit down."

Smothered smothering of shratten shattering. Her voice was plummy in a way that reminded him of an overpowering perfume.

When he looked at the woman who had borne him, there was nothing familiar there, only too much skin on too bony a frame. And yet... Feeling compliant, he obeyed her. He walked through the elaborate set of double doors, like the gilded mouth of a cave, into their dining hall. A carved monolith of mahogany stretched the span of six men over a Pazirian carpet—too far for a canopied man to traverse without revealing himself. It felt like the walk of a prisoner toward certain execution. Niklaus's mother, smug Hashod Gorovich, and his maiden daughter Rebethel were as wardens, staring as he made each step with meticulous care—*don't stumble*—toward the high-backed chair at the table's head.

Niklaus sat. The chair seemed to suck him in like it had been enchanted to add gravity to his limbs, and his world progressed around him like liqueur in winter. Rebethel, her seat adjacent to his own, raised her dark, angled eyebrows at him, looking down her nose the way she always did. His mother's puckered mouth drew down. Hashod's wolfish white smile widened in clashing contrast to the black curls of his beard.

Fated Hashod. If he could turn back time, Niklaus would make it so that he'd never met the man. That he'd never invested his father's inheritance into fated Aethertech Mechanics. How different things would have been...

His mother cleared her throat, and he realized he'd been sitting idle for some time, staring into the space where mind touched matter. "Eat. You must be starved."

Niklaus glanced at the spread before them. A feast of exquisite delights lay in delicate serving bowls, interspersed with fruits of every size and color scrupulously cut to resemble geometric shapes or flowers.

It made his mouth go dry.

Hashod spoke from the seat obliquely across from him. "Niklaus, it is a pleasure to join you on this special occasion. Are you well?"

Niklaus looked to Rebethel, who admired her freshly manicured hand while twirling a lock of sable hair. She might have been lovely, could he see anything past paint and powder and jewels. He spoke through a mouthful of parchment. "Fine, thank you."

His mother sighed, covering her face with a lace-gloved hand. "Since Niklaus doesn't appear to be in the mood for food or conversation, let's move on to it."

Hashod placed a stack of papers on the table. A harrowing feeling settled in Niklaus's stomach that was unrelated to his state. Papers from this lot were never good. Papers meant betrayal, slander, manipulation. What could they possibly want from him now?

"What's this, then?" he asked.

"You could read it," his mother scoffed.

"It's a marriage contract," Hashod replied. "To secure your and Rebethel's future together. And to ensure the continued well-being of Aethertech Mechanics."

Was this a hallucination? He wasn't in the right state for this. Had they... planned it this way? Presenting him with a marriage contract at a time they suspected he would be inebriated? "No."

Hashod's mustache eclipsed his blazing smile. Rebethel rolled her eyes.

"What else do you plan on doing with your life?" his mother snapped.

Something scrambled inside Niklaus's chest, a rat in a barrel set to flame, desperate for freedom. "Literally anything else."

His mother's jowls tightened. "This will ensure Aetech continues to prosper. It's taken a hit in the last year since the release of your fated Groundling work."

"Yes, that was the whole shratten idea." He'd done what his father would have done, had he lived to see the monster they'd birthed. Niklaus had tried to burn it to the ground with paper for kindling and a pen as his sword. But he was a lone soldier on that battlefield, and the enemy wielded cunning and greed in equal measure.

"Sabotage was the whole idea? Niklaus, do you even listen to yourself?"

Yes. He was the only one who listened to himself. He'd been screaming at the top of his lungs for a year, and no one had heard a whimper.

His mother's anger broke through the veil of propriety. "Aetech was crippled by your foolishness. If we don't do something, the company could go under. You can't seem to come out of your fated rooms, but Rebethel is dedicated to keeping Aetech alive. Do you want to lose everything?"

Niklaus hadn't felt more sober in the last year than right now. Did he want to lose everything? What else did he possibly have to lose?

He opened his mouth to ask that very question but closed it, looking to Rebethel instead. She avoided eye contact.

"And you?" he asked her. "This is what you want? We never really got on, even as kids. Do you want a contractual marriage with me?"

Finally, Rebethel's brown eyes locked onto his. She gave him a pitying look, like he was a sick and shriveled thing. "The way I see it, this gives us the opportunity to ensure additional funding goes toward the oligarchy's most crucial projects. You and I aren't obligated to spend unnecessary time together just because we are married."

For the blink of an eye, Niklaus imagined Latouda there. He imagined her backhanding Rebethel flat out of her chair. But it was only that: an imagination. Even to Latouda, he'd only ever been a tool to manipulate.

Heat flushed through his limbs. "What you're saying is, you're willing to take me on as a house pet to add the additional cushion to your purse."

Rebethel turned from him. "Don't be dramatic."

"Mother, I won't stand for this," Niklaus said, his breath stuttering in his chest, his fists clenching and unclenching. "The suggestion of this union has lingered for long enough. The answer is no. An—and that's final." Fates, if only the statement hadn't been stamped by a hiccup.

"Clearly, you're too intoxicated to think straight," his mother said.

"If I were sober, I would have had the wit to incinerate those papers on sight."

His mother pounded two lace-covered fists on the table, her face contorted in rage. "Niklaus Meyernes, you will sign those papers!"

"Or what?"

She stared at him with eyes like ice, and he realized the answer without her having to say it. The desperate creature in his chest turned to lead, a dead thing weighing against his empty stomach.

"Or you'll sign them for me? Like the last ones? And hire lawyers against me if I claim it to be a forgery?" Considering his history, no one would believe him anyway.

The room grew so still that the silence became a tangible entity, sitting with them at the table to pour tea. Crisp. Cruel. The kind of silence which screamed truth.

That maid was right. No one really did have a choice. The four Fates were set for him, like pillars of stone, and they were not kind.

Chapter 3
Calverous

Calver raced through Chira'na's grasslands, his eyes on the distant treeline that marked the refuge of the Sharinash forest. Dread prickled his skin into perspiration, despite the cool air of pre-winter. One by one, bodies emerged in pursuit, shadows against the setting sun in the hills between him and the city's imposing walls.

Flee. Why had he elected to flee with all the pride of a mouse in an open field?

Because he was being chased, naturally.

But why not fight?

Because slipping away quietly seemed the less risky option.

Less risky than eliminating the Tera'thians that would in all likelihood continue to hunt him?

Fates, he didn't want to kill anyone else if he didn't have to. And killing them in the grasslands would raise attention. And—

{Let me.}

No.

He shoved the Survivor and all its bloodlust back into the well it had crept from. The mind-djinn had been in control for months—years—leading to today. He needed one fated hour to think straight about what he'd done. And how to fix it.

He ran ahead of them for almost a league, doing all he could to keep control of his own mind by keeping it calm. He focused on his dowaga, patting against his back with each step. His steady breaths, in and out. The sound his footfalls made against the high grasses of Chira'na's hills.

The Sharinash forest's edge came to life as he grew closer, its ancient woods spilling into the golden fronds around him. The thickness of the flora alone should intimidate his pursuers. If that didn't turn them away, the wood's horrific lore might lend a hand. To the average man, the forest was uninhabitable.

Dashing into the brush, he paused, listening for the enemy. The forest brimmed with sounds and smells: growth and rot and the millions of teeming lives which hid in perfect view.

His pause gave him a chance to remember how horribly he'd just failed.

Failed. He rode his panic like a wave. How would they possibly recover from this? It should have been a brainless thing for him, the Hand's Reaper: destroy one shipment, come forward with their own distortion tech to fulfill the shortage, stir the pot of Aetech's monopoly with a giant, choice finger. Now Fankalo would be sitting on a million silver notes' worth of inventory with a different finger to point.

There had to be a way to mend this. To repair this.

A crack of a branch.

The thuds of footfalls.

But if these men put him back in Cul'Mon's clutches, if he risked fighting back and got caught? That would be the end of it all, for all of them.

Pushing down his alarm and the Survivor's tandem attempts to seek control, Calver darted deeper into the forest. He wound through game trails like veins, fully encompassed by the thick foliage which branched out from the heart of the forest. Every so often, it seemed as though new paths opened to him. A chill ran down his spine despite his body's heat from the chase. At times like this, it felt as though the Sharinash was alive; a single entity with a heartbeat rather than a collection of billions of individual life forms. Even after all the time he'd resided here alone, he found it unnerving.

Almost as unnerving as his continued pursuers, evidenced by the telltale crackles and snaps of foliage behind him.

Calver quickened his pace.

He'd hoped the terrain would throw them off by now. Clenching his jaw, he turned to his last resort, veering onto an alternative course.

His mind-djinn skittered along its newfound surface tension. *{If you'd let me lead you...}*

Fuck off.

He steadied his emotions—a trifle, really, when running for one's life after sabotaging one's future. One step. Then the next. Crisp piney musk sucked in, desperation exhaled: motions he practiced every day alongside the swings of his dowaga.

The canopy overhead grew thinner, the late afternoon sky becoming more visible, until the ground plummeted away at the edge of a cliff. He skidded to a stop, crunching pebbles below his feet and sending plumes of dust careening into empty space.

Far below, a secluded lake waited, still as a painting in the breezeless air. A crater-formed cliff face rimmed the body of water on three sides. Calver's chest heaved from the flight, which was long enough to have brought the sun to the horizon, as he searched for the rockpile that marked his target. In a scramble of nails against sweat-flecked dirt, he dug into the earth beneath it until his fist clenched around another Aetech lamp, tampered with and buried more than a year prior as an assurance against Cul'Mon. The sight of it brought warmth into his core. Distortion was the one thing which had never forsaken him.

They were seconds from him now. The men advanced at a run with cosalts raised and tankas fixed on him. They thought they had him cornered. Perhaps they had yet to be warned of the things he could do.

The small details on their faces became clear as they prepared to surround him. Calver activated the lamp with a flip of his thumb and set it onto the stone. Then he turned and hurled himself over the edge.

His stomach rose into the hollow well of his mouth.

Behind him, a tanka launch clicked into place before its barbed arrow released. He spun in midair to dodge the projectile, too late.

As the metal bit into Calver's side, a man screamed in Tera'thian, "Pull back! It's a trap!"

Calver plummeted. Lights blossomed behind his eyes, and he reeled into a poor position for one who did not want to break bones when their body hit water. His attempt to straighten was both belated and in vain, and he squeezed his eyes shut for the crash.

It was as porcelain smacking into cold iron.

His shoulder was ripped from its socket, the air forced from his lungs. Calver teetered in a ship of agony, threatening to take on water. He fought past the shock of pain—an old friend at this point—orienting himself down and away from the surface with whatever parts of his body would function. The lamp would ignite at any moment, and he didn't want to be near the surface when the cliff collapsed.

His wherewithal didn't last. His lungs burned. He needed air.

Pivoting, he thrashed back toward the surface. As though expecting him, a resounding *'boom'*—another old friend; he had few, and none of them were friendly—announced that his tampered Aetech lamp had done as he had bidden it.

His head erupted from the trembling surface, and he gasped for air. A wave of heat hit him from above; debris from the blast hurtled toward him. A single breath was all he dared to sip before diving back under to escape.

His body was too shallow. A chunk of stone shattered his right leg beneath the knee.

Death is not an option. He stated Fankalo's first rule for strength, willing anything to take away the pain. Desperate, he cast down the barriers at the midpoint of his mind against the Survivor. It rode forward to take over a degree of control.

The pain faded—one of the few advantages of his submitting to the creature.

{See how you are incapable?}

The Survivor's takeover, the dilution of his physical and mental sensation, was more familiar than he wanted it to be. He understood that he was desperate for air, that his whole body was writhing in an agony he couldn't feel. His limbs moved of their own accord, as though controlled by puppet strings. His recognition of it all was a dull blur, like he was only half-awake.

He struggled down and away from the surface, his only chance at escaping the debris raining from above. *Death is not an option.*

He fought away negative thoughts that threatened his full submission to the mind-djinn. Searched for anything to cling to, to keep one hand in his headspace. Once he lost himself beneath the Survivor, there was no telling when he'd surface again.

{You will live. And you will submit to me in your agony.}

The surrounding water was a war zone. One colossal stone broke through with the froth of a hurricane. Calver spun out from under it just before hitting the lake bed, but sucked in water in his maneuvering.

Did a chest make a sound when it imploded? Or was that more crashing debris?

The Survivor forced him to resist the urge to hack out the fluid surging into his lungs. Using his good leg, he pushed against the lake bed, orienting himself toward the light from the setting sun. Its orange glow barely penetrated the murky water at this depth, a guide as to which direction promised life.

Calver clawed toward it with mutilated limbs. A mere hand's breadth of liquid remained between him and precious oxygen when a shadow eclipsed the warm evening light. Then the surface above him broke as the limbs of a gargantuan tree crashed into his skull.

The Survivor seethed.

Calver's world blackened to a final silence like the onset of a thunderclap. Sudden. Shocking. But it was time enough for the hollowing disappointment of knowing he'd failed Fankalo, too, in the end.

Calver's breath puffed into the air: a warm cloud, ransacked from his chest and disseminated by the heartless steel of winter. At first, all he saw were dark shapes blended together like ink on a waterlogged letter. With time, the wicked outlines of tree branches became more defined, illuminated by the crescent moon which hung low above the treeline. The first pinpricks of stars pierced the early veil of night. If the air hadn't chilled him, that awareness alone would: being wet in the wilds on the first day of winter was a warrant for death.

Calver's subconscious self-defense leaped ahead of his creeping awareness, screaming in alarm that his body was more ice than organ. He held his breath for fear that the dregs of his warmth might spill from him, should he exhale again. His muddled mind clung to the sensation by its teeth.

He shouldn't be able to feel fucking anything. Shouldn't be alive. And, sure as Preservation's beard, shouldn't be in full control of a body whose utmost concern was the weather.

He wouldn't be alive for long, his anxiety prodded. The very blood that seeped into his heart threatened to congeal.

{How is this possible?} the mind-djinn questioned. Its words were faint.

It's not. Calver's head throbbed with every panicked beat of his heart, another assurance the Survivor was not in control.

The bit. The rock. The water. The tree.

No. Nope. No. He distinctly remembered drowning. Calver cringed against the memory he would rather be rid of. It had been agony.

Still-rising anxiety surpassed his exhaustion. He lifted a frozen arm, the one which he knew had dislocated, and felt at the tanka wound with numb fingertips. The telltale hole was still present in his clothing, heavy with cold water, but the skin beneath was smooth.

He focused on the leg, which had shattered at the femur. Its bone was perfectly intact. He bent his knee, wiggled his toes, rolled his ankle to convince himself otherwise.

{*Impossible,*} the Survivor reiterated.

Fates help him. Even the voice in his head was so dumbstruck, it was repeating itself. There went any flicker of sanity he might have had. Calver's terror peaked. This was wrong. Dead wrong. He shook his head. The motion brought the thing beside him into view, setting every hair on his limbs to stand as rigid as the individual, frigid fronds in the Sharinash.

Another body.

Calver bolted into a seated position and skittered backward until his back crashed into a tree. Its bark clawed like talons against his frozen skin, even beneath his wet cloak. His heartbeat pounded in his ears. The world turned to stars before his eyes, and he fought off a wave of nausea. Vomit—a third old friend. Fates, if the company he kept indicated anything...

He forced a slow inhale to calm himself and avoid falling unconscious again, then blinked the black veil of shock from his eyes, blindly pulling his dowaga from his back. His frosted hands could hardly hold it.

When his vision cleared, he saw that the body was both bloody and unmoving. And then he saw the lake beyond, black as oil by the light of the stars and moon. He was still on its bank. The belt around his chest loosened a notch.

The jagged face of the cliff towered over the lake's far side. His jettison point from that afternoon stared at him like the blackened hull of a walnut. The charred skeletons of trees stretched into the night or teetered along the ledge.

Calver's eyes darted back to the body, now several paces away from him. Not one of the Tera'thian soldiers, but a... girl? Young woman? The petite creature wore a bone-colored turban and the emerald robes of a cenobite. Calver's brow furrowed. There was no such thing as a female cenobite. As he scanned her, her chest dipped with the slightness of a flower beneath a child's breath.

Not just a body. A live person.

Calver's hands trembled against the steel of his weapon. Fates, his threadbare brain was fraying at its edges.

He couldn't stop staring. Her hands were a crimson smear. The sight caused his own blood to curdle, chilling him deeper than the watery cold set into his bones.

It wasn't possible.

A wave of dizziness passed over him again. His eyes sought the sanguine clouds which darkened his clothing. It was his blood. This tiny person was his rescuer. Or—his skepticism reared—she belonged to Cul'Mon. Another one of his tricks. Something to throw Calver off guard.

He shuddered. More soldiers could be upon him at any moment; they'd followed him this far. He couldn't stay out in the open. If the cold didn't kill him, somebody else would.

Still, he had yet to tear his eyes from the stranger.

What was she doing here? She was a thing that should not be—a woman, alone and undefended in Nelfindar's most dangerous forest. Like a knife, levitating by no means of its own. And it jabbed at him and jabbed at him until he could no longer stand it.

He latched the dowaga onto his back and crawled closer on hands and knees, his body groaning in protest, his limbs like chunks of ice. She was soaked. Gooseflesh covered her sable skin, which was spattered by mud from the embankment. Her lips were the telltale pastel of a person with too-little time.

There was a satchel at her hip. He patted at it. Empty. The wheels of his trepidation sped. Why? Why was she here, unequipped, empty-handed?

Calver gave the girl's arm a tentative prod. She didn't budge.

Kretch. The moon was fast rising and the temperature dropping. His Sharinash refuge was not far. Calver bit at the inside of his cheek. What would he do with her? Fankalo's second rule rattled through his mind. *Don't involve anyone, and stay away from people.*

But she would freeze here.

And soon.

He was the Hand's Reaper. He killed people. What was killing one more very small person who had clearly sacrificed herself to save him? He'd be sparing her the terror of waking in a cave in the clutches of a mute assassin—or, worse, the Survivor. Who could say which of them would occupy "him" by then?

Even if he could speak, even in the impossible chance that she was literate, like him, you didn't just say "Hello. Thanks for rescuing me. You're a captive forever now. Can't have you destroying eight years of reconnaissance. It's not you, it's me."

His heart still beat like a hummingbird's, causing his uninvited shadow to creep forward in his mind. But its motion was irresolute, a far cry from the usual anvil of its presence at his fear.

{She dies, or you die. Leave her, Calverous.}

Was it also—dare he suggest it—afraid?

The right thing to do in this situation would be to forget she had ever been here. Or maybe to end it for her, quickly, so she wouldn't suffer.

His dowaga lifted. His frozen heart fell.

Then the night shifted and slowed around him, as though it had gained sentience and awakened from a deep slumber. The eyes of the world—the wind, the lake, the stars—turned on him, all awaiting his next action. They pulsed, an echo of something just around the bend of memory. That feeling...

Take her.

Limbs tingling and trembling, he returned the dowaga to its holster again. One did not, even if they wanted to, disobey the biddings of destiny.

Calver heaved her brittle form into his arms and staggered to standing. More stars flashed before his eyes; he inhaled slowly to push back the new wave of nausea.

He looked down at her face, calculating and recalculating. His disquiet heightened with the knowledge of what he was doing: listening to voices again—to destiny. That was what had fucking put him here in the first place. The Fates had never known a better madman.

Her eyes fluttered open.

He nearly dropped her.

The woman's irises were a brilliant shade of silver, like the plated caps on Chira'na's skywalk buildings. They locked on him, gripping his soul like bark grips a tree. His gut lanced with a feeling akin to lightning.

She was a Ruxian.

Her face was expressionless for the space of an exhalation. Then she whispered, "Methu'su...?"

Calver became hyper-aware of the hollow behind his lips. He could no more answer her than he could stop his limbs from shaking. *Methu'su?* A feeling of loss and longing pinned him, its origin untraceable. It wasn't a word. It was a name. Familiar, but tucked out of reach. Just like this feeling...

Her eyelids drooped, and she sagged in his arms. Calver stood still, his breath caught in his chest. Whatever this was, it was far beyond anything he had the resources to deal with. There was no way he could become involved with a *Ruxian*. His mind ran in a circle. Fankalo had given him rules. The second rule was to not involve anyone.

Fankalo, whom he'd failed. Who would never accept him back, after this disaster. His sorrow at his dashed hope for redemption surged like a tide, and with it came the Survivor.

{Kill it.}

The Ruxian?

All perturbation gone, the mind-djinn's weight crashed into his resolve with the strength of a mountain. It was so sudden, Calver nearly broke without a fight. He cried out at its pressure. His knees buckled. He panted to control his breath, to control his state.

If he submitted to it, as he usually did, no more Ruxian. No more social apprehensions. Problem solved. But...

His mind found the void mantra of his childhood dowagian instructor, Mesu Callisto. *Victory over the mind can only come with an embrace of the void. For only in nothing can you find everything.*

Void.

The Survivor tensed as he fell into a meditative trance, despite the agony it pressed against him. *{Listen. You don't under—}*

Void.

It screamed.

Void.

It ebbed into nothing, far more easily than it should have.

Calver stayed there for long minutes, untrusting of his ability to maintain control.

Fates. He was a dead man.

But he had already been a dead man, living on borrowed time that would see him dead all over again. That had been determined long ago.

Going against every lesson he'd learned in the last fourteen years, every loyalty he owed, he hoisted the young woman over his shoulder. Dangerous cold aside, Cul'Mon's agents were bound to come again, and it was only due to luck that they had not found him yet.

He strode east, into the thickest part of the forest, as quickly as his stiff body would allow.

Chapter 4
Attilatia

A girl never grew up expecting to be an assassin... until someone tried to assassinate her.

A humid breeze tinged with salt and sea tugged at Attilatia's white jumpsuit as she proceeded across Seraphinden's skywalk toward Aetech headquarters. Whirring distortion lamps and the soft glow of the crescent moon illuminated the shimmering path, flecked with dazzling quartz and shining agate. She felt exposed out in the wild open air, like another attack might come at any moment. After sixteen years as an Azadonian expatriate—if one could say that of being a glorified hostage—she had never grown accustomed to living aboveground. Now, her paranoia only compounded her discomfort.

In contrast to the dark sky, the skywalk practically sparkled. As if being out in the open weren't bad enough, the glowing walkway lit her up like the fated sun, shining against the whitewashed buildings lining the path and the fragrant tendrils of their hanging gardens. Orange and blue flowers blossomed year-round, watered by an elaborate system of fountains and aqueducts. They crisscrossed overhead, in a superfluous lattice that connected to the homes and businesses of Seraphinden's elite. Even when she wasn't worried about receiving a free stab to the back, Attilatia couldn't appreciate such things, knowing the debauchery which afforded them. As if to prove their wealth to anyone who wasn't already impressed, the buildings were all capped in glistening silver—a tribute to the Ruxians who'd once ruled there.

How far this country had fallen since.

The closer she grew to Aetech, the more leaden her footsteps became. How she dreaded the snare around her freedom, and the waste—of time, of passion, of energy—which could otherwise be spent rooting out whomever had tipped off the Kovathians. But she had to work to keep up appearances: put forth minimal effort for a science these *chikotos* thought was magic; hold her tongue while the Nelfinden patriarchy abused and subjected its people; sit back and let the blood and milk and water of her enemies flow around her. Business as usual.

Thank Preservation, it was aftersun and the skywalk was nearly empty of civilians. That was the only way she could tolerate it. The patricians who inhabited Seraphinden's skywalk believed themselves above the rest of the world, their living structures a literal monument to that belief. Fates, at least she knew she was a villain. She wholly understood the price she'd paid to get where she was. Attilatia pulled the zipper of her jumpsuit, the uniform all Aetech employees wore, a little tighter against her throat.

As she approached the iron gate of Aetech's front entrance, the silhouette of a man stepped before it. Her heart made as if to plummet into her stomach. Broad-featured and thin-tempered, Hashod's presence at Aetech so close to highmoon was inauspicious at best, condemning at worst. She hid her disturbance by continuing at her usual brisk pace. *Don't make eye contact. Don't acknowledge him.* Aetech's chief operator had no reason nor right to speak to her outside of their weekly summaries.

Dread entwined itself with her innards as he stepped forward to slow her path.

"Sesu Mitar, access to the building has been shut off for the remainder of the evening."

That brought her up short. As Aetech's chief engineer, her access had never been shut off. Chaos, if it weren't for her, the building wouldn't even function.

"An aqueduct vein broke, and the main level flooded. I wouldn't want for our most talented"—Hashod's spectacled eyes scanned her from turban to toes, leaving the sensation of insects crawling on skin in their wake—"Inventress to work in such conditions, of course."

Her jaw clenched. Preservation help her. Hashod spoke truth as often as cattle took wing. His amber countenance lied just the same—too gaunt in some places and too plump in others. Still, she would take part in this same old, treacherous dance with him with her best foot forward. She needed to pilfer from Aetech's stores tonight, or she'd lose yet another strikapa antidote test.

"Why, Hashod, are you to say I can no access my distortion circuitry?" she asked in broken Nelfinden. The language was idiotic, its mechanics never a priority.

Her relationship with Hashod was simple: a continual exchange of formalities and threats. She seethed every time she looked at his perfectly groomed visage. And the way his eyes licked every inch of her, stripping her of any dignity... Nelfinden men were disgusting. His daughter had to be near enough to her own age. In her country, women married younger men to compensate for the deficit in their life expectancy, and because all men—prone to barbarism on their own—needed another mother after they'd grown out of the woman who birthed them.

Hashod's wrinkled skin tightened over his cheeks, and her dread cut deeper. "I thought you would be pleased to hear you have the evening off. Go back to your hole. Enjoy whatever it is your people *do* during the daytime."

A jab at her heritage. She wasn't the only Azadonian who fell into the stigmata of a nocturnal lifestyle.

Attilatia twisted her mouth. Tonight was her last in the work week. An extra day of sitting on her ass drinking tea and fortifying her home's defenses would be tempting, were there not additional repercussions. "Actually, I do not mind the wet. Is important I work tonight."

She started toward the gate, but a guard sidestepped from behind the connecting stone wall. He lowered his cosalt, a long-shafted weapon with a barbed tip, in her direction—the gall.

"What this?" she spat. "Fated *chikoto*! Let me in."

Hashod showed no response to the Azadonian slur, which had no Nelfinden equivalent but translated to "born from an asshole." His arms folded behind his back. A corner of his mouth quirked up. "What do you so urgently need to get into Aetech for, Attilatia?"

She needed two ounces of a specifically formulated chelator, which was *only* kept in Aetech's medical hold. If she didn't add it to her antidote by morning, the entire batch would be wasted. But if Hashod discovered that she'd been stealing Aetech's property for months, that would be the least of her problems.

"I let you decide how urgency it is," she snapped, making something up on the spot. "Three ruxechorin cell need replace. Would you like east sector to lose all power for next three day?" With a less-than-subtle glare at the guard, she moved past him toward the entrance.

"Tell me what you'd like out of the medical stores, and I'll have it brought out to you."

Attilatia froze. The enmity in his eyes made her heart want to leap from her body. She had covered her tracks meticulously. There was no way he could possibly conceive that she—*No*. Hashod was up to something, as she'd suspected he was for some time, and he was gaslighting her to cover it up.

Hashod gave a nod, and an icy grip clamped around her forearm. She gasped against the sharp crack of pain as her arm was contorted behind her back. Her gut turned. Had she misjudged this dance? Hashod had always been a barking dog, but now he was foaming at the mouth.

The guard turned her to face Hashod, and Attilatia blinked back tears. If there were ever a time to be insufficiently backboned, this was not it.

Aetech's chief operator smiled in a way that dissociated from the rest of his face. "If I were you, I would keep your pretty head down and your mouth shut."

If only her words could carry venom. "I know you hide something! I see my station disturbed when you think I away at highsun. You really think you slip my own technology past me? What you conceal inside right now that is such big secret?"

He chuckled without mirth. "You are imagining things. But I will tell you what I am not imagining: extra digits added to certain ingredient orders to our pharmaceutical supplies. Ordinarily, I would never suspect you, of course. But seeing as you are the only one who works such fated hours..."

Chaos. The accusation was far from latent. "Sorry I no like to burn my retinas like you sun-worshiping *chikotos*." Like any Azadonian, her sensitivity to light caused horrific headaches.

"I suggest that you don't concern yourself with Aetech today, Sesu. That is, if you don't want to be tried for theft as an Azadonian. Do you know how quickly I'll have you imprisoned for the advantages you have taken of the Nelfinden Oligarchy when they're exposed?"

"You wouldn't!" she spat. "Where are you to find someone else with my capability maintain distortion circuit, cah?" She tugged away from the guard, whose grip constricted like a snake. "No happen. Now, let me in this fated building."

Hashod clucked his tongue. "Oh, but I have finally found someone to replace you. One with your skills, but who will push the circuit further. In a way that you cannot even begin to fathom."

She pinched her lips to keep her jaw from dropping. Surely he was lying.

Hashod's eyes lit like suns at her poorly veiled horror. "Aetech is about to change. You are fucked, Attilatia—and not in the way you beg for it. The reign of terror you've had over this company is about to see its end. Nothing will ever be sweeter than seeing you get what's coming to you."

Attilatia fiddled with the glass bead on her bracelet. Threats and more threats. Hashod had convinced himself he was brilliant, and yet he was so predictable. Hadn't he learned that blackmail only gave her argument and ammunition to destroy him?

She jutted out her chin. "And you know how much credibility you go to lose the moment I expose you had your own blood mother bagged for effort in groundling education?" His smile fell, her heart elated, like opposite ends of a scale. *Got you, motherfucker.* She kept dirt on everyone who might have a thimble of control over her. "Were you to worry about losing your position by association?" she sneered. "Blood traitor. If I am to go down, I drag you into Destruction with me."

Hashod placed the end of his nose a thumb's width from hers. "You, of all people, have the nerve to call me a blood traitor?" He slapped her across the face.

The hit stung, but the hypocrisy more so. Attilatia bit her tongue, holding back any cry, and leveled her chin. What she'd done was different. In the long run she would help, not hurt, her people.

If her plan actually worked... and that was a colossal *if*.

"I know why you're so sour," he continued. "Your little nest rat leaves with the Red Wing recruitment next ten-day, doesn't he? Don't think that your collaboration with Roskaad Thyatira changes anything. He is still within my grasp." He meant her adoptive brother, Thedexemore, and the reminder made her chest ache. Thedexemore was the one the Kovathians were after. Not her. And his enlistment came as her last resort. "One wrong move, and that boy is out of the Red Wing and deported into Kovathian hands before he can say 'Jenolavia.'"

Attilatia flinched at the name and its bitter reminder. One wrong move? She'd only made wrong moves ever since...

A sudden suspicion licked at the periphery of her awareness. Hashod's fury was uncharacteristic, even for him. He was projecting. *He* was the one who was sour at Thedexemore's departure—that she'd snuck him right out from underneath Hashod's hooked nose into transient safety.

Chaos. Was Hashod the one who had set the Kovathian assassins after them in the first place? That couldn't make sense. Unless, of course, he had somehow found a replacement for her as he claimed. Attilatia swallowed and stared at Aetech's chief operator like a vulture stared at a wounded beast, but she held back any wayward remark. He was right: Thedexemore's survival, his longtime bartering tool against her, was still at his mercy.

Hashod took a step back and dabbed at his sweating brow with a kerchief from his breast pocket. He looked exhausted. Why? She narrowed her eyes at him. Something had not gone according to plan for him, and he was dealing with the repercussions now.

"Go home, Sesu Mitar," he said, his voice relenting. "Whatever you planned with that stolen chelator, it will have to wait."

The guard released his grip. Attilatia stomped hard on the man's toes. He grunted as she skirted away without a backward glance. She hurried from the skywalk, her head down and hands stuffed deep into pockets all the way to her home on the outskirts of the city in Poqualle District. When she crossed her threshold, alone and safe, she slammed the door shut behind her—and began to scream.

Attilatia had always been told that she needed to learn to control her temper. The very thought made her laugh. If only they knew how much of it she *did* control. One would think that after all her rage had cost her, she would have learned to overcome it, yet her loss only fanned the flame.

She fell to her knees, the heels of her hands pressed into her eyes. Her formula was useless without the timely addition of the chelator. Two weeks of research completely wasted. Two weeks further from finding a cure for the strikapa. Two weeks further from a chance to save her homeland. To liberate Thedexemore.

Surely, Hashod would take caution to prevent her from sneaking back later that night and seeing what he was hiding—something she suspected would help him have her removed. And by the next morning, when the regular crowd came in to work, whatever he'd done would be covered up.

Calm, Atti, she told herself. *You've waited sixteen years.*

Two weeks were as significant as the foam that clung to Seraphinden's walls at low tide.

Chapter 5
Calverous

FOURTEEN YEARS PREVIOUSLY

Life in the Kaidechi slums was slow, as life tended to be when there was little for Calver to do but stare at the dust floating in the crack of light between wall and curtain. Or perhaps that was simply how all time spent waiting to get back to Callisto's dowagian studio—which was all Calver did—passed.

The shanty he shared with his mother and sister made it worse, like it knew he wanted to leave and purposely stretched the time spent there. Every draft-prone corner spoke of disappointment; every rotten rafter supporting the tin ceiling—and there weren't many rafters in a space so small—knew he resented them. The only window sat beside a crooked door in a more crooked frame; a faded curtain was kept across it day and night. Their home would have subsisted on the skywalk if his father had been the man he was supposed to be. The man his mother still claimed him to be…

But then there were moments which didn't pass as slowly, for the love his mother poured into them—at least what little she had left to give.

"Natoluphut Seraphindo stood at the edge of the sea. His long silver hair whipped in the wind. His silver eyes locked on Tera'thia's almighty fleet. Over *three thousand* ships sailed toward him, prepared to bring Nelfindar to rubble and ruin." His mother's brown eyes lit up as she softened her voice to a whisper. "But Natoluphut was the most powerful Ruxian to have lived since the Cataclysm. He lifted a hand to the sky and commanded the sea to swell and cast them into the water."

She gave a dramatic pause, eyes shifting between Calver and his sister, who were in contest for who could slump the lowest in their chairs. Then her hands flew wildly in the air, mimicking a tumultuous sea. The effect was entirely for Arleena. His sister used to giggle when their mother did that, a rare crack in her otherwise commanding demeanor. That ship, too, had sailed.

"And then, the miraculous! A great light shone down from the sky, striking deep into the ocean. The water rose, thrashing and crashing about, tearing at wood and flesh until there was nothing left of the Tera'thian fleet."

She stopped flailing, instead stirring the pot over the hearth with one hand and stroking Arleena's head with the other. His sister's eyes, once trance-like during these tales, now found the sunken roof in painted disinterest.

"After saving our people from the Tera'thian threat, Natoluphut reigned over Nelfindar for years to come, creating an age of *prosperity* and *good*."

She enunciated the last few words in a sing-song voice before quickly chirping "The end!" and bopping Arleena on the nose with a finger, eliciting a scowl.

Calver had heard the tale countless times. The version she'd just finished had been clipped, abbreviated so they could focus on something other than their gurgling stomachs. And to warm Calver's ears while he sat on his hands, waiting for the Red Wing recruitment at highsun.

Their mother plopped two wooden bowls, brimming with thin porridge, on the table. Arleena dug in like a predator, pulling the bowl to her lips and tipping her head back. The action was an instinct: not to feed herself, but to find yet another way to infuriate their mother.

"Ah, ah! Shame, Arleena! A lady uses a spoon." She removed the bowl from Arleena's hands, set it back on the table, and placed a wooden spoon in his sister's palm.

With a cheeky snort, Arleena set back to eating properly, though she made sure there was still porridge running down her chin.

Their mother's hand buried itself in her hairline. "I don't know, Calver. It's like I'm raising a tiny monster. Destruction take her." It was a thing she used to say with eyes that glittered with mirth. No longer. She sat back with her chin set in her hand and sighed.

"RAAAAAHHHKKH!" Arleena snarled in victory over their mother's resolve.

"A terror if I ever met one."

Calver fought back a smile. Arleena only set to mischief because she was bored senseless sitting around in this hut. She was like a battle commander trapped in a six-year-old's body. Their mother had taught them their letters. Arleena was reading and writing at a level Calver hadn't reached until the age of nine—and he'd been advanced. He supposed that didn't mean much in the slums, where the Oligarchy's laws, which privatized education, made most of the groundling class illiterate.

Calver ignored the cramping in his stomach, his own animalistic impulse to dive in face-first. He raised his spoon toward Creation, as taught when they'd lived along the skywalk, before digging in. The porridge was more water than anything, but it warmed him almost as much as the look of approval his mother gave him. Arleena rolled her eyes.

Their mother turned toward the stove and scraped at the bottom of the pot with the serving spoon, taking a single mouthful. Calver caught her expression—one that had become more and more common on her face: a lowered brow, the corners of her mouth drooping. She only did it when she thought he wasn't looking.

"A-are you going t-t-t—" He stopped, frustrated with himself.

"To what?" His mother brightened again, like a candle in a pause between gales.

"T-tell what happened n-next?"

"Hmmm." She pierced him with a look that made his stomach turn. "Why don't you finish it?"

Calver didn't reply, continuing to shovel breakfast into his mouth, head down, while Arleena made overly dramatic slurping noises beside him. Today was going to be a perfect day. He didn't need any reminders of his inadequacies over speech therapy.

The corners of their mother's mouth turned up weakly, and she pulled her threadbare shawl around her shoulders. She batted him on the shoulder. "We can do it together, Cal, and alternate lines. It will be good for practicing your words." She wasn't suggesting; she was telling him. "When you get tripped up, just remember that sometimes you have to stop focusing on the ones you can't save and focus on the ones you can."

Line by line, he stumbled and stuttered through the story of King Seraphindo building the capitol of Seraphinden with Ruxian magic. It might not have been agonizing if he hadn't already been itching to leave.

Arleena brandished her spoon like a cosalt, her licked-clean bowl now resting on her head like a helm. "Don't forget Seraphindo's army. If I'd inherited legions, I could convince people I was magic too."

A six-year-old skeptic. Where had Arleena learned deductive debate? Their mother shot her a glare.

Calver wondered if she begrudged Arleena all the ruthless confidence Calver lacked. As a dowagian prodigy and his father's son, the expectations for him were higher than he was capable of leaping. He was too gentle, always fearful of pushing during combat, despite his natural talents. Whenever the time came to land a killing blow, even a practice one, he hesitated.

But Arleena... she was always sure of herself. And smart. And funny. Calver couldn't even stand to be jealous. Arleena was like light, packaged in brown eyes and skin framed by black curls that were a perfect mirror of his own. She was the only thing that sustained him in those long hours between sessions at the dowagian studio.

"There wasn't r-really Ruxian m-m-magic, was there?" Calver looked around at their desolate home. Even without his younger sibling's skepticism, he was beginning to understand the difference between his mother's tales and the truths she would keep from him forever, if she could.

She frowned. "The histories tell us that there were once hundreds, even thousands, of Ruxians who had the power to manipulate matter. Even more who couldn't. Though I expect the stories of Natoluphut are exaggerations."

Calver picked at his nails. "If they were so m-m-magical, why aren't there any left t-today?"

His mother sat in the spare chair, which creaked in protest under her slight weight. Her eyes lifted, as though constructing her response carefully.

"The Ruxian gene was recessive, so some think they dissolved, over time, into the genetic pool. Others believe the Tera'thians began hunting them. Or they *could* all be in hiding, waiting to come back to save Nelfindar in its next dire hour." She winked at him. He took it to mean *it's a story, Calverous, don't read too far into it.*

A horn sounded outside, prompting him to his feet. Any melancholy slipped away as his chest bubbled in excitement.

"Ah," his mother sighed, "the recruitment."

She peeked outside from behind the thin white linen she hung over the window to keep out the dust—along with the eyes of the slums' less-than-desirable onlookers. Then she reached into her pocket and pulled out five silver notes.

"I saved them, knowing how much you look forward to this day. Go have a snack with your friends."

Calver gaped at the notes. "M-ma!"

He looked for Arleena to tell her he would bring her back a treat as well, but she had moved, huddling in the corner of the room where they bundled pillows and blankets for sleep.

"Arleena?"

She didn't look at him, preferring to wrap her skinny arms around knobby knees with her eyes screwed shut. Their mother hardly ever let them leave the hut, for all her terror of the world out of doors, especially Arleena. She was probably furious with envy.

"Hey, l-little warrior. I'll bring s-s-some-some." He found himself stuck at a hitch between words, the most frustrating thing about his stutter, before stomping his foot and stopping to breathe. "Something for you," he finished.

Her wet eyes flicked open and met his with a stare that pinned him into place. "Don't go, Calver. It's bad luck."

Calver rubbed the tips of his fingers together. Arleena had been speaking to him about "luck" a lot lately, almost as one might speak on a weather forecast.

He squinted at her. "This is the l-luckiest day of my life. D-don't worry about m-m-me. I'm always going to be here for you. I p-p-promise." It was a promise he made daily, endlessly. He would not be like their father. He would never abandon her.

He tickled her toes until she cracked like an egg, her arms falling away from her knees. A strangled giggle escaped her throat, a sound like sunlight and honey.

Their mother took the opportunity to scoop Arleena onto her hip, which she was too big for.

"I want to go with Calver," Arleena wailed.

"Hush, dear, not this time. It's too crowded." Their mother turned back to him. "You don't talk to anyone you don't know, you understand me?"

He nodded.

"And you come home to me before it's dark."

"I kn-know. I know!" He was practically bouncing in anticipation.

Her seriousness broke, and she beamed at him. "The Fates counted me lucky to bless me with you as a son. I—" Suddenly distracted, she looked down at Arleena, who was gnawing at her bicep like a tiny lion in want of being set down. She sighed, placing a hand over the girl's face, who rebelled by licking the entirety of her palm. "Well, get going, or you won't find a good spot."

Calver flashed a grin at her and stashed the notes in a pocket of his tattered trousers. He pulled playfully on one of Arleena's toes as he jetted toward the door. Her squeal of laughter peeled into a sob which followed him across the shanty.

"B-bye! See you t-t-to-to—" He broke off and dashed out of the home before finishing. It wasn't worth the extra few moments it would take him to say; he'd see them in a few hours.

Calver dashed through the Kaidechi slums at a breakneck pace, his face stinging from an immobile grin. A twelve-year-old boy in rags was invisible in such a place, free to do as he wished. The rabble around every corner, flooding the alleys, took as much notice of him as the grime below their feet.

But he slowed before reaching the main square, where the same boy would be chased down by the guard without question. Having notes in his pocket would not help him, either. He paused at the corner which marked his slum's gateway into the city's central street. His mother had taught him the correct way to take in his surroundings: listen for too much quiet, or too much noise; scan for eyes that met his; search for someone walking too fast or too slow. One could never be too cautious. Though cautious of what, he never understood. He was a dowagist, and a good one at that. What could possibly hurt him?

His eyes followed a gull riding the currents toward the central square, and another eager grin conquered his face. For the next few hours, that was what he'd be, too: an insignificant, dirty scavenger, unhindered by anyone's rules but his own.

Calver couldn't imagine a city more magnificent than Kaidech, poised like Creation's own sandcastle along the easternmost coastline of Nelfindar. But in the two years since the instatement of the Azadonian quarantine, it had fallen into obscurity. As the closest port to Azadonia, Kaidech's main source of economy had been pulled out from under it. Calver's wasn't the only family who'd been thrown into the slums. And the city itself had come to exist as its Azadonian counterpart—diseased, as though it had lost a heartbeat but somehow still lived on. Now, half the buildings, once cafés, bookshops, tailors, and ale houses, were boarded up. The markets kept guards posted at every corner to cut down on thievery, but the thievery went on, and the guards only added an aura of bleakness.

But today, the center streets rippled with activity. The Red Wing recruitment this year was expected to be the largest ever seen in Kaidech. Men were desperate to join the Nelfinden military: a way out of the city, which was otherwise bordered by wastelands. Calver couldn't enlist until he was seventeen, but the next five years would find him like the last ten had—watching, as he had since he was old enough to walk and his father had been the one to lead the recruitment.

This year's would be led by Roskaad Thyatira, which was almost too good to be true. That an actual general—the most famous general—would give the recruitment speech in a now-obsolete corner of Nelfindar. Calver had spent the past two weeks biting his tongue to prevent himself from continually gushing about the man to anyone who would listen. He was Calver's idol. Thyatira was every ground-level Nelfinden's idol, for that matter; the golden man fighting to change the military system so that people from the groundling class could earn their way into leadership positions. People like Calver.

He made his way to the dowagian studio, a small adobe building bordered by vacant shops on either side. Pim and Darion were waiting for him. It was the only place he ever met them, though once or twice he'd gone to Pim's house without his mother's permission. It had left him feeling so wholly out of place that he'd made an excuse—Arleena was sick—to leave. Something to do with the abrasiveness of his ragged linens pulling at silk seat cushions.

His mother never wanted people to know where they lived, nor that he trained at the studio on scholarship, as it cost more than they lived off each moon cycle. That he understood; she was ashamed for anyone to know how far they had fallen. But with a single glance at him, compared to any of the other boys that trained there, they knew. They all knew.

Darion, whose presence alone was an embrace, clasped forearms with him. Pim's wiry arm swatted at the nape of his neck. "We'll be cozy in the back where we can't hear a fuckin' thing if you don't get yer ass to move a tenth the speed I know it can."

Calver didn't say anything—the good ones didn't expect him to—but flashed Pim a sheepish grin and tilted his head toward the city's center.

They scurried off, weaving in and out of the bodies teeming through the open pavilion and into the streets with the adeptness only twelve-year-old soldiers possessed. The eager crowd sat atop buildings and garden walls and dangled from trees, all to listen to what Thyatira had to say. Calver, Pim, and Darion squeezed through it, nearly to the front, where they climbed atop a desecrated statue of Jenolavia. The likeness of Azadonia's last Prime Matriarch looked over the city square with a vacant expression, her arms spread like an eagle's wings to form the perfect perch.

After waiting for an unbearably long time, the young Red Wing general took to the erected stage. The crowd roared in appreciation. Thyatira was tall and muscular with neatly trimmed dark hair. His clean-shaven face boasted a broad jawline and a cleft in his chin so deep it almost looked like a battle scar. The man gave a short, cordial wave before breaking into his speech.

His words were impossible to hear, even as close as they were; the crowd was too massive. Calver had never seen so many of Kaidech's citizens in one place. It didn't matter. Every recruitment speech was the same. Fragments of Thyatira's words, such as "honor to serve" and "duty of the common man" were barely audible over the hubbub. The words didn't matter—words were overrated—but the general on the platform did.

The speech ended. The crowd dispersed.

And Pim nudged Darion on Jenolavia's opposite arm. "Dar, I swear I'm so hungry, I could eat at least three halouchas. I want a yam one. I want a bean one. I want a fish one. But I want dates and ghee too. Fates." He clasped his head with his hands.

Darion huffed. "About what I'd expect from a hungry shrimp. I could swallow five halouchas whole right now if I had the chance." The fried Nelfinden street food was famed for its size, if not for its grease.

Glad to have a few notes this time around, Calver was about to chime in with his own superfluous claim when another boy climbed up onto the statue beside them. The limited contents of Calver's stomach soured. Leave it to Thero to ruin a perfect day.

"They would never let you enlist," the boy said quietly enough for only Calver to hear. Calver looked away from the malicious glint in his eye. "They wouldn't risk it, seeing as surrendering military secrets runs in your blood."

"Fuck off, Thero," Pim growled without even having heard. "You might get dirty out here without your entourage to clean you up."

Thero smirked, but did put space between his perfectly tailored tunic and the stone of the statue. His embossed boots reflected the unclouded sun as he shifted. "I'm just building proper expectations. Your boy's sitting here all starry-eyed, like he thinks he stands a chance."

Darion stepped in. "See where that mouth lands you when Calver's leading this thing."

Calver cringed. His dream was no secret: to take up command one day. He'd proclaimed it enough times when he was younger, before he'd learned to keep his mouth shut. Before he'd learned Major General Thadinar Curtaim had betrayed his family and his country in one fell swoop. Before he'd started to stutter.

Thero shifted to face the two of them. "That's a big claim for a kid who can't string six words together."

Pim came to his defense the way he seemed to come at everything: flailing. He threw a fist toward Thero's wide-eyed face.

Calver experienced a flash of insight: a false mental image of Thero's body toppling a full story to the ground below, his neck connecting with broken cobbles at an angle no neck should. He lashed a forearm forward, narrowly saving Thero's nose from becoming gravel in a bag. And Pim from committing a homicide.

"Stop," he managed without stuttering.

Pim cursed and shook his wrist. "Chaos, you're fast."

"S-save it for s-st-studio," he muttered, his galloping heartbeat slowing back to a trot. He and Pim were set to go against Thero in a double next ten-day.

Thero's smirk found its way back to his face. "Lovers in a quarrel? I'll leave you two to it." He scrambled down the stone and lost himself in the crowd, at least as well as any rich boy could. Still, he took any elation Calver had felt that day with him.

Darion elbowed him in the ribs. "He's only scabbed because you're the only one he has yet to throw to the mat. Callisto's giving him private lessons, you know?" No one had beaten Calver in a duel in over two years. Not even the older boys. "And because you kissed Penale Warla behind the studio. Had a thing for her, he did."

Who didn't?

"You kissed Penale Warla behind the studio?" Pim's echo came at a volume that all of Kaidech could hear.

A furious burning rose into Calver's ears.

This time, Pim's flailing took the form of a string of curses foul enough to make an old woman below them threaten to find their mothers.

Two gulls screeched overhead, fighting over a scrap of food. The woman made her grumbling way down the street, and Pim turned to look at him with eyes like a dog watching its dinner bowl.

"Well, how was it?"

"It was f-fine." Calver's hand found the back of his neck.

It was amazing.

Pim leaned back against Jenolavia's colossal stone head. "Damn, I knew it. She's only interested in tall guys."

Then, without warning, the world around them stilled, as if time turned in on itself so that Calver might experience every fractal heartbeat as though it were a full moon cycle. A peculiar spark ignited in the center of his skull. Familiar. Inviting. Strange. And he was struck by a longing so profound that he tightened his grip around the statue's neck to keep himself from falling. Fates, he would dive headfirst into whatever *that* was, if only he could.

He was acutely aware of the sun shining at his back, the birds in the sky, the people below. But they were of no consequence compared to *that* feeling. He leaned into it. It leaned back. He wanted it; he'd never wanted anything like this. The internal phantom flowed, wavering back and forth as though inviting his attention. Then it tilted. He followed it to his right. His eyes trailed around the backside of the stage, visible only from their vantage point.

Thyatira pulled the hood of his cloak over his face and glanced in either direction. Then he turned briskly from the Red Wing's ranks toward a northeast side street. It was the glance Calver's mother had taught him: the glance of a person who didn't want to be seen.

The spark danced, its sentiments contagious. Calver's blood coursed through him like hot oil in a chute. He turned to his friends. Oddly muted, as with the rest of the city around them, they had returned to escalating the number of halouchas they wanted to an amount likely to feed the entire Red Wing. They hadn't seen.

When he looked back, the general had darted out of his sight. The spark tilted again, in the direction he had disappeared. Then it too faded, as if it had never been there. The world returned. Calver's heart pounded in his ears like a palm against a barrel. A jolt of excitement struck his bones.

He had to follow.

He'd been warned about such happenings: phantom voices; talking with entities he couldn't see. His mother told stories about the things in the world that were evil beyond measure. Things a dowaga couldn't protect him from, and only the Fates could control. But they were just the same as her telling him about Ruxian magic. Or not to speak with people he didn't know. Or not to go anywhere outside of their home and the dowagian studio, and to always alter the paths he took between. Paranoia.

Calver addressed his friends. "I-I-I don't think I c-can eat that m-much."

Heat touched his cheeks the instant the mortifying words left his mouth. Pim and Darion raised eyebrows at one another before proceeding to goad him with a series of insults and profanities in the way only friends could.

He shrugged and slid-scrambled to the ground. "I'll g-g-get with you l-later at Callisto's!"

Pim's jaw dropped in disbelief. Darion muttered something about Penale Warla. Calver ignored them and slipped away.

As he dashed in pursuit, his thoughts flitted to Arleena: her unwarranted fears and his promise to her. But this, if anything, was lucky.

Whatever this was, it was destiny.

Chapter 6
Calverous

"Aay... can you... wake up?"

Calver battled with the ebbing and flowing tide between him and a rarely reached depth of sleep. Then something touched him.

Touched him.

His skin snaked with fire. Hands pressed into his arm, rattled him. The bite of alarm chased any dregs of slumber from Calver's body.

Not again. Never again.

He snapped upright, lashing forward through the dim light of the cave to immobilize the threat. His fingers clenched around the Ruxian's wrist like a metal trap. A knife was in his hand before his next heartbeat.

She gasped.

His blade's edge did not quiver when it came to a stop less than a thumb's width from her throat. The Ruxian recoiled, sucking air through her teeth, but had nowhere to go.

"Easy! What, you dragged me to your fox den just to slice me open?"

Calver blinked away sleep. They were in the safehouse: a series of natural tunnels, once temporary shelter that he'd made his permanent living space when he realized he couldn't be around people. His back rested against the door he'd built over the rocky cave mouth. It was the only way he ever found sleep.

The Ruxian stiffened when he didn't respond, but Calver stared unceremoniously. He couldn't help himself. Bright silver eyes and hair—she'd removed her turban—consumed his field of vision. He was not yet convinced she, or any of it, was real. Even in the dim cave, those eyes seemed to emanate a faint light. Their stare penetrated him, seeping beneath skin and tissue to seek something private within him.

{Kill it.}

Void.

He released her.

"Thank you." She exhaled, retracting her hand to her chest. But she didn't retreat. She remained crouched in front of him, absorbing him as though he were an equally strange specimen.

They were like two wild cats, hackles raised, at a standstill after an unexpected encounter. He hadn't thought this far ahead. What had he been thinking in the first place? He'd brought the woman back to his home. A rule violation when he was already unredeemable.

Fankalo would find out.

Would think him a fool for taking this risk. Fates, he deserved his exile.

She was likely an agent of Cul'Mon. He had no means of communicating with her to find out.

They wouldn't—

"I have to pee," she said.

The bluntness of the statement shocked him like a dousing of cold water. He pulled himself to standing, sliding his back along the door for support. Tiny spots popped before his eyes as the blood rushed from his head. He stabilized himself with a hand on the adjacent rock wall.

Her eyes watched him all the while. Eyes like starlight incarnate. Fates help him, what had he gotten into? Calver fought to stay calm. He had to keep his mind his own, or there would be very little point to having rescued a Ruxian and more bloodstains to deal with.

Once steady, he motioned for the woman to follow him. They wound soundlessly through the lead tunnel into his safe house. A sequence of untampered Aetech lamps lit the way, casting shadows against the natural curvature of the ceiling and its stalactites. He was sure each one led the Ruxian's imagination to believe worse things than the last. *Run.* By all means, this shiny little human should run—*would* run from him, when she got her chance.

They hobbled into the first cavern down from the entryway, where he kept a bucket for a chamber pot. He motioned toward it and had already moved several paces away in a poor gesture of decency before she called after him.

"Well, I have to do more than just pee."

His feet took root in the cave floor, anxiety in mortal combat with reason. He gestured to the bucket again, albeit halfheartedly.

One side of her face scrunched in affront. "You're. *Not*. Serious."

He couldn't let her outside, could he? She had to be involved in whatever had happened at the locomotive port. If he let her out, she could immediately run and expose... He blinked away the fog blurring his brain as it jumped from conclusion to conclusion. What could she even know?

Nothing.

A Ruxian couldn't be an agent of Cul'Mon's.

But, then again, she could be an agent from Aetech, on to Fankalo's schemes. Disassembled Aetech lamps littered the far cavern. More than enough to condemn him, and Chaos knew how long she'd been here, awake, unattended.

The woman must have drawn her own conclusions about his thoughts in the moment that stretched between them. She shook her head and lifted a finger like she was scolding a dog. "No."

No. That didn't make political sense either. Why would a Ruxian work for Aetech?

A Ruxian shouldn't exist.

His hand found his hair, a thing he hadn't thought about in some time, overgrown and under-groomed. Fates be strayed, she didn't look like a spy. The young woman was like a strand of willow. She wouldn't be hard for him to pursue, even if she did make a run for it, even in his weakened state.

{Kill it. This creature is a ploy against you.}

He tried not to acknowledge the likelihood of the Survivor's logic, giving it a mental shove to the back of his mind. This was bad. He should have left her. But he hadn't. Now would he just keep her imprisoned here forever, or—?

"I'm dead serious. I'm about to lose it on your floor, guy. You can hold my hand if you deem it necessary, but I need to go outside. *Now.*" She growled the last word with an urgency that made him inadvertently jump toward the door.

{You will die.} The Survivor was persistent. Calver cringed as its unbearable weight pressed against him, trying to take control. *{Eight years of planning, worthless, for your weakness.}*

Calver pushed back. How long could he keep this up? He'd only kept the creature at bay during the demolition to prevent it from taking victims. Hoping that maybe, just maybe, it would prove he wasn't a liability—enough to warrant Fankalo's invitation back to sea.

That chance was gone now.

His body did the exact opposite of what all reason pleaded of him, and he ambled back up the stone hallway to open the door. Fell to his knees. Worked at the locks. A bubbling alarm filled the pit of his stomach. Did Ruxians have the power to control minds as well as matter?

She stood behind him, closer than his boundaries of personal space permitted, silver eyes following his every movement as he clinked open four unique lock configurations. He cracked the door and peered outside. It was nearing nightfall—they had slept through what was left of the previous evening and the entire day following. The deep-blue twilight was still. Undisturbed. But it could be lying. Anything might wait for them beyond the trees.

Calver turned to address the trap he'd set the night before: a distortion-triggered wire that would release a keystone holding back a landslide over the entry, just one of several defenses. The Ruxian was practically bouncing up and down behind him. He held up a finger for her to be patient. Then he meticulously deconfigured the ruxechorin core that powered it to prevent the arrangement from crushing her the moment she stepped beyond the threshold.

With a sigh, he pushed the door open. The girl darted past him, skittering into the woods. His stomach turned over in panic. Fates. She was gone. Escaped, like any sane person would want to after a glance at him.

He was fucked.

He made to pursue her, but she called out to him. "I'll be right back, I promise! I'll... I'll knock seven times!"

His hands found his hair again. Fates behave, he was at the mercy of her word. Words meant nothing. He stood inside the door, staring into the vacant twilight, rendered incapable of motion by his own internal storm. Why couldn't he move?

The Survivor screamed at him. *{Kill it!}*

Yet again, his body didn't listen to his idiot brain. He turned and stepped inside to wait for her return. Mind control. It was mind control. He wasn't this fatedly stupid.

Chest rising and falling in short, panic-induced swells, he locked the four locks back into place and pulled his dowaga into trembling hands. Trembling, because he didn't remember what it felt like to think for himself without the Survivor anymore. And he couldn't tell if his inability to act in his own interest was a Ruxian enchantment or just unwillingness to kill the thing which would get him killed. Each prospect was equally frightening.

He stood by the door for what felt like an age, but might have only been a minute. The stillness was broken by seven knocks, as promised, lilting like a melody. Relief flooded him like water in a drought. Calver opened the locks, the door, and the girl stumbled inside, looking as though the excursion had drained her. She was insane. Either his rescue had been contrived, or she was completely insane to have come back here. She was—

She was dying.

"I need to sit down," she gasped. With a hand braced against the wall to steady herself, she lifted her chin to look at him. The spaces beneath those starlight eyes were dark and hollowed. Her matching brows furrowed in an expression nearing pity. "By Preservation, and you do, too. Let's both go have a sit, then?"

She stumbled past him, into his own safehouse, as though she knew where she was going.

Calver followed the Ruxian through the low-ceilinged caverns of his living space. They stepped through shadows and shallow pools, the silence broken only by the echo of their footsteps and her ragged breath, until they reached an opening where the rock ceiling swelled to two stories. He kept his simple utilities here: a hearth which vented through a cobbed chimney, cooking supplies, meager food stores, and hundreds of books taken piecemeal from his trips into the city. Books on war, on weapons, on political strategy. Books that confirmed the need for violence. They littered the earthen floor in stacks, interspersed with stalagmites.

The Ruxian collapsed against the far wall beside a makeshift desk he'd fashioned from a stack of old Red Wing command reports stolen from Chira'na's Repository archives and a plank of rotting wood. He didn't have a bed or chair. To an outsider, his cavern home, which he'd never considered home, might seem…

It was pure savagery.

Terrifying.

He was terrifying. How fitting, for a traitor, murderer, psychotic—

{Kill it.}

As if to prove his point.

Calver fought away the insurgence and studied the woman's reaction. She didn't seem to care for her surroundings one way or another. She shook, her eyes bloodshot around their silver centers, her frame skeletal. His stomach tugged inward. He doubted she had concerns for creature comforts over simply continuing to breathe.

What was the social protocol for interrogating dying refugees after they rescued you? Calver's skin crept with discomfort. The Survivor normally weighed against him like a stone in such a circumstance. He was far from calm: Cul'Mon's men could be footsteps away. So why did it hold back?

"You can't speak, can you?" Her voice had a resonance he couldn't identify: airy, lispy, with rounded vowels. Somehow foreign, but Nelfinden all the same. She glanced up at him from beneath hooded eyes as though for confirmation. Calver realized he'd been staring at her again. He dropped his chin once.

"I had to resuscitate you yesterday. Saw you didn't have a tongue."

Chaos. As if this entire situation weren't awkward enough, she had sussed out his deepest insecurity before he was even conscious, seized it in her cold-prickled fist, and was waving it about like a fucking battle flag.

The Ruxian looked down at her shaking hands, still matted with his dried blood, and then back to him. The corners of her mouth twitched in a motion too weak to be a smile. Her silver eyes bored into him.

Calver had always imagined how he would react if the Survivor didn't intervene in nearly every interaction he had. But left with the opportunity now, he found himself awkward and impotent.

"Can—can you write?" she asked.

Calver's heart picked up speed. Ninety-seven percent of the Nelfinden population was illiterate. He nodded again, relieved to have anything to distract himself from thinking about how far his life, his hopes of ever seeing Fankalo again, had gone sideways in a single evening. He pulled a notebook and a stick of charcoal from an inner pocket. The pages were still stuck together with water.

'Can you read?' he scratched, the charcoal extra dark against the damp paper.

He pushed the notebook across the stone at her and backed away before realizing the idiocy of the question.

She squinted at his scribble, and her face drew inward. "Why would I have ask—never mind. I'm from Tennca'Pui. Script is mandatory."

Tennca'Pui was a sovereign commune of eunuchs: cenobites who dedicated their lives to studying the Fates. Her emerald robes argued in her favor, but it made about as much sense as a Ruxian refugee in the heart of the Sharinash. Not only were they explicitly male, but they were forbidden from leaving the monastery.

A strange, uneven discourse began, during which she waited for each written response. Compared to communication through nods and gestures, it was effortless.

'You're from Tennca'Pui?'

"Yes." Her body shook and she sucked through her teeth as though the very answer pained her.

'You are not a man.'

"Well I know that already, thank you. Is this a conversation or a stating of the obvious?"

He blinked at her remark. He wasn't used to candor from anyone but Fankalo. 'Are there more that look like you there?'

She pulled her knees into her chest. "You mean women? In Tennca'Pui? Creation, no. Women are forbidden."

Chaos. For all his lack of social wisdom, even he knew this conversation was a failing experiment.

The Ruxian's eyes unfocused, and then she began to chuckle. The noise started low in her throat and built in a crescendo until she was in hysterics, half-laughing, half-crying. "I—sound like—a lunatic."

At least she was aware of it.

She slipped into another fit of laughter, silent this time, her chest heaving against the spasms of her diaphragm. "And I'm talking to a lunatic. A murderer. Bathed in his blood like it's nothing out of the ordinary. Fates..."

A part of Calver cringed beneath those words. They were true, but no one had ever said them to his face.

Another part of him nearly reached out to her. Nearly.

Instead he scribbled faster, as though she'd never swayed in her composure. 'I mean Ruxians.'

She looked at the word, tears streaming, shaking her head. "I—I don't know. I don't—"

He snatched back the paper, cutting her off. 'Silver eyes. Silver hair.'

"No. There's only ever been me." She paused. Her lip trembled. Then—"Are there more who look like me in Nelfindar?"

Not in living memory. He shook his head.

The young woman sagged against the cave wall like a rag doll.

With the Survivor oddly inhibited, Calver's thoughts flashed to his mother. What would she think of this? A Ruxian. Androtia Curtaim's face flowed to the forefront of his brain freely for the first time in years. He stopped it. That was an emotion he was not ready to feel.

'What are you doing here?'

"I need help." The Ruxian looked up at him with eyes glazed by fear, and Calver, with all his slowness, realized she thought he was about to kill her. *Fuck*. Who knew? Maybe he was. "I've been traveling alone for weeks, and... there are people... hunting me. But I can't keep moving like this."

Certainly not. She was indisposed, and he shouldn't have invited a lost cause into his refuge, when the Survivor would kill her the moment he let his guard down.

But his hand moved across paper in opposition to his stream of thinking.

'I do not intend you harm unless the intent is mutual.'

Why had he written that? It wasn't true, nor was it particularly helpful. This woman could destroy everything. Who knew what she already knew about him? Calver's throat hardened. Something about killing a Ruxian seemed like an act against nature. Like tearing the wings off a rare butterfly—or returning her favor of saving his life by ending hers.

He'd done worse things.

She gave an apprehensive nod. "What is your name?"

Calver blinked. No one had asked him that since childhood, and those who knew him as the Hand's Reaper needn't ask. He hesitated. "Hello. I am the Reaper." didn't seem appropriate; it might give her a heart attack. Chaos, at least his frayed social graces could remember *that*...

'Calver.'

"Calver what?"

Why ask?

'Just Calver.' He sliced his hand sideways through the air to indicate for her not to persist. Curtaim was a name lost to time.

The girl chewed at her lip before extending a trembling hand, cracked with his coagulated blood. "We have something in common. I am also a just. Raimee."

Just. A word that meant so many things. That she, like him, didn't belong anywhere. That she didn't have anyone. That if she went missing, no one would mourn. Calver stared at her hand for too long. She seemed as though she might retract it, but he pushed down the part of him that shied from physical touch. She'd saved his life; he'd save her the humiliation. He gripped her hand.

In the instant they made contact, his skin prickled, not unlike what he'd experienced the night before at the lake. His body expanded in every direction. The time between heartbeats stretched. His blood roiled. The sensation was alien and horrifying and invigorating all at once.

What in Creation?

Calver lingered for longer than what would be considered standard decorum before he became aware of it. He snatched his hand back, blinking to clear his head—and that feeling. The Ruxian gazed at him with parted lips, slowly withdrawing her own dirty palm. He attempted to cover his reaction by bumbling with the paper.

'Are you hungry?'

She nodded so furiously her silver hair thrashed around her head like a sea. He held out a hand in the universal gesture that meant "wait." Then he stood and bustled to make a fire.

The Ruxian remained silent while he prepared food for them, his mind on an endless loop. He turned his thoughts over like river stones, searching for one that would hold reason. One that would make sense.

A Ruxian in the Sharinash. A Ruxian... spy? And a Tera'thian infiltration, and—

His stomach turned over.

Where had the contents of that Aetech shipment been distributed?

Chapter 7
Niklaus

TWENTY YEARS PREVIOUSLY

The Meyernes manor was, by Seraphinden skywalk means, modest, and its cloistered garden brimmed with an impossible number of flowers for such a small space. They spilled all the way to the marble of the balcony overlooking the Casowhatan sea, perfuming the air with their sweet botanic scent. Niklaus sat beside his father on the lip of the garden fountain, his calloused fingertips steadied over the fingerboard of the five-stringed kwitra. The strings steadied him back, like the touch of an old friend.

Niklaus plucked at them experimentally to elicit the impossibly divine resonance of metal reverberating through the hollows of a carved gourd. Some notes were supple delights, others twanging burrs. All were marvels.

His father leaned back to gaze past heavy eyelids at the clouds overhead, honeyed by the glow of the lowsun. A smile tugged at his lips. "Do you know why I asked you out here?"

To the garden, where his father had all of his difficult conversations, as though the roots might soak up some of the tension? On the day that another of Niklaus's tutors had decided to quit on the spot? As if they could be out here for any reason beyond a lecture his mother had forced his father to give? "Ah—bonding?"

A cheap answer. All things were bonding. Eat dinner, call it bonding. Play a game of stackers, call it bonding. Talk about responsibilities, call it bonding. It was what his father did, and it seemed important to him, so Niklaus went along with it.

"Yes, that. I also wanted to talk to you about family matters and what to expect."

And there it was. His tone held all the levity of a courtroom lecture in a way that was distinctly *not* bonding-like. But it didn't seem as though Niklaus were in trouble. His father's words were heavy, but fringed with excitement, not reprimand.

"You're leaving Mother?" Niklaus asked, aghast, before thinking twice.

Fates, what an asinine thing to say. It was common knowledge his parents' union had been an arrangement, and one of far more economical benefit to his father. And sure, the two hardly spoke to one another. But insinuating a separation, as their heir, was the uncouth sort of spewing his mother would rap his knuckles for.

But his father did not reprimand him. He only laughed, a sound with more power than the wind and more depth than the sea, which helped to ease Niklaus's shoulders away from his ears.

"Nothing so lucky, Niklaus." He scanned the array of blossoms around them as though they might give him the right words to say. "A flourishing garden is indicative of a well-tended gardener. One savvy enough to recognize the weeds and pry them at their roots as sprouts. One that will fertilize and water, not salt the beds."

Kretch. This was definitely not a conversation about flowers. This was serious. Niklaus set down his kwitra and turned to face his father, a man in his middling years who was perfectly average—in height, features, and temperament. In stark contrast, his sense of humor had always been second to none, which was why the moment had all the rigidity of a child caught five-fingering in a pastry shop.

Niklaus's father shifted, his words hitching with hesitation. "Every boy… starts with a dream. Some reach it. Most don't. My hopes have always been that, if I provided the financial backing, you would have the opportunity to pursue anything you wished. But… I am seeing that lost opportunity has its own cost, and that those expenses, well, they're inherited. Not only by you. But innumerable others."

And it wasn't a lecture on why Niklaus should stop intentionally triggering psychological breakdowns in his tutors, either. This was beyond serious. His brows pinched together. "What do you mean?"

His father clasped his fingers in his lap. "I am leaving the service of Colonel Limtush."

Niklaus's chest felt like it expanded back to its full width. Was that all? His father had served as Limtush's Hand—an honorary assistant in noble circles—for almost a decade, but hated every moment of it. "Oh. Well, that's great."

"Is it?"

"You told me that Baem Limtush was more crooked than the front teeth of a Shrokan hooker."

His father raised his white-flecked eyebrows. "You have a knack for memorizing my least savory statements, don't you?"

Niklaus shrugged and picked up the kwitra again. He strummed a chord—not the one he'd intended, but it sounded nice anyway. "I write them down."

His father laughed again and cleared his throat. "Nikla, I have been presented with an opportunity—a gamble—to invest in an alternative means of our livelihood. And I wanted you to be present with our prospective partners before I chose to take it."

Niklaus moved his finger up the neck of the gourd, plucking as he went. "Me? Why? If you want to change your Fate, just do it."

His father waited out the steady rise in pitch and then its subsequent fall. "If this venture fails—and it very well may—it will mean a lifestyle change. For you, your mother, and I." He worked his jaw like there was something caught between his teeth. "And it will not be a happy adjustment."

Niklaus shrugged. Maybe if they didn't have to keep with the skywalk status quo, he could become a teacher like he wanted. "I—I don't really care."

Did that come off as infantile?

"But you should."

Preservation. Yet another conversation steering back to his faulty motivation. The disappointment he was, considering the resources he'd been lavished with.

Infantile or not, he'd rather disappoint his father than lie to him to please him. "But I don't."

The housemaid happened to select that moment to walk across the balcony, a basket of linens in her arms, on the path between one room and the next. Her daughter, four years junior to Niklaus's thirteen, ambled after her, trailing a sheet through the dirt of the garden beds as she went.

The girl caught sight of Niklaus and her eyes sparkled, teeth capturing her lower lip in a mischievous smile. She slipped a glance toward her mother, already departed indoors, before skipping over to them and settling with legs crossed at their feet.

"Hello, Latouda," Niklaus's father said.

"Mesu." She nodded at him before turning to Niklaus. "Play me a song, Nikla!"

She couldn't have had better timing. Niklaus's chin bent toward his newly emerging Adam's apple. "Last time you told me it wasn't any good."

Latouda grinned. "Well, it wasn't, but I still liked hearing it."

He strummed a dramatic chord. She clapped her hands, bed linens tossed on the grass beside her.

"Don't do the one about the codfish," his father warned, "it's inappropriate."

Niklaus flashed his teeth. "Wouldn't dream of it."

He toyed with a couple more chords before breaking into melody.

"In the southern docks of town you'll find the worst kind of offender,
She trades illicit, tender-alchemy for a legal kind of tender.
Now, law is based on reason, and therefore free from passion.
But that might imply what's legal lacks a level of attraction.
When the Fates divvy up riches, how do they cast their votes?
I invite you, look no further than to those with all the notes:
How do immortals feel about a legal kind of tender?
Just look at those they give it to, who trade passion for splendor!
Yes, the Fates give wealth to people with a legal kind of teeendeeer!"

The final notes rang out through the garden, caught and diffused by the breeze. And then by the overstuffed silence of his meager audience shifting the crossings of their legs.

"I didn't get it," Latouda said.

Niklaus shrugged. "I wrote it, and I'm not sure I get it either."

"And I don't think passion specifically rhymes with attraction."

Fates, but the maid's daughter was a worthy critic. "It was a bit of a stretch, wasn't it?"

Her aquiline nose scrunched into a smile. "But it was funny, wasn't it?"

"As long as you think so."

A cawing call came from the open doors beside them. "Latouda!" The girl jumped to her feet. "There are sixteen beds to strip, and you have yet to do anything but trudge dirt into all the spaces I've washed!"

Latouda winked at Niklaus and wiggled her slippered toes, which were, in fact, filthy. She turned to his father. "By the by, Mesu Meyernes. I was supposed to tell you that your visitors have arrived."

"Splendid. See them through." Niklaus's father chuckled as she darted into the manor.

"It wasn't very good, was it?" Niklaus asked him.

His father's hand found his chin. "Once it's had a little... massaging, insinuating that all patricians are prostitutes is bound to ruffle some feathers."

Niklaus smiled. A higher compliment couldn't have been bestowed.

A soft knock sounded at the paned doors behind them, leading from the manor's antechamber. Nikalus turned to see a man standing with a girl, perhaps Niklaus's own age, a pace behind him. Her shrewd brown eyes encircled the garden, as though calculating its worth, before falling on his. She blinked at him before looking out at the Casowhatan as though she hadn't seen him there.

"Mesu Gorovich," Niklaus's father boomed, welcoming as ever. "Thank you so much for coming." He stood to greet their guests, and Niklaus followed suit, the neck of the kwitra slack in his grip. "This is my son, whose opinion I value in this matter."

Niklaus's chest expanded, yet again, at his father's words.

Mesu Gorovich was too broad to be a businessman and too narrow to be a military man. His dark eyebrows were thicker than eyebrows had any right to be, and they seemed to cast a shade against his otherwise milk-white smile. "A pleasure, young master."

Niklaus gripped the newcomer's hand and returned the smile. "Niklaus Meyernes the third. At your service, mesu."

"And this is my daughter, Rebethel." Mesu Gorovich inclined his head toward the girl.

"Lovely to meet you," Niklaus chimed, reaching for Rebethel's hand. She placed it into his, but it sat there without grip, like it wanted to be there as much as any good burr wanted to be in a sock. She didn't respond, but her eyes trailed to the kwitra in his opposite hand. One corner of her mouth drew into a smirk. Niklaus's insides roiled in discomfort, and he rubbed his palm against his sirwal.

His father grinned like split citrus at Mesu Gorovich, his exuberance nearly catching. "Niklaus, Hashod has a business partner in Chira'na with a lot of influence in Azadonia's Kovathian sect. He claims that they are weeks from passing into law the ability to sell their distortion patents."

Niklaus cocked one ear toward his shoulder. "Distortion… like the energy technology?" With the restrictions the Prime had placed on foreign trade, distortion was the most expensive commodity on the skywalk.

"The very same. Imagine not only breaking Azadonia's monopoly on the science but being among Nelfindar's first to produce it nationally."

It sounded too good to be true. Why come to a family at the skywalk's lowest tier to invest in something so promising? Why not go to the top? Unless, of course, it was a gamble.

His father seemed to read his thoughts from his expression. "Of course, we would make our investment once the technology is confirmed."

Niklaus swallowed. His father was rational. He wasn't so desperate to leave Limtush's employ that he would jump into something perilous.

"Keep in mind, it might take some time. We are expecting weeks, but Azadonia's Matriarchy continually pushes back on these matters."

"Of course," Niklaus said, fighting to maintain a smile, if anything for his father's sake. He'd never seen him so excited.

"Mesu Meyernes!" A frantic scream sounded from the side of the cloister, shattering the moment and setting frost around Niklaus's bones.

A courier in Red Wing uniform burst through the gardens—directly through the beds, like he was a creature from the wilds, not a human who understood that flowers were not to be trodden upon. He came to a stop on a cluster of poppies. They crunched beneath his boots with a sickening sound.

"Mesu Meyernes." The courier doubled over, chest heaving as he gasped the words. "Colonel Limtush has need of you this minute. Make ready to depart for Casowhatan. The Chori navy is on the horizon."

The color left Niklaus's father's face. He gave Mesu Gorovich an apologetic look and said to the courier, "Walk with me."

Niklaus tagged after his father as he burst through the double doors into their foyer.

"We're under-prepared," the courier said. "Limtush is pulling together a civilian militia until we can receive support from our southern forces."

Niklaus had never been one to pay attention to the politics behind the Kath war, despite his teachers' best efforts. But he knew their Prime had sent their main fighting force to aid their allies, the Pazirians, against the Tera'thian-aligned Chori raid on their capital, Yalusa. Which left Seraphinden at a tenth of its usual northern fighting force.

His father's face contorted as he set a brisk pace through the reception hall. "Support from our southern forces? Weren't our southern forces supposed to prevent a Chori force from getting through the Rollard straight in the first place?"

They swept through the front doors and onto the skywalk.

"They were caught unawares. It was Major General Curtaim, mesu. He ordered the fleet to dock in the Rollard Isles just before the attack. A-and then—he disappeared."

"Disappeared? What do you mean, disappeared? Red Wing Generals don't simply vanish into the aether."

"We can both imagine what happened."

"Fuck," his father growled, like Niklaus imagined a seafarer skewered by his own hook might. It was so uncharacteristic that Niklaus might have laughed under different circumstances. Now, the sound enacted a strange gravity on his intestines.

With the suddenness of shattered glass, an alarm sounded across the skywalk: a piercing horn that sent shivers down Niklaus's spine. His parents had taught him years ago that a horn like that signified the need to take shelter. It might as well have meant 'kiss your loved ones.'

"Father, what's happen—?"

"Nikla, go home."

He shook his head so violently, his dark hair caught in his eyelashes. "But what about you?"

"I will attend Colonel Limtush."

Panic clutched in Niklaus's throat. Limtush was only a reserve colonel. It was more of an honorary title than a military position. Limtush's main focus was his family's pharmaceutical operation, not his acute military influence. He wasn't ever supposed to see combat, let alone bring his Hand into combat. A combat where they were impossibly overwhelmed and outnumbered.

Niklaus gripped his father's arm. "Wait," he nearly said, but didn't. There had to be a way to prevent this. His father was getting ready to leave Colonel Limtush anyway. Why go to Casowhatan? Why not stay here?

"With any luck, I'll be home before you wake," his father said.

Niklaus knew his father's principles. Principles that, in the face of a genuine threat, seemed far less attractive. His father tore his arm away and marched off with the courier without a backward glance.

The skywalk's civilians moved like the wind was at their backs, seeking shelter. Niklaus returned home. He meant to find his mother, who he was sure would be searching for him, but somehow found himself back in the garden. The Goroviches had disappeared, and the space felt smaller and darker than ever before, despite the amber glow of lowsun. He ran to the balcony, a burning stone rising in his throat. The black ships which cloaked the sea where it met with the sky were too numerable to count. They darkened the horizon like a menacing fog of timber and sail and steel.

Nikalus stepped back from the balcony with buttery knees. He sat on the fountain's lip again and stared at the poppies, squashed by the courier. The scarlet petals, victims to violence, were smeared into the dirt beneath their once-stems in a way that was horribly wrong. He could almost hear them screaming.

War was a thing that happened to other countries. Other people. War was not a thing that should ever touch the capital city of Nelfindar, the most powerful nation in all the world. And it was certainly not a thing the Hand of a pharmaceutical tycoon should ever have to rub noses with.

Niklaus lifted a broken stem that nothing would ever mend. He could have said something. Could have told the courier to stay out of the beds. He'd seen him coming from half the balcony away, hadn't he?

But he'd been silent. Compliant. And inherently, he'd seeded this violence.

Chapter 8
Calverous

Calver stoked a fire in the hearth, then pulled water from a rainfed cistern to set pearled sorghum to boil. Porridge was routine. Routine was good.

Unlike the events of the last twenty-four hours, during which eight years of planning with Fankalo had gone awry, his position had likely been compromised to Cul'Mon, and a living—half-dead, if he was being honest—Ruxian had fallen into his confidence. The Ruxian in question—Raimee—remained slumped in the crook where cavern wall met cavern floor. He could not tell if she slept. She kept her head cradled in her arms, her face obscured by a silver nest.

Calver searched a small hearthside pot for honey, already knowing it to be empty and wishing it wasn't. Unembellished it would be. He ladled a bowl of the gruel and set it into Raimee's hands. She jerked in surprise, then looked at him as though he'd set a diamond between her palms.

By the time he sat on the floor across from her with charcoal in hand, she was already half-finished. Calver's own stomach growled ferociously, but with a single bowl he'd thought it best the starving one ate first. She was so thin, as if a too-hard poke could punch a hole right through her.

How to approach this? He hardly knew how to interact with Fankalo anymore, let alone a Ruxian stranger.

{Kill it,} the Survivor hissed from its depths.

And that was why.

But the Survivor exerted no pressure over his will, as it usually did. Just another oddity to add to the pot.

Calver watched, his fingers caressing the hilt of a knife for comfort, as she gulped down the rest of the porridge. He stood, refilled it for her, and sat again. She watched him back over the rim of the bowl as he firmed his resolve enough to jot on the writing pad again.

'Someone is hunting you?' He tapped it for her to read.

She nodded. "Which means we have two things in common." She studied him, as though hoping her boldness would make him give something away. His stomach turned.

'I am not asking to sympathize.' How did she know he was hun—

He gritted his teeth. Only an imbecile *wouldn't* assume so. People did not live tucked away in the wilderness unless they didn't want to be found. 'Explain how someone like you comes from Tennca'Pui?'

She understood his meaning: why she broke their gender norms. "I was brought there as an infant—my mentor, a councilor there, had been friends with my mother. They made an exception for me, even though—" Raimee gulped. Her sentence finished itself. "And—and I didn't want to leave the monastery. I had to. Something terrible—" Her eyes darted around the perimeter of the bowl in her hands. She shook her head. "It was compromised."

Calver furrowed his brow. Tennca'Pui compromised? Surely Fankalo didn't know, or he would have received word.

But Fankalo knew everything.

The thought scratched at him, worse than the barbs in his back. He didn't need to wonder *why* the attack had occurred, if Tennca'Pui had been harboring a Ruxian for two decades. He knew too well the person who would find reason in butchering a neutral territory, one sworn to non-violence, in search of a Ruxian descendant if he knew one were sheltered there.

He started on a new sheet of paper. 'When?'

Raimee discarded the bowl and hugged her knees into her chest. "Nearly a month ago. We were invaded by foreigners. I don't know who they were." Her voice caught in her throat. "The cenobites have sworn oaths against violence. We were defenseless. And I—I don't understand…" She sniffed into her tattered robe.

'They came because you are a Ruxian.'

Fury and offense mingled with the tears brimming in her eyes. Shit. Stupid. He'd written it with all the sensitivity of a wolf chatting up a rabbit before biting into its neck.

"What in Chaos does that mean?"

But perhaps worth the information her response gave him.

Not a lie, this time. She had no idea what she was. But how could she have made it here? Tennca'Pui was a two-month-long journey by road. A Ruxian refugee would not go without notice. The only explanation would be that she had walked the entire way through the Sharinash, a third the distance.

And that was impossible. She wouldn't have survived.

At least, not alone. Which meant he could be in bigger trouble than he'd thought.

'It means you are unique, dangerous, and a highly desired bounty.'

Her lip trembled, but her eyes didn't waver from his. "Is that why you brought me here?"

Without the Survivor in control, every possible threat fell short of his fingers. 'I brought you here so the wilds wouldn't claim you.'

Her shoulders fell in a visible sigh of relief.

'Do your attackers know you escaped?'

"Yes? No? But if they came because of me, as you say, they obviously didn't find me there."

Something in her story didn't add up. If she meant to stay alive, she wouldn't have wandered into the Sharinash. If she meant to stay hidden, she would have gone west into the Tsorlap, not ventured so close to Chira'na, a metropolis with a population near a million people. He gestured for her to continue, but she bit her lip and fell silent.

'Are you an agent of Cul'Mon?'

She dragged a hand across her face. "I don't know who or what that is."

'Then why were you at the lakeshore with his men?'

Raimee gaped at him, like she couldn't believe someone would have cause to not believe another. He locked her in a deadpan stare.

"You have a funny way of showing gratitude. I was walking, not conspiring against you." Yet she fidgeted with the hems of her sleeves.

'You pulled me out?'

"Yes. I saw you fall..." Her gaze found a place that existed only on another plane. The place where people sometimes found the right words to say. "And then—" She stopped again, as though she half-expected the cave to answer for her.

'How did you—' His hand hovered over the paper, equally unsure of how to communicate what he thought had happened the evening prior: the impossible.

She gripped her elbows like they might anchor her to a reality where magic was still the talk of lore. "Fix you?" she finished for him. "Because when I pulled you out of the water, you didn't have what most people would recognize as a functionable head."

Calver looked sideways, hoping she didn't see the way he flinched. He nodded.

Raimee sighed and slumped further. "I... don't know. I thought maybe you were the one that did it, not me. It nearly killed me."

True enough, she looked as though she'd escaped death as narrowly as he had. It was an honest response, though it only hastened his heartbeat.

"I... I can't explain it. I tried to revive you—we all receive medical training—a-and it was like you—" She swallowed and moistened her lips. "You took the life out of me. And I woke up here." Her eyes darted around the inhospitable cavern, still more shadow than solace, even with the flickering light from the hearth and his distortion lamps.

"Calver," she whispered. It was so strange to hear his name. "Please help me." Her words were failing. "Please, please..."

A shiver racked her body. Fever. She was ill, exhausted, and bereaved. Perhaps she would respond better if the questions were from curiosity, rather than an interrogation.

'Are you seeking Chira'na?'

The Ruxian read his message and closed her eyes. "Y-yes. I came this way looking for someone named Abiathar Methu'su. My mentor tasked me to find him..." Again, she paused as though the answer pained her. As though she knew recounting it would be useless. "In Chira'na."

Abiathar Methu'su. A chill coursed from Calver's head to his toes. That name.

How could something so significant to his recollection be so clouded? To hide his recognition, he stood and paced. What were the chances that the one man she was looking for was someone he knew?

Unnoticing of his epiphany, Raimee continued to grip at her elbows as though they might grip her back. Then she curled like a cat on the floor in a feverish stupor. The abandoned bowl was still at her side.

Calver's stomach protested just looking at it, despite his hunger, but he filled it anyway and brought it to the floor to eat. It had been over a day since his last meal, and he did not want Cul'Mon to corner him without strength.

He sat beside the comatose Ruxian at first—it only seemed proper. But everything about her unsettled him. He moved to the far wall and dined in silence for some time, trying to steady the gale that buffeted his mind.

He didn't know how long into the night he sat there, porridge cold and forgotten after a few force-fed bites. The Fates were laughing at him. He'd failed Fankalo, again. Failed everything they'd fought for. And now, he'd broken the simple rules set for him.

"Whatever you do, Cal, don't involve anyone, and stay away from people when you're not on assignment. You're just too much of a liability."

The memory punched into him. Salt and smoke in the humid air and Fankalo on the beach, calf-deep in the river of blood that chased the rain into the sea, tanka leveled between his eyes. *"Don't make me test my aim, brother."*

There had to be a way to fix this. A way to find that shipment, wherever it had been dispersed, and finish the job. He couldn't continue to spend his abating days alone. He didn't think he'd make it.

Calver put his palms over his eyes. Without Fankalo's protection from Cul'Mon in the time he'd lived in exile, he'd been meticulous, preparing for anything.

But what could have prepared him for this?

Chapter 9
Attilatia

Now that Hashod was watching the materials ledgers, Attilatia was forced to spend her day off dredging around the Shrokan district in search of supplies. Shrokan's streets smelled of rot and worse—of the beggars who babbled on the corners, their grime-covered fingers extended. Attilatia pulled a hood over her turban to hide her face, though it was impossible to conceal the dark oculars shielding her eyes from highsun. They marked her as an Azadonian more clearly than a sign around her neck could.

The Azadonians had never let any of their tunnels fall into such conditions, even after the strikapa took its toll. There was always a place for any who fell on hard times. A way to keep their hands occupied, their bodies warm, their bellies full. Such was not the case in Seraphinden. It was a solemn reminder as to where she would find herself if she pushed her insolence too far with Hashod.

After stealing from Aetech for the better half of a decade to fuel her personal projects, having the option taken from her was a crippling loss. Now her work was all chicken, no egg. She would have to spend from her own pocket—precious funds she'd been saving so that, when the time was right, she and Thedexemore could escape.

She'd wallowed on it all morning, sour as a crabapple. Not that her mood was ever particularly saccharine these days, what with being cornered into putting her only family at the mercy of the Red Wing, the recent Kovathian assassination attempts against him, and dealing with Hashod's harassment. But, given the choice, she would have rather danced the lethoso stark naked on the skywalk balcony than spend daytime hours awake and in Shrokan, of all places.

She fingered the outline of the dagger nestled against her ribcage, then tugged at the waist of her traditional tipiana to loosen it in hopes of appearing bulkier. As a woman, a foreigner, and especially an Azadonian, she would be a target for anyone having a particularly bad day.

That said, she couldn't deny groundling prices on a beggar's budget. So, Shrokan it was.

She found herself outside an apothecary, indicated by a crude sign by the window. The stores in Shrokan all hosted signs painted or carved with images of whatever the shopkeepers sold to aid the mostly illiterate population. The apothecary should have what she needed for her antidote tests. Her distortion experiments were another story. Though she could always disassemble completed Aetech lamps for their raw materials, the idea was not only barbaric but expensive.

Raw, synthetic ruxechorin—the chemical which fueled all distortion devices—and the components to produce it were Nelfinden contraband. Legislation Hashod had enacted, no doubt, to eliminate any threat to Aetech's long-standing monopoly. As if anyone could possibly identify the stratum ruxechorin was attuned to distort from out of the trillions the Fates had to offer. There were no threats.

Still, if there was a dark market item to be found, Shrokan was the place to find it. And the very fact that a law had been enacted to prevent the sale of ruxechorin meant that someone from the city's seediest groundling district had probably made it their personal goal to break it.

Attilatia pushed her way past the curtain which served as a door and, away from the glare of natural light, slid her oculars to her forehead. The shopkeeper, more hair than man, sat on a stool behind a counter and spared her a glance before settling back to rearranging an assortment of rune-stamped bottles.

"Calcium Disodium, please," she asked him.

With a sigh, as though he'd rather not stand, the man prowled behind the counter and rummaged to retrieve a small vial of white powder. "Seventy-six silver an ounce. How much you want?"

Attilatia didn't try to hide her scorn. Either he was out of his mind, or trying to take advantage of her. "I not born yesterday."

"That's the going rate. You can take it, or you can leave." He returned to sit on his stool.

Not a ploy. He was serious. "Chaos abound, what create such increase?"

"Last two shipments of it to Seraphinden were taken by raiders," he grunted, picking at his fingernails.

Unlikely.

"What, Nelfinden charter ship were pirated by herd of sea rat?"

"That was the fourth shipment I've lost supplies from this moon cycle. Word is, the raiders have united under a queen. With full-size charters themselves, now. And they come armed to the teeth. Everything's gone up."

He heaved the corpse of something cat-sized and furry unceremoniously onto the counter and took a pair of pliers to its teeth. Attilatia wrinkled her nose.

"Queen would imply nation," she said. "And raiders, they just that. Raiders. Individual bands of bottom-dwellers." She thought about her own thievery of Aetech materials, shrinking inwards only slightly at her own hypocrisy. What she did was different. "How do you mean they have queen?"

The man sighed in exasperation. "I'm just telling you why you're paying an arm and a half for metal detoxers." He dropped a tooth into a jar on the counter. "That's all."

It was a clear dismissal, but this was the first conversation of interest she'd had in moons. The Nelfindens prohibited international travel and trade. In the time she'd been in Seraphinden, she'd never had a real way out, short of building her own ship and casting off into the night—which she'd considered. But a raider nation might just be able to take her from Nelfindar to Azadonia. Or at least know if Azadonia still existed outside of Kovathian control. Maybe. All things had their price.

"Surprising such dogs would have guts to put woman in charge." She put the requested notes for the chelator on the counter and pushed them toward him. "But what make them unite?"

"What do you think would make them unite? Same as makes anyone else unite. Fear."

"Fear of what?"

He shook his head, his eyes narrowing on her dark oculars. "You should really come out of your hole more, moon worshiper. That ignorance will get you into trouble."

"Fear of what?" she repeated.

The shopkeeper hesitated. His face scrunched in self-admonishment. He'd said something he'd clearly thought to be vacuous. "Listen, woman. I have nothing else to say to you and business to be made." He nodded at the scraggly mass of fur on the counter. "If you have what you need, I suggest you be on your way."

"There is other thing…" Attilatia lowered her voice and took her chances. "I need raw ruxechorin. Where you think I—"

His chin lifted, eyes blazing. "Get out."

Attilatia bristled. "Is just question. Friend of mine sourced in Shrokan before when—"

The merchant slammed his hand on the counter. "Get out! Before I call the guard to haul you back to where you belong."

Heart thumping in her ears, Attilatia snatched the bottle and stuffed it into her bag. She stormed from the apothecary without another word. That was an overreaction, if she'd ever experienced one. As if he were above contraband, when the shop held all the telltale signs of a moss den.

She stopped short outside the shop, her attention caught by a utility pole three body lengths from her. Its Aetech lamp was in disrepair, as was usually the case in the groundling districts—they hadn't been maintained since their installation over a decade ago—and its light flickered despite the mid-lowsun. A weathered paper had been nailed to the post, more splintered than driftwood, bearing the countenance of the new General Prime, Roskaad Thyatira. Beneath it was the lettering "Groundlings Rise." She stepped forward and traced the lines of Roskaad's face with a taupe finger. The flashing light above filled the portrait's inky eyes with fire.

How fitting...

There were those few among the groundlings who could produce such literacy. But why would they? Doing so would be risky. Seen as a sedition by the oligarchy. *Chikotos*. Some people couldn't think far enough ahead to keep themselves out of prison.

Thyatira's eyes stared into her, bringing to the surface all of her hopes and all of her fears: Nelfindar was on a collision course with revolution.

There were so many trapped under Thyatira's spell... Attilatia's lips rolled in over her teeth. Could one man, raised at such a disadvantage, truly accomplish what he had set out to in this hopeless society?

"Sssssspare chaaaange?"

Attilatia clutched at her dagger. She'd been so entrenched in thought, she'd lost sight of her surroundings. A middle-aged woman stood an arm's span away from her, head lolling, face and hair weeks from their last wash. She stroked the fabric of Attilatia's tipiana with fingers caked in—*better not to think about it*. The woman was clearly descending—an effect from the moss.

"No," Attilatia said.

"Azadonian slick," the woman spat with teeth bared. "Greedy. Dirty. You deserve to be—"

Attilatia didn't hear what she deserved. She tore away with her eyes down. As much as she wanted to find synthetic ruxechorin, where there was one mosser, there would be more.

She bit into her lip. Was it possible the raider problem had caused a ruxechorin shortage, too? The timing couldn't possibly be worse. After sixteen years, Aetech was no longer a guarantee to her and her brother's safety. When Thedexemore left with the Red Wing, it would buy her three months to figure out who'd sent the Kovathians to assassinate him. Or otherwise secure a way for Thedexemore to escape the country... for that, she needed all the bargaining power she could muster. Which meant distortion intelligence, and the ruxechorin that fueled it.

If she couldn't buy it in Shrokan, she'd have to barter for it elsewhere. Her insides burned as she considered her alternative—the one she'd sworn off, yet again, thinking she'd garnered some amount of self-respect. Who was she kidding? Where she'd left space for self-respect to grow, she'd only cultivated malice.

A pivot down a sloping, cobbled side-street took her in the direction of the great green wall at Seraphinden's northern limits. Within fifteen minutes, the usual eclectic aromas of turpentine, shellfish, fried dough, and sulfur heralded Seraphinden's wharf—like a codfish had opened a bakery, then set it on fire.

Attilatia made her way to the messenger station—an oddly decorative structure, with dragonflies carved into its swinging parlor doors—that connected with Seraphinden's dock. She paused outside, her fingernails biting into her palms as she considered disassembling some of her existing inventions to salvage their ruxechorin cells instead. A short distance down the street, a groundling beggar coughed, cradling a baby which coughed even harder into her chest.

No. There was no point in repairing the damage she'd done to herself for pride's sake. Not when it put Thedexemore at risk again. Some cracks were simply too big to patch.

Attilatia pushed her way through the swinging wooden parlor doors to the messenger station. Its usual attendant, Celestar, sat behind the single shanty desk in its overstuffed office. The nearly spherical man wore an apricot women's turban and rouge, and took a bite from what had to be the greasiest haloucha Attilatia had ever seen before batting his eyes at her.

"Atti? Haven't seen you in a few moons, honey. Who are you here for this time?" he managed to say around whatever was in his mouth.

How Celestar managed such amiability when he spent all day bathing in the wharf's rotten-egg smell as if it were Pazirian perfume, she would never understand. But she appreciated it almost as much as his ability to keep a secret.

Attilatia inhaled deeply through flared nostrils.

"I need speak… with Sarko." Fates, she hated the words as they passed over her lips.

Celestar raised his eyebrows, their piercings glimmering in the lantern light. "You're in luck. His ship came into port two days ago. He leaves for Steila, day after next."

"When could you get message to him?"

"Tonight?"

She'd seize her opportunity while it lasted. "Tell him meet me at highmoon. Same place."

Celestar clasped his hands beneath his multifaceted chin and beamed at her. "He'll be delighted."

Chapter 10

Calverous

Calver woke early the next morning, as normal, and left the cave and the still-sleeping Ruxian to practice the dowagian arts. The forest around him was silent with the contemplative pause of winter. He built his own heat, which the cold air licked greedily from his skin. The exertion gave his mind an outlet, short of letting his mind-djinn take control and bring the death it promised.

Pivot. Parry. Catch. Throw.

He spun the dowaga through a series of movements, holstered it, and repeated it a dozen times. The rigid routine was how every day began. It was a consistency he could control. He moved faster, pushing his limbs to match pace with his mind, still whirring madly from the previous two days' events. He sweated, straining against the abnormal exertion. *Good.* It would make him stronger. Mental fortitude was just a bonus to the main objective of his training—to stay alive. To stay at least one step ahead of Cul'Mon. Until he didn't need to.

Four hundred and twenty-one days.

The demolition failure had been a colossal waste of time and resources. If Cul'Mon was behind it, it was entirely Calver's fault. His face hardened. To think he'd dreamt of redemption. How many more times would he screw things up for Fankalo in the time he had left? He spun the dowaga a little faster. A parry left, a hook right. As if that weren't enough, there was a fated Ruxian in his safe house. To track the shipment, he'd have to leave her unattended.

Kretch. Why had he let her live? There were rules for a reason. No happy ending would come of this scenario. Interaction was something he couldn't afford if he and Fankalo were going to dethrone a dictator next year.

"You're just too much of a liability."

Fankalo had meant that as a liability to the Shadewalker's Ghosts—her fast-growing list of recondite acolytes. Calver took it as a liability to anyone with a heartbeat.

Like the Ruxian.

He had no idea what he would do with her. No idea what he would write when she invariably made eye contact with him. How he would tell her that he knew about the man she was looking for, but then again, he didn't. Tell her he could help her find him on the condition, of course, that she would get out of his hair, keep his secrets, and pretend she'd never met him. Then they could both get back to what they needed to do. No harm in it.

{It is more likely to rain in the Jiradesh.}

Calver's grip tightened on the dowaga. The Survivor was back to its full strength again. It pushed its way past his disturbed thoughts. Requested control. Requested to do the task that he could not.

Void.

He scrambled to lock onto a new thought pattern, picking the first thing that flitted into his mind.

Methu'su.

It wasn't much better, but the Survivor's bloodlust ebbed to a dull roar, enough for him to think through. The name haunted him, locked away somewhere, just out of reach. Raimee came from the community of cenobites, so it made sense that she was looking for a scholar of sorts. It was possible that he'd simply read it somewhere... not that that narrowed things down. All he did was read. If he was reading, he could keep himself level. It was when he relapsed into idle thinking that things went badly.

Calver glanced at the cave. He didn't have to say anything to the Ruxian about Methu'su. He could leave now. Never have to look at or think of her again. He'd be free to let the Survivor take control without risking her life. Free to return to Chira'na, unhindered, to write to Fankalo and explain why, while the target shipment remained in pristine condition, and their shot at replacing it with Fankalo's Dreiden Corporation technology was demolished: completely and utterly fucked.

A heat in his stomach combusted into a guttural roar. He hurled his dowaga into the forest. It spun about its three perfectly balanced points, reflecting light from the low morning sun in a thousand directions. It looked like a shooting star until it lodged itself into a tree with a dull *thunk*.

Calver exhaled. Hung his head. Sighed. And proceeded to collect it. Holstering the weapon, he plodded to the cave entrance. When he'd first found the space, some eighteen moons ago, he'd framed a door there with cob and timber and covered it with lichen until it was invisible to the untrained eye. An insurance policy, to be sure no one caught him unawares. As if anyone would. He'd not seen another living person in the Sharinash until two days ago.

Without really knowing why, he knocked seven times, as she had—weird—paused, and creaked the door open to enter. He crept through the entry passage before peeking around its bend. The Ruxian was still lying as he'd left her: on the floor in front of the fire, of which only glowing embers remained. She lifted her head, watching him with effervescent eyes. One of her silver brows raised. Calver's stomach clawed for purchase.

"So what, we have a knock now?"

He shrugged.

Calver walked past her and threw a couple of logs from the stack beside the hearth onto the fire. He kneeled to stoke the flame back to life.

"Where did you go?" She analyzed him with discernable distrust.

He found the paper pad where they'd left it, on the floor beside her. 'To think.'

"What did you think about?"

How, at the moment everything he'd been working toward for the better part of a decade took a nosedive, the Fates had thrust a Ruxian under his guardianship. 'How you have terrible timing.'

Every trembling span of her body curled inward. "All things considered, I'd think you'd find something to appreciate in my timing." Her voice was strong, but she had all the posturing of a bleeding rabbit. Kretch. What was he going to do with her?

His charcoal hovered over the paper. He was going to do the thing he shouldn't. And should. 'I'll help you find Methu'su. I've heard the name, I just don't recall where.'

Raimee's eyes came alive. It was as though an invisible barrier between them crumbled. A portion of his anxiety ebbed, too, having made a decision that didn't involve blood or strangling.

For now.

'I think I may have read of him. I'll look through the volumes here. You're welcome to help if you're feeling well enough.'

She scrambled upright and away from the hearth as though astonished the space was not where her body would make its final imprint. "Yes! Yes, of course. I mean, I am."

A moment passed, and the blood drained from her eager face before she re-seated herself.

"To a certain capacity."

The task began.

Over three hundred volumes constituted Calver's personal library, if one could say that of his hoard, all accumulated during his stay outside Chira'na. Methu'su, if he were a living person as indicated by Raimee's mentor, could only be present in historical accounts from the past seventy years. He stacked a pile for her to pick through, less-than-subtly including any that held political information regarding the Ruxians.

Despite her ailment, Raimee moved through books at a rate without precedent. In two hours she completed four volumes, end to end. At first he assumed she was skimming each page, hoping the words she was looking for would jump out at her. But every few minutes she would slow down to read aloud to him a passage she found interesting. Always amicably, like his offer to help her made him no longer a danger. Like she wanted his opinion. Like he was her long-time research partner and sitting in the wilds, caked in mud and blood, was a thing they'd always done.

He'd be doing her a favor in staunching those sentiments.

Then she quieted again. Raimee stopped, shaking her head, her silver brows furrowed at a compilation of Seraphinden's oligarchical decrees. "They lied to me. Blinded me."

Calver set his own read, so far fruitless, to the side.

"I've spent a lifetime studying biology, discouraged from any focus on world events or politics because they weren't 'relevant.' 'A deviation,' they said. Time wasted that could otherwise be focused on specializations that brought funding." She gulped. "But that was a lie. They hid this on purpose."

So, she was as ignorant as she had appeared. Calver frowned. An act would have almost been better. Once she left this safe house, she didn't stand a chance. She was dead—dead as he was.

Her jaw quivered, and she pinned him into place with the stare he simply couldn't get used to. "Calver, you think I am a Ruxian?"

The question he'd waited for. He nodded.

"And you've never met another person that looks like me?"

'No. And I am well-traveled.' If she hoped to see more than a dozen sunrises alone, he would need to tell her everything... and in a way that did not invite familiarity. 'There are many who would give anything to control you. If not for power, then for riches.'

She gulped again and tilted her head. "But... it's not right. From what I understand, what I am doesn't exist anymore. And when it did..." She trailed off and looked at him.

She hovered too close for comfort as he scrawled the words onto paper.

'Ruxians were heralded as royalty manifested by the Fates themselves. They ruled Nelfindar. And then they were hunted to extinction by those in Tera'thia who hoped to take away Nelfindar's advantage.'

"Advantage, because Ruxians could distort matter on a whim?"

He nodded. 'They were living weapons.'

She shook her head vigorously. "No—no. Calver, I may look like a Ruxian, but I don't know anything about distortion, other than that it powers Aetech's mechanisms. You're mistaken. I—I can't..." Her eyes went wide. Her hands covered her mouth.

She understood.

'If you are brought to light by any governance, it might as well be a declaration of war.'

She stopped and gaped at him for a moment, considering him differently. "And you." She paused, carefully selecting her next words. "You knew I was this when you took me in. What, in all honesty, are you thinking? This puts *you* in danger."

Danger.

A low laugh rumbled in his chest—a sound that took him by surprise. Raimee's expression darkened. The situation was distinctly not funny, but she'd caught him in the one question he couldn't answer: what *was* he fucking thinking?

'You are a bit of a problem for me. But, luckily for you, I also prefer not to get mixed up with the Tera'thians or the Nelfinden government.'

She stared at the note, her mouth twisted with lack of conviction. Did she think he lived this way for fun? "How can I trust you aren't just planning to sell me?"

She shouldn't trust him. She should run for the bleeding hills if she had any mind to her. Hadn't he entered this discourse with a goal of straying from familiarity? Calver scowled. 'This lack of trust goes two ways. It's as I said before, you have terrible timing.'

The woman searched him like she was looking for something to grab onto. So different from every associate he'd known in the last eight years, who'd learned not to make eye contact with the Hand's Reaper.

'You're safe,' he assured her. He hoped. It wouldn't be the first promise he hadn't been able to keep.

Raimee's shoulders fell from her ears. She moistened her lips like she was tasting her words before giving a response. "But you don't believe I'm trustworthy because..." She seemed to reconsider what she might say, but still plowed forward. "*You're* obviously some kind of spy."

Calver's hands balled into fists, a futile grip on his-fast slipping control over their interaction. 'I think we should continue our search.'

He turned the paper to her and thumbed open another book, but he noticed one corner of her mouth rise in a clear smirk, and his stomach roiled. Fates, wasn't she ill? She was testing him now. Or toying with him? Enough time in isolation, and he couldn't tell one thing from another. *Don't take her bait.* The time stretched between them. He flipped a page. She didn't look away. Her stare cut deeper. Deeper. Until he could no longer bear the incision. 'You're walking a precarious line.'

"Precarious or not, I have no ego that prevents me from knowing when I'm at a person's mercy. What you choose to do with me has already been determined. So I may as well know the man holding hands with my fate. Are you a good spy or a bad spy?"

It was an outwitting he couldn't stumble around. So he resorted to empty threats. 'Keep messing around and you'll find out.'

She crossed her arms. "No, I'm certain I've already made my assessment."

Chaos it backfired. It was lucky he wasn't a spy. One would think a man who couldn't speak would be a half-decent discretionary. *'Help me read, or the food supply will run out before we find this Methu'su.'*

Her face dimpled at his response. His insides burned. This conversation was an experiment, and he was the test subject.

{You've lost control. Let me.}

Void.

"Let's talk about that. Did you learn to cook from spy school or elsewhere?" As if to prove she'd championed over his intentions to scare her.

He rolled his eyes. One piece of paper, too many things to write. 'I don't want to talk'—technically a lie. 'Making gruel is hardly cooking'—an invitation to keep talking. 'You're pushing your luck'—she'd already seen right through to the core of him, and it would only be a redundancy. 'My mother taught me to cook'—definitely not a door he wanted to open. 'There's no spy school'—stupid. 'I'm not a spy'—what he *was* had more layers than a skywalk confection and even he wasn't sure of it.

He settled on, 'Stop with the questions.'

Her face fell. "I've never met someone from outside the monastery. And I assumed a hermit might enjoy some amount of banter."

The rules hung like a weight around his neck. 'A hermit is a hermit for a reason.'

She pouted.

He held up his hands, smoothed his fingers across his brow. 'You can ask whatever you want. Just don't expect an answer.'

She perked her head up. Fates, she was like a puppy. "Alright... then I have a question."

He raised an eyebrow at her.

"Will you teach me to make food? I always wanted to learn, but it wasn't my assigned duty at the monastery."

Calver snorted, and then stiffened in surprise. He hadn't done that in half a lifetime. 'You have no self-control.'

She shrugged, eyes crinkled at their corners, as if to say, *you wouldn't be the first to tell me that.* "Does that mean this is one of the questions you won't answer?"

{End it. Now.}

Calver set the book down, considering, and found a *want* there he'd never expected to. No one had ever...

Teaching someone something? Not that he had any skill—three daily meals of fortified porridge hardly qualified as cooking. But what harm would come of it? He would still pass her off when they found what she was looking for. It wouldn't affect his plans, and it...

'I'll teach you. Tomorrow when I return.'

Her smile was like light, clear and bright against the dimness around them and incongruous to her ailment. "Where are you going?"

'Chira'na. But you are too weak to join me.'

He would need to tell Fankalo what had happened, sooner or later. And find out what was on that shipment that had made it important enough for Tera'thian agents to shepherd it into Chira'na.

"How long will you be gone?"

{Watch now how she prepares to stab you in the back.}

Void.

Why was it that every question made him more uncomfortable than the last? He remembered an old social evasion tactic Callisto had taught him, and turned her earlier statement around on her. 'What was your assigned duty at the monastery?'

"Tending the gardens."

'Sounds nice.' It really did.

"It was... while it lasted." Raimee's silver eyes blinked away from him, her brow furrowed.

With her stare broken, Calver felt like he could finally breathe. He returned to skimming books for a reference to Methu'su. Raimee did not join him but gazed into the fire, hugging her emaciated limbs into her chest.

Calver considered removing himself from the anguish of his predicament to consider hers. She'd lost everything. Everyone. Despite her obvious efforts to appear coherent, she was sick enough to require medical attention. Medical attention he couldn't provide her with, given the risks. His fingers twitched for the charcoal, and he nearly scribbled a message of comfort. But he stopped himself.

He'd overcome it alone. She could too.

Chapter 11
Calverous

It was firstlight when Calver exited the Sharinash and caught sight of Chira'na. The tall grasses leading away from the treeline spilled down toward the city's fortress walls like a golden carpet. Beyond them, the silver-plated spires and domes from Chira'na's skywalk reflected the pink morning sunrise.

Aside from the dowaga slung across his back, his traveling cloak was all he wore openly. But beneath it, dozens of pockets and fixtures were sewn to discreetly stash the usual essentials: knives of varying lengths, tampered Aetech orbs, distortion discs, paper and charcoal, dried fish, notes for market, two vials of potent oil, and forged identity papers.

The usual queue waited outside the Eastern wall at the gate for entry. Beggars, travelers, businessmen. Calver waited for a full hour just to reach the documentation station. After paying the standard entry fee, ten silver notes, he was ushered into a separate line to wait yet again. Nelfinden bureaucracy at its finest.

His papers registered him under the name of Dallard Friyal: a designated disabled—deaf—citizen from the town of Minden, one day's journey north bordering the Jiradesh. It was a more-or-less believable cover identity for one wearing a traveling cloak and bearing a dowaga. But there was a new guardsman present, and he inspected the papers for a gut-wrenching minute longer than the usual glance. He was young, hardly older than the minimum enlistment age, and sported a patchy black beard as if to prove otherwise.

Calver rubbed at the dark overgrowth on his own face, suddenly self-conscious for the first time in as long as he could remember. He hadn't groomed himself in–

It had been a while. No wonder the Ruxian thought him insane.

Fuck. Among other things, idiot. A beard had to be the least of her concerns.

The guardsman narrowed his eyes at Calver. "Why the dowaga, traveler?"

Calver tapped his ear and shrugged.

"Chevek, the deaf man's a regular. Carries a dowaga every time." One of the usual entry guards came over and rapped him on the back of his head. He snatched the papers from the boy's hand and shoved them hard into Calver's chest. "Next."

Suspicion was a problem. *What was he looking for?* Calver tucked the papers into his cloak and gratefully passed through Chira'na's gates. They opened into a grand cloister with colossal stone statues of rearing horses lining the path. It bordered a sprawling lawn of manicured grass, rimmed by thousands of rose bushes. Citizens lounged and picnicked, blissfully unaware that a war was coming, and it would not discern between those at work and those at leisure. And if he didn't find that Aetech shipment and right his mistake... it might be even deadlier than he imagined.

Calver wove his way across the lawn toward the city center, where he would receive news from Fankalo. He was following the main avenue into the heart of the city when his skin itched with the too-familiar feeling of eyes on his back.

There were still Tera'thians in this city.

He kept moving, heart pounding, scanning the crowd for anything out of tune. A sudden tug came at the back of his cloak, and he drew a knife beneath it.

An urchin fell into step beside him.

Calver slipped the blade back into its sheath.

The boy was away from his usual haunt, an alleyway behind a northeast quarter butchery. Probably in search of food—or of Calver himself, he realized with a sinking feeling. By the looks of him, it wasn't likely that he had many other benefactors. Calver side-eyed the wiry child, who wrung his hands, eyes shifting like he'd developed a nervous twitch from being kicked at as often as anyone looked at him.

Great. Charity once, and now Calver had a tag on him. Why couldn't this kid be a pickpocket like the rest of them? Calver slid a single note into his hand. The boy, catching his discretion, brushed up against him to fist it.

"Fo' an itcher, yah's sure alrigh'." The boy peeled away.

Calver assumed that by "itcher" the urchin charged him to be addicted to moss.

Better that than what he really was.

He watched the boy disappear in the crowd, feeling strangely reminiscent. The days he'd spent begging in the Kaidechi slums had been the good ones. What did that say about the rest of his life, where wealth had been of no consequence?

He ground his teeth and lengthened his stride.

The Repository, Chira'na's central library, rose like a tower before him, casting a shadow over the city square. Its hulking mass was carved from the same stone as the city's walls and rose twenty stories high. It was said to contain over twelve million entries—a combination of books, ledgers, articles, and scrolls. Mammoth stone pillars carved to look like sentries adorned its face. Its sides displayed intricately sculpted murals depicting the four winds of Fate battling the forces of nature, and King Seraphindo, with his hand raised over the sea, plated in silver.

Calver's chest tightened at the depiction. Teach her how to cook? Chaos, he couldn't afford a distraction right now. The sooner he had the Ruxian on her way to Methu'su, the better.

He entered the Repository and skipped the line for the distortion-powered lift, hiking the twenty stories up to the publicly accessible roof. Killari knew to find him there each week, bringing him news from the Shadewalker's Hand at sea. Fankalo's vessel would be stationed near Karval, now, allowing them faster communication for their recent objective.

The failed one.

Calver removed one of the oil vials from within his cloak and popped the cork. The smell of rosemary wafted into the air. He heard Killari before he saw her; alerted by the whooshing of air against wings, he lifted his right arm and widened his stance. Her weight hit him with a rush. A few of the surrounding roof-goers looked at him curiously before going back about their business.

Fankalo's creature was a beautiful Pazirian falcon, and as intelligent as she was lethal. Her talons tightly gripped the leather guards covering Calver's arm beneath the cloak. He reached into a pocket to grab a dried fish, which she gulped eagerly, purple lowlights in her brown plumage glinting beneath the sun. Calver capped the rosemary vial and gave the bird several appreciative strokes before reaching for the canister tied to her leg.

Fankalo's note was lengthier than usual. Calver sat with Killari, teasing the encrypted message out by dissecting and rearranging its syllables.

'I had an unlucky feeling about the North gate demolition. Assure me it's something I ate?

'Bad news first. Special forces from Bovahk Ani's wing are moving west. Somewhere between two to three thousand heads.

'They invaded Tennca'Pui, of all places. Wiped it clean. Left the monastery labeled with the Shadewalker's Ratka. Cenobites aren't exactly a strategic target. So what is this,

Cal? Some sort of psychological warfare? A way to keep you looking over your shoulder? A taunt? A tag, you're it? We're missing something that Cul'Mon clearly wants you to know.

'My spies report their forces are headed for the isles of Solutium. The timing will align with the Nelfinden recruitment rendezvous in Steila and my move inland to bolster the Dreiden Corporation's distribution outside Seraphinden. Follow my logic?

'I don't like this. We need to make our countermove now. I've been trying to determine where to put you. If there's going to be carnage in Steila, I'll need you out there to glean information before Cul'Mon gets too close. I've arranged a ship for you at the south dock in Karval in three days. The owner will respond to Jarah.'

Calver re-read the message. And again.

So, Fankalo did know about Tennca'Pui. And the Ruxian was telling the truth…

But he kept staring at the words 'I've been trying to determine where to put you.'

The world around Calver dissolved. His breath clutched in his chest, paralyzing him. He was just a problem to be dealt with. Even if the demolition had been successful, as Fankalo insofar assumed it was, he was still going to be kept at a distance.

Killari took to startled flight as he backpedaled into a stone maintenance shed atop the roof, sank down until his backside hit matter. His knees found his chest.

He'd inflated a false dream, hoping that after the demolition was a success, Fankalo might think he'd changed. Might bring him home—not that a raider ship had ever really been his home in the first place. But Fankalo was.

It was a fantasy.

What leader would ever take another chance on him after what he'd done?

He tried not to think about the incident—a medley of blood and burn. He'd fallen too far. The Survivor had taken full advantage before he was even aware of what he was doing.

It wasn't me, he told no one, with the tongue he didn't have. *It wasn't me.*

He'd only tried to protect them. But when he'd regained control of his own mind outside of Nelfinden territory, Cul'Mon had come for him—he always fucking came—and left only char in his wake. Letting the Survivor control his mind had been the only defense Calver could give them… until it wasn't.

The Survivor purred at his pain, relishing in it. He considered letting the mind-djinn bring him into a place of non-feeling, but refused it. He deserved to feel this. In the end, it was still his fault. None of it would have happened if he'd chosen to die in the Kaidechi grasslands all those years ago.

The other roof-goers didn't notice the giant man cowering beside the shed. People were not prone to seeing the things they weren't looking for. Killari hopped back over to him and prodded his hand with her beak.

Calver found the strength to steel his mind.

What had happened had happened.

There was nothing to be done for it. He didn't have to feel this way: to try to save a thing which couldn't be saved. He was choosing to.

No longer.

Four hundred and twenty days. Soon enough, he wouldn't have to feel anything.

He fed the bird another fish as he mentally composed his response. He couldn't be in Karval in three days. He'd promised the Ruxian he would find her Methu'su—and it was the least he owed to her. And the events surrounding the Aetech's shipment didn't sit well with him. He'd failed. Now he would find out why.

Honesty, he decided, was the best way to go about this. One did not lie about business with Fankalo, though he chose to omit any details about the Ruxian.

'The demolition failed. Trace your steps. We have been crossed, or we are in the dark with regards to something larger.

'That shipment was escorted by a Tera'thian special unit. Either they foresaw our interception and wanted the original shipment to be successful, or they replaced it with something else. Put a hold on your Karval transport. I want to investigate where the shipment went first. I may still be able to destroy it before it's dispersed.'

Good. His words were strong. Altruistic, even. Definitely not an echo of the desperation he felt.

Calver rolled the paper up and stuffed it into the tiny canister. Killari pecked at his pocket for more snacks. He fed them to her one by one until they were gone, then drew the second oil vial from a pocket and popped its cork. Lemon.

Killari erupted from his arm, off on her quest. He watched after her as she flew southwest over the city, remembering the days he'd spent watching her soar over the ocean from the deck of a raider ship: the home she now returned to.

It had been a good enough life, while it had lasted.

The Survivor suckled at his longing. Calver changed his line of thinking. There was work to do. If the attack at the distortion locomotive port hadn't been a means of capturing him, then what was it? Why would the Tera'thians risk exposing themselves over an Aetech shipment?

The easiest answer would be that he and Fankalo had been infiltrated, but it was unlikely. Only two souls knew the specifics of his now failed demolition: Fankalo and himself. No room for betrayal there. The Tera'thian operation *had* to have been planned separately from their own... But why? It had the happy effect of throwing years of planning into the metaphorical ocean. While Calver wouldn't rule out the possibility of coincidence, he would tear Chira'na apart for information before he fell back on it.

He looked over the city with arms crossed. Whatever had been on the distortion locomotive was important enough that sixteen Tera'thian agents had transplanted themselves into the Chira'na guard to ensure its delivery.

So what if the shipment *wasn't* simple Aetech lamps for the city's elite?

The thought sent him stumbling forward. He gripped the balcony's ledge with white knuckles.

No. *No.* Fankalo wouldn't have kept something like that from him. If anything was contrived, he and Fankalo were in it together. And, Aetech lamps or otherwise, he needed to trace the shipment to its delivery point and eliminate it.

He released the balcony and paced. Fankalo had an insider, Greeny, who could access the port's shipment records. Calver had met with the man here and there on some of Fankalo's more reprehensible errands. Greeny was the largest dealer of moss within the groundling class of Chira'na, hence his namesake, and well-connected. He owned the city's largest warehouse, which wasn't subject to legislative investigation. Something to do with paying off the city's officials. Fankalo stored much of the Dreiden tech they didn't keep at their headquarters there.

Calver sighed; the slow dispensing of air warmed his nostrils but stole resolve from the rest of him. Willingly going to Greeny's, without being tasked to, spoke volumes of his desperation. Everything about the thug made his mouth sour. But nearly all Calver's work was discretionary, and the type of individual who would volunteer silence in exchange for tender hardly deviated.

He suppressed an urge to itch at the barbs chewing into his back. Given the things that he'd done, what did the quality of those he consorted with matter? Greeny was just a means to an end. That was all any of this was anymore.

Calver kept his hood pulled forward past his ears as he made his way into Chira'na's moss district: a chaotic street in the northeast quadrant which wound far too tightly around shanties and alleyways for its number of pedestrians. It was not the slow degradation in the quality of infrastructure that signified his arrival, nor the smells, which turned from bread and oil, perfume and sweat, into rot and waste.

It was the sounds.

Groundlings begging, braying, singing, muttering, crying, haggling. Their various noises lacked inhibition, and with that, no one really seemed to listen to them. After fourteen years without a tongue, Calver had come to realize it wasn't so much a handicap as one might think. Some people would talk and talk without ever truly saying anything. In the same sense, those who had the most to say were the least often heard. Words were a commodity. The fewer there were, the greater their value.

In the moss district, everyone was destitute.

Calver glanced down every side alley; it was not a place to be lost in thought. These streets went largely unpatrolled by Chira'na's guard. It proved how little the oligarchy actually cared about the health of its groundling inhabitants—everything was anarchy here. Fankalo loved it. Called it "freedom." It made business easier for them, sure. But to Calver, anarchy was only a constant state of heightened unease.

Two guards bore cosalts at the doorless entryway into Greeny's domain. The anxiety which coiled in Calver's stomach was invisible to them. He had a reputation, after all: the Hand's Reaper. They nodded him forward, postures almost reverent, and Calver ducked through several sets of curtained doorways. He ignored the stares of the rooms' inhabitants, all of whom were packing moss. Greeny could almost always be found at the rear of his shanty palace, in his Stones parlor.

The drug lord sat beyond a crowd of players on a pouf at a low table in the corner. He faced the door, as was his preference and also where Calver's commonalities with him ended. Greeny's table was occupied by a wall of muscle resembling a man, a minstrel with a beard braided past his midline, and three harlots. A short, wiry man, marred by an array of ugly scars and even uglier tattoos, Greeny glanced up when Calver walked in. His eyes fluttered in a knowing blink.

Calver sat, unannounced, on the cushion between Greeny and a curvaceous girl in red. She spewed a stream of hardly distinguishable curses at him, then slumped onto the ground in a stupor.

One had to love the social graces of mossers.

Greeny's only acknowledgement of Calver's presence was to throw his cup of Stones down on the table.

Six blues.

"Oof. Bad odds," commiserated Muscles.

Greeny shot him a derisive look. His weathered fingers drummed on the table. A low hum of noise sounded through the parlor around them, but their table had fallen quiet enough to hear the dead.

At last, Greeny sighed and raised eyebrows at Calver. "You got rid o' my good luck charm." He shrugged in the direction of the displaced girl.

Calver picked up the Stones cup from the table. The game was exceedingly stupid, which spoke volumes of its popularity in a moss den. Players tipped six dual-colored—one side green, the other blue—river stones onto a table. Whoever had the most green stones won.

Calver cast the rocks gathered inside his cup onto the table.

Five green. One blue.

"Fates be damned. Never seen you roll anythin' less than four green. That ain't right." Greeny shook his head. "What you want'n, then? Tryin' to store more of your boss's distortion trinkets?"

Calver lifted his writing pad and tapped it twice. He needed a translator.

"Your man gonna give me a lot fo' this one. Times nasty."

As Calver understood things from Fankalo, their wallet was virtually bottomless at this point. He inclined his head.

Greeny clapped, and the room fell silent. "Eaaahhh... who here has their letters?"

Several sets of eyes fell on Calver before darting away. The chamber's roughly three dozen patrons remained still, holding their collective breath.

"Pissants," Greeny mumbled. His voice rose. "I've got sixty tabs for the guy that's got 'is letters."

This time, silence greeted the query for only a pause.

"That's me, Greeny." A tall, fair-complexioned man in his mid-twenties raised his hand sheepishly and stepped forward.

Greeny barked a slow, stilted laugh. Most of the room joined in. "Agnod, I should have guessed you was a high-brow from the start. Never walked quite right, did ya?"

Acknowledging an education was risky and, honestly, idiotic. There were spiteful feelings directed toward those with skywalk schooling in this district. Calver didn't know how much sixty tabs were worth—he didn't follow the moss trade, nor did he care to—but it couldn't be cheap.

Agnod stepped over to them—and Greeny was right: it was a proper walk, rigid, unlike the saunter all too common in a moss parlor. *Sloppy.* He tugged at his worn, silk-trimmed tunic, which might have once been expensive. Calver had seen the type, usually his own age, who had fallen into moss because of an excess of time and finances. Most never came back from it. As Calver understood it, the withdrawal was as excruciating as it was deadly.

Greeny waved the table's other two men aside. They stood without complaint to meander away, while the remaining women shared a knowing look and grabbed their fallen companion, vacating the room entirely. Agnod sat on the floor cushion beside Calver, opposite Greeny. A nervous smile painted his face, but his eyes darted around as though he worried Greeny was playing a trick on him.

He had barely crossed his legs when Greeny lunged across the table like a predator, knocking him flat. The moss lord straddled Agnod's chest, pinning his arms with his knees. One hand gripped his neck; the other held a knife to his throat. Calver didn't flinch. This was protocol among the Shadewalker's Ghosts. He wouldn't have written a word if Greeny had acted any differently.

Agnod did not struggle, though a timid whimper strangled its way from between his teeth. Calver watched to be sure he didn't miss any gestures between them that would give away anything contrived.

"Listen to me, boy," growled Greeny. "The conditions are these." He licked his lips and tightened his hand around Agnod's neck. The man's eyes were so wide they looked as though they might burst from his skull. Tilting his head toward Calver, Greeny kept his voice low. "Outside of this moment, you never talk to him again. You never mention him again. And you never think about him again." He pushed his face closer. "He don't exist, see? You understand the words I'm sayin'?"

Agnod managed the smallest of nods.

Greeny lurched off his chest and slumped back into his corner seat. Agnod sat up, rubbing his throat. Calver noted his slow expressions, indicative that he was falling down from the canopy. Before long, he would be as useless as the woman in red. Chaos curse his luck. Of course the only literate man in the room *would* be impotent minutes after his arrival.

He scowled and rapped his knuckles on the table.

"We begin," Greeny said.

Calver scribbled in haste.

"He needs to access the distortion port's shipping records from the last two weeks," Agnod said flatly, emotionlessly.

Greeny planted the tips of his fingers together under his chin and leaned back. "Specific information, you need?"

Specifying exactly what Calver was looking for would give too much away.

Agnod read Calver's response more slowly this time. His words were slurred almost unintelligibly. Fates, the transition to the fall was fast. "All the data available from the passst two weeks—inbound, outbound, delivery datesss.... n' personnelsss involved. Locationsss. All hard copy, original accurate recordsss. Not word... of mouthhh."

"Heh." Greeny leaned in toward Calver, close enough to see the numerous hairline scars adorning his brow like wisps of smoke. "I got respect fo' you, Reaper. The rest of these fuckin' itchers," he gestured around him, "they don't understand the complexity of my capabilities. But you—you know. You got faith in me to do this crazy thing, eah?" He dragged out the last sound and clapped a hand on Calver's shoulder. His voice was rough as sand. "You n' me a lot alike. Not easy to buy nor sell. We steady. We capable, eah? Not crup-heads."

Calver massaged his handful of Stones, face expressionless. His stomach squirmed. Sometimes, he tried to rationalize his past actions for the sake of his own sanity. The greater good was a primal god which accepted human sacrifice. He was not *actually* the Hand's Reaper; those morbid acts belonged to the Survivor, helping the real him to set his plan in motion for the Tera'thian coronation. He did them for Fankalo. He did them to free the tume'amic children forced to bear his genetic scars.

But a part of Calver knew that if one acted a part for long enough, they became the very thing they were embodying. That part of him had trouble distinguishing where he ended and his mind-djinn began.

Despair clouded his sick, silent heart. The Survivor purred knowingly.

"Yea, I do this thing for you," Greeny continued. "Gon' be paid like mad for it. But it mean more to me that you give me something of a challenge, eah? Just in time too. I was startin' to get bored."

He winked at Calver. At the same moment, Agnod's eyes crossed. He slumped to the floor with a dull thud. While mossers could remain in the canopy for several hours, the fall, once it began, only took a matter of minutes.

"Give me four days, alright, friend? Six max."

Calver blinked his understanding and turned to leave.

"Hey, you wanna stick around and try best two of three?" Greeny rattled the stones around in his cup.

Calver continued on his path out of the room.

"Hm. Your choice," Greeny muttered indifferently from behind him. A few onlookers stirred as Calver passed by, but not for long enough for Greeny to notice them doing so.

They knew better.

Chapter 12
Niklaus

FIFTEEN MONTHS PREVIOUSLY

Niklaus nestled snugly under a low-hung canopy of sheets, his bare limbs twisted with the maid's. Latouda was as good a lover as she was confidant. The morning had come and gone as quickly as their present game of thumb over thumb—a thing she was ferociously keen on besting him at. After a third round of victory, she sighed and lifted herself from his chest to sit, legs crossed, and signal.

<Have I served as a muse well enough for you to finish the fated papers?>

Her fingers and wrists moved just slowly enough for his untrained brain to understand. The signal language mimicked speech rather than resembling an alphabet or stand-alone words. There was a hand sign for each possible syllable in the Nelfinden Language—just under two hundred in all. It was a much simpler alternative to speech than traditional sign language for people like Latouda, who understood spoken Nelfinden but had become hard of hearing.

"You weren't half-bad, for a groundling maid," he responded.

She frowned and signaled her incomprehension. Latouda could read lips, but she wasn't explicitly good at it. Her skill for it was somewhere along the lines of his own at the signal language: passable.

His hands gestured crudely. <It's better you didn't understand that one.>

She scoffed at him, but her mouth twisted into a smile as she planted her bare foot on his chest to push him toward the edge of the bed.

<Taking your lazy, entitled time as always. When will they be finished? You'll let me proof them first, of course?>

<Another week?>

She narrowed her eyes.

He cringed. <*I went on a bit of a detour.*>

<*Detour for what?*>

The story would be too difficult for him to signal adequately. He pointed to his lips and spoke slowly as she watched, unblinking. "Hear me out. I was diving into Aetech's financial delegations. Three months ago, a huge resource allocation shifted from the private sector to the military."

<*The military?*>

He nodded.

<*Why?*>

<*The sky is red if I know,*> he signaled back to her.

<*Aetech is your company, idiot.*>

"Founding investor, not owner," he corrected her, waggling a finger before switching back into gestures. <*And you know I've never given a thumb's width about it since. Likely why it's taken me three months to notice in the first place.*>

Latouda giggled in a way that indicated he'd signaled a syllable incorrectly or, more likely, inappropriately. He had no idea which it was, so he cleared his throat in favor of speech. Latouda's almond eyes found his lips.

"So, I looked into it. Checked the visitation logs... and found that Lieutenant General Roskaad Thyatira had been paying Aetech's main complex a visit nearly every day for weeks."

Latouda fell still. He took a moment to appreciate the smoothness of her bronze skin, the lustrous sheen to her raven hair. His thoughts first stumbled, then slipped toward other things entirely before he noticed the smear of disappointment on her otherwise perfect face.

<*The groundling general?*>

"You look like someone kicked your puppy." The look only confirmed that he was right to have his suspicions of a man who was otherwise infallible. "Why, do you have a thing for him?"

She winked at him. <*He is rather handsome, don't you think?*>

Niklaus shrugged. Thyatira employed his handsomeness like sharks did their teeth: a tool to use to his advantage.

<*In all seriousness, that doesn't seem to ring true,*> she signaled. <*He's fighting for groundling rights. Your fated company works to impose the opposite.*>

"I thought the same. So I started investigating, and went down a bit of a rabbit hole."

<In true Niklaus Meyernes fashion.>

He grinned. The only thing which excited him more than chance encounters with his maid was plucking the worst of the oligarchy's family gossip from their secret vines and spilling them onto the streets for the rest of Seraphinden to lap like wine.

She raised an eyebrow. *<What did you learn?>*

Fates above, how was it that Nelfindar's best listener was a deaf woman?

"The public record on him is almost nonexistent. Obsolete. An anomaly." A bubble of excitement, newly reforged, formed in Niklaus's throat just thinking about it. "Every other general has a skidmark leagues long for me to sniff out. This one, not a thing. And no public record, no census record—no one that even knew him before he was fifteen and found 'wandering the streets' by Colonel Limtush before the battle of Casowhatan." But, inconveniently, after Niklaus's civilian father had been butchered by Chori forces.

Latouda's chin lowered until it was at risk of merging with her neckline.

"Hang on... let me get the paper," he said.

Shedding their sheets, he strode in his purest form to his writing desk. He pulled open its center drawer, rifled through its contents for a moment, and removed the aged article of reference, its corners yellowed and curled.

"This is a statement from Colonel Limtush." He cleared his throat before skimming the details out loud: *"The scavenger, Roskaad, was astounding. Brilliant. Offered a perplexing analysis of enemy resources, which helped us to combat the Chori's navy in our most dire hour. The fifteen-year-old's strategic direction was a large contributor to Nelfindar's unlikely victory."*

Why had he just spoken in a mock military voice to a deaf person? He folded the paper and tucked it back into his desk. Latouda looked at him expectantly and circled her hand in the universal gesture of 'get to your point.' Niklaus's chest tightened. Didn't the article seem suspicious enough?

"So he enlisted at fifteen, before he was legally of age. Then he was promoted to Lieutenant General by twenty—the youngest commanding officer in Nelfindar's history. In the sixteen years since, he's fought every bit of legislation the oligarchy put forth in his attempts to keep the military relevant. Even during peace times."

<Yes. To provide additional work opportunities for those in the groundling class. He's a hero.>

"If he's a fated groundling hero, then why is he fraternizing with Aetech? Think about it, Latouda. If I'm going to write these papers exposing Aetech for the monster it is, you can't tell me Thyatira's behavior is irrelevant."

<You don't know what you don't know.> Her reply came painted with disinterest. <Which someone like you, always on the hunt for the next conspiracy, can't seem to understand.>

"Yes, but you can't tell me something isn't off here. This man has no negative press. None. In what world does that happen?"

<Just because you're a terrible person, doesn't mean every individual of notoriety has bad press.> Her eyes sparkled. <Is it possible that he's just perfect?>

Niklaus held up a finger in playful warning and she flashed her teeth at him. He shook his head. "I've spent weeks searching now... and I can't find anything on the man."

<Weeks?> She huffed in frustration. <Nikla... We've talked about this. You tend to do this. Is the paper's delay really worth one of your tangents?>

He ignored her. "No record of his family. His birth. His schooling. It's like he popped out of the ground at the battle Casowhatan and decided he wanted to be a military mastermind. It doesn't sit right with me. I'm trying to uncover details on where he grew up so I can talk to his family or neighbors from before the battle. I've got an errand boy on it now."

<Errand boy?>

"It will only be another week."

Latouda blinked several times, waging some genre of internal battle, before she chose to exhale and smile. <Well, if it has to be another week, perhaps you should come back to bed?>

He scanned her enticing form, splayed across his four-poster. Fates, she was perfect. He was tempted to call it a day and nestle back into her arms. He opted for lying down at the foot of the bed with his arms crossed instead.

"Preservation, but I would like that. I shouldn't, else I'll be late. My mother's arranged afternoon plans for me with the Goroviches again." He wrinkled his face in disgust. "You know, she's proposing an engagement? To that goat of a woman, Rebethel."

Latouda snickered. <Isn't that something the man is supposed to do? Not his mother?>

"Traditionally. I haven't done it yet, and made it clear I don't want to. But, kretch, my mother is getting desperate. Wants to be sure the future of Aetech is secured with those of 'like-minded' interests."

<*Maybe you should just get married to someone else, then she'll leave you alone about it.*>

The most inspiring shratten words he'd ever heard. Niklaus bolted upright.

"Fates above, you're right," he said. Latouda didn't see him speak, as he was facing away. He saw her signal a brief *what?* from the corner of his vision.

<*You're right!*> he repeated in signal, and suddenly he began laughing. Once he started, he couldn't stop. "Right" did not do her justice. She was a genius.

Latouda shimmied toward the headboard of the bed and drew her knees into her chest. <*You're a fucking madman.*>

He crawled to her through their field of tangled sheets and pulled her into a hug. Then he pushed her out at arm's length, his hands firm on her bare, sculpted shoulders.

"You! My lifelong maid. My best of friends. You will marry me!"

Latouda responded with her usual eye-roll. <*That's normally posed as a question, not a statement.*>

Niklaus looked into her eyes, then gripped her left hand for a moment before releasing it to signal. <*Latouda, marry me. I'll make your wildest dreams come true. I swear it.*>

Her brow shot toward her hairline. <*You're being serious.*>

"Serious as the strikapa."

She laughed herself this time. <*Of all the crazy kretch you say, this takes the stage. Nikla, I'm a disabled groundling! You can't marry me.*>

"I'm the richest man in Nelfindar. I can do whatever I want."

She held up her hands, her face distressed. <*Stop. Stop. You're not some all-powerful Fate. There's something serious we need to talk about. I haven't been completely honest—*>

He spoke over her. "Fates, this is so much better than Rebethel Gorovich. We can make this work. We really can. It will be the last thing anyone ever suspects. And it will be hilarious!"

Whatever she'd wanted to tell him went forgotten. Her face was a blended brew: a shot of fury, a pour of amusement, a sprinkle of refute, the way it often was with him. They'd spent a lifetime arguing with one another, and it was always play, but the punches still hurt.

<*Listen, you high and mighty shrat,*> she retorted. <*Maybe I don't want to get married to you. Maybe I don't want to simply be better than your least desirable option. And maybe I don't want to be 'hilarious.'*>

In that moment, a frantic knocking came at the door.

"Come back later!" Niklaus yelled, and grunted as Latouda slammed knuckles into his ribcage.

"Mesu Meyernes. I have an address," a young man's voice called back, muffled behind the solid mahogany.

Adrenaline shot through Niklaus's veins. So quickly? He'd assigned the task to one of their newest servants, an eager young man more legs than anything else, having just reached his teens. He'd thought some new blood might be the right way to get the information quickly and without spreading gossip, the way their veteran staff tended to.

"Come in!"

The servant rushed through the door, skidding to a stop the moment he saw them and averting his eyes. Latouda pulled the sheets up to cover herself and palmed her forehead. He caught her signal something along the lines of, <*The shratten worst...*>

"I... I have the address," the boy repeated, color rising in his cheeks.

Niklaus hopped to his feet, stark naked. "Excellent, boy. Where?"

"In Casowhatan. The Western Market."

"That's not more than a few hours with a good coach. What time is it?"

"Just past highsun, mesu." The errand boy shrank slightly, stilling his eyes on the ceiling.

Niklaus moved to look out the window. Sure enough, the highsun blazed bright over the green Casowhatan. This was it. This was his chance. Maybe it wouldn't take another week to finish the papers. "Preservation keep me, I can make it there today if I leave right this moment. Prepare me a coach!"

The boy didn't waste another heartbeat in removing himself from the room.

Niklaus threw open his wardrobe and fumbled with a mess of clothing, tripping into trousers and pulling an embroidered blouse over his head. Clashing. He was always clashing, but that was by design. Just another easy way to get an easy rise.

Latouda gave his outrageous display a coy smile and shook her head. He turned and feigned a gasp. "Latouda, in bed at this hour? Don't you have cleaning to do?" He pounced on the bed to give her a fleeting kiss.

She punched him again, having read his lips. Then returned his kiss, though reluctantly. She caught his hand as he pulled away.

<*Wait,*> she signaled, biting her lip. Her eyes pinned him in place. <*There's something I still need to tell you.*>

He took a step back, a familiar excitement roiling in his stomach that only digging into a secret could appease.

<Not now... I've got to make it there today. This story is just begging to be told. We'll talk tomorrow, darling. Or any time you like, really. Don't we have the rest of our lives?> He winked at her.

There was no eye roll. No banter. No insult. She hesitated, her fingers fidgeting with the sheets before they rose to signal. <Ok.>

Chapter 13

Calverous

FOURTEEN YEARS PREVIOUSLY

Calver rounded a corner in time to see the whipping fabric of the hooded Thyatira dash around another turn through crowded alleyways. He trailed along, just out of sight, for what felt like an hour.

They traveled into the farthest reaches of Kaidech's eastern limits beside the sea, and Thyatira slipped through an open gate and into a seaport junkyard. Calver crept after him, careful his steps didn't crunch in the mess around him. As he maneuvered on tiptoe, every heartbeat dispelled more of his excitement in exchange for apprehension. The smells of rotting fish and rust clung to the air off the tide. Filth seeped through the holes in his canvas shoes to squelch between his toes. His brow lowered, his lips pressing into a line. What would a general want all the way out here?

His imagination ran wild with childish fantasies. Thyatira might have a special mission, one the Red Wing depended on. One Calver could help with…

And then he considered the stomach-shifting alternatives. A knifing regret twisted into his core.

The figure stopped at a clearing in the junkyard where three men waited. Two wore Red Wing uniforms; the other was garbed in a black tunic and sirwal displaying the silver badge of the Prime's circle.

Calver crouched behind a discarded metal sheet, once part of a distortion locomotive wall. It was pocked with dents and rusted holes. A buzzing energy flooded his limbs as he peered through one to watch. They couldn't see him here, but he couldn't help but wonder if they'd hear the pounding in his chest. The midsun beat down against his skin, causing it to slick with sweat. If they didn't hear his heartbeat, surely they would hear the beads of his perspiration pattering against metal and earth.

Thyatira let his hood fall. Only a dozen paces away, every feature of his face became visible in exquisite detail. He was trembling with rage. "How did he find out?"

Calver shrank down. This had been a mistake.

"General Thyatira." The Prime's representative bowed. "The Prime's intelligence sources are his own. Bovahk Ani's troops will arrive in three days' time."

Calver's eyes narrowed. Ani? As in the Tera'thian emperor Ani?

"And he's asked us to pull back?" Thyatira snapped. Calver winced again, as though the general's fury were directed at him. "Continue on schedule with the recruitment tour? Has he lost his mind? There are thirty thousand people in this city!"

"A sacrifice to preserve the current livelihood of millions of Nelfindar's citizens and prevent this single episode from escalating into war," the representative responded.

The large, bald soldier beside Thyatira grimaced. "Just to be clear," he asked the representative, "the Prime expects us to move along like it never happened? How is it that the leader of a nation can give orders for us to enact treachery against it and expect obedience? He's tied our hands."

"It would be of great benefit to both of your careers." The representative folded his hands.

"My *career*," Thyatira hissed the word, "will benefit from us winning a war." He threw his arms out in exasperation. "*Nelfindar* will benefit from us winning a war. You agreed to this. You had my back!"

Calver's shoulders pulled forward. His limbs tingled. Winning a war was one thing. Starting a war was another.

This wasn't right. He had to be mishearing things. He—

"The Prime's wishes have been stated." The paunchy representative shook his head. "I expect you will follow them, General." Then he turned toward the balding soldier. "And I expect you to keep your young protégé in check, Colonel Limtush." Thyatira's hands balled into fists. "I appreciate the work that we have done together thus far, but this notion simply will not progress." The representative's words held an air of finality.

"If not now, then when?" Thyatira argued. "So long as Nelfindar is blanketed under Prime Taranil's foolish technological priorities, this military will dwindle until our forces are too small to combat even the Chori's diluted numbers. What good will Aethertech Mechanics be to Nelfindar if we're all dead?" His words held the same passion they had when he was on the podium, but their meaning had changed. Twisted.

The representative raised his voice, leaning in toward the general. "You argue only to your own political gain. In entering a war that we would otherwise be immune to, Nelfindar would lose countless lives and deplete valuable resources, taking away from the economy that—"

"Taking away from *the Prime's* economy," Thyatira interrupted.

"Roskaad," the bald colonel—Limtush—warned.

Thyatira didn't heed him. "The oligarchy's economy. *Aetech's* shratten economy. Maybe this move will gain him favor from the patricians, but what happens ten years from now when the rest of the nation bottoms out, following its current trend? The Prime won't be able to handle the unrest and there will be no military left to deal with it."

"Then the population will downsize of its own means. That's how nature works." Nature. Not civilization. The Prime's Hand sneered, "Aetech's economy is the new path. Your military economy has been weighed and voted against."

"And how is the Prime going to cover up the massacre of an entire port city? Kaidech may have fallen off the map since the quarantine, but this isn't something that will go unnoticed."

Calver's heartbeat kicked up a notch. The Red Wing was going to abandon Kaidech to Tera'thian forces.

"Simple," the Prime's Hand replied. "Cross-contamination. A strikapa outbreak in Azadonia's closest port."

And then cover it up.

"Thacklore has been working to—"

"Thacklore?" Thyatira was sputtering now, his voice so different than it had been on the podium. "You would trust the word of Deshpian Thacklore over my plan to fight when—"

"You are below station to question this decision. Either you follow command, or you will be stripped of title." The representative's voice had more steel than a dowaga.

Thyatira practically convulsed in anger. He shook his head. "Then the blood of this entire city will be on the Prime's hands. I will keep my mouth shut, but know that one day—"

"That's quite enough, Roskaad," the representative interrupted again. "I've worked closely enough with you to realize that you don't understand when you've lost. You dare threaten *us*? Tell me, who leaked to the Tera'thians that there were conduits hidden in Kaidech?"

Calver bit at his lip. What in Chaos' breath was a conduit? What could be worth invading a city over? A weapon? He'd explored every inch of Kaidech without his mother knowing and never seen anything resembling a weapon. Especially not since the quarantine.

Thyatira froze. His eyes were fixed on the man like a hawk's on its prey.

"That's right. The blood of this city is on *your* hands." The representative turned to leave. "Remember your place, Roskaad. You are lucky to be where you are. And you might even stay lucky, so long as you cooperate. We look forward to your arrival in Seraphinden after the recruitment—"

Almost faster than Calver's eyes could follow, the bald man—Limtush—flipped a knife from his belt. He assaulted the representative with a fanatical series of jabs to his back, connecting with sounds of stiff resistance, like punching a sharpened stick into a melon. Calver stifled his own scream. The representative fell with a gasp and a shudder and lay still. Limtush hovered over the body, the bloodied knife still in his grip.

Thyatira swore. "How do you expect us to explain the Prime's Hand going missing after a contracted meeting with us?" The three Red Wing soldiers remained rooted in place, their faces stern but not revealing that they had just done anything out of the ordinary.

Limtush straightened his uniform. "I'll deal with it. He's become less and less trustworthy. That, and the threat for the information you fed to Bovak Ani... We can't afford to be weighed as Tera'thian spies."

Enough.

Calver's esophagus bulged. He had seen enough. He shouldn't be here. Couldn't. He had to tell someone—

Callisto. Callisto would know what to do.

He stepped backward. In his haste, his heel scraped against metal. The stumble sent a pile of scrap clattering onto the earth around him. He froze, limbs refusing to obey his screaming thoughts. The blood rushed from his head. When he regained motion, his ankle rolled as he misstepped; his torso met the ground, skin smearing against a soft pillow of scum. Overhead, the sky was a perfect blue. Serene, and without a single cloud to witness what would happen next.

"Seamolt! Behind the panel," Limtush growled.

A hand clenched at the collar of Calver's frayed tunic, and the third, bearded soldier dragged him into the open before his panicked senses could get his feet beneath him.

"Bad luck for you, kid," the bearded soldier said, reaching to unholster his dowaga.

While everything else seemed to exist in a haze, those words rang in Calver's ears, a clear echo. His mouth went dry. Bad luck? Arleena's face pooled into the center of his mind. Her worries. Her warnings. Her genius. He wouldn't ever see her again. And he'd promised. Promised—

He did not hesitate.

He twisted away and, using the tilted metal panel he'd been hiding behind, launched himself into the air. The bearded soldier was mid-gasp when Calver's foot chopped into his throat. The man's larynx folded beneath his sullied sole. He clutched at his neck, his eyes rolling back into his head, as Calver aimed a second kick at his diaphragm. The man fell to the ground with a sickening thud.

Calver scrambled away several paces before his shirt was yanked backward. He was ready this time, and prepared to attack—only to discover that it was Thyatira himself. Calver used every defensive maneuver he had ever learned in an attempt to wriggle free, but the general pulled him into a headlock.

Limtush rolled up the sleeves of his uniform. Calver's chest heaved. He panted as he struggled to slip away, to break the hold.

He screamed.

Thyatira covered his mouth. Limtush's arm drew back.

Calver felt pain like he'd never known in all his years of training as the man pummeled him in the face. In the neck. The diaphragm. The groin. He ceased to struggle. He couldn't see; he couldn't breathe. He'd never even had a chance to beg.

He hung loosely in Thyatira's grip before the general discarded him on the ground like a heap of garbage. "That's enough. It's just a kid."

Rise. That was what Callisto always said when they went down. *Rise.* Just like the sun. A simple thing. When a person fell, they got back to their feet.

Calver did not rise.

Adults weren't supposed to do such things to a child. He curled into the fetal position, his face pressing into the filth coating the junkyard grounds. His ears rang. The tang of copper moistened his tongue.

Remembering what Callisto had taught him, he breathed slowly, taking his focus away from the pain. *"Your mind only has the ability to focus on one thing at once. Take your focus away from the pain and replace it with something you can control."*

His fantasies had been right. There *was* a secret mission: his own. He had to save Kaidech. It was up to him. Only him.

Rise... Rise!

Thyatira spoke, his words drawing Calver's attention. "Ok, eavesdropper. What are you doing here?" He crouched down to look Calver in the eye.

Calver tried to speak. "I-I-I-I-I—" The words kept sticking in his mouth. He stopped. Against his every will, a moan escaped his bloodied lips.

"Sack of kretch." Limtush spat onto the ground Calver writhed on. "Got a mean fight in him." He nodded over to their companion, who was coughing and clutching hopelessly at his neck, face turning purple. "Jugular. Seamolt won't come back from that. Just kill him."

Thyatira eyed Calver. His expression was unreadable. Why hadn't they butchered him yet? "He could be someone's child. We must tread with utmost care covering this up."

Rise! Why couldn't he rise?

Limtush gave Calver a rib-crunching shove with his foot. "Kid just killed another one of my Hands, Roskaad. I doubt he'll be missed. There's whole tribes of sons of whores in this city."

Thyatira nodded, his eyes lingering on Calver's tattered clothes, the holes in his shoes. Something pinched in his expression, and he looked down. Then he turned away from Calver. "Regardless, the whole city will be ash this time next week."

Calver tried to speak again. "S-s-st," he gasped, rolling over on the ground, blinking away tears. "When I-I-I-I—" The words would not come.

"He's touched," Limtush sneered. "Can't even talk." He crossed his arms. "Thinking on it, I could use another subject. Might be best not to leave another body, anyhow. It wouldn't hurt to just take him for testing."

Calver's desperation shifted into the clutches of unbridled terror. He fought to speak again. This time, the words were spewed between blood and spittle. "W-when I'm a g-g-general, one day." He stopped to gasp, glaring at them before spitting out a mouthful of blood. "I-I'll t-t-tell them what you d-d-did." The words erupted from him with a ferocity he hadn't been physically capable of moments before. Thyatira froze, a cold fire lit in his eyes.

Silence cut through the three of them, filled only by the rolling of the sea, the gurgle of Seamolt suffocating, and the unsteady wheeze of Calver's final moments of freedom.

Thyatira broke the stillness, speaking like a mother shushing a child. "You have trouble with vocal expression, don't you, boy? Not a standard for generals, I'm afraid. It's all a matter of the things one says."

What about the things one did?

Calver seethed with every ounce of hate he possessed for this man. This false hero, just like his father. His veins ran hot, boiling over with anger at having been tricked yet again into idolizing a traitor.

"Do us all a favor, and make his problem disappear," Limtush said.

Calver unfurled. Tried to squirm away through the dirt. Opened his mouth to scream for help. He knew by his father's example what happened to military men with information they weren't supposed to have.

They died.

Limtush kicked him hard, twice, before straddling him to pin him to the ground. He forced Calver's mouth open. "Roskaad, do it."

"Is it really necessary?"

"If I'm taking him, we need the precaution."

Thyatira grimaced. "It's not that I want to do this, boy." He brandished Limtush's knife, not yet wiped clean of the Prime's Hand's blood. "I simply don't have a choice."

Calver fainted as the man who at firstlight had been his idol sawed out his tongue.

Chapter 14
Calverous

Calver made good time through the Sharinash, even with the large bag of goods bouncing across his back. He flipped it from one shoulder to the next, switching when its pressure against him dug too deeply into the disciplinary barbs implanted there. He usually made a point of traveling light, but the Ruxian had a monstrous appetite. She'd cleaned out his previous food stores quicker than should have been strictly possible.

He'd purchased enough food in Chira'na to feed three people for a ten-day to be safe, though he expected to return in a few days to receive Greeny's information. It seemed like too long. Time was a thief. Who knew what opportunities it might steal from him and hand-deliver to Cul'Mon while Calver waited for answers?

The barbs in his back itched, grinding against muscle with every twist, every step, a constant reminder of the capture that would be worse than death. If he weren't so distracted with fostering the Ruxian, he could have stayed in Chira'na and tried to trace the shipment himself. The options he weighed were each as lost a cause as the next: his impossible redemption, staying out of Cul'Mon's grasp, and keeping the last of a legendary bloodline alive.

But maybe this time, he would keep one promise he'd intended.

He quickened his pace.

Calver approached the doorway to the cave and stopped to knock, just as before.

"*We have a knock now.*"

But no answer came.

His face fell. Heart hammering, tense fingers reaching for the lip of stone that disguised the entrance, he creaked the door open. It was unlocked, the cave dark as night.

An all-consuming trepidation itched at Calver's chest. He clicked on the Aetech lamp activator by the door and hurried down the cavernous hallway, following the line of circuited distortion lamps as they burst to life. His throat ached.

Please still be here.

The Survivor writhed into being, preying on his panic. It pressed into him, seeking control. *{I warned you.}*

Calver rounded the corner to an empty room. The fire was an ember; the books untouched since the night before. And the girl was gone. He sank down onto his knees.

Shit. A quiet rage surged from the pit of his stomach until it filled his limbs with fire. The Survivor pressed, ever stronger, its weight unbearable.

{She was a liar. A ploy. Let me fix this.}

Calver palmed his eyes. The circumstances of her arrival had been far too acute to have been a coincidence. Why had he even for a moment thought that he could trust her?

Because he was weak. Emotionally skewered by his failure at the demolition. By the final reaping of the fate he'd planted for himself eighteen months before in a separate moment of weakness. He cried out under the pressure, grabbing at his hair, willing it away. *She was destitute. Starved. Desperate.*

The Survivor pressed harder.

He'd been infiltrated, and he'd *let* it happen. He sat there for long minutes, wallowing in horror at his own stupidity. How would the ripples of this affect Fankalo?

The mind-djinn's pressure compounded. *Four hundred and nineteen days.* Fates, he couldn't wait that long. He didn't want to do this anymore.

Calver broke.

The mind-djinn surged forward.

Regret.

He wrestled for control again with a roar. His head seared like it was splitting in two.

Void.

Like music, a delicate rapping of seven knocks came at the door.

Calver couldn't break free. The Survivor pulled the dowaga from its latch.

Raimee rounded the corner. Her hair dripped with moisture. Her emerald robes, all mud and tatters, were balled beneath one arm. She wore his single spare tunic, so large it fell down past her knees.

"You're back," she started brightly, but her eyes fell on the dowaga and her smile faded.

{Kill it.}

The Survivor was weaker than usual. Calver almost had it. He just needed to find something to cling to that wasn't this.

"Calver?" Raimee asked him. *Him.* Not the Survivor. *Void.*

He whipped out his writing pad. In the struggle to keep his body, he scribbled so hard he nearly broke the charcoal. 'Where did you go?'

"What—what happened to you?" She looked at him differently than she had the day before.

Void.

He shook the paper at her to elicit an answer.

"I needed to bathe. Fates, I've been wearing your blood for days." She took a step back from him.

'Where?'

Her brow furrowed. "A stream. Chaos, I didn't realize I was a prisoner."

{Kill it.}

"Victory over the mind can only come with an embrace of the void. For only in nothing can you find everything."

Calver won.

Whether it was a matter of his own mental fortitude or the Survivor conceding, he could not tell. He took a moment to meditate on non-feeling, pulling it in like oxygen.

'Fine,' he wrote.

Raimee shook her head and took another step in the direction of the door. "Is this a normal thing for you? Flipping between night and day?"

No. Normally he lost. Normally he was the one submerged, not the Survivor. And normally no one else noticed a difference.

He dragged a hand across his face before responding. 'I have a lot to protect.'

Raimee shook her head. "Calver, look at me. I could barely make it to the river." He did look at her. Her body was skeletal, her face gaunt. "I couldn't be a threat to you even if I intended to be."

He clenched and unclenched his hands; rolled his shoulders. Closed his eyes for an inhale. An exhale. Then nodded.

They both stood awkwardly staring at each other, much like their first meeting. Raimee wavered, her frail form like a tall blade of grass blowing in some unseen wind. Could she...? But no. He was intimidating enough; he couldn't just ask this woman if she could tell that there was a voice in his head which seized control of his body. Like you asked a person to check for ticks.

"I... prepared a surprise for you. For when you got back," she began.

Calver blinked, cocked his head.

"I didn't read through the books you set aside for me to look for Methu'su because—well—I found this one." She turned from him cautiously—like he might bite her should she present her back—and hobbled toward the hearth, where a gargantuan, mustard volume lay. Raimee rotated the tome, which he recognized intimately, to display its title. *A Collection of Standardized Signals, Fourth Edition.*

His heart picked up speed.

"Years ago, I petitioned for a sea kelp research contract for our monastery, which should have put me on a six-month voyage across the Casowhatan. The funding fell through. But I started learning to signal because, well, the seafarers invented its code. And I was so excited. And I—" Her eyes glistened. "That's not important." Her cheeks darkened. "I assumed you wouldn't—you know—because—well—no one does. I mean—except seafarers." Then, with her usual awkwardness, she tucked the book under an arm to signal slowly and sloppily.

<*I practiced all day.*>

Calver's body felt like too-thin soup. Seconds passed by as he remained immobile, incapable of doing anything but gulping. His hand found his mouth and clung there. He hadn't been able to signal with a person since...

It didn't matter. He shouldn't have the right to communicate like others did.

Raimee's brow furrowed. She signaled again with imprecise fingers. <*Can you understand?*>

He nodded, trying to keep his expression controlled. Expression determined emotion. Emotion summoned the Survivor. At least, bad emotions did. He wouldn't let the Survivor take this from him.

She slipped back into speech. "Is it alright? I didn't mean to upset you."

It was better than anything he deserved. Anything he could have hoped for.

She fidgeted with the sleeves of his tunic—which she'd rolled to keep from covering her fingertips—like she was worried he would transform into the beast again at any moment.

Calver took a steadying breath and nodded again.

A smile swept across her face, and she bounced once on her toes. "I am so relieved. For a moment I thought you were... Well, I'm not sure what I thought you were."

Calver still hadn't moved. He didn't know what to do.

Thankfully, she broke the awkwardness again, tilting her torso toward him, her hands clasped behind her back. "I flipped through the book as much as I could, but it's been a long time. Maybe you can help me practice?"

<Yes. I'll help you practice.>

Eighteen moons had passed since he'd last signaled. It felt clumsy to him, but she didn't seem to notice.

"That was... fast. Let's start slow, eah?" Her eyes eagerly inspected the bags he'd brought back from Chira'na.

<Sure.>

"Is there anything more I can eat?" Almost on cue, her stomach made a loud squelching sound.

<For the shiny, magical human with no end to her belly? There might be just enough.> He held each motion for longer this time.

She seemed to understand, as indicated by her embarrassed recoil. "I've never been as hungry in my entire life as I've been in this cave. I can't even begin to understand why."

<I can't believe...> he started. Stopped. Started again. *<I can't believe you can signal.>* Calver nearly cringed. He sounded stupid. Stupider than if he'd tried to talk past the stump of once-organ behind his teeth.

"I will say that reading them seems to be easier than forming them. But practicing will help, I hope? Rote memorization was a fundamental skill at the monastery. I'm a quick study!" She waved an arm in an overly enthusiastic gesture before snapping her limbs to her sides and blushing again.

It had taken Calver several weeks to develop any amount of proficiency. Even if she had learned them before, how had she—? He reined in his rising suspicion. They were at a crossroads. Either he trusted her, or he didn't.

He shouldn't trust her. Not for any reason. And yet...

He nodded. *<We will cook. And practice.>*

They cooked and they practiced.

<Here are the stakes,> Calver signaled to Raimee as she pulled dozens of ingredients from the sack he'd brought from the market.

The sick Ruxian went rigid like her spine had turned to steel. "Stakes?"

He nodded, keeping his face impassive. *<Everyone learns faster with stakes. Right, scholar?>*

Her voice did little to hide her wariness. "Of course. I—what kind of stakes?"

<*Well, the way I see things, there's only one bowl. One spoon.*>

Raimee's arms fell slack. She released a breath with a relieved chuckle like a tittering bird.

<*So if you get a signal right, the spoon gets passed to you.*> He took the wooden utensil and slid it into her fingers. <*But if you get a signal wrong, or I can't understand it, the spoon returns to me.*> He plucked it from her fingertips, causing her face to split into a gap-toothed grin. <*Whomever has the spoon when the food is ready gets to eat first.*>

Raimee lifted her chin, a competitive light in her eye. "Challenge accepted."

For the tenth time since scouting out a recipe that wasn't fortified porridge in Chira'na, Calver quelled his rising excitement by forcing his facial muscles into stoicism.

<*Signal in answer*> he instructed, and held up an onion. <*What's this?*>

<*An onion*> she responded. Her movements were slow and hesitant, but accurate.

He nodded, handing her the spoon. Raimee clapped her hands together—the most childlike thing he'd ever seen from a grown woman—threatening an early slip in his resolve. He hid his face under the guise of an exaggerated twist to flip a knife from his hip holster.

<*Chop it, there on the stone.*> He tilted his head toward a flat stone set beside the hearth.

Raimee's nose scrunched toward her brow, and she looked at the knife as though it had grown fur. "Has that been sanitized?"

<*Everything is getting cooked.*> He thrust the hilt toward her.

She only looked down her nose at him, an impressive feat, considering she didn't even rise to his shoulder.

<*Nothing has died on this blade,*> he assured her.

Recently.

With a look of reservation, she took it from him, her fingers loose on the handle.

Fates help him. She'd never used a knife before.

"I've never—" she started, stopping as he began to signal.

<*Give it back. Watch first.*>

A lesson in safety proceeded before he entrusted her with the blade once more. Then began a volatile dance of signaling words for anything and everything between chopping, sauteing, seasoning, boiling, and snagging the single spoon back and forth with such vehemence, Calver feared it might snap.

Whenever he signaled a syllable she didn't recall, she would let him know, and he would write it down for her. She drank the knowledge unfailingly, though she had fallen into a habit of mixing up sh- and th- sounds; both were made with the same motion, but with the difference of using the pointer or middle finger.

He slid the spoon from where she had not-so-subtly shoved it behind her ear in lieu of a genuine hiding place. <*You'd better be careful. The food is nearly ready.*> He raised his eyebrows at her. <*And I eat very slowly.*>

Her jaw dropped in mock horror beneath narrowed silver eyes. "You wouldn't," she said aloud.

<*Take the tip from me. It's better for your digestion.*> He'd only ever seen the girl shovel food into her mouth as though it might disappear if she didn't.

"Forgive me for losing my manners while starving to death."

Stilling his cheeks from tightening had never been more difficult. <*You'll never win the spoon back if you just keep talking.*>

Raimee's fingers flew into a quip. <*You could let me win, and at least we'll both get to eat before it's cold.*>

Not only were her signals flawless, but her hands worked continually faster than they had less than an hour ago. He returned the spoon with a lazy toss into the air. She fumbled to catch it before gracing him with a glare.

<*Those are done.*> He nodded toward the pan.

In a moment of carelessness, he crossed space with Raimee to reach for a pinch of salt while she took the initiative to ladle vegetables into the bowl. Scalding broth dripped onto the sleeve of his tunic.

Calver sucked air through his teeth. Raimee gasped, as he shook the sleeve and rolled it away from his skin, but her apologies fell short, her eyes fixed on the other burns along the crease at his elbow. Eight digits stood there, enduring as diamonds, each the length of a bean.

She fell back into speech. "That's a brand."

Even before she'd made the comment, he'd already begun to tug the sleeve back down. *Stupid. Stupid.*

She stared at him with wide eyes. "What's it for?"

<*You've lost your spoon again,*> he motioned, but the tease came without his prior mirth.

The Ruxian's brow furrowed, and then her eyes grew wide as realization dawned on her. Her voice shook slightly. "You—you were tume'amic? But they—but you're—"

Too old? Should be dead, thrown in a Tera'thian pit somewhere? Everyone knew the tume'amic were milled at eighteen. Children didn't usually lead uprisings.

"You're Tera'thian?"

<Nelfinden,> he corrected her, her insights and accusation causing a flare of panic. <Not Tera'thian.>

She pulled away from him, eyes darting in thought. "What, so you were stolen or something? How? How can that be possible?"

Fates, had this unraveled. He wasn't meant for a halfway decent social interaction. He shrugged.

"And that means you escaped?" Raimee cupped both hands to her mouth in horror.

Calver couldn't avoid the tide of fleeting memories. The smell of his own burnt flesh. The feel of skin on skin. *Shit.* The Survivor pooled into him as though on command.

{It knows too much. Let me. I'll—}

Void.

Calver cringed. He didn't want the Survivor to intervene any more than he wanted the memories. He wanted to rewind the evening to the moment before he reached for the salt.

<Little Ruxian of many questions, you are letting your dinner burn.>

Her hands lowered to reveal a twisted mouth, but she listened. Turning away, she removed the pan from the hearth.

Raimee did not ask again. He scooped rice and lentils into the ladled sauté and handed her the bowl. She took it from him with a nod of gratitude, her lips pressed into a line as though trying to keep something contained.

After an evening of conversation, the sudden silence—or lack of hand signals—was unbearable to him.

<What did you study as a cenobite?> he asked, looking for anything to break his mind away from the still-lurking Survivor.

She seemed equally grateful for the new topic. "Well, because you asked, you are looking at the world's leading expert on Casowhatan sea kelp."

And the only one, he was sure. The monastery commission she'd spoken of earlier probably wouldn't have lost its funding if sea kelp enthusiasts had been in demand.

<Impressive.>

Raimee gave a mock bow. "I also studied anatomy. Surgery. Childbirth. Medicine." She spoke freely; he didn't correct her. She'd already acquired the target of their game, and needed her hands to eat. "And then, of course, zoology, dendrology, herbology, fungi. Just about everything that lives and grows."

<*Is that why you can heal bones instantly?*>

She tucked a curl behind her ear. "I told you, that seems to be something of a... new ability for me." She quickly changed the subject. "And you study history. War. Or so I've gathered from your collection."

<*How and why people kill other people.*> He paused, then cast his eyes down.

The Ruxian shifted, bowl still undisturbed in her hands as she watched him. What would his life have been like if he'd studied biology instead of the dowaga?

He'd be long dead.

The scent of their dinner wafted from the bowl enticingly, ready to be enjoyed. The Ruxian looked like she was on the verge of falling over. <*Eat,*> he signaled.

She responded with a cheerily signaled, <*Hooray!*> and sat with a groan of relief.

It should have been enough for two dinners each. But, of course, Raimee burned through most of it in a matter of minutes, slurping as she went.

When the bowl changed hands, she asked, "Did you have a difficult day today?"

A sheath of ice stole around his heart. <*Why?*>

She looked at him thoughtfully before responding. "Well, even after you got over—whatever your earlier personality shift was... and even when it was all going well, you've had one of—one of these"—she reached for her face and pulled down at the skin beside her eyes—"going on."

The motion was so ludicrous, he felt the ice crack. <*Have I?*>

Her head bobbed, and she pulled the skin around the rest of her face down to make a point. "Yeah, big time."

He snorted, and she smiled at him, brighter than the highsun.

The fire crackled behind them. Calver took a bite of the dinner and swallowed slowly, the only way he could.

<*I received some bad news today,*> he signaled.

"I'm sorry," was all she responded.

She looked away, allowing him to eat without further scrutiny. It was only after he'd finished and reached for the next book in their pile that she signaled. <*Did I help?*>

<*Yeah. You did.*>

Chapter 15

Attilatia

By the time Attilatia returned to the small adobe dwelling she shared with Thedexemore, the horizon of Seraphinden's distant green wall had swallowed the sun. Darkness settled over the gardens her brother tended around their residence. The humid air was stiff as canvas, sticky with the familiar perfume of puspas and jasmine, hibiscus and moon orchids.

Attilatia tiptoed across the threshold into the embrace of the earthen structure, moving with care so as to not alert Thedexemore of her arrival. The door to their home opened directly into a modest kitchen. She set her oculars and turban on the table.

From the corner of her vision, something moved.

Blood turned to ice, heart hammering, her hand clenched on the dagger she kept beneath her tipiana—

—and the frightened alley cat, like a burr with legs, darted around her and out into the night. Attilatia dragged a hand across her face as the lump in her throat loosened. An animal in the kitchen? Fates, at least when Thedexemore left she wouldn't have fur in her tea to look forward to.

With a silent curse, she lifted the russet rug at the room's center. Beneath it, a wooden hatch sat with all the innocence of a bloodied knife. Despite her ability to afford living space elsewhere in the capital city, Attilatia liked to keep herself at arm's distance from Aethertech Mechanics. But the real reason she'd chosen to build their home in Poqualle had nothing to do with her distaste for all things skywalk. It had entirely to do with the district's subsoil.

She lifted the trap door from the floor, begrudging the fact that she hadn't made time to grease its hinges, and descended a ladder into the dark, quiet haven of her subterranean lab. Over a span of six years, she'd carved out the earthen space beneath her home until it was the size of a Blue Wing vessel. It was the only place she could distort however she wished, away from Aetech's prying eyes.

But tonight, she was not focused on distortion.

Attilatia pulled the calcium disodium she'd bought in Shrokan from her belt and set to work on a new strikapa test antidote. She'd thrown out the last batch after failing to add the chelation agent in time.

The gear she donned when tackling the strikapa made Aetech's jumpsuit look like a lady's gown in the skywalk's courts. Intestine-lined gloves extended to her shoulders; a vest stretched from her neck to her toes. A mask shielded her face. Spread by skin contact, if even a drop of the culture touched her, it would mean an excruciating death.

She separated the strikapa solution, prepped the evening before, into five separate dishes. The motions were a dance she'd practiced countless times. Tonight, she performed them with the careful silence of a prowling fox, hoping Thedexemore had not noticed her arrival. Between the trapdoor and the cat—

A knock—far too lazy to be an assassin's—sounded against the wood overhead. *Chaos.* His ears were like a hound's.

"Go away," she said in Azadonian.

The trap door pulled open with a screech. A pale face with stark black hair like a violent thrashing of ink popped upside-down through the hatch.

"You went into town today," Thedexemore commented in perfect Nelfinden. That language from his lips poked at her nerves.

"I am busy," she grumbled. She only had an hour at most before she needed to use the far tunnel to meet with Sarko.

"Where'd you go? Korshuva? The Archives? The Port?"

Attilatia despised going into town, and it wasn't one of her market days. Dense as her brother could be, the things she didn't want him to know were becoming more difficult to slip past him. "Shrokan."

"Chaos. You went to Shrokan? Did the shratten moon fall from the sky?" He still spoke in Nelfinden.

Attilatia gritted her teeth. Fine. But she would not turn from speaking her own tongue in her own home. "How did you know?" Even fully covered, she moved slowly to be sure that not a drop went where she didn't want it to.

"I saw the turban. Good idea, that. No one would ever know you had a, ah, psychotic episode." Thedexemore hopped the final three rungs of the ladder which descended from their kitchen. He leaned against it casually, face smug, as if he thought he looked like more than the skinny wood he slouched on.

Attilatia set the beaker down. She flipped up her face mask so he could see her pursed lips. "That's not what that was."

He held a hand to his throat in mock horror. "You nearly stabbed me."

A ten-day prior, she'd chopped her waist-length hair to the tips of her ears. A thing done in haste, perhaps; Nelfinden women only wore their hair short if they were so impoverished they had to sell it. As an Azadonian, it was dangerous. But Hashod had grabbed her by her braid... and she wouldn't let him do it again.

"And the lesson learned? You shouldn't try to wrestle the scissors from me, Dexe."

He grinned.

Attilatia steered from the subject. "Tell me you didn't intentionally allow that animal into the house while I was gone?"

"Toronoff? He only comes when he's hungry."

"You named it?" she said, instead of *you're feeding it?* She didn't know what was worse: that he'd named the cat, or that he'd named it after a Nelfinden theologian.

"He spends enough time in the garden."

Thedexemore was purposefully lingering. As if she didn't have enough to deal with. "Go to bed. You have school tomorrow."

The private education she paid for so he would have somewhere to be and something to do every day was their largest expense.

"I don't care about school. I'm in the Red Wing now." He said the words as if entering basic training made him a war hero. Fates, when had he gotten an attitude?

She snorted. "Yeah, I see you. Too good for me now that you're learning to swing a stick for a no-good oligarchy with no anticipation of real combat, eah?"

Thedexemore groaned and gripped his hair. "Aw, Atti. Why did you choose to ruin everything?"

"Because I told you to go away, and you chose not to listen. And because I think you are a *chikoto*. How much are you going to get paid there, anyhow?"

"It's not about the money."

Attilatia chuckled. "Which is another way of saying that you're paying them, eah?"

"I'll make twenty silver every ten-day."

She didn't hide the way her face drew down at the paltry wage. It might buy fish for a family at the market. "That's it? How did Thyatira recruit record numbers with that for incentive?"

"Lodgings, too."

"You mean gruel and tents."

"And it goes up after training ends. Ah. They said." She raised her eyebrows at him, and he brought a hand to the back of his scrawny neck. "Work's hard to come by for most of the groundling class, Atti. And me. Even being literate, no one around here would put me to work, considering... well, you know."

That all of Nelfindar treated Azadonians like they were livestock with tainted meat?

Of course, the Red Wing wouldn't have enlisted him either without her meddling. It wasn't legal for their kind to join Nelfindar's militia. Thedexemore might have been the first to propose the idea, but his recruitment was not his doing; she'd just let him believe it was. Why not? A boy should dream, when he had little other opportunity.

No, the only reason Thedexemore would be joining the Red Wing was because she'd called in her favor with Roskaad Thyatira to put him there, away from the dangers that he was still oblivious to.

She snapped the mask back over her face, preparing to return to her antidote testing. "You don't need to work. I will work."

"And what am I supposed to do all day when the recruitment ends, come spring?"

Attilatia shrugged. "Whatever you want. Go find a girlfriend. Boyfriend. I don't care."

"Atti. Look at me."

She did, and managed to see past her mask—and her affection—to the pale, sheltered thing that he was. He had Jenolavia's thin lips and hooked nose. His father's diminutive stature. His slight shoulders hunched forward as if guarding something even slighter, as much as to be invisible, at the center of his chest. Were Thedexemore a thing to be put to market, the motives of any prospective buyers should be held suspect.

Something withered inside her. "That's why you're on this harebrained escapade?"

"Yeah. I figured it might give me... make me... something."

Thedexemore's eyes found the earthen floor. He didn't know it yet, but the Red Wing would not train him. He would never be allowed to fight. It was part of the arrangement that Attilatia had made with Thyatira. It would blindside her brother, sure, but he would certainly be safe. Safer than he was here, where Kovathian agents had somehow discovered their identities and location.

"That's not a logical line of thinking." Fates, she couldn't even look at him.

She knew she hadn't made an ideal parent to Thedexemore. She wanted to be. But her wants and her actions were magnetically charged, constantly spinning around one other, and she forever lacked the force to marry them.

"I never argued it was. It's just—it's what I want."

He'd grown up sheltered. Isolated. Understimulated. In their situation, there was little option otherwise. How could he possibly know what he wanted?

"Go to bed, Dexe," she whispered. "It's late." And she had work to do that couldn't involve a teen boy who talked too much for his own good.

"Why were you in Shrokan?"

"Dexe," she growled.

"Atti." He mimicked her tone perfectly.

Chaos, was this *chikoto* unaware that she had a deadly pathogen inches from her fingertips? "If I tell you, will you leave me in blessed silence?"

"Maybe."

"Buying chelators." She held up the beaker and waggled it carefully.

"Don't you normally get those from Aetech?"

Her nostrils flared. "Hashod has chosen to stop accommodating my extracurricular usage."

Thedexemore snorted. "It's not like Aetech can function without your cooperation. Or that you've ever listened to Hashod."

Attilatia shrugged.

Hashod's threat to replace her still darkened her headspace. It had only been a scare tactic, of course; his statement was invalid on two accounts. First, no one could replace her. It wasn't arrogance that led her to believe this, but logic. Aetech held a monopoly on the distortion market for one reason: her. And the secrets she held hostage. If anyone else had discovered how to build a distortion circuit, which was impossible, it wouldn't be guarded information. It would be competition—a public economic war waged against Aetech.

Second, Hashod didn't have the slightest inkling as to the extent to which she *had* pushed the circuit. At Aetech, she held herself back. After all, her aim had never been to advance Nelfindar's technology.

"What batch is this, anyway?" Thedexemore asked, nodding at the culture.

Attilatia sighed. "I—I stopped counting." *After three hundred.* It lessened the pain to not count them any more.

"That—is distinctly not Atti-like behavior."

It was appalling, truth be told. Not at all scientific. But her experiments in search of an antidote were no longer science. They were chasing a hopeless thing, like a dog chasing a bone into fast water.

"Go to bed," she said for the third time, as it occurred to her for the first time that the reason he was no longer obeying might be because he was no longer a boy.

"Look, I know you're mad about Hashod. But I'm not tired. And I'm not going to school tomorrow. Pointless now, eah? But I am going away for several months in a few days. Can't we just... talk?"

No. The sooner she dislodged him the better. "Did you ever once stop to think that maybe I'm angry because, after spending half my life fighting, scraping, clawing to give *you* the life *you* have, you would rather go on a walk through the Jiradesh to make twenty silver a ten-day?"

His brow furrowed. "You *are* mad I've enlisted?"

She had withheld comment when he'd first suggested it. What could a person say when the fraying strands of their heart strained to cling together? "I don't want to talk to you about this, Dexe. Go away."

"Well, you can't stay mad forever."

She chuckled to herself without mirth. "I don't know about that. If you count my entire life, I've already been mad forever."

"Come on, Atti. I haven't seen you all week. You sleep when I'm home. And It's an off-day. I thought—"

"I'm in the middle of something important."

His spindly arms crossed over his chest. "Are you even going to say goodbye to me?"

Preservation, they had a few more days. Why so dramatic? "Yes. Chaos. Yes. But you know my rule—don't talk to me when I'm in the lab!" Attilatia turned to face her work, unwilling to see his expression as she dismissed him.

The wooden rungs of the ladder thunked as her brother ascended it and shut the trap door behind him with another screech. There was silence—which hollowed her, despite it being exactly what she wanted—followed by fading footsteps. Then a deeper silence.

The growing culture at the workstation blurred as Attilatia blinked back tears, hotter than they had any right to be from a person so cold. She hadn't been prepared for this. The anticipation of his departure bore a hole in her. He probably thought she would be glad to have him gone, given the way she treated him.

But at least he was alive, whatever the quality of living that afforded. It was better than being in the final cavern.

Attilatia set a thin pane of glass over each of the variably chelated cultures, five in all. She glared at them as though they were responsible for her troubles. If that *chikoto* boy got himself killed, on the other hand, it *would* have all been for nothing. The voices in her head whispered that it already was. That Azadonia was more than silent. Dead. Wiped out by the strikapa in earnest.

No. She couldn't believe that: that the life she had given up, betraying her people, the disclosure of Azadonian technology, had been without meaning.

But eighteen years had passed since the Nelfinden quarantine. Azadonia was still a black zone to the Nelfinden oligarchy. The Nelfinden Prime, Taranil, xenophobic as he was, took no chances.

They were indefinitely stranded. With no way to communicate with the homeland.

Deshpian Thacklore's dark market confidants assured Hashod that there was still an Azadonia to be had. Of course, Hashod could be lying to her just to ensure her continued cooperation. Attilatia's fingers tightened around the chelation dispenser.

Or Thacklore could be lying to fuck with her.

The memory of blood-spattered crystal stemware flashed behind her eyes. She had the sudden compulsion to clean her hands. Moving to the sink, she dumped the beaker and the chelator, washing them, her gear, and her hands. She stripped her protective layers to hang to dry.

With the chelator added, it was just a waiting game. Perhaps this batch would be a success. More likely it would not, as with the hundreds of its predecessors. It was certainly nothing to be nervous about. Even if the antidote was successful, she didn't know what she would do with it. It wasn't like she could blindly skip back into Azadonian territory to deliver it.

Sometimes it seemed the only reason she did any of this was to make herself feel better. To communicate, in the only way she could, that she had regrets, and that she wanted to do what was right, but she was incapable of expressing it otherwise. She was damaged in that way.

A misanthrope.

She moved from the thought, her body moving with it toward the long tunnel. Time to meet with Sarko.

A standard Aetech lamp marked the back wall of her lab, fastened like a sconce. But it was no standard Aetech lamp; it was another seed of her mind. She twisted it, making a clicking noise. The wall parted. Colossal masses of earth shifted, like beads of water skittering across a hot pan, to reveal a tunnel. Attilatia's chin lifted as a current of air rushed around her. At least there were some things she could control.

She stepped across the freshly turned earth of the threshold that led into her greatest insurance effort. Another decoy lamp existed on the other side. With a turn, the earth compacted behind her again, settling her into the hugging comfort of pure darkness. She ignited a third, specialty lamp, dim enough for her to wield without oculars, and began the thirty-minute walk to the shore.

The longer she moved, the more her tension abated, as if it trickled down through her limbs to be deposited in the soil beneath her. Every ten body-lengths, she passed beneath another reinforcing arch to retain the tunnel's integrity. They were the only points to tell her how far she had come, how far she had to go. Each felt like a testament to what one woman could do with unbridled distortion: a power only she would ever possess—so long as she had the ruxechorin to sustain it.

Her slippered footsteps echoed softly through the vein of cleared earth around her. The ceiling dripped with condensation from the cool air, a great contrast to the Seraphinden heat. It was an invigorating change. And by the time she had walked long and fast enough to not feel the nostalgic prickles of cold against her skin, the tunnel ended.

A ladder stretched three stories toward the open air above. Attilatia ascended, rung by rung, until she reached a hat of solid earth above her, and the final decoy lamp. She twisted it, and the earth and sand overhead coalesced outward in a ring. Light from the moon and the stars caressed her skin. The mineral scents of salt and shell wafted on the warm breeze, vacuumed into the cool air of the tunnel.

The ladder had an extension fastened to the wall beside her, which she locked into place before climbing the final rungs toward the world beyond. Hovering at the liminality between above and below, she stilled herself with a breath. Its sound mingled with the crashing of the Casowhatan waves beyond. Then she peeked over the edge.

A set of brown eyes peered back.

"Chaos, Sarko!" she screeched in Nelfinden as the wind off the ocean whipped his dark hair across his weather-eroded face. "Is you try to break my neck?"

The rumble of Sarko's familiar hacking bark blended with the sounds of the sea.

"Let's get on with it," she muttered, after giving him long enough to have his laugh.

Sarko coughed to clear his voice, which was too old for his age, but its gravel remained. "Charming as ever. Did you cut your hair?"

"What does it look like?"

"It looks like kretch."

Attilatia narrowed her eyes. Charming as ever, indeed.

He grinned at her. "What do you need this time, love?"

"Ruxechorin."

"*You* need ruxechorin?" One eyebrow cocked, highlighting chiseled features which might have been handsome were it not for his eternal smirk.

She held her tongue at, "Yes."

"No."

Attilatia's eyes narrowed. 'No' implied that he had access to the resource, but wouldn't retrieve it. "What you mean, no?"

"There's no chance my source will part willingly with ruxechorin right now."

Worse yet, it implied that not only was there ruxechorin on the dark market, but someone else was making use of it. Hashod's threat to replace her echoed in her ears.

"What is point in keeping pet thief if he unwilling to steal for me?" she grumbled.

Sarko cupped her chin. He licked his lips. "For one, I can still bite."

Chaos, he was nauseating. Allowing herself to slip into a smile, Attilatia leaned forward. Her lips parted to encompass his.

Sarko tasted of salt and smoke, and he drank her kiss like it just might give him everlasting life. And she pretended it would—for a moment, she played the game. Made him think he was a god among mortals. That she would submit to his every desire.

Then she pushed his scruffy face away before he could get ahead of himself, separating them with a husky breath. "Tell me about this source."

"I—" He winced. "Can't."

But he would. Attilatia trailed a finger down the side of his neck and toward his stomach, then flicked him in the chest. "Ah. Then I no can either."

"Atti," he moaned as she began her descent back into the tunnel.

"Happy Fates until next time, Sarko. I no can say it has been pleasure."

"Atti, wait," he tried again, his face a silhouette against the moon.

She did wait, a body-length below him on the ladder with a hand on the decoy lamp.

But Sarko did not fold into compromise, as she'd expected. The corners of his eyes fell in concern. "You need to be careful asking about ruxechorin right now. It's... it's not a good time."

Not an attempt to get her to resurface. Not an appeasement for them to make a new deal. A warning. Attilatia's chest tightened as she thought about the Shrokan merchant's overreaction.

What was happening?

"Is that all?" she asked.

Sarko shrugged. "I came a long way," he tried sheepishly.

"That make one of us. Here. One for road." She blew him a kiss and turned the lamp, sealing the space between them heartbeats later. The rasp of shifting sand and dirt stopped as the opening congealed like stone, shrouding her in darkness.

Attilatia's mouth twisted. Irritation had gotten the better of her. It wasn't the first time she'd left Sarko both abruptly and unsatisfied; if she wasn't careful, she might lose his services. But she couldn't help but feel that this time, she'd gotten the worse end of the deal.

Why would he warn her not to look for ruxechorin? What else was she supposed to do?

She descended the ladder into her tunnel, thoughts descending with her into darkness. Could Hashod be behind this, pooling dark market ruxechorin for another project with a different engineer at its helm? And Hashod *was* hiding something in Aetech's facility on the nights she didn't work. She knew someone had been going through her workstation.

Attilatia rolled the glass bead on her bracelet between the thumb and forefinger on her opposite hand. She didn't have the headspace to unravel this Aetech issue right now. It was something to figure out once Thedexemore left with the Red Wing. With him gone, she might even be able to breathe freely enough to uncover who had ratted them out to the Kovathians, remove them, and figure out if Hashod's subversion was behind it. But right now she had limited time with her adopted sibling, whom she'd cast aside for a worthless meeting. As if things weren't strained enough between them.

On the trek through the tunnels to return to her lab, she resolved to brew Thedexemore tea when she returned. To tell him some generic words that didn't really resonate with all the things she felt but seemed appropriate. Like that she was proud of him. She scoffed—"proud" was too limited. It would never be good enough for the sweet, innocent—and, true, imbecilic—boy she'd given her life for. But maybe it would mean more to him.

When the earthen passage closed behind her, she made haste for the culture across the room. No harm in taking a peek before surfacing to the kitchen. A single hour was not enough time for definitive results, but—

Her heart hardened to stone in her chest. The culture had tripled.

Attilatia sighed and started to clean the dishes in her workstation sink. Her throat swelled in her neck against a constricting pain; her fingers trembled. *Kretch.* Everything she did seemed set up for failure. And now she'd set Thedexemore's fate in the same way. He would be but a decoration in the Red Wing's ranks. In four months, he would return home dismayed and defeated, having had nothing of the experience he wanted. Fates, she was a monster.

But at least he would be in one piece.

One day he would understand that he had a larger purpose than dying a warrior. She turned off the sink and dried her hands before dabbing at her eyes. Tea. Maybe she just needed some tea... to fix everything.

Attilatia lifted the trap door, pausing with her chest at floor-level. Thedexemore sat at their table, elbows resting on the wood, hands laced behind his neck. The space before the skinny teen was already set with a pair of steaming cups and food for two.

He turned in his chair at the sound of her, and the corners of his mouth twitched into a smile. His black eyes were forgiving in the way that only his ever were.

She smiled back. Then she climbed out to wrap him in a hug, trying not to remember that it was one of the last she would receive for months to come.

Chapter 16
Niklaus

FIFTEEN MONTHS PREVIOUSLY

Niklaus's spirits rose as he sped out of the capitol city toward Casowhatan, creaking of carriage wheels against the road beneath him, clopping of horseshoe against stone ahead of him: harmonies to his exuberance. He kept the shutters of the carriage thrown open, allowing the salty breeze off the sea to paint his face with freedom. Appreciation was a thing which ought to be practiced in threes. He was about to solve a mystery, he'd ignored his mother's afternoon call, and he would marry Latouda.

Latouda.

Fates, but she was brilliant. Why hadn't he considered simply getting married to halt his mother's scheming himself? Thinking of the crone's reaction was enticing enough to make his mouth water. It was a little early for libations, but with celebration on the horizon, a good drink was in order.

A near hour passed before the bubbling in his chest began to fizzle. They'd passed outside the city's green walls and the line for the exit guard checkpoint, taking an oceanside route to Casowhatan. With little to look at other than dunes and sea, he pulled his kwitra into his hands and dallied across the strings in accompaniment to the wheels and horse hooves.

Another hour, and the clopping and creaking came to a stop. The driver rapped twice upon the carriage door. Setting the instrument on the cushions beside him, Niklaus exited with a jaunty hop onto tan cobbled stone to find himself in an outdoor square. The raised corners of his mouth pulled down.

It was a quaint, middle-class locale. Mothers toted belligerent children as they shopped the various stands and displays: a rainbow of fruits and vegetables, trinkets and tonics. Food carts sold halouchas, mashed yams wrapped in plant fiber, fava beans and millet, and the air was filled with the blended aromas of every spice a man could name. A musician standing near the square's center attracted a modest crowd.

Lovely. Fascinating from a cultural standpoint, as with any groundling venue. But wrong.

Niklaus scouted the area with disappointment. Not a residence to speak of. Stands, a few restaurants, an inn, a bank. His messenger boy had more legs than brains, too, that was certain. The infrastructure looked modern, its buildings coated with fresh paint, its road free of potholes. His mouth twisted. Then again, perhaps he was the one lacking in gray matter. He should have questioned the boy further before loping off like a hound with a bone to bury. Niklaus reread the scrap of paper the boy had given him.

'Casowhatan. Today's Western Market. The third townhome down on the main street.'

His eyes lingered for the first time on the word "today's", and his insides wilted. "Today's" seemed unnecessarily specific.

Niklaus stepped into the path of a man with salt-and-pepper hair and skin like a dried apricot. "Ah, excuse me, mesu. I was wondering if you could direct me to today's Western Market?"

"You're standin' in it," the man grunted, looking past Niklaus toward the wharf. The gruffness of his voice and the maritime flare of his clothing suggested a life at sea. He carried an empty bucket. The sudden smell of brine punctured the air, and Niklaus couldn't tell if it came from bucket or man.

"Yes, but see, this is a market."

The seaman eyed Niklaus's clothing and carriage, likely to determine whether he should give him the time of day or curse him with Chaos. "Well, that's likely why it's called the Western Market, mesu."

Niklaus chuckled at his own expense. Why was it that he always selected the words that made him sound like a lunatic? "I was told I would find townhomes. A residential street, maybe? And this market looks quite new. I was expecting something a bit more, well, horribly dilapidated."

The man stared at him with all the exasperation he deserved.

Niklaus corrected himself. "Something more seasoned."

"You're about twenty years too late. Everything was rebuilt after the fire."

"A fire?"

The man shifted the bucket under his opposite arm, eyes still set on the wharf. "Look, I'd like to chat, but I've places to be."

"Tip for your time?" Niklaus pulled a ten-note from his pocket purse and waggled it. "Eeeeeah?"

The man shifted from one foot to the next. "I've got a few minutes."

"What happened in the fire?"

"Half the row burnt into cinders. A few families died in the blaze."

All this talk of fire, yet Niklaus was pricked by a chill. He'd spent weeks interviewing associates and searching through written records. Nothing had ever been said about Thyatira losing his family in a fire. The man was a public figure; wouldn't that have been common knowledge? It could only serve to make his story more interesting—a man who'd overcome poverty, overcome loss, to become a martial hero.

"Can you remember their names?" he asked.

"It's been a long time."

The unusual surname 'Thyatira' was absent from every census Niklaus had searched prior to the battle of Casowhatan... but, having made the trip, it was worth asking. "Was one the Thyatira family?"

The seaman recoiled and shook his head. "I don't remember any names. None. I can't help you." He might as well have screamed "Yes" and pumped his arms, bucket and all, into the air.

But the reaction unexpectedly turned Niklaus's chill into the cramping spear of guilt. He'd been looking for negative press on a man who was simply trying to outrun his trauma. This wasn't a buried secret; this was a grave, unfrequented by someone not willing to mourn. This story was one he should let lie in peace.

Something he'd never been good at.

Niklaus rolled his lips in over his teeth. "Do you know where I might be able to find some of the residents who did live here?"

"I'd help you if I could, but the residents from Western Market aren't around anymore." The sentence didn't seem to be a lie, but it *was* an evasion.

"What do you mean?" Niklaus squinted against the afternoon sun.

"They left. Moved away."

"What, the whole street?" Niklaus shook his head. "That doesn't just happen, does it?"

The man paused, as though deliberating whether to invest himself in the conversation. "Well, not all at once. It happened over some time. Within a couple of years after the incident. The residents that lived here started to go missing. Those that didn't moved away. No one wanted to stay. Casowhatan's municipality tore down the remaining homes and restructured it into a marketplace."

This was it. This was the kind of information he'd been looking for all along. Something off. Something wrong which he could tie back to the groundling hero, adding spice to the already savory injustices revealed in his Groundling Papers. As he chased the thoughts around his head, Niklaus felt his hopes sink. As interesting as this was, what was the use of the knowledge if there was no one left alive he could interview?

He tried coaxing. "Do you know of anyone—anyone at all—who might still be around I could talk to about the fire?"

The seaman paused again, thinking hard, before he shook his head solemnly. "Sorry, mesu."

"That's quite alright," Niklaus replied. "My thanks to you." He flipped the note toward the man, who aptly pocketed it.

"Fates bless," he said with a nod before beginning to walk away, only to halt after several steps and slowly pivot on his heel. He stared at Niklaus for a moment filled by the screeching of seabirds crossing overhead. "On second thought... I might know of someone."

Niklaus tried not to let his excitement show. "Please do share."

The stranger eyed Niklaus's pocket. With a sigh, Niklaus drew another ten-note from the purse within. *Of course.*

The money elicited an immediate response. "Meridana. She's in a sunset group home called Preservation's Nest in the northwest quarter now, but she lived with her daughter's family at the time of the incident. When her children passed, well... she ended up in geriatric care. Didn't have much of a mind left, if you understand my meaning."

Who could keep their mind after seeing their children into the realm of the Fates?

"That was almost twenty years ago, but she might still be there."

Fat chance. If the old woman had been losing her mind two decades ago, it was more likely the oligarchy would vote him Prime tomorrow than that he'd find her still alive.

"Thanks," he muttered.

"Don't mention it, mesu."

Having accomplished far less than he'd intended, Niklaus decided he might as well call on Meridana in the unlikely case that she was still breathing.

If a town could have corners, Meridana's sunset home was tucked away into the furthest of them. The near-empty street seemed entirely forgotten by the rest of Casowhatan. An uncomfortable lump grew in Niklaus's throat as his carriage approached. It seemed an unbefitting place to house those who would remember not to be forgetful, if they could remember anything at all.

His carriage came to a stop in front of a cracking adobe structure which he might have thought abandoned if not for an elderly man seated on its stoop, smoking paper rolled with tobacco. All groundling buildings in coastal Seraphinden and Casowhatan had stairs like this—a precaution against flooding—but Niklaus didn't see any reduction of hazard when the staircase might swallow a body whole with an improperly positioned footstep.

Niklaus descended from his carriage with a thanks to the driver and approached the stairs with the tentativeness of a man who may or may not be lost, and waiting for some dear to tell him so. The man atop them watched him. His eyes seemed to hold their own sentience compared to the rest of him, which looked all too similar to the thing he was smoking: pale, wrinkled, and charred in some places. Those carob irises shouted at Niklaus, proclaiming they had seen things he would never know, nor want to know. He cringed beneath their silent rebuke.

He climbed step after creaking step. The geriatric said nothing, and Niklaus asked him nothing, knowing that the man would not respond should he ask. He opened the front door and allowed it to slam shut behind him.

It was even quieter inside than out, the room's air stifled by the smell of rotting wood... and people. The sunset home's attendant looked up at him as he entered, like she wasn't entirely sure he was real.

"Meridana?" he asked.

She nodded immediately, like her head was loose on its hinges. "Right this way," she said. Chaos count him a cat in a cooking pot, he'd expected to be shooed across the threshold by now. The attendant cocked her loose-hinge head at him as he failed to disguise his own surprise. "Meridana doesn't usually get visitors. She'll be so pleased."

What had been a desire to run from the place boiled into barely contained excitement as Niklaus followed her down a dim corridor. The floorboards beneath his feet protested with every step. There were only a handful of doors in the hall, and they made their way to the final one on the left. The attendant stopped and rapped her knuckles more loudly than Niklaus would have imagined necessary, a sudden burr in her placid demeanor.

"Meridana!" she barked. "Visitor!"

No answer came.

"I'm letting him in!" She turned toward him and, at a quarter of the volume, said, "I'll leave you two be. Go ahead."

Niklaus pushed open the door, which complained even louder than the floorboards at being disturbed. Fates, none of the residents could ever dream of making it past the front door without waking the rest of the building. On second thought, it was likely the attendants wanted it that way.

Inside the room, a small person gazed out at him through a mask of wrinkles. Meridana was an ancient relic of a woman. She resembled a too-hard raisin that had sprouted a hairy nose and half a dozen teeth.

"Hello, Meridana. My name is Niklaus Meyernes."

The woman's visage of crumbling stone broke, replaced with the punched-out smile of a street grappling champion. She extended a withered appendage as though Niklaus were the Prime himself. "Meridana. Meridana Demundia, dear mesu. Preservation's blessings to meet you."

Niklaus clutched a hand over his heart, clasping her fingers with the other. "Fates have mercy. Nobody warned me that you were the prettiest girl in Cassowhatan."

The corners of the old crone's mouth lifted so high that they pulled at her nose and caused her eyes to become lost in her weedy brow. He could have sworn that dust flew from her lungs as she coughed a slow, drawn-out laugh. "There's another chair here, dear... somewhere... Please, sit with me."

Niklaus scooted his seat close to her, pulling out a notebook and a charcoal pen. "I'm writing a report on some of the families who used to live in what is now the Western Market. I was wondering if you might be able to share some information with me."

Her face fell, like a hard mask had been stripped from beneath her now-hanging skin. "That was a very long time ago..."

"Can you remember it well?"

Her gaze went distant, and a pang of guilt grew into a stone in Niklaus's stomach. The woman had lost her entire family. Children. Likely grandchildren. She hadn't had a visitor in Fates knew how long, and now he was making her relive her worst moments.

"I don't know about well..." she drawled. Then she chuckled toothlessly, the brunt of her own joke. For that alone, Niklaus decided it had been worth the trip. "But I would be happy to tell you about it."

He grinned. "Wonderful. Wonderful. Please, could you tell me about the Thyatiras?"

"Ah yes," she recalled with a nod, "a lovely baker's family. They had a son and two daughters."

She recounted unending details about the confections they'd sold, stuffed with figs and yams, honey and tahini. She told of how the couple had met, their taste in wine, the flowers they'd kept in the windowsills, the daughters' affection for hummingbirds. On and on she went. Meridana spoke ploddingly, as a great stone might should it ever have the desire to tell a tale. Her cadence progressed in the way that dust falls, and she hummed distractedly between sentences. All the while, her body slowly rocked, causing the chair—as old as she was—to creak, as though the steady motion might move her somewhere she'd like to go.

"Such a sad thing," she croaked. "What happened to them. All of them. Couldn't live next to lovelier people."

Niklaus had been hesitant to interrupt, not wanting to control what might be her best conversation of the month. He listened, waited, until he couldn't hold the surge any longer. "Could you tell me more about their son?"

"Oh, that boy..." She shook her head. "Just awful. He died a year before the fire, even. Taken too young. An accident."

Niklaus started. Impossible. She had to be mistaking him for someone else. Who knew how reliable any of her recounting could be? "You're saying their son passed before the fire?"

Meridana nodded. "He was out playing with his friends in the farmlands. Fell backward from a haystack. Rake went right through his heart." She clucked her tongue. "I wish I could forget it. No one ever wants to help a mother prepare their child's body for the ground. Horrible tragedy."

Niklaus's mouth went dry. That couldn't be right. The address had taken him to the home of the Thyatiras—they had to be the same ones. And Roskaad was clearly alive, so... "What was the boy's name?"

"His name was Paeltin. Paeltin Thyatira." She nodded calmly.

"And you're sure that the Thyatiras only had one son?" He tried to keep the consternation from his voice.

"Yes. And two daughters," she repeated before beginning to hum idly, eyes glazing.

"You don't remember a Roskaad Thyatira?"

"No... No, I don't... Not one of the baker's children. Though that name does sound familiar," she said, suddenly looking at him as if she'd forgotten he was in front of her and had been conversing with the chair he sat on. "Would you like to stay for teatime, dear?"

Niklaus considered it, but with a glance at the lowsun thought better of it. "Ah. I'm so sorry, my lovely. I have a long way to go before dusk."

"You can stay over." She winked at him and cackled. He joined her.

"As tempting as that offer is, I'm engaged to a lovely woman who would likely disapprove, and I have work that must get done while it's still fresh in my mind." He beamed at her. "Here, something for your trouble." He placed a hundred-note into her palm—likely worth more than she lived off in a month. Her pupils gave it an empty flick, as though it were a rock, before she beckoned him to her and placed it back in his palm.

"I'm old. Did you know that?" There was a sadness in her eyes which spoke to his own.

He kneeled and clasped his hands around hers. "Do I know that each mural fades, and each mind jades? That each bloom wishes to endure as the moon with a passion, so like their own fleeting nature, sparked from tinder and then burned? What if I had envy for such a thing, to be so nearly an ember to exalt each burgeoning breath? Else be cursed to abandon them with the callous cruelty only conceived by those without learned perception. Did I know that you are more beautiful than the brightest burning star?

"A man can duly hope, lest he be less than a man."

Meridana's laugh was like a storm. It began low, slow, and roared into a hurricane. She clapped her hands, coughed, and, once recovered, cried, "Do it again!"

He scoffed. "To answer your question, you've had me completely fooled, Meridana. I would've had half a mind to marry you instead of my maid if you hadn't told me that."

She threw her head back and cackled once more, tears in her eyes. Then she curled his fingers around the notes. "I've no need for money, Niklaus. I'm on my way out. Where I'm going, it will only weigh me down."

"Ah," he replied, her frankness causing something vital inside him to wither. "Well. No bother. I'll just spend it on something that will get me into trouble, then."

"Please do." She nodded, her whole body rocking as she did so. "And come back to visit, dear? I do love visitors."

"Yes, Meridana. It would be a dream to see you again. I'll be back soon, I promise."

He looked forward to it.

Latouda had disappeared.

Fates. Niklaus couldn't blame her, idiot that he was.

She ignored any messenger he sent her way, and he tried not to think about it, immersing himself instead in the papers she'd been so keen for him to release. A ten-day passed, and he found no further information on Roskaad Thyatira, despite an all-consuming search. He hardly slept. He denied audiences with anyone. A piece of him told him to drop it. He could no sooner drop his heart from his chest.

He returned to visit Meridana, shortly before the Groundling Papers' scheduled release, hoping he might be able to tease out any scrap of new information concerning General Thyatira—something to soothe the raging flame which consumed him.

She'd died.

Niklaus stepped down the treacherous staircase outside the sunset home, each plank bemoaning him, the same soundless old man's eyes at his back. His skin prickled beneath the first cold drops of a front off the sea, a counterpoint to the burn behind his eyes. A sense of foreboding crossed over him, as if Chaos had just placed a curse on him, one he would never be able to shake.

He took to his carriage, poured himself a drink, and opened a book.

It was only a feeling.

Chapter 17

Calverous

"Let me get this straight," Raimee began over a breakfast of fruit and toast—things Calver never would have made for himself, considering the time it took to chew them. She closed the book in her hands on Chira'nan legal ordinances. "If I want to enter Chira'na, I have to prove what I do for a living? And pay the city's entrance fees, whether or not I have work?"

<*Yes.*>

She shook her head like it was the silliest thing she'd ever heard. "But what if I don't have a job and I've simply come to the city looking for one?"

<*You wouldn't be permitted inside. You'd have to submit for one first.*>

"Then how do I live—eat—while I'm waiting to hear back?"

<*Common issue. You'll see the camps of refugees outside Chira'na's walls.*>

"What if I'm coming to visit family? Or an associate, as with Methu'su?"

<*Your representative party is required to send a letter to the city officials. It would need to contain proof of their own employment and a request for your entry.*>

She scrunched her nose. "Fates be strayed. That's a fear-based system if I've ever heard of one."

Calver nodded. <*The Prime's Corporatist policy. Better to control the flow of goods and people and information. Keep everything national. Anything that doesn't work for this agenda stays in the wilds.*>

Her lips pressed into a line. "Then how am I supposed to find Methu'su?"

He waved a casual hand. <*I'll get you in.*>

"You can... do that?" She leaned forward eagerly. "You would do that?"

He nodded again. He hadn't ironed out the details, but he would have the proper documentation forged.

She gave him a winning smile. "There's a lot more to you than I expected."

Best not to think too hard on that comment. Calver hoped the mind-reader couldn't sense the burning at the back of his neck.

"When will you go back to Chira'na?"

<*Tomorrow.*>

"What do you do there?"

Again, with the personal questions. <*Business.*>

"So, you have an employer?"

<*In a loose sense of the term.*>

She eyed him from head to toe. "And you are their... hired muscle?"

<*I am many things.*>

"Impossible to talk to, being one of them," she muttered.

The woman was completely incapable of filtering her thoughts. <*I liked you better last ten-day. You didn't talk nearly as much.*>

Raimee snorted. "Guess you got the wrong first impression of me when I was, you know, about to die and figured you were the one that would take me out."

<*I'm thoroughly reconsidering. I didn't realize you'd be so noisy.*>

She rolled her eyes. "You know, it was pretty easy for me to realize that you're hardly as intimidating as you try to put out." She stood and paced like a lion preparing to pounce on her prey. "As a matter of fact, and I hate to break this to you, you are downright likable."

Calver leaned against the cavern wall and put his book over his face. She was so forward it was painful. Why did she act like this? He had to be the least likable person in Nelfindar.

"I know. It must be intolerable to discover about oneself."

<*Let's just read.*>

"Nope. For the first time in my life, I'm tired of reading. Let's talk about Chira'na," she said, now pulling her effervescent hair off to one side and attempting to remove its knots with her fingers. "Will you teach me how to blend in?"

His stomach cringed. Again, with the *awkward* questions. <*Hardly.*>

Not only was he the worst possible teacher for such a thing, but the Ruxian would blend into society as well as ink into Azadonian silk.

"Come on, really though! My mentor once told me that if I ever left Tennca'Pui I would be—I'm trying to remember the exact phrase he used—not properly socialized?"

If a greater understatement had ever been proclaimed, he had yet to hear it. <*Have you ever had any peers that weren't castrated old men married to science?*>

"Oh." She held her fingers to her mouth. "No. I suppose not. Women were never allowed inside the gates. And they weren't strictly my peers. Most of the cenobites ignored me because, well... I was technically taboo to them. But I've read a lot of books on conversation and books with conversations, and I—" Her eyes widened. "Oh, I *am* talking too much, I think."

A lunatic was what she was. She fidgeted, like she always did, attempting to re-braid the half-tangled mass of her hair yet again.

<*You may encounter some social difficulties,*> Calver agreed.

She harped on his previous comment. "So you knew that the cenobites at Tennca'Pui were eunuchs? Is that unusual, then? Do most men in Nelfindar keep all of their parts, you know, for mating and the like?"

Something bubbled rapidly from Calver's stomach into his throat. It escaped his body like a bark, but not, having more in common with an expulsion of gas than a genuine laugh. That was a thing he hadn't done in recent memory. Raimee's speckled cheeks darkened, a reaction he was sure he mirrored. Fates, she didn't even know what she'd said wrong.

<*This is a perfect example.*> Calver tried to control his face for her sake. <*That's not a question you ask. Anyone should know this. Anyone socialized.*>

"Well, I didn't. And I was only asking out of curiosity!" She put her hands on her hips. "Don't socialized people ask questions?"

<*Not weird ones.*>

"How would you know the difference? Are you expecting to convince me that *you*"—her eyes ran a lap of the cavern— "are properly socialized?"

<*I've had exactly enough socialization to understand when a question is weird.*>

"Well, if the answer is so incredibly obvious that it made you lecture me on the protocol for asking socially acceptable questions, I should know it." She crossed her arms.

He sighed. <*Yes, we have all of our parts.*>

Raimee slapped her knee. "Well, I didn't ask you about your particular situation, but thank you for informing me." She stared at him, and he had half a mind to shield his groin. Fates, this conversation couldn't be any less comfortable. "Don't you find them to be distracting?"

Apparently, it could.

<*Please, don't go around asking men about their genitals. It can only end badly.*>

Raimee doubled over, eyes scrunched, mouth helplessly open. It was a tinkering laugh that brought butterflies to mind. Her recovery was less than graceful. "Alright, I have duly noted that men who have genitals don't like talking about them."

He nearly told her that was also an inaccurate statement, but thought better of it. <They're only occasionally distracting,> he admitted.

She scrunched her flat nose. Calver fought against the twitching of his lips.

"You know, I've seen you smile at least three times today, which, I have a feeling, is a record for you. It's kind of nice to have a friend out here, as opposed to a featureless boulder."

His fingers launched to correct her. <I am not your friend.>

"Oh? A true boulder, then?"

<We find Methu'su. We part ways.> She had to understand. Help her? Yes. Lead her astray? No.

Raimee's eyebrows raised. "So, by your logic, we should dislike one another up until that point to ensure that the separation is an *enjoyable* experience?"

Why was it that every time he tried to distance her, she closed the fucking gap like a seamstress? Calver chose to re-open his book. The stack was growing smaller; soon he wouldn't be able to use it as an excuse. But he didn't know what to say. Saying nothing was so much easier than attempting to signal the storm raging inside him into meaning. Reading was safe. Reading was routine. Reading would achieve an objective.

She allowed him to lie in blessed silence for a fleeting second before—

"Calver?"

That tone.

He knew it was going to be an uncomfortable question before she even asked. He peered at her around his book. She was clutching her own tome nervously, eyes cast to the ground. Her feet shifted from side to side.

He sighed and nodded at her to go on.

She kneeled in front of him, less than an arm's distance away, locking eye contact. Her closeness made his stomach squirm, but he held her gaze.

Raimee was an aesthetic oddity Calver could only describe as having too many things vying for his attention. Her nose was broad, yet her facial features were oddly angular. A gap between her front teeth afforded her a constant lisp. Speckles and bumps spattered her umber skin, like constellations he'd first mistaken for dirt. Then there was her hair—like violently curled moonbeams, waist-length and voluminous as her body doubled.

But her eyes were different. They did not compete. Looking away from them was more difficult than banishing the Survivor had ever been.

"What happened to your tongue?"

Like it was totally normal to ask people about their missing organs. He ran his fingers through his hair to grip the back of his neck.

Raimee shrank. "That's probably one of those questions I'm not supposed to ask."

She was trying to better understand him. That didn't mean that she was an enemy. It meant she was human. And stranger and lonelier, even, than he was. He released a breath.

<I was a kid. I found out something I wasn't supposed to know. The knowledge couldn't be removed. My tongue could.>

Raimee put a hand up to her mouth. "Oh. Creation. I thought…"

<I know what you thought.>

What anyone thought—that it had been an act of justice against a criminal. Fuck, why had he even told her? She had no right to ask the question. What did he think he had to prove?

Raimee reached out to touch his shoulder. He pulled away before her hand could fall on him and stood to leave.

<I have to go. Business to attend.>

He'd be lucky if Greeny already had information for him, but he couldn't stand to sit here with her pity.

"Right now?"

Calver didn't respond. He'd done this to himself. He'd let her get familiar. And he had the power to stop it, too.

What he still lived for—what he would die for—was more important than befriending a fated Ruxian.

He left the cave. Mesu Callisto had always said that sin stemmed from either ignorance or passion. But the things done to him… They had been neither. They'd been precise. Calculated.

It made his stomach churn.

The makings of a martyr were a crude recipe. Sliced once, burnt twice, salted thrice, and propagated enough times for him to be sure he had offspring—children he'd never know, but who would meet a similar, if not worse fate.

For the way he'd been forged, he would burn down the kitchen.

Calver pulled his cloak tighter against the wind as he clipped though bustling city streets toward Chira'na's Repository. It was never quite cold enough to snow in this part of Nelfindar. But when the wind blew in gales like this—like the Fates' fucking breath—in winter, it came with bite.

He patted the encrypted letter to Fankalo in his pocket, anxious against all reason that the gale might somehow blow it out and away. A reassuring crinkle caught in his ears amidst the howling rush of air. Wind like this did strange things to a city. Calver could not deny the darkness nestled within the walls of Chira'na; more a feeling than a tangible thing, but it existed all the same, harbored like a dormant sickness. The air stirred it out into the open, where it pooled about him; hope, desperation, and fear all riding a fanned current of aether. He recognized it as intimately as his own shadow.

He lengthened his strides without concern for suspicious eyes. Who wouldn't want to get from one place to the next in *this*? He had hoped that receiving communications from Greeny this morning would still the galloping of his heart. It only drove a whip against its flanks.

He made the journey to the Repository's rooftop in record time. Killari already waited for him, tucked into an alcove in the frame of the maintenance shed. She commanded his attention with a shake of feathers that, caught in the wind, nearly threw her off-balance. Calver joined her behind the relative buffer the shed provided.

The note at her ankle was scribbled in haste across hardly more than a scrap of paper.

'I want you out. The original shipment has been distributed regardless. Your staying can't correct that. I'd rather cut my losses than risk you further. If we do have a rat on our hands... Fates know I'll find him and make him squeak. Leave for Karval today. I'll expedite your transport.'

Calver's heart faltered.

Short, to the point, and seeded with a latent manipulation he now understood. Just as the words were encrypted, so were their meaning. Fankalo didn't want him to investigate, because...

His teeth clenched together.

Because he wasn't ever supposed to find out what was really in the shipment he'd been instructed to destroy.

Heat flushed through him despite the cold. Killari pecked at his ear as he rolled up the note. He had waited hours for Greeny to find him a translator this morning, and didn't have time or mind to buy any fish. Without tithes to offer that would lessen her reproachful stare, he gave her a sorry shrug and, shortened by his temper, an inadequate stroking of her chest. The wind pulled her plumage into a lion's mane, making her look all the more irritated.

He tried and failed to light a matchstick a dozen times over in the unstoppable gale. As he could not burn it, he was forced to look at Fankalo's message again. For as long as he held the note still in his hands, he couldn't stop turning it over in his mind. His grip tightened until the paper tore. Unwilling to break protocol, he dropped its halves into his canteen instead. He would make the return journey without water.

He pulled a charcoal pencil from his pocket and rolled it between his fingers as he considered the response he'd already written that morning. He couldn't leave for Karval now. Not with his deal with Raimee left unfinished. One did not challenge Fankalo—not even him. And yet...

{Fankalo is keeping secrets,} the Survivor whispered.

No.

But how could he argue false truth to a thing which already knew his innermost thoughts?

{Betrayed you. Never disclosed the shipment's contents. She knew—}

Void.

He rubbed a hand across his eyes and looked at his reply.

'Greeny reported the Aetech shipment to contain twenty-five thousand military-issued defensive shields bound for Chira'na's Red Wing headquarters. Please tell me you didn't know what the inventory was before the demolition attempt?

'Greeny is still working to uncover who else might have taken interest in its records. I'll track down the plates and see whether they were tampered with. With a Tera'thian unit shepherding them, I guarantee this is related to the Steila rendezvous. This isn't just our problem anymore. It's a national emergency. One needs only a nose to smell what's been sowed.'

Calver nearly threw it in the canteen, too.

But no. He wanted Fankalo to know he knew. And how it made him squirm.

Instead, he added a postscript:

'Give me a few more days.

'A favor. I need fast information about a man named Abiathar Methu'su.'

Rolling it again, he set it in the canister. He popped the vial of lemon oil and Killari wasted no time taking off with his response, wings flapping vigorously to keep her from blowing sideways. He watched her fly over the thousands of red flags rippling in the streets below, newly erected in anticipation of the Red Wing recruitment which would soon enter the city. His stomach writhed. Fankalo was going to be pissed.

The feeling was mutual.

Before long, Killari was a small black spot against the low-hanging sun. Calver squinted against the orange fire its retirement cast across Chira'na. It was late. He'd half-expected the urchin to have paid him a visit by now; it was rare that he spent a full day in the city without encountering him. Perhaps it was the weather. He thought about the boy's torn rags, his bone-hugging skin. He'd have taken better shelter today.

Calver shook his head. Why was he dwelling on this? A week ago, the trials of a street urchin wouldn't have taken harbor in his headspace.

The Survivor stirred, a predator looking for anything to sink its teeth into. Calver pushed it down. A week ago, he'd hardly controlled his headspace at all.

He left the Repository on a straight path for the city's gate. He could search the Red Wing's headquarters for the shipment, but more information from Greeny would be worth the wait. The Red Wing wouldn't leave for another week yet. Besides, he wouldn't make it to the safehouse before sunset as it was. Darkness in the Sharinash was never ideal. For some, it was a wish for death.

He considered the events of the past week in a spinning mental wheel, with the Survivor's submission as its axis. Not in fourteen years had he spent so long with agency over his body, his thoughts, without it crippling him with internal pressure. He'd accepted the Survivor before. It made it so he didn't have to think about things. And it shielded him from whatever tracking magic Cul'Mon possessed.

He turned his mind from the conundrum. And from any thoughts of Fankalo, knowing they were an equal invitation for the Survivor to assault him. Instead, he wondered for the hundredth time where he had heard the name Methu'su, tracing the tangled threads of memory to their origin. How long *had* it been? They weren't finding him in the books in the safehouse, which meant they would need to search in the Repository.

Raimee would need to come with him—it was her journey. And soon, though her healing had gone slower than he would have assumed. Ready or not, she would need to be exposed. To society. To Kath...

A strange feeling clawed its way around Calver's chest as he thought about the perils the world would present her—a fated botanist, totally defenseless and more decent than anyone deserved. The feeling changed, claws melting like ghee in a hot pan.

He quashed it.

Fuck. The sooner she was off to Methu'su, the better all around. How would he get her in? He could hardly march around Chira'na in broad daylight with the only Ruxian to exist in seventy years. Fates, the girl wasn't exactly inconspicuous.

They would need to come up with a way to disguise her...

He trod the weed-strewn path from Chira'na's outer gate toward the distant treeline. The ghostly blue-green glow of the twilight was just enough to see by. He turned to catch a glimpse of the north wall beneath the fading light.

His breath condensed in a cloud around him as it vacated his chest.

Blood trickled from his extremities, displaced by tingling cold. His every thought surrendered to horror.

Two gargantuan horizontal lines with an oblong diagonal slash running through them were charred against the port gate wall.

Something visceral shifted within him in a way that spoke of bile; the Survivor rippled against the bulwark between them. The Ratka. The mark of the Shadewalker. Again.

Calver turned into the forest. An icy dagger snaked down his spine, as if to guard him from the Ratka's eyes on his back. He needn't guess why. It was Cul'Mon's reminder that he was still one step ahead. And things were about to get worse.

Chapter 18
Calverous

FOURTEEN YEARS PREVIOUSLY

Calver awoke, immobilized at the wrists and ankles, lying prostrate on a cot. A shallow pool of blood matted his face to the canvas, seeped from his mutilated mouth. The smell of antiseptic bit through the air to blend with the metallic tang of his essence. It clogged his nose, his throat; simply breathing was strenuous. His stump of a tongue throbbed angrily, made worse by the fact that the surface he lay on rattled like a cart over cobbles.

Calver tried to orient himself with a slow series of blinks. He couldn't see past his dark eyelashes, the stark white of the cot, and the crimson which soaked it. His ears rang. He couldn't draw his thoughts into a line. It felt like he was floating. He would've believed he was, too, if he couldn't see that he wasn't. He wanted to keep his eyes open, to look around, but just thinking about it made him dizzy, so he let his eyelids fall.

Time passed like an endless melody to the beat of a rattling cot. Jarring. Throbbing. Tearing.

His mouth felt cavernous, with nothing to fill its space. By the time Calver's thoughts returned to their full sharpness, panic set in—first as a trickle, then as a flood.

His tongue was gone.

Gone.

He had no tongue.

What was he going to tell his mother?

Kretch. *How* was he going to tell his mother?

She would be devastated. And Arleena—the thought stabbed at him—he'd left her.

Left her, the thing he'd promised he would never, ever do.

Calver's skin flashed hot with anger. Over his dead body.

For the first time, he remembered to think as Callisto had trained him: like a soldier, not a victim. If they had wanted to kill him, they already would have done so. But any use they might have for him now... Fates, he didn't even want to think about it.

He summoned the will to roll to his side. It was agonizing. Surely that colonel—Limtush—had broken his ribs. His mouth was even more excruciating. He tried to spit out more blood, but had trouble working the correct muscles to do so. Crimson spittle dribbled grotesquely onto the cot below him.

As he looked around, he experienced a sensation familiar to a dowaga pressed against his chest. The space he was in was constructed entirely from steel. A train carriage. That and the clattering beneath him could only mean he was no longer in Kaidech. The distortion locomotive route to the port city had only been completed four months ago. The city officials had hoped it would help elicit a rise in the shattered economy. This guide rail connected others all across Nelfindar; he could be anywhere.

From where he lay, he could see a set of drawers, a mirror, and a plush rug. This carriage was someone's private quarters. A different kind of panic set in. He wasn't going to wait to find out why they wanted him here. Testing the strength of the ropes which bound his arms and legs, he tried to wiggle around. They were excruciatingly tight.

The mirror.

He wormed to his feet with a gurgled moan, ignoring the spots in front of his eyes; ignoring the agony in his chest, his face. He hopped to the mirror and rammed his shoulder into it.

Again.

The mirror splintered. So did his ribs.

Again.

Its crunching was like music, a ballad promising freedom.

Again.

It shattered, its shards cascading to the ground in harmony with his agony, like ecstasy.

Calver dropped to his knees, then flopped to the ground. He rolled to his back to grasp one of the larger shards with his bound hands. His fingers, numb from the bindings, could barely hold it, let alone use it to saw at anything.

He arched his back to place the long shard between his heels instead, fumbling. Sometimes he made a cut, moving his wrists across the shard held in his feet, but mostly he just fumbled some more. Sometimes he paused to rest for a ragged breath against the threat of passing out before returning to the labor.

The rope frayed away, bit by painstaking bit. There was no way to track the time that passed. Five minutes. An hour. At one point, he began to count his breaths. More than two hundred passed before the final fibers snapped with a tug of his wrists. He suppressed a gasp, his heartbeat skittering in anticipation of who might hear him and what they would do.

It took his purpled hands several minutes of stretching and massage to regain an acceptable amount of feeling. Calver was excruciatingly aware of the passage of time, his only real resource, slipping away with each heartbeat. Once he was capable, he sawed off his ankle bindings, too.

He stood, braced himself against the set of drawers. Then he wobbled to the door.

Dead-bolted from the outside.

He thumped his head into its cool metal. It felt good against the side of his face. Maybe he could just stay here for a while. Rest until he had a better idea—

Footsteps rang against steel. He bit into his bloodied lip and scrambled backward. A dagger of glass from the broken mirror reflected his swollen face. The spark in his mind flared. Limbs shaking, he snatched it and the discarded rope and hobbled to the cot. He lay back down, arms pressed behind his back as if tied.

A stocky man in Red Wing garb entered the room, shutting the door with a screech. His bushy black brows leaped toward his hairline when he looked at the mirror and then to Calver on the cot.

"Ye'r awaaake? Shoulda lasted for another hour or two yeeet... What did yeh do, yeh li'l braaat?" The man's speech was painfully slurred. He waddled toward Calver, like he didn't even notice the shattered fragments of mirror littering the floor, breathing loudly through his mouth. He pulled a small, white tablet from his pocket. "Open upsss. It'll make this eeeasier... for the both of usss."

As the man leaned in, Calver snapped up and stabbed him in the eye with the mirror dagger. He reeled, howling in pain, reaching to unhinge a dowaga from his back. Calver kicked him in the kneecap, knocking him backward. It gave him enough opening to grab another shard from the floor.

Ignoring his aching body, Calver lunged forward toward the man at the same instant he flipped his dowaga out in front of him. The stocky soldier's face was contorted with rage, the glass still stuck in his bloodied eyeball. He swung blindly with the weapon. Calver dodged it and circled behind him. He hopped onto the soldier's back, gripped him around the neck with one arm, and plunged the shard into his throat with the other.

The man slumped down to the floor with a gurgle.

Calver gasped, both in pain and horror. He looked down at his trembling hands, covered with the man's blood mingled with his own. The force with which he had wielded the shard had sliced both of his palms open.

Two. Two people he had killed now.

Calver fell to his knees. Then he hunched, spine pulled into an arch by a means beyond his own will, and vomited across the steel floor. His watery stomach contents made fine company for the glass and blood there. The acid burned the open wound in his mouth. His chest hurt. It all hurt.

When the heaving stopped, he wiped his mouth with the back of his lacerated hand and looked at the body. Dead. A still-warm thing, temporarily suspended from its imminent decay by its own shock at the sudden meaningless of its existence. A body was meant to carry a life, after all. This one didn't.

He pulled the dead man's head into his lap and cradled it for long minutes before he managed to control the sobs afflicting his body. Their agony was like Chaos seeking retribution for things he had done.

Breathe. Breathe. Breathe.

In training, it had been easy. Callisto had never warned him how much more difficult it would be to breathe with his own body mutilated and a dead man in his lap. But, ever so slowly, it helped. He re-found his calm. His clarity. Because if he was caught here, he wouldn't make it out alive. He had to live. He had to get to his family at any cost and warn them what was coming...

He dried his eyes on the back of his tattered sleeve and spotted a canteen at the man's belt. Only then did he realize how thirsty he was. He clutched the canteen with trembling digits, trying to steady them enough to drink. The water stung as it ran over the gaping wound in his mouth and, Fates, it was nearly impossible to swallow. But he gulped tenderly once—twice—without coughing any of it up.

Then he shifted the belt and canteen to his own waist. He took the dowaga, too, unlatching its holster from the dead man and strapping it to his back. The movement pulled at the torn skin and muscle in his palms; he sucked in through his teeth. The pull was nothing compared to the tearing at his conscience.

Calver stared at his injured palms.

Bad idea—it made his head spin. He turned away, searching for something to use to cover them. He decided on canvas from the cot, which he cut using the dowaga, its grip braced against his fingers alone. Calver wrapped the strips of cloth around the wounds with three loops. He tried palming the weapon.

Bearable. Just bearable.

He'd wasted too much time.

He rose to his feet and shuffled to the end of the carriage. Apprehensively, he pushed the door open. It swung outward with an ear-splitting screech that he imagined the inhabitants of the entire machine would be able to hear. When he peered out into the next room, however, he found it to be dark and empty.

It was an extension of the same carriage he had been held captive in. At the far end there was another door with a window to the outside. There was a leg-long gap between this carriage and the next, entirely open to the elements.

Now was his chance.

He scurried to the windowed door but quickly pressed himself flat against the wall alongside it. He had seen movement in the next carriage through its window.

The door slid open, flooding the space with light.

"Taking his time, of course. Probably testing the moss for himself. He canopied last ten-day when we were working on the other subject. A right slob."

It was Limtush. There were three others with him. Calver crouched, hiding silently behind the open door. If he was lucky, he would go unnoticed and could slip out past them before the door shut...

"Fates above, the kid is here!" exclaimed the third man who filed in, just as Limtush reached the door to the private quarters where he'd been held. *Kretch*. Calver unlatched the dowaga and brandished it defensively.

One of the soldiers laughed. "Aay, listen, boy. Come over here."

Calver ran the blade end of the weapon straight through his gut.

An unnatural sound erupted from the man's throat, raising the hairs on the back of Calver's neck like soldiers at attention. The other men snapped out their weapons and swarmed him. Their comrade fell to the ground, writhing, as Calver scrambled for the door.

"Don't kill him! I need him alive!" Limtush screamed.

One of them caught Calver around the ankle, tripping him. He crashed agonizingly onto his damaged torso, but grabbed for the lip of the door frame.

"He's got a shratten blade, Colonel, what in Preservation do you want us to do?" shrieked another.

Calver gripped the door frame with one hand and took the pommel of the dowaga in the other. He swiped at the hand on his foot. The man released him, and Calver bolted through the door to suspend himself between the two carriages. Sunlight momentarily blinded him. Wind roared into his ears, ripping at his dark hair. Still blinking against the brilliant day, Calver could make out the grassy hills streaming by.

There was no way to know how fast they were moving or whether leaping from the side would kill him—

"No!" Limtush bellowed from inside the carriage. "Grab him!"

—and there was no room to deliberate.

Calver leaped from the machine into midair, tossing the dowaga away from him so as not to impale himself when he landed.

It was a man-high drop to the ground, though when Calver hit the earth at a sideways roll it felt like he'd fallen from the clouds. He screamed as his bones rattled against the ground, body bouncing as it went. He rolled over a dozen times before coming to a stop in the high grass. The sound of the locomotive whooshing into the distance continued for a time. Then there was silence.

Calver couldn't catch his breath. Each time he tried to inhale, a suffocating pain bit into his chest. He tried to spit blood from his wounded mouth to make space for air, but he couldn't manage it. He choked helplessly on the warm fluid as he inhaled convulsively, causing his lungs to spasm even more in an endless cycle of pain.

He prayed a silent prayer to the Fates for it to stop. For the pain to go away.

It went unanswered, so he prayed instead for sleep. After several agonizing minutes, it came. He lost consciousness in the heat of the blazing sun, lifeless in the grass.

Chapter 19
Calverous

When Calver arrived at the safe house, its door was locked from the inside, thank Preservation. From beyond it came the faint warble of Raimee singing—if you could call it that. He'd never heard someone sing so off-key. Something inside him cracked, like the breakdown of a thermal vent. The corners of his mouth tipped skyward.

He rapped seven times, loudly, hoping she would hear him over her own racket. The singing faltered. Moments later, she was rattling at the locks behind the door. She threw it open and greeted him by doing the same with her reedy arms.

"You're back!"

Said like he might not have come back. Like he might have just left her there to find her own way, despite his promise to help her, after the way he'd stormed out.

Raimee suddenly put a hand to the cavern wall as if to support herself amidst a dizzy spell. *Still so weak.* The corners of his mouth drew down.

When she noticed him staring, she straightened.

And faking otherwise.

<Use more caution.> Calver cleared the entryway and, peering behind him, closed the door. <It could have been anyone.> He stressed the last signal with a shake.

She rolled her eyes. "Really? We have a 'secret knock,' don't we?"

<And it's not exactly complicated.>

"You want to change our knock?" Her attempt to hide her grin was pitiful.

<You're toying with me.> He pushed his way into the cave, heaving the bags along with him.

"And you are an absolute genius at reading people, for a grouchy caveman." Raimee trailed him around the corner into the main room. The fire was ablaze in the hearth, and there was a pot of something cooking on the stove. It smelled...

Well, it smelled.

<You cooked?>

"Seeing as you taught me, I gave it a go on my own," she said, her face glowing in the hearth's light. "I thought you'd like to have something warm in your belly."

Her excitement rubbed at him. He flicked it away. <*I think you were just impatient to get something warm into your own belly.*>

Her face pinched.

<*I didn't think there was enough of anything left to make a meal?*>

"I just threw everything left in one pot," she admitted with a shrug.

He fought not to wrinkle his nose at the mixture of oats, fish, carrots, beans and... when had he ever bought garlic?

"I think it's ready, too!"

They sat to eat. The food was just palatable enough to get down.

She inquired about his day; he answered in clipped, single signals. She recited to him what she had learned from his books about the political climate, and the history of Nelfindar, Tera'thia, and their surrounding nations. She went on to cover the basic theory behind distortion mechanisms and the Azadonian quarantine. She'd ventured further into his library than what he'd set aside for her. Throughout her retelling, she repeatedly interjected her own thoughts and opinions on what she'd learned with: "This food is abominable, isn't it?"

<*No tongue means no taste buds,*> he lied. He could still taste some things; the sense was merely diluted. But as he attempted not to gag on another noxious bite, he decided tonight was the first time he'd ever been glad for it.

"I've been through the majority of your library, Calver, and—and I'm not seeing him anywhere. You're sure you remember the name?"

<*Yes.*> He put the bowl down to use his hands with some relief. <*I'm sure of the name. But not sure it's from these books.*>

"Hmmm." She pursed her lips, drumming her fingers against the stone. "Well, that's troublesome; maybe you should have mentioned that *before* we spent a ten-day searching them. If it's not here, then where?"

The question poked at him. His recent memory was impeccable. How was it possible to blank on this one crucial detail? Could his recollection of Methu'su's name be even older than he'd thought? A ghost from his old life—the one he'd tried miserably to extinguish from memory?

He remembered the taste of his blood in his mouth. A dowaga coated in entrails. The sickly feel of flesh on flesh. His sister's fingers laced into his own.

Void.

He didn't think about those times for a reason.

He changed the topic. <*How are you able to read so quickly?*>

She snorted. "Admittedly, I've wondered how it's possible that you read so slowly. You don't seem mentally damaged."

Fates, was she ever wrong.

Every muscle in Calver's face felt like it took on water. He pushed what would have been a bruise to his pride aside. He was sharp. Maybe not Fankalo sharp, but more so than many. This was an opportunity to learn something of value. Impulsive, naïve, and maybe a bit unorthodox she might be, but this woman had spent her entire life studying among the scholars at Tennca'Pui.

<*I what?*>

Color pooled into Raimee's cheeks, and her shoulders drew forward in what had become a noticeable habit. She opened and closed her mouth several times before deciding on how to recover from her earlier statement. "Well—alright, yes. You're a tad, teeny bit slow." She sighed. "It's almost like you look at *every* single word."

That was what reading was, right? <*I do.*>

She clapped a hand to her forehead a little too forcefully, and rubbed it awkwardly afterward. "You're serious?"

Calver blinked.

"What a waste of time! Chaos, you only need to scan the very center of the page, you know? Who taught you to read?"

His mother, he didn't signal. But he cocked his head for her to continue. His reading 'ineptitude' had her flustered, like he'd gone about life with his shoes on the wrong feet. She needed to wear it off.

"Look." Raimee stood and headed toward the books scattered at the opposite side of the cavern to retrieve *A History of Nelfinden Primes*. She opened it to a page displaying the mustached face of Claudiois Felippe, Nelfindar's first Prime, instated seventy-six years previously. "We start easy. Ignore the first two words and the last two words on each line of the page. Just read the text between them."

Calver did, allowing his eyes to glaze over the very ends of the lines and focus only on their centers. He read a page from top to bottom and sat back, making eye contact to confirm that he had finished.

"So?"

<*I didn't lose anything.*> It was a simple solution, and efficient. Though he doubted he could achieve her proficiency.

She beamed at him. "Your peripheral vision will pick up on the outside words, and your mind will automatically fill in the voids with the most logical algorithm." A response he was sure she'd memorized from a textbook. She paused and kicked one foot back and forth. "Sooo... Now you can read twice as fast as you used to. You're welcome."

He hummed approvingly and signaled, <*Thank you.*>

Raimee leaned forward, studying him like he was some genre of fascinating beetle beneath a lens. It made him shrink inwards, feeling smaller than this creature who weighed less than the sack of food he'd carried home. "It is so strange to hear you make sounds."

<*I won't make sounds, then.*>

"No, please! I didn't mean that. It just—caught me off guard. You have such a—a normal-sounding voice. For humming, anyway."

<*False.*>

Again with that look. With that face. He braced himself for more questions.

"So you can talk. You choose not to."

He shook his head. <*Sound and speech are not the same.*>

"Let me hear you. Give it a go."

Calver's stomach roiled in a way that bespoke whatever it was he'd just eaten. She might be a fast reader, but she was a slow learner. <*I'm beginning to wish you were still sick and silent.*>

But she is still sick, a part of him nagged. She'd been faking otherwise for days... despite clear signs of continued affliction.

"Come now. Then what good would I be to you? You would have had to make your own dinner." She barely choked out the last few words. They both looked to the half-eaten batch of food that remained, unwanted, over the hearth.

Calver's mouth strained to keep its corners down.

"I caught you. Your. Beard. Moved."

He masked his face. <*You're delusional.*>

She sighed. "You pretend like you don't want anything to do with me. But what you don't know is that I've spent a lifetime around people that *actually* don't want to do anything with me. And I have a gift for telling the difference."

<*You also have a gift for gabbing incessantly.*>

She narrowed her eyes. "You're having fun being rude, aren't you? You secretly enjoy me being here."

He imagined, for a moment, telling her how much worse off he would be if she weren't here. How the things he'd been through in the past few days would have pushed him so far into darkness, he wouldn't have come back. How he'd forgotten how easy life was when there was someone else to buffer its burden, strange as they might be.

He didn't.

<*Only about as much as I enjoy your cooking.*>

It elicited another tinkering laugh. He smiled again and didn't hide it, Preservation help him. How was he going to get out of this cycle?

He attempted to take back what little control he had over the evening's conversation. <*As it stands, you are poorly equipped to leave in search of Methu'su.*>

Raimee raised an eyebrow at his abrupt return to pragmatics, but didn't interrupt.

<*I brought you essentials. Clothes. Shoes. For your journey, once you have the information you need.*>

He retrieved his market bags from where he had abandoned them earlier. Feeling suddenly vulnerable, he thrust them toward her—<*Here*>—and leaned against the cavern wall with arms crossed.

Raimee's eyes grew wide, then narrowed. She turned the goods over in her delicate hands. "These are new." She searched his face. "You stole them."

<*No.*>

"Then how..."

He couldn't blame her for her line of thinking. <*I've told you before. Money is not a concern.*>

"Then why—?" Her eyes trailed around the cavern to finish her train of thought. Comprehension crossed her expression. She moistened her lips. "How long have you been here?"

Questions. Questions.

He shrugged. When her eyes didn't move from him, he signaled, <*Eighteen months. Six days.*>

"Alone?"

He shifted.

"Where were you before that?"

<*It doesn't matter.*>

The tension was cracked glass, just waiting for the next breeze.

Clearing her throat, Raimee held up the bag he'd given her. "Well, get out, then. So I can change."

He obliged with warming cheeks, thankful for her redirection.

A change of clothing made Raimee more human and less like some creature on the brink of starvation in the winter wilds. But even with the level of tameness that simple, durable clothing added to her bearing, she still didn't resemble the women in Chira'na's streets. It might have been her hair, or her eyes, or—no, it was all of her. She possessed fatal levels of weird.

Of which she was entirely unaware. Her elation moved her as unceasingly as the very winds outside. "I've never owned a winter kaftan. Or sheepskin boots. Or anything, for that matter. Our robes were communal at the monastery." The taupe garment billowed as she twirled like a child, stopped herself, nearly fell over in the process, and placed a hand on her forehead. He'd chosen the least ostentatious color for a reason: to compensate for the rest of her. It hardly helped. She squinted at him before twisting her hips again to watch the fabric whirl. "Fates be strayed. I was half-naked, wasn't I? I don't know that I'll be able to repay you, Calver."

He wasn't sure how much more twirling he could take—or, considering her condition, how much more she could. <I just wanted my spare shirt back.>

It worked. She stopped spinning and screwed up her face at him, but... <My debt outweighs yours.> Had he ever thanked her? <Call it even when we find Methu'su.>

"Deal."

She reached out her palm, and the world tilted around him. The thought of gripping her hand—of willingly touching another person—made him cringe. But this was not just any touch... this touch meant Ruxian magic. His fingers twitched once before he clasped her palm.

Every tissue in his body launched into a tailspin. *This feeling...* if he could just reach whatever was on the other side of it, all the world would be at his command.

Then he remembered it was a handshake.

He retracted as quickly as he could manage without evoking her suspicion. Raimee's lips parted. Her gaze lingered on the place where his hand had been a moment before. Calver wiped his palm against his cloak.

She shifted. "So, what now?"

How was she so unbothered by all of this? Like *that* had been normal. As if casually chatting with a mute—as his all-but-hostage—was normal. As if he wasn't an exile, murderer, traitor, monster.... He must have drowned a ten-day ago, and everything since had been his imagination. <*We go to Chira'na. Expand our search.*>

"Together?"

<*Yes.*>

Raimee's gap-toothed smile was impeccable. "You know, my mentor told me that most of Nelfindar was absent of altruism. I think this is the first time I've found a reason to disagree with him."

She searched his face. His eyes found his feet.

<*Nelfindar is absent of altruism.*> Nelfindar would tear her apart if he told her anything else.

"But you're not."

<*Only for you. Because you remind me of my mother. She was—*> Calver's throat caught. He hadn't realized it was the truth until it was written out by his hands. <*Very positive, despite adverse conditions.*>

"Oh... I... thank you?" The question lingered. "Can you tell me more about her?"

He couldn't remember anything else to tell. He'd shut his mother away, never wanting to imagine what she'd think of what he'd become. The Survivor stirred, like a serpent uncoiling.

Calver exhaled. <*She was also obnoxious most of the time, like you.*>

Raimee's expression soured, followed by a playful swatting of the air. "She sounds lovely. I never met my parents. Did you have a father?"

Allegedly.

A sudden jolt of insight extracted itself from the void and struck him at his core.

Methu'su.

Kretch. Methu'su.

It was the name of the man who had hand-delivered the last words of his father alongside the news of his death. A note which asked Calver for his forgiveness. Calver's hands balled into fists. Had his father not been a traitor, there would be nothing to forgive.

He forgot himself. Forgot anything but his own anger and the Survivor's lapping of it, like nectar. Chaos abound, that was why the name had seemed so significant. And also why he couldn't remember it: because he didn't want to.

If he had never heard the name Methu'su, he might still have a father.

Raimee's expression returned to blushing regret at his lack of response. Calver chose to move his hands to move him from the conversation, rather than physically leave her to wonder if he'd ever return again.

<*You should read more before we leave. On Nelfinden history. We'll look for Methu'su in Chira'na's archives. It's more important for you to understand the social climate if you're going to be traveling through the country.*>

She stiffened but nodded seriously. "Alright."

Calver stepped away from her, pulled three Aetech lamps he'd bought in town that day from the bag, and carried them to his makeshift armory. He began to pull them apart, the familiar motions easing at his tightly wound nerves. Distortion had always felt like the thing he'd been put on this earth for. Unlike his own self, he could dismantle any distortion apparatus and forge it into something new. Something useful. It was a thing which took him closest to that ever-fleeting feeling called hope; it was the only thing which didn't make Fankalo look at him like the monster he was. From what had once been his idle tinkering, Fankalo had forged the Drieden Corporation that would fund their dreams all the way to the Tera'thian coronation.

As he worked, Raimee dutifully dove into a stack of books, but she positioned herself where she could see him around the bend. Every few minutes, she paused in her research to pierce him with that silvery gaze. She never asked what he was working on.

She knew.

Kretch. Of course, somehow, she *knew.* He bit into the inside of his cheek and continued to twist at wires.

After a time, he noticed she had disappeared. He set his work aside and moved from the armory to find her curled in sleep before the hearth, turned to face the fire's embers.

Taking the tip, Calver moved to retire by the door. He could use the rest.

"You know, Calver..."

She was still awake. Hearing his own name spoken aloud was still strange—startling, even. And he realized with a stab in his chest that he loved the way it sounded as it passed across her lips. That he *could* listen to it over and over and over again: Calver, not Reaper.

But he wouldn't.

Raimee didn't turn to face him, but continued to stare into the hearth's embers. He heard her swallow and then speak at hardly a whisper.

"I can teach you more things—if you'd like. Things like reading quickly. Skills for memorizing. Cataloging. Writing in shorthand... If it's helpful, that is. Just as something I can—even after we find Methu'su... I mean—if you want to learn more."

A stone sat in Calver's throat. She was insinuating they stay together?

She would be valuable. The translator that he'd needed on so many occasions.

Then he fully comprehended the suggestion: the words of a person desperate for companionship. Desperate to not have to go through it alone. So desperate she would ask them of a murderer who couldn't even speak. A man who was counting the fucking days until he killed himself. Fates, he'd nearly let the Survivor murder her a half-dozen times. He'd be doing her a favor if he went back on his word and disappeared into the night.

Raimee never turned to see whether he was listening. Calver could have done her the kindness of acknowledging her suggestion; he didn't. He rounded the corner, made it as far as he could down the passageway before crumpling like he'd been hit behind the knees with a sparring blade. Curled into a ball, hands gripping his hair.

It could never be. His heart slammed against his ribs. *A Ruxian should not be.* His breath locked in his chest. A person who could communicate with him should not be. His lungs heaved. Communicating with him about a future that would not be.

A future that he knew faded to black. To darkness. To silence. To that same silence, planted in him fourteen years ago like a cancer; a mortal illness without cure; silence that begot silence. The Tera'thian coronation was hardly more than a year away.

She wanted them to be more? He had obligations to fill. What was more than a martyr? A martyr had to be more than the emerging ties that wove them together, needled right through his almost-dead man's heart.

Memories from years of unbearable loneliness surfaced all at once, causing the Survivor to crash down on him in an angry tide. He rocked in the fetal position. The pressure was too great. It pined for her blood. It would do anything to get it. And it would all be so much easier if he just gave it what it wanted...

He kept trying to stifle its advance by replacing his turmoil with the old mantra. *Victory over the mind can only come with an embrace of the void. For only in nothing can you find everything.*

It didn't work. The pressure remained.

Fine. He could take it. He deserved this pain.

He deserved this pain.

Chapter 20
Attilatia

TWENTY-FIVE YEARS PREVIOUSLY

The distortion lamp cast sparkles across Attilatia's father's dark eyes as it whirred to life in his hands. She clutched at the lip of the cool slate counter, pulling herself to stand on tiptoes, which caused the beads from her dance hukata to clink against stone. The garment was a mess of brilliantly dyed skirts. A horrid thing—not in any way pragmatic nor discreet for slipping past her mother on her way into her father's workspace.

Ever dramatic, her father lifted the lamp toward the cavern ceiling of his lab as though it were a newborn. That light would be but a simple globe of glass, if not for the synthetic chemical her grandfather had formulated nested inside. She'd been told that a grain-sized pellet of ruxechorin was worth a fortune. That was silly. She'd gladly trade some for the right flaky bean puff.

"You see, Atti?" her father said, pushing his spectacles higher up the bridge of his delicate nose. "This lamp is now calibrated to distort flow from your selected stratum to create a constant stream of energy."

She pulled away from the counter, shifting her long black braid from one shoulder to the other. What tedium. He said the same thing every time they created a new distortion lamp together. Chaos, her father tended to act more like a grandfather than a man in his thirties. He did have that slight, hunch-shouldered posture of the elderly... and those who dedicated their lives to looking through a microscope. And he spoke so slowly, repeating himself over and over.

A part of her knew it was done in an attempt to calm her, but that only made it all the more aggravating. Everyone else saw her as the councilor's angry and impatient child. A "misanthrope" was how they'd diagnosed her the year prior. He didn't see her that way.

He knew she was smarter than anyone gave her credit for and simply irritated that no one else could keep up.

"I know this, Dasha," she pressed. "We have built many progressive models of the distorting lamps. I'm ready to build my circuit, eah?"

He chuckled, patting her hair as if to say, *Oh, you delightful little thing*. She crossed her arms. He might understand her better than most, but even he sometimes treated her like an infant.

"Forgive me, Starshine. You have to remember that your dasha still wakes up each day thinking he has a seven-year-old, only to rediscover he has a brilliant scientist instead. Distortion is—" He scrunched up his face as he thought, like he was trying to fit it into a beaker. "A sensitive thing. In the lamps we have something simple and something good. We want to keep distortion simple and good. With too much experimentation, and in the wrong hands... distortion may not be so good."

He must have seen the look on her face, because he raised both hands in a placating gesture. "Be patient. We may build something new, but not tonight."

Why did he even invite her to the distortion lab if they were only going to do endless repetitions of the same fated thing? "Why? Because you prefer a seven-year-old to a scientist?"

He chuckled again. "No, my sweet *hakuni*. We do not begin tonight, because the moment your mother finds out you spent two hours in the lab with me when you were supposed to be practicing the lethoso, she will put rocks in my stew."

Attilatia's mouth twisted. "You don't believe my distortion circuit will work."

"I think it is an excellent idea in theory, and I will not form an opinion before it has been tested."

"Which is just another way of saying that you don't believe it will work," she muttered under her breath.

If he heard her, he didn't show it. "Best not be late. Your mother's work in Legislation was a monster today."

Her temper sparked. Mother had put him up to this. She was so focused on Attilatia's future as a politician, she quashed nearly every opportunity Attilatia had to distort. "When can I build my circuit?" she pressed.

"When you have mastered your lethoso dance."

The fated lethoso dance. She wished their queens had never invented it. Seething, Attilatia grabbed the lamp from where her father set it on the counter and turned it twice over in her palm.

"Careful—"

She glared at him and slammed it onto the floor, where it shattered, the precious liquid from its core seeping onto stone.

Her father, ever patient, sighed once, unbuttoning his blue lab tunic and setting it on a hook by the door. He lost some of his magnificence without the coat. He became plain—ordinary—like a beetle that shed a brilliant exoskeleton to reveal a colorless underbelly. Attilatia's stomach crinkled in regret, but she maintained her air of resilience.

Her father stooped to pick up the pieces of the lamp from the floor, then went to the sink to wet a cloth.

"We succeed in life by balancing our passions with our duties," he said, cleaning her mess with the damp rag. "Your lethoso will one day be the pride of all Tentika. Perhaps of all Azadonia."

"And my distortion circuit will be the pride of all the world."

He set the cloth in the sink and reached for her hand with still-wet fingers. She did not take them.

"Come now," he said, hand dropping to his side. His eyes held sadness. She knew she'd put it there. She didn't want it to be there. But she didn't know how to collect it. "Let's change out of your Hukata before dinner, before your mother puts our heads in a hole."

※

Dinner was absent of the usual warm conversation that rose between her and her father like the clouds of steam from their stew. Attilatia's stomach had yet to un-crinkle. She pushed her bread in circles around the bowl, soaking it. Perhaps some of the night's tension might drown with it.

"Atti, I saw the pool was dry. Did you not practice your water step today?" her mother asked.

Attilatia shifted in her seat. She'd forgotten. An additional hour of water step was a standard after regular dance lessons every other day. "I did not."

Her mother pursed her lips, holding her teacup tightly to her chest. "I spent thirteen hours working in Jenolavia's administration today. Your dasha produced distortion lamps for the next Kaidechi trade. You had one responsibility: the lethoso. Do you mean to tell me that you have already perfected your water step?"

"No. I—"

"She was in the lab, Teichi," her father cut in to her defense, sipping his stew. "It was my fault. A few lamps broke, and we were up against the Kaidechi export. I thought we could use her help."

"What place does a seven-year-old girl have in a distortion lab? Trade is a man's place. My daughter will be a politician. Politicians dance the lethoso."

"She's good at distortion."

"And I might be good at tying my tipiana backward and walking on my hands, but you wouldn't see me going into the caverns that way."

"Maybe you should." Her father's eyes glittered.

"Yes, maybe you should," Attilatia parroted with a laugh, momentarily forgetting her anger.

Her mother swatted at her dasha. "Hush, *chikoto*! Three years I've been pushing for Jenolavia to take Atti on as caretaker for one of her heirs. I want to set her up for success. Playing with distortion can't do that."

Attilatia's father came to her rescue again, changing the subject. "Speaking of Jenolavia, what kept you so late?" He pulled at the hem of his shirt where it met his neck as though suddenly distressed.

Her mother grew serious. "We had a Kovathian engagement today."

The Kovathians were the divergent sect her mother claimed to 'kiss the toenails of the Tera'thians.' It was all the council ever seemed to deal with anymore.

"Again?"

She nodded. "And it got… ugly. They're furious with Jenolavia's refusal to sell our distortion rights."

"Black-hearted Kovathians."

Attilatia's eyes clung to her father. He looked different. Like he'd aged. Small beads of sweat sprouted from skin gone white as down. His eyes held a confused look.

"Dasha—" she started, but her mother interrupted.

"Can you blame them? It's potentially costing us millions. The incredible things we could do if we—"

"The incredible things we could destroy. And what if the Kovathians use distortion to start another Cataclysm? What then?"

"No need to get upset, I'm not taking their side. I just think Jenolavia could…" Her mother trailed off. "*Hakuni*, your face," she whispered, noticing what Attilatia had just moments before.

Attilatia watched in horror as her father's cheeks and neck swelled before their eyes, red and yellow pustules blossoming over stark white.

The strikapa.

Her mother clapped a hand to her mouth.

"Mother—" Attilatia started in panic.

"Preservation help us. It came on so fast. Breathe, *hakuni*, breathe!"

Her father wheezed, his panicked eyes darting about like they were trapped within his skull.

"Atti, run for the medical ward."

Her father slid from his seat and slumped onto the ground.

"Dasha!" Attilatia cried, rushing to his side. She reached for him, her fingertips nearly grazing his before her mother grabbed her square by the shoulders and yanked her backward.

"You know how it spreads. Just go, Atti. Hurry!"

Panic clutched Attilatia's heart as she took a final look at the man on the floor, transformed in just a minute from her father to a monster. Biting her lip, she tore away from their home and into its adjoining tunnel. *Preservation*. Another outbreak. There were still mourning shrines at every cross tunnel from the last, which had exterminated the entire southern cavern.

The trip to the medical bay would have only taken a matter of life-saving minutes, had Atti made it there. She couldn't get within throwing distance. There was only so much room in the vein-like passage, and hundreds of Tentika's citizens flooded through it, all rushing toward the medical ward like rubble cascading in a tunnel demolition, each stone piling in contest for a small, single outlet. Attilatia was thrown forward then backward, a small boat in a storm. Only she didn't float above the waters of the surging crowd, but fell beneath them.

No. No. No.

She couldn't breathe. She couldn't see. A mass of bodies pressed against her, fighting, shouting. It was a scene incongruous with the ideals of her people—civilized, gentle, strong. Attilatia screamed as she slipped and was dragged by the crowd, her knees scraping against the ground. She prepared for her bones to break when, in an act of Preservation, the waves split around her. She scrambled for the tunnel wall before they crashed back together where she'd kneeled only moments before.

Step by step, she sidled away from the medical bay, her back to the tunnel wall, toward the dome-ceilinged gathering cavern beyond. She could not tell if her sobs were silent, or so overpowered by the cacophony from the chaos before her that they were drowned out.

Once free of the crowd, Attilatia sank to the floor, knees hugged to her heaving chest. She could not return home now. How would she find the words to tell her mother she had failed? How could she move herself to a place where her dasha no longer existed?

Screams and wails reverberated through the ceremonial sound chambers of the gathering cavern around her. They continued into the night, and Attilatia's eyelids grew heavier, even, than her heart. She tried to imagine starting the day over: practicing her water step instead of sneaking into Dasha's lab. Making him and Mother proud. Spending dinner without crinkles in her stomach.

But it was not the whirl of skirts from her dance hukata that filled her mind as exhaustion overtook her for sleep. It was the not-whirl of the broken lamp on the floor. The not-whirl that had made a home in her chest, and she was sure would never ever leave.

A hand shook Attilatia awake. She blinked to see a woman hovering over her, mouth drawn, eyes pinched in concern.

"This one's alive," she said, the relief in her voice palpable.

"What?" Attilatia mumbled.

The woman wore a sash embroidered with the insignia of Tentika's emergency guard over her tipiana. "Sixteen trample victims, five of them even younger than you. The Fates have blessed you. Does anything hurt?"

Yes, but Attilatia couldn't objectively identify what it was. She shook her head.

"Head home, *hakuni*. I'm sure someone is worried terribly for you."

The woman began to pull away. It was only then that Attilatia saw the forms piled at the center of the gathering cavern.

"Wait," she gasped, latching onto the woman's hand. "What—what happened?"

"Another strikapa outbreak. Anyone who came into contact with the water from the western vein was afflicted."

Attilatia's stomach pulled inward, like it was being sucked into a place that didn't exist. That vein ran through both the lethoso pools and the distortion labs.

"You should get home." The emergency guard dismissed her again, turning toward the dead. "Tell your family we've started a boil-only mandate until further notice."

Attilatia didn't remember the journey home. She didn't hear the shriek, hardly noticed her mother clutching her, tears falling on her skin, when she entered their cavern.

She had killed a man, inadvertent as it had been, and it was all she could think about. She had killed her father. The only one who'd ever understood her.

It seemed a fitting punishment for the Fates to deliver a misanthrope like her. She had a keen enough mind to understand that society progressed through collaboration, not isolation. The thing she was... it didn't belong.

And now, without Dasha, she didn't belong to anyone.

Chapter 21
Calverous

Raimee started to stagger just two hours after leaving the safehouse, tripping over every other stone or fallen branch. Calver had worried the trip to Chira'na would prove arduous for her. While she'd grown stronger over the past weeks, she remained frail. Navigating the dense foliage, rocky peaks, and boggy valleys of the Sharinash was no small feat, even for someone healthy. Their speed hadn't been helped by her early desire to examine every leaf and bush, bug and mycelium.

"I think I need a moment, Calver. My head hurts," she gasped, collapsing onto a boulder.

Calver pulled his canteen from its holster and handed it to her. <*Then rest. Less than an hour to go. The hardest portion is behind us now. The Sharinash ends here.*>

Ahead, the treeline thinned into the golden grasses and hulking rock forms that hallmarked the stretch toward Chira'na. Between trees, he glimpsed the city's massive walls on the horizon. His eyes hunted for the Ratka he'd seen there not two days ago.

It had been removed.

<*You're doing well,*> he lied. <*This is a healthy change from reading all day, Cenobite or no.*>

"Is it true that the Nelfinden oligarchy doesn't sponsor its citizens' education?"

<*Only in the groundling class.*> Which was most of its people.

"So... You must have been born into privilege?" Raimee sat up, leaning toward him with interest.

<*Maybe.*>

"Hmm. Then how did you end up a grouchy caveman?"

Through mutilation, enslavement, and a hundred other sins the Survivor had drunk from his memories like water from a mountain stream.

He shrugged.

"Worth a shot." She snapped her fingers. "It will remain a mystery. Alright then, where did you learn to read? Where are you even from?"

<An old Azadonian trading outpost. You probably haven't heard of it.>

"You don't mean Kaidech?"

Fucking mind-reader.

Her mouth hung open as she took his silence for an answer. She looked up at him in a way that made his insides squirm. "Kaidech? You mean strikapa-decimated Kaidech?"

<You really do read too much.> Maybe if he kept her out of breath, she'd stop prying into his life. <Let's keep moving.>

Raimee crossed both arms and legs. "Now, hang on. I've been trying to put you together for almost two ten-days. You can't just walk off when I find a missing piece." How could he explain this was a game she didn't want to play without resorting to violence? "I learned about this in my epidemiology studies. Years ago. Nobody survived. So... what happened? You managed to wind up in Tera'thian hands. And you're fighting against Tera'thian agents, that much I've been able to draw from the books you have on their command tactics. So does that mean..."

Calver shook his head. She'd pried further than he'd anticipated. The liability she posed was worse than he'd ever imagined: a literal scholar placed in a situation where the only thing she'd had to study was an agent of espionage.

"Really? You can't lead me up to that one and then just choose not to answer."

<You bet I can.> He hoped his hands wouldn't spell out too much of the truth.

"You look upset," she said, leaning toward him as though she might try to touch him again. "I'm sorry. It was insensitive. I—"

<I'm not upset.>

"Yes, you are."

<I'm not upset.> He signaled again, with enough aggression to put a dent in a tree trunk. <Kaidech was ravaged by the strikapa. That's what you'll hear from anyone you ask. That's the answer you'll get from me.>

"You're insinuating that Tera'thia—" She broke off at his glare.

<Strikapa.>

"But then how did you become tume'am—" She faltered again beneath another seething look, clearly biting her tongue to hold back from asking anything else.

Calver redirected the conversation, before she could continue to pry. <Do you remember the plan?>

"What plan?"

<*The Chira'na plan.*>

"You mean the 'follow me and don't say anything or look at anything or touch anything like you're a good, domestic goat' plan?"

<*Yes.*>

He handed her a set of papers forged by one of Fankalo's associates on his last trip to Chira'na. Raimee turned them over. Her narrowed eyes relaxed and then crinkled at their corners. She began chuckling. The longer she looked at them, the harder she laughed, until she was unable to contain herself.

Calver had half a mind to leave her on the rock, where she could study its moss while he single-handedly retrieved Methu'su and brought him to collect her.

<*What?*>

"Alright, so let me get this straight," she finally managed to breathe. "You are my husband; a deaf, mute businessman. And I am your... blind... housewife? How could that possibly make sense? Think about it, Calver, really."

His cheeks grew hot. He knew it was a gambit. Everything had become riskier the moment he'd taken her from the lake shore. But what other option did they have? He'd weighed the possibilities, and chance was the only solution that presented itself. <*They don't scrutinize the papers very closely. No one will think twice on it.*>

"Calver, here I thought you were cautious and, sure, borderline paranoid. But this is a terrible idea." She wiped a tear out of the corner of her eye, still giggling. "I keep trying to imagine how they met. I mean, what does she *see* in him? Priceless."

Calver sighed. <*Do you have a better suggestion? We need to hide your eyes. I considered listing you as Azadonian. It would give us an equal excuse to use oculars. But you don't look Azadonian.*>

"I could just wear the fated oculars and *not* pretend that I'm blind, you know."

<*Anyone could ask you to take them off if they suspected you.*>

"Anyone could ask me to take them off regardless. You know, to prove that I'm blind or whatever."

<*Who in their right mind would ask a blind woman to take off her oculars?*>

Raimee rolled her eyes. "Is this another cultural taboo I need to learn or something?"

<*It's common courtesy.*>

"And it isn't common *sense* to ask why a deaf man has a blind wife? Who *wouldn't* want to know more about that? What happens if they ask?"

Preservation help us. <No one will. And if they do, you'll be the one talking. Tell them it was an arranged marriage.>

"Well, that's not very romantic, is it?"

Calver threw his hands up, and Raimee backed down.

Of course it was flawed. But they had their hands tied. How could she take this so lightly? What did she not understand about him telling her that she would be sold to the worst of humanity, if not murdered on sight?

He pulled the blacked-out lenses from his cloak and thrust them toward her. She had already tied her hair up into a turban which, conveniently, was in fashion among Nelfinden women at the moment, and they'd stained her silver brows dark before leaving the safe house. She placed the final piece of her disguise on her face and wrinkled her nose.

"Splugh. Do I really have to wear these horrible things all the way to Chira'na? They're quite annoying."

<Now you know how I feel having to tote you all the way to Chira'na.>

She tipped the oculars down her nose and looked over them at him. "Well, that's just not nice."

<Can you see?>

"Just enough to not trip and kill myself, for now. How do I look?"

He paused. She looked... odd. Did she look too odd?

"I must be gorgeous. Just look at you, you're speechless."

Calver forced his mouth into a line as she chuckled at his expense. <Well. You don't look Ruxian.>

"I'll take what I can get."

<It's the turban. It's too full.> He pulled a dagger from his belt. <We'd be better off keeping it slim.>

She scuttled away from him. "No, no. Nonono. Cenobites do *not* cut their hair."

Well, that certainly explained a lot.

He flipped the knife away. <Alright, scholar. Let's hope that it can pass as excess brains in your head. Ready to carry on?>

"Let's go," she said, but he caught her quickly controlled wince, the way her foot nearly twisted as she stood.

A façade. Fates, there was something wrong with her. Something she wasn't telling him, and it—

He had enough problems. He wouldn't make this one of them.

Without having to navigate through the thick of the Sharinash, they moved twice as fast. The grasslands were open and unobstructed; they could see for leagues into the empty space which became the Jiradesh. Small groups of travelers moved in and out of the city, though no one else came from the east as they had. The Sharinash was a territory left untouched for its density and lack of resources.

A distant caravan headed southwest toward Karval. The sight of it made Calver's stomach turn, and he tried to turn his mind to anything other than Fankalo keeping secrets from him.

Which, conveniently enough, became the legendary Ruxian walking ten paces ahead of him as he kept a rear guard.

Raimee moved the way he imagined an aethersprite would, or a wind dancer; barely making a sound as she padded across the ground, her hands brushing the tips of the waist-high grasses on either side of the thin footpath they traveled. Dragonflies wove in and out of her steps.

He stopped.

The insects were common in this area; renowned, even, for their fuzzy sky-blue thorax and inky black wings. But he had never seen them behave like this. They flew in and out around her ankles in ellipses, perfectly timed with her every step. Calver's skin tingled as she meandered along the grassy path, oblivious, humming out of tune to a song he thought he might recognize.

She continued for a time before realizing he'd stopped. She turned. "Calver?"

He shook his head, awe subsiding, and jogged to meet her.

"Why'd you stop?"

<*Thought I saw something.*> He shook his head at the stupidity of his own signals. <*Do you like dragonflies?*> Fates, that was worse.

"Yes, well, as much as I like any other bug," she laughed. "And I love bugs, they're just so pretty."

<*If you say so.*>

"Dragonflies are especially amazing." She grinned as several of the insects which had been weaving around her feet rose to encircle her head like a crown. "According to entomological study, they've been around on this planet a million times longer than humans have. Some of the oldest beings still alive. So, to me they've always been kind of a reminder of endurance. Perseverance, eah?" She shrugged and tucked a flyaway strand of silver back into her turban. "I've never seen them act like this, though. Is it normal for this particular species?"

He shook his head.

Raimee cocked her head toward one of the blue and black bugs, which had landed on her shoulder. "They're not doing it to you," she noted.

He hummed in agreement.

Ruxian magic. What else could she do that hadn't yet manifested?

"Your face is doing that thing again. Are you jealous you don't have a dragonfly crown?" She nudged him with an elbow he failed to dodge.

<*Yes.*> Calver couldn't control the muscles contorting at the corners of his mouth. Raimee giggled.

They walked on. The team of dragonflies swayed in pace with her for another half-hour before dispersing. Calver hoped that, in his dwindling days, he never forgot the sight of it.

Raimee dove into an extended lecture on dragonflies and their relatives, and Calver tried to listen. But no matter how hard he focused, his thoughts kept turning back to the demolition.

Why would Fankalo hide what was on that train?

Replacing military defense technology, rather than Aetech's standard technology, would have required extensive planning. They'd been producing replicate technology for Dreiden for over a year.

So this had been kept from Calver at least that long.

And to get hands on the plans to replicate those defensive plates, Fankalo would need to have a contact deep in the Red Wing's ranks.

How deep...?

"...but the migrations of mayflies and dragonflies are completely different, too," Raimee continued. "You see, mayflies die almost as soon as they reach adulthood. They mate and expire without even eating."

Like tume'amic. Like what would have happened to Calver, if it hadn't been for Fankalo. Cold doused the fire which had begun to spread into his limbs. Where was his faith?

<*No eating?*> he asked.

"I know. Miserable, eah?"

The shadow of Chira'na's gargantuan walls fell upon them. Their size at a distance was deceptive, as compared to the low hills of the surrounding topography. When one stood directly beneath them, as they were now, the stormcloud of stone more closely resembled a feat of nature than a structure of man.

"Creation's den..."

So, some things could get her to stop talking.

She drew close to him, her hand lacing around his forearm for support. Covered by his cloak, he felt nothing of her magic, and the gesture only made him feel queasy. But he couldn't very well let her stumble and attract unwanted attention. He handed her the cane he had been carrying for her guise and took a subtle glance in either direction.

<*Don't say a word from here on unless you have no choice,*> he signaled discreetly.

Raimee nodded and took the cane, though she did not release him; rather, she clung to his elbow as though she might otherwise wash away in a flood. Then he understood. Any amazement for the city's walls dissolved the moment a person saw the refugee camps at their feet.

Countless sets of hollowed eyes watched them pass by the lean-tos and small fires of their disheveled encampment. Fates, her fingers were worse than talons. They were too close to the gate now for him to risk signaling for her to let go. He wriggled his arm. She loosened her grasp and felt forward with the cane in her opposite hand, moving it in arcing sweeps. He sighed in relief—

—and then nearly groaned in dismay.

The young soldier with the patchy beard was standing at the front of the line again, scowling at each person who entered. On Calver's previous sojourn into the city, the man had scrutinized him for nearly a minute—as if they maintained a personal grudge—before his superior called him off again. His forgery was superb. It always stood its test. He could only hope that traveling with Raimee might get this guard off his back.

He was wrong.

"Papers," the guard demanded, holding out his palm. He didn't wait for the space of a blink before snatching them from Calver's hands.

"Oh no." The guard sergeant stepped toward them to intervene. "Not this again. Chevek, leave the deaf man alone. He's been coming through here without issue for more than a year."

"Yes. And now he's brought a collaborator." Chevek pointed an accusing finger at Raimee, who wore an aloof expression.

"Chevek, he's cleared. He's *been* cleared. Leave it." The sergeant rolled his eyes and gave a not-so-subtle swipe to the back of his inferior's head. He turned to Calver, his speech so loud and slow that it stood as its own insult. "I'm sorry, Mesu Friyal, please continue on your way."

Sergeant Leena turned to assist an old woman behind them; Calver stood still, hoping his thundering heart would do the same. Eighteen months of establishing routine trips under this guise had paid its dividends.

Raimee gave him a little tug on the arm. He responded by reaching out to take the papers back. Chevek glared at them without returning the documents. Then his eyebrows rose.

"Wait a moment," he said, pulling back.

Calver's gut turned. Neither of their secrets would withstand five minutes of interrogation. He blanked his face, took a mental inventory of his most readily available weapons. His eyes darted to their periphery, recounting the guards stationed along the wall. *Don't reach for the dowaga*. Not yet.

"Chaos's unruly bush," Chevek scoffed. "I knew there was something strange about you. This is either a theft or a forgery. And a shit one at that. How is it shratten possible for a deaf man to have a blind wife?"

He'd turned to call back to his supervisor when Raimee intervened. She threw her head back in a laugh. "We get that all the time, you know? It's only to be expected." Her voice was lilting and sweet. She turned toward Chevek. "Can I feel you?"

Without waiting for a response, she reached out and, rather sloppily, patted the guard's upper body until she found his face. Her fingers danced across his cheeks, his nose, his brow. If Calver's gut had turned before, it made a hard dash for escape now. He was pretty sure blind people didn't actually do that, and that his insides might catch flame.

Chevek's mouth contorted into a snarl as Raimee chimed, "Ah, there we go. A little tactile exploration helps to put a face to a voice, you know?" She let her hands fall away. "As it is, we met at a school for the gifted nearly a decade ago. He was just so wonderful. Never one to start an argument."

"Fathom that," Chevek grunted.

Fuck. They needed an out. Why did she keep talking?

"I know our situation is unusual." Raimee leaned in toward Chevek, almost intimately. Her eyes must have actually been closed, because Calver didn't think it would be feasible for her to withstand the look Chevek gave her otherwise. "But, in my situation," she lowered her voice in a mockery of 'best not let the deaf man hear me,' "options have always been limited. And I still wanted children. All disadvantages considered, especially that beard, the lovemaking does not disappoint. We have three."

The guard's face turned to stone. Then it crumbled.

He threw his head back, chest heaving from a laugh that could have belonged to a giant. Raimee's tinkering giggle joined in a moment later as she patted the guard on the back.

"I'm sorry. We've all been on edge," he said. His lips rolled inward. "We've... well, never mind that. I'm still going to need you to step to the side, though. A brief questioning of you separately, as a precaution. I imagine your story will stand and I'll send you on your way."

Miraculously, he handed Raimee the papers. She thrust them sloppily into Calver's chest as though she truly couldn't see him beside her. Calver didn't twitch, maintaining as blank an expression as possible while his stomach cartwheeled.

That had been too easy. Did she have some sort of sway over the guard's mind? He still wasn't convinced she didn't have sway over him. The guard turned to address Calver again when, in a moment of pure luck, a refugee from the encampment threw an elbow into the sergeant's nose at the gate behind them. The bedraggled man made to dash into the city.

Chevek sputtered a stream of curses. "Move along," he shot at them before drawing a dowaga from his back and bolting to the gate to intercept him.

Calver didn't hesitate, tugging Raimee along. He wanted to put as much distance as possible between them and the young guard before he reconsidered. They had better find Methu'su quickly. In Calver's experience, good luck didn't strike twice.

Once they reached the crowded inner cloister, out of eyesight from the gate, Calver exhaled in relief. Raimee clapped her hands together, laughing.

"That. Was. Thrilling!"

Away from the scrutiny of the guards, he let their act fall. Amidst the throng of Chira'na's populace, no one would notice. He signaled discreetly, <*That was horrifying.*>

"It was quite funny, wasn't it?"

<*No,*> he signaled, trying to void a bubbling anger he worried might summon its mental counterpart. <*I told you not to say anything.*>

"It worked, didn't it?" she argued.

<*By the winds of Fate.*> He shook his head, running his fingers through his hair. His body trembled and he realized, with surprise, that it was from suppressing his own laughter.

It was relief. Glee, not anger. Had he forgotten how to tell the difference?

<*What's wrong with my beard?*>

"Well, nothing. I suppose. It's just—well, the cenobites never kept facial hair. It's been an adjustment."

<*Having to look at me has been an adjustment? You just told me cenobites don't cut their hair.*>

"Head hair."

<*Men wear beards here.*> The signals, his defense, only made him more vulnerable.

"Thanks, Raimee, you did a great job back there. Saved my arse from shit forgery, you did, Raimee," she mimicked in a low voice, elbowing him in his ribcage.

<*That's not what I sound like.*>

"No kidding, loudmouth."

<*Shut up and act like a blind person.*>

"Be still and stop signaling things for a blind person to read."

<*Fair point.*>

Chapter 22
Attilatia

EIGHTEEN MONTHS PREVIOUSLY

Attilatia sat down at her lab station in Aetech headquarters after finishing a routine check of her numerous circuits—one which controlled the skywalk's power, one which treated the city's sewage, one which evaporated saltwater from the Casowhatan before cooling it back into freshwater for the aqueducts. The work floor was abandoned: empty, and the lights turned off. Moonlight shone serenely from the arching windows that spanned the entire ceiling. That ghostly glow was all she needed, both to see by and for company.

Seraphinden had been a technologically backward relic until the Aetech Corporation bought Attilatia's mind from Deshpian Thacklore—for the cost of an island—fourteen years before. Since then, she'd given Aetech riches: a gravity which allowed the patricians whose economy orbited it to live a life of beautiful simplicity and function.

And Aetech had given her the night shift—after the first five years of knuckle-kissing in the hopes they might lengthen her leash, at least. Now she could work in a way that didn't involve sunlight or people, which she detested in equal measure. The small privilege was less likely granted for her comfort than because most of the staff despised her presence.

She was blessed, she reminded herself begrudgingly. Her circumstances today were far better than her first year in the thrall of Deshpian Thacklore after fleeing Tentika. She tucked a loose strand of long, raven hair behind her ear before diving into an outline for the updates to Seraphinden's cargo locomotive.

Something beside her stirred, and her spine stiffened like a book's. No one else worked at this time of night, and no one had access to the building without a corporation-granted distortion key. She narrowed her eyes.

"Hello?" she called out in Nelfinden to the dim workers' floor behind her. Like any Azadonian, she could see in the darkness as well as any feline predator. There was no one here. Feeling foolish, she grumbled to herself and turned back to her desk.

A man cleared his throat from the workstation directly across from her.

Attilatia gasped and stepped back from her chair. It tilted and crashed to the marble floor with the echo of a thing much larger.

"I apologize." The man held out a hand in a peaceful gesture. "I don't mean to bother you, and I most certainly didn't mean to frighten you. You seemed busy when I first arrived, so I simply waited for you to return to your desk."

Attilatia spewed a slur of Azadonian curses, backing away as her jumpstarted heart attempted to settle. It was not the first time she'd been followed. Nelfinden men had little respect for women and, with the face the Fates had cursed her with, she was the subject of frequent torment.

"Of course I were busy! I working. How do you get in here?" she demanded.

The sinister expressions of a stalker were absent from the man's face. He didn't move toward her; he only gave her a calming smile. "Hashod suggested I come to speak with you directly. Don't worry, it is for an entirely professional matter, though you would do me a great kindness in keeping it to yourself, if it's all the same."

Hashod wouldn't have allowed just anyone to access the building at night. Attilatia abandoned her retreat, though the prickled fine hairs on her body refused to do the same. The man was dressed smartly—in uniform, in fact. Handsome. Well spoken. More or less her own age—maybe older. She righted her chair and sat back at her desk.

"I see." She straightened her jumpsuit, keeping the zipper pulled high past her collarbone. "And what this professional matter Hashod could no tell to me himself at my private work times?"

"Allow me to make a proper introduction, Sesu Mitar. My name is Roskaad Thyatira, Lieutenant General to the Red Wing. I have heard so much about you—namely, that you are the mind behind Aetech's tremendous success."

A sycophant. She crossed her arms with a derisive huff. "That what you heard about me? You seem want something. I suggest you speak honestly, and we see from there if I can give you whatever is you came for. What have you *really* heard about me?"

The general blinked. "That your mind is even sharper than your tongue."

She rolled her eyes. "You speak too kindly. Surely *that* is only best of talk."

Thyatira spoke in her direction, though she imagined she was only a silhouette to his Nelfinden eyes. "That you are a thorn, disguised as a flower," he added.

Thank Creation, a Nelfinden who could speak honestly.

"In your country, people cut the flower," she said, letting the words roll off her tongue like thick syrup. "Put it in jar of water, where it wilt and die. I think, better to be thorn and left alone than made object of adornment at my expense."

The general did not shy away. "Might I ignite a lamp?" he asked her. "I know you can see me. It would only be fair if I could say the same for the purpose of our conversation."

"You know, there is reason I prefer to work in moonlight," she shot at him.

"I will keep it low," he assured her.

"Fine. You Nelfinden only do as you want anyway."

He flicked the tiny orb's activator, and she cringed as it cast a brilliant light over the room. But Thyatira covered it with a cloth from his pocket so she could see without squinting. He looked at her with a blank expression. Uncharacteristic of most Nelfinden men, he didn't fuck her with his eyes from tresses to toenails. Even that wasn't comforting.

She cut to it. "So, what you are needing, then?"

"I'd like to know what you might be able to create for me."

"Probably anything," she speculated, not caring of how haughty she came off. "Though I no have the time or the worry to do so."

"Humor me."

Did he mean he wanted her to make him laugh? His tone implied it was a Nelfinden expression, which was almost more frustrating than his interruption.

When she didn't respond, the general continued, "You are in a powerful position, Sesu Mitar. With your capabilities, you could make a huge impact on Nelfinden society."

Her mouth twisted. "Please, tell me something I no already know. This what I do every day, *chikoto*. I make impact."

"Tell me, who it is that you have an impact on?"

"I... Everyone. Aetech powers city. I power Aetech."

"Everyone?"

Her arms tightened across her chest. "I do no play the mind games, General. I, unlike Hashod, do no speak in questions as means of try to prove my intelligence or dominance. In fact, I think doing such thing proves opposite. Please speak plain or leave."

He offered her another smile. It wasn't patronizing, sly, or leering; it wasn't kind, either. Just plain. As though it were a reactionary expression with no real emotion behind it.

She had liminal feelings about it.

"Thank you for correcting me," he said. "What I mean to say is that, while you power Aetech, which does a great deal of good for the patricians, much of Aetech's resource allocation negatively affects the groundling class. Do you follow?"

So, he'd come here to guilt trip her into charity work. She knew it had to be some sort of trap.

"Listen, I just work here," she snapped. "I no have time for your project."

"I realize that. But if you were given an opportunity to create something, while at your job here, not in your leisure time, which might benefit all class levels—an expression I believe the Azadonians would use would be 'to even out the millet'—would you consider it?"

His attempt to build rapport with her by drawing inference from her homeland resuscitated her irritation, but she pushed it down. At least he was trying. "Why you ask me this?" she sighed. "Why no ask Hashod? I just do what I told."

"Hashod seems to think you are limited. That you wouldn't be able to do what I've imagined, which is why I thought it might be easier to get the answer from you directly. I find that I am persuasive."

The fact that she was still allowing him to stand in front of her was a testament to that.

"You aren't limited, are you?"

She spat out a laugh. "Oh, I am certainly limited."

"But not by distortion's potential. The technology is your hostage. If I have a correct understanding of energy manipulation, there shouldn't be a limit. You are enforcing one."

Attilatia rolled her eyes. "What brilliant conclusion you come to after speaking with Hashod about my fallibility. With mind like that, it a wonder they have no promoted you to General Prime."

The general ignored her barb. He stepped closer to her, squatting down to eye level where she sat at the desk. "You misunderstand me, Attilatia. I admire what you're doing. I really do. And I'm hoping that what I need will align with your personal goals."

She turned from him to address the locomotive plans. "What you know of my personal goal?"

"Only what I've drawn from inference. You want to stagnate distortion to a place where it progresses society, without becoming destructive."

She didn't look at him. What did she care if this stranger discovered the leash to her fickle allegiance to her father's creed?

"If there's so much potential, why does Aetech let you maintain control of its secrets? Why not just discover how to progress the technology for themselves?"

She looked at him. Narrowed her eyes. He watched her back. He knew exactly what she was doing, but the way he'd laid it bare... it wasn't a threat of exposure. He was marveling at what she'd gotten away with. Fates, at least somebody could appreciate it instead of reserving it as future fuel for when they finally set her on fire.

"Think about genealogy," she started, both terrified and justified in her open admission. Even Thyatira's shoulders rolled back in unveiled surprise. "You open one door. Two more open. Finding every offshoot of original thread feel impossible. With distortion, you open one door—far, far more open. The chance of person simply stumbling into the ruxechorin attuned stratum I lend Aetech to operate from is... one in seventeen trillion."

Why had she told him? Her limbs boiled with regret—

"You are a marvel."

—and her heart lifted in gratification. After years of insults and scrutiny, was she so desperate for recognition for all that she'd worked for? All she'd kept hidden? "Go stroke someone else's ego, eah?"

He didn't back down. "Help me help people, Attilatia. I won't ask anything of you that moves you from your creed."

"I—" She cut off her usual biting response. She'd never had a chance to help people. Yes, of course she was aware of the discrepancy that Aethertech Mechanics created in Nelfinden society. But she'd barely been able to help herself. She couldn't concern herself with it if there was any risk of revealing to Hashod what she was capable of.

But... if she might find her own advantage in aiding this general?

She considered him.

"And Hashod will approve this thing if I say it can be done?"

"Indeed. It only rests in your capable hands to devise the solution," Thyatira said.

"I think... is something you tell me more about. I will listen to see, eah?"

He pulled a chair with a screech across Aetech's work floor to sit beside her. Attilatia did not balk at the approach, despite her better instincts, but crossed her arms and legs more tightly. She had given him an invitation, after all. She could allot him five minutes.

"First, I want to learn from you. My understanding of distortion technology is rudimentary at best. My career has always kept me so busy, I've hardly had time to pursue my interest in the sciences." Thyatira's eyes sparkled with excitement, and Attilatia realized what had seemed so off about him: he'd been holding himself back. That was why he'd seemed so stiff and stilted? A fear of coming off too strong? "Talk to me about distortion, and if what I am envisioning is something possible, I'll explain it to you."

Attilatia's forehead wrinkled in surprise. No one had ever asked to learn from her out of genuine intrigue—only to steal her ideas. She looked down at her workstation. "Well..." She could put off the improvement outline for another hour. "I give you overview. Though I no sure you understand, as my Nelfinden is no good and is very complex in theory."

"I'll do my best, and I would be delighted to listen," he assured her.

Her mouth twisted. Was he really this eye-rollingly earnest, or just trying far too deliberately to win her favor? Better to assume the latter. "Well, my *delighted* pupil, let us go for walk. My people no do explain while seated. Body should move when mind move, or you grow the fidgets."

"Become fidgety," he corrected her.

From anyone else it would have sparked ire, but the general's intentions seemed genuine, not derogatory. He had asked to learn. Perhaps she could stomach helpful tutelage in exchange.

She shrugged. "Strange language. And one I no care practice."

"Don't care to practice," he assisted.

On second thought, she'd had her fill. "I am teacher here. You want explanation or no?"

They strolled through Aetech's industrial halls, Roskaad's cloth-covered lamp brightly illuminating what must have been a dim path for him. The dark silhouettes of vents and ducts and machinery arched above them like a mechanical canopy, a physical testament of human progress. Looking up at them never grew old. Attilatia revered them amidst the symphony of their echoing footsteps. They were the most beautiful thing on the skywalk.

Thyatira watched her appreciatively. Not objectifyingly, but as though he were admiring her very thoughts. Her pride. Put on exhibition, it only intensified her feelings. Attilatia's chest swelled; heat rose into her cheeks as a rare smile tugged at the corner of her mouth.

"The universe made up of infinite number of parts. When you break these parts into more parts, small enough, eah? They act differently than they wholes. You follow?"

Thyatira nodded.

"The typical laws of nature state that one reaction elicit following reaction," she continued. "But these small particles no act like this. They act entirely off probability.

Potential, or you could to say…" She racked her brain for the correct word in Nelfinden. "Intention."

"You mean to say small particles act of free will rather than according to the laws of nature?" Thyatira asked her with a sideways glance.

"You could phrase it that way, if it help you better understand, yes."

"How fascinating. And this is *proven*?"

Their wander had brought them to the distribution warehouse. Rows upon rows of standard configured Aetech lamps lay before them, their sizes ranging from small as a pea to large as a bull. She picked up an apple-sized lamp and activated it, squinting against its light as it whirred into life. Caressing the lamp with a thumb, she addressed it rather than the general himself. All of Aetech's products were old friends to her.

"Is anything *proven*, General? My only evidence the distortion technology before you, but even that does no *prove* anything. Is only evidence to support single perspective.

"If were to use myself as most basic, and terrible, example…" She deactivated the lamp and let her gaze meet Thyatira's dark brown eyes. "There is ninety-nine percent probability that I will no to eat a haloucha from vendor cart on my way home for dinner. Is cuisine for *chikotos*, eah? Every object, like me, has probable and improbable path." She gave him a closed-mouth smile, shrugging one shoulder before continuing to pace. He followed.

"In distortion, we call this path 'flow.' Flow is force, like, aaaahhh…" She searched again for the correct words. "Gravitation. Magnetics. So if I take my probable flow-force, I will go to my house and make good, nourishing, Azadonian food. Remaining one percent probability, however, improbable flow, it don't to just disappear. It stay as potential, or become actuality somewhere else. But remember, we are not talking of me or halouchas, we are talking of the parts very small."

Thyatira held a hand to his chin. Attilatia waited to see if he would interject with a question, but he only nodded for her to continue. Quiet for a man in a position of power. An unexpected tingling washed across her skin; her teeth dragged over her lower lip. Fates, who wouldn't appreciate some ice water in the Jiradesh?

They made their way through the supply halls.

"There is infinite 'somewhere elses,' in same way there is infinite parts in the universe—one generated for each probability no taken. Each forms energetic iteration called a 'stratum,' and stratums are infinite in equal proportion to the probabilities, eah? And so when we distort, we are to take the flow potential path of minority stratum from somewhere else and using to generate energy. Free, unlimited energy to power buildings, aqueducts, and the public transports."

"This is the theory behind circuitry?" he asked her abruptly.

"No. This is theory behind simple distortion technology. Is for individual, disconnected devices. The theory behind circuitry is mine, and mine alone."

"Understood." He nodded and didn't press her any further. "I have a question on simple distortion, then. How do you detect the flow to be distorted? How is it measured?"

She smiled approvingly. "Is good question. Flow is thing beyond human senses. And because it associate only with the very small, there no exist cause and effect which we can perceive. It were previously impossible to measure. We only discover it because of Ruxians." She recalled the way her father had explained distortion technology's origins to her. She hadn't believed him at first. "They lived, you know? One hundred years ago, Azadonian scientists work to develop what is call 'ruxechorin syndicate.' Ruxians had unique neurological feature in central gland of brain. Is unique organ, like eye or ear. It secrete this chemical, raw ruxechorin, which allow them to sense flow. Is how they manifest their rumored powers."

She watched his baffled expression with amusement. These people had been utilizing the technology for over two decades but hadn't a lick of understanding for it. They'd adopted it like some mystical power, never seeking an explanation before accepting it as a fact. That was half of Aetech's lure: the patricians thought they were purchasing magic. With the Nelfinden education system as corrupt and debilitated as it was, it was no wonder. They were trained *not* to think.

"The Azadonians, we copy this chemical signature released by pineal gland of Ruxians and reproduce it synthetically. Ruxechorin lie at heart of every piece of Aetech technology. It distort flow from minority probability from other stratum and into whatever we so chose."

Thyatira stared at her in wonder. He spoke softly, as if worried he might break a spell. "It's a replication of Ruxian magic."

"No. Is science," she corrected him. "The universe is no in chaos, General. Only in chaos could magic exist. Everything happen for reason. Is no random. Is only that we can no sense or conceive of the correlation, the intent. We, as humans, are too small, too limited to see larger picture." He listened respectfully, hands clasped behind his back, as she carried on. "For each small thing, there is pattern which drives flow. Pattern which spreads across infinite stratums in way we could no perceive any easier than tiny ant perceive Seraphinden's city street plan. You follow me?" He nodded. "There is intricate pattern to infinite tiny parts which are infinitely small across infinite stratums of probability untaken. My people, we call this pattern, in your translation, the dragonfly."

"I have heard of the dragonfly," he interjected. "And each wing represents one of the four Fates?"

Attilatia's guard, temporarily forgotten, rose at his question. She chewed at the inside of her cheek. Thyatira was too eager to display his limited knowledge of her heritage; it was almost as though he'd picked up a book on it before coming to meet with her. Cute. But if there was one thing she'd learned, it was that no Nelfinden man put willing effort into an interaction that wouldn't give him the greater benefit.

"There are only three Fates, now. Since Cataclysm," she corrected him. Given that it was the very belief in the Fates which caused them to exist, she would not be a contributor to Destruction's resurrection by admitting his existence.

The general didn't seem to register her last point, or at least he didn't question her on it. "So your religion is rooted in science?"

She rolled her eyes. "Religion is word you use. Nelfinden concept. We have no such thing. Our 'religion' *is* science. Religion imply creating explanation for something behind which there is but randomness. No explanation. As I say before, nothing is random, though much misunderstood due to lack of perspective. And the dragonfly is science, as are the *three* wings of Fate," she said with conviction. "Your people heralded Ruxians as gods, mistaking distortion for magic. Is same way you replace science with your 'religion.' They are no gods. Not like Fates. They only have ability to sense the Fates. In flow. And some of them could learn to manipulate it, in time. Not all."

"So what are the Fates, in your definition?"

She raised an eyebrow at his continued curiosity. "I will play your language questioning game this time, general. You tell *me* what Fates are, in my terms. It prove whether you paying attention, eah? Guess correct, and I will listen your idea."

Roskaad laughed at her challenge, but not to mock her—more like he found genuine joy in it, a thing which caused warmth to take root in her belly—then lifted his gaze in contemplation. They walked for twenty paces in silence, but for the echo of their footsteps in the empty lab, before he responded.

"Speaking in terms of your science, then, rather than religion," he began, "the Fates are a pattern among the intentions of small particles which might determine an outcome in probability on a large scale."

Attilatia stopped walking and crossed her arms. Her mouth drew to one side. Kretch. And here she'd been planning the perfect snarky remark to usher him out the door. Would taking on Thyatira's project cause her trouble down the road? She didn't have bandwidth for political involvement. A woman could only stretch so far...

She looked at the general and lifted a finger. "Perhaps all Nelfinden are no entirely thick-skulled." She sighed, dropping her arms to her sides. "Ok. What is it I am to create for you, General Thyatira?"

Chapter 23
Calverous

Raimee would have played a fine blind woman, had she the attention span for it. Her head jerked every which way like a deranged chicken as they walked along the rose-lined path into the heart of the city. Calver remembered hearing that Tennca'Pui's entire population of cenobites rarely rose above two hundred. Here, people gathered by the thousands. With the way Raimee moved, he imagined a bystander noticing her for what she was at any moment.

But that was paranoia.

People didn't see what they weren't looking for. And no one was looking for a Ruxian seventy-five years after they were thought to have—

False. There were still Tera'thians in this city.

Fates, they might already be tagging him.

The streets were busier than usual, as vendors and city officials bustled to prepare for the festival surrounding the Red Wing's recruitment. Calver's anxiety deepened as he guided them toward the Repository—both to receive word from Fankalo, and because it was the only thing he could think of to keep the bookish girl occupied while he consulted with Greeny again.

"Those walls!" Raimee pointed at the side of the Repository depicting the Ruxians, whose silver-plated hair and eyes splintered the sunlight. He pushed her finger down. "Those are the Seraphindos?"

<Those are why we stay discreet and don't point at things.>

Her lips rolled inward. "When I escaped the attack, my mentor told me to stay out of the public eye. I thought it was a cenobite thing—we don't leave the monastery, it would look bad. But why not tell me to go to the Nelfinden government? I'm sure they would help me, wouldn't they?"

<If you were hidden in the first place, I expect there was a reason. After decades of rule, the oligarchy has its own agenda. Your mentor was wise. Stay out of the public eye.>

"Forever?"

<Until we find Methu'su. Then we'll see.>

She raised a skeptical eyebrow. "And you plan to search aimlessly through a mountain-sized building of archives to find word of him?"

Most citizens didn't have access to public census records without a warrant from the jurisdiction. But Fankalo wasn't most citizens, and Calver had received access at the tail-end of his last trip.

<As a backup plan. But first we go to the roof. I may have a better lead. If that doesn't work, there's always the census.>

Raimee's mouth popped open and promptly shut. He couldn't see her eyes to read what went through her mind. "The census. Oh... I didn't think of that."

They passed through the elaborate curved doorway of the Repository into its lobby, where the tiles of the muqarnas vaulting glinted down on them from twenty stories above. Raimee tilted her head, mouth open. Calver put his thumb to the nape of her neck and nudged it back down. The first floor was designed to be an attraction—a sea of ancient volumes and ledgers—and she fell into it, feet dragging as though someone had tied them with stones to drown her.

<Be patient, scholar. And blind.>

"Please. Just give me five minutes to read—"

He hushed her with a hand. *<First the roof. I want you to meet a friend of mine.>*

That got her attention. "*You* have friends?" She cocked her head as though it was the most astounding thing she'd ever heard.

<You'll like her. Come.>

They surmounted to the roof, stopping twice over twenty flights for Raimee to gasp for breath. Calver eyed the way her legs shook. Convulsed, even. Nearly two ten-days had passed since he'd brought her to the safehouse, and she was still skeletal, despite continued rest and nourishment. His stomach pinched in on itself. He remembered a time, back in Kaidech, when his sister had brought a wounded gull inside to try and heal it. She'd given it water and scraps from her own meager bowl, read to it, and stroked it like a fated baby.

It had died while they slept.

Calver closed his eyes, pulled in a breath, and continued to march. When they reached the top, he handed Raimee the canteen and a small muslin sack filled with dates and tiger nuts. She took it with a pinched expression, until she looked inside.

"Oh, thank Creation." She started crunching and, through a mouthful, accused him. "Have you had this the entire time?"

Today's breeze was mild, tugging lightly at his hair as they crossed from the dark staircase and into the blinding sky. The sun glinted off the thousands of silver-capped domes sprawling across the city below like diamonds in a display. Flapping red recruitment festival flags pooled like blood around them—a reminder that made muscle grip bone. He needed to find that shipment before the Red Wing's caravan moved north. He had three days.

Raimee fidgeted, her head swaying from side to side. Calver restrained himself from what felt like a hundredth reprimand and popped open the rosemary vial in his pocket.

"Is your friend here?" she asked, continuing to eat and fumble with anything she could. The glasses. Her kaftan. The pebbles underfoot.

<Not yet.>

"Didn't we just agree that I'm supposed to stay away from other people?"

<I imagine you'll make an exception for her.> He walked with her to the edge of the roof, where she could admire the view. Perhaps it would help her relax.

"That bird..." Raimee whispered. "Its... intention is set on you, Calver. How is that possible?"

Calver followed her gaze. Sure enough, he spotted Killari swooping in their direction. Raimee gasped, and as always, more than a few heads turned to stare at the huge falcon as she landed on Calver's forearm in a whoosh of wind and feathers.

"She's your friend!" Raimee concluded in awe. "Oh! She's so beautiful!"

<How did you know she was coming down to me?> He signaled awkwardly, one arm still outstretched. Killari touched heads with him in greeting.

Raimee ignored him, but lifted her hand in eager hope. "May I?"

<She'll bite your fingers off.> He'd seen her do it. The bird responded to few besides him and Fankalo.

"Oh." Raimee lowered her hand, but Killari leaned toward her. Cooing and chirping, the bird hopped from his arm and onto the Ruxian's shoulder. Raimee gave a squeal Calver imagined was a mixture of both excitement and pain. His mouth dropped open before he had the sense to close it.

<She usually hates people.>

"Is that why you two are pals?" Raimee teased, stroking the bird's head with delicate fingers. Killari nuzzled into her hand.

Calver's fingers twitched. Killari always favored him. Always. She was the only creature that did.

"Don't worry, I'm not going to steal your sweet little birdie." Raimee raised her pitch as if speaking to an infant and addressed Killari. "Am I, you sweet, beautiful thing?"

The bird cooed back. Trying not to feel envious, Calver reached into his pocket to grab a few fish.

<*Want to feed her?*> he asked reluctantly.

"Yes!" But she winced. "Can you hold her, though? She's a tad pinchy."

Calver reached out. Killari obediently hopped back to him. He was embarrassed at his own relief.

"Ah." Raimee gritted her teeth as the bird's talons released her. "And I imagine your arms are made of metal?"

<*I wear a guard.*>

"Lucky you."

He handed her a few fish. Raimee fed Killari with delighted praise while Calver examined the script from her ankle. It was long this time.

"What's that?"

Calver frowned at her. Responding with the bird on his arm was difficult. <*A letter.*>

"Well, I know *that*." She peered over his shoulder and pursed her lips together. "It's... gibberish."

<*Correct.*> He mentally unraveled Fankalo's encryption. Its spacing told him Fankalo had taken a long time to write it, as though careful in selecting which words to say.

Raimee stared until Killari nudged her for more fish, and she stepped back to tend to the bird. Maybe she was learning what questions not to ask.

'I knew the shipment was defensive tech for the Red Wing. I produced it at Dreiden, too. I wasn't strictly hiding this, though I worried you would react this way. This has been warfare from the very beginning, and the defense industry is always in business. And it's not as though we're affiliating with the Red Wing directly. Their General Prime doesn't wear your mark.

'If you want to investigate, fine. If you find the perpetrators, dispatch them.

'I received word back from a Chira'na associate who has a lead on Methu'su. Deshpian Thacklore. A gossipmonger. He knows everyone who's passed through Nelfindar's upper stratum in the past forty years, what they eat, and who they're sleeping with. I've made you an appointment with him for tomorrow at highsun. The address is on the back.

'A warning. This one is trouble. Be wary what you ask him. What you reveal. Deshpian fell from the graces of military command for a reason. He's a snake.

'And let's discuss the things you learn.

'Fankalo.'

<Good news,> Calver signaled after memorizing the address on the back, though it felt like anything but good news. He reached within his cloak for a match, struck it, and set the message alight. Raimee watched curiously as the flames engulfed the paper and spread toward Calver's fingertips. He almost hoped the flame would burn away some of the worry tugging at his gut. That it might abate the Survivor's creep at the first scent of fear.

Void.

He cast its embers over the side of the roof.

<*Traction on Methu'su.*>

"Really?" Raimee bounced on her toes.

<*We have a meeting with an old associate of his tomorrow. With luck, he'll tell us where to find him.*> He added, <*We'll need to stay in Chira'na tonight.*> They couldn't risk the gate again. <*The Repository provides lodging for traveling scholars, if you're ok with resting here.*>

Raimee gaped in disbelief. "And this you learned from... that gibberish?"

<*Yes.*>

"Who was it from?"

<*Nobody.*>

"Fates, why do you have to keep so hushed about all these things?"

<*To keep us alive.*>

"If that's good news, then what did you read that bothered you?"

Between the lines? That Fankalo was keeping secrets from him. Certainly more than one. <*Let's go.*>

Killari took to the air. Calver pulled Raimee toward the descending staircase, noticing a moment later that he'd done so willingly and without flinching. He released her.

<*Now you can read whatever you want.*>

Chapter 24
Calverous

FOURTEEN YEARS PREVIOUSLY

Mesu Callisto had once said that the line between Creation and Chaos was sometimes too thin to walk on.

The sun was a thing of Creation's quintessence. Calver had often basked in it, spending long days at the beach with Arleena, combing for salvage in secret when their mother went out on an errand. Now he baked in it.

Of all his ailments, it was his thirst that woke him. His entire body felt like fruit left to dry in the sun, but all his world was misery now. His torso panged from cracked ribs. His head ached. And, of course, there was the endless throbbing at the back of his mouth to remind him that he was unchangeably marred.

He would die here.

Kretch.

The pain was too much for him to move.

There was no way for him to know how far the locomotive had taken him. Kaidech could be days away on foot. The city was an Azadonian trade outpost; there were no other towns in the grasslands that stretched toward his home. He was on his own.

Well... on his own with the little spark again. It was back—more of a feeling than a physical sensation, but he could still give shape to it: pea-sized, sitting right in the center of his skull. Calver shuddered. It *had* put him here, but it had also enabled him to learn that Kaidech would come under attack.

Kaidech.

Chaos take this shratten pain. He had to get back to Arleena. Whatever unknown leagues it took to get there, he'd crawl them if he had to.

The spark flickered gently at him. Consolingly?

He'd take every edge he could. Calver let it embrace him, and to his surprise, it warmed. Not like the baking heat from the sun above, but like a cup of steamed milk on a cold evening. The spark wavered like liquid.

An encouragement?

Calver mustered his resolve and reached a shaking hand for the canteen. He grasped it with grime- caked fingernails, his fingers fumbling as they unscrewed the lid. Without sitting up, he drew it to his lips, swallowing coagulated blood from the stump in his mouth as he downed it. Calver gasped when it was empty, then groaned.

The spark flickered. Congratulating him? Then it beckoned him again, the way it had in Kaidech.

Fates. He didn't think he could move. But then again, he hadn't thought he could drink either. The spark kept beckoning with increasing insistence.

Arleena.

Where? he asked it.

The spark flowed and then stopped, returning to its normal, flame-like waver. Did that mean close? Could the spark understand his thoughts? It flickered again, an implicit response. *Yes.*

Calver stiffened. He was hallucinating. The pain was driving him mad. He panicked. This was only the beginning. This pain would endure, perhaps even worsen as he fought his way home. Fates help him.

The spark flickered consolingly again. *Friend. Help,* it insisted.

He had no idea how he made it to his feet. He couldn't separate the steps into individual moments; the experience passed in a single blur. The lowsun cast an orange glow against the threads of hip-high grass, spread like an endless sea around him.

A mound of earth raised the locomotive track to half his height above the ground. Its guiderail stretched in either direction into the distance, and the spark beckoned him to walk along it toward the setting sun.

With a ragged breath, Calver clenched his jaw and followed until the spark directed him to stop. At his feet, the dead man's dowaga glimmered innocently in the grass.

The spark danced. *Take.*

He did.

The spark continued to beckon.

He walked, slow and staggering, for an hour, maybe less, before he crumpled to his knees. The phantasmal being had grown brighter, more tangible as he went. *There. Just there*, it said to him, pulsing. He lifted his eyes. A colossal obsidian stone rose over the grass in the distance, shrouding it in darkness. It was the length of the Kaidechi dock away. He could do it. Calver crawled through the grass on his hands and knees toward it.

Closer, it consoled him.

He kept going until the black rock loomed over him, obscuring the green-blues of twilight in exchange for shadow. The ground at the base of the rock hollowed beneath him.

A cave.

Calver rolled into it, coming to rest on his back, all energy spent. The earth was cool and dry and utterly dark, so he closed his eyes, embracing the stillness.

I'm here, he thought to the spark.

{Hello, Calverous,} it answered.

His eyes sprang open. This was no longer an odd little thing with implicit movements and feelings. His heart spiked into his bulging throat. It was an actual voice in his head.

{You're not crazy. You've simply found me, and so you can hear me properly now.}

What are you? he thought as his empty insides twisted into knots.

The thing fell quiet for many breaths before it spoke to him again. Its voice echoed in his head: soft, like a hiss or a whisper. But it possessed a sharpness, too. While mimicking a human tone, the sound was not quite right.

It didn't answer his question.

{I've been watching you for a long time.}

Why? he demanded.

{You're special to me. It's why I saved you. Brought you here.}

Saved me? How could it suggest such a thing? *You've destroyed everything!*

{Don't be angry, Calverous. I'm here to help you save your sister. Your mother. Friends.}

He squeezed his eyes shut. This couldn't be real. *I don't understand.* His breath came in short spasms. Panic felt as though it were a physical thing closing in on him from every corner. Stepping on his heart. Crunching at his bones.

{You don't need to understand. Just know that I can help you. And you can help me too.}

How?

The voice had no body. It existed only in his mind, but somehow he felt it smile the same way he'd felt the spark console him.

{Share your mind with me. I'll take away all of your pain. I'll help you get back to Kaidech without any feeling. Any fear.}

His eyes narrowed. *I deserve to feel this.* For breaking his promise, he deserved worse.

{But it weakens you. I know all futures. You cannot make it without me.}

Whatever this thing was, he couldn't trust it.

{Let me. You can have your feeling back any time.}

No.

{Calver, you're dying.}

The reality of those words threatened to break him. He wouldn't ever leave this cave. Would his bones be found here? If Kaidech was invaded—destroyed—who would even remember a boy from the Kaidechi slums? His dreams of changing the world would decompose alongside his body.

{I'll keep you alive. I'll take you home.}

The thought of not feeling anything was more frightening than it was alluring. A disembodied voice was a thing of lore, the kind where monsters lurked in the tides and grasslands. Where men were led to their deaths by aethersprites.

{I thought you wanted to be a hero? A general?}

The words bit at him. It was a trap... but recognizing it didn't make it any easier to resist.

{It's a shame I saved you for nothing... I'll leave you alone now. Have a nice death, Calverous.}

The voice was gone. The spark was gone. And Calver was suddenly and completely alone with his pain.

Fear eclipsed him. More terrifying even than hearing voices in his head was the thought of dying alone. His body screamed for death, embraced it with open arms. But not him: he couldn't die. Not now.

Wait. Please come back.

The sun beyond the rim of the cave fell below the horizon, and the space around Calver settled into consummate darkness. At his plea, the spark flickered back to life. He wondered then if it had always been there, unnoticed. Waiting. Watching.

It didn't matter. Anything was better than being left alone here in this darkness.

I'll do it. How do I do it?

The voice sounded through his mind with the impression of a smile. *{Imagine opening your mind to me. I need only permission.}*

Calver did so. He imagined his mind welcoming the spark to spread, extend. Moments of agonizing silence slipped by.

Had he... done it? Did he even want to have done it?

Then an overwhelming presence, one that intermingled with the darkness of the cave, pressed in around his head. His pained muscles recoiled; he swallowed. The motion pulled at his stump of a tongue, a reminder of how little time he had left. There was no other way to go.

The spark spread from the center of his brain like an itch in liquid form, extending through every span of his extremities. It thrummed gloriously as it circulated his veins, sharing memories and emotions in the span of a heartbeat. It had been here for lifetimes, alone, immobile, waiting.

No. Nononono.

Calver shrank in fear as invisible marionette strings ran through his bones. They pulled him to sit upright.

This was wrong. This was the wrong decision. He willed it out, willed it gone, but it kept permeating.

And then, with the same suddenness the experience had started, Calver felt nothing. Nothing from his ribs, his tongue, his hunger, his thirst. He gasped, or thought he did, but his body made no sound. He no longer controlled it. It was...

A marvelous relief. Even his fear, incapacitating just moments ago, ebbed into nothing.

Calver fell backward further and further until he landed in the mental equivalent of a fetal position. Everything was still. Easy. He could see through his own eyes, barely, but didn't feel a desire to focus or pay attention.

Is this... ok? he asked the voice.

{Yes. You have done a good thing, you see? No feeling. No weakness. And because of it, we will stay alive together.}

Calver numbly realized that they had already left the cave. He was—they were—walking along the locomotive guiderail into the twilight. A miniscule, diluted panic hit him. With it, he ascended to the intangible threshold of his own mind.

Where are we going? His vision cleared as he rose. A dull ache from his body returned. The voice faded behind his own thoughts ever so slightly.

{We're going to Kaidech. To save your people. Remember?} it reassured him.

Arleena.

Calver hovered in his state of semi-control, feet moving beneath him without his direction. His tongue throbbed with each beat of his own heart. A heart he now shared.

{Trust in me, Calverous. It will all be alright.}

I'll take it back. But he sank even as he thought it. The rocking from his own steps threatened to lull him to sleep. He gave away all of his control until, once again, blissful numbness consumed him.

{It will all be alright.}

Time passed.

Calver wasn't sure how long they traveled. The voice kept him alive, as promised. It found water by digging deep into the earth with Calver's bloodied, dirt-caked hands. It hunted the small game which quivered in the tall grasslands, eating it raw like an animal. The sun rose, then set again. Calver faded in and out for what might have been days or even weeks. There was no way to distinguish time.

It was the smell which reawakened him again. He crept into the commanding headspace to discern the stench of smoke and something else—something rotten, which assaulted his nostrils. Beneath him, the port city sloped from the horizon to meet slate-colored seafoam. A sky of billowing, black smoke strangled the struggling rays from the highsun.

Horror obstructed Calver's airway.

He was too late.

The voice acknowledged his return to their mind with a soft purr.

No more. No more. He thrashed away from it. He'd been numb for too long. He'd let go of himself. *I want back in. You said I could have the control, the feeling back, if I wanted.*

{Then take it... if you can bear it.}

Calver pushed his way forward through the tar pit of comfort which clawed for him to stay huddled in his inner mind. A ragged scream tore from his chest. He was usurped again, this time by a pain so immense it caused him to teeter onto his knees. There would be no relief for him here. No mother to aid him and heal him. His home—

Memories bloomed and faded behind his eyes. Mother cleaning an apron in the ocean, Pim pulling him up from the floor after a grapple, Arleena releasing a fox-like cackle. All burnt into ash. Arleena...

Calver hunched over and retched. He hadn't known a person could throw up so much. Something bloody surfaced which he couldn't remember eating. It made him retch again.

In the distance, Kaidech was a stage with thousands of glowing coals for actors. Their smoke billowed skyward in midnight clouds.

What had she thought of him? That he'd abandoned her? That he'd—

Calver wailed, a sound that should have been "No!" But the noise was deranged: a strangled vowel which closer resembled a moan. He hated the way it sounded, and he loathed himself for it. The dialogue internalized.

No, nononono.

He stumbled down the hillside into the outskirts of the city—his slums. But for the crackling flames, which licked around the few buildings that stood, a strange silence hung over once-familiar alleyways. He staggered through vacant streets where ashes settled over cobbles in a cloud-like layer.

At the city's central square, where he'd laughed with Pim and Darion just days ago, he arrived at the source of the smell. Calver had known what he would find beneath the smoke the moment he'd seen Kaidech from the hills, but a part of him had hung onto the hope for something different. Anything but this: corpses piled by the thousands in a single, still-burning pyre.

When he drew close enough to see features on individual faces, Calver's knees hit cobblestone. Some of them were still whole enough to stare at him, their glassy eyes cast in vacant surrender to whatever guarded the liminal plane between consciousness and nothing. But most were a byproduct of carrion birds or flame, each indiscernible from the next. He gathered himself into a trembling ball, unwilling to look for that pair of small brown eyes.

Arleena.

It was the one thought that surpassed the rest; the betrayal he'd never, *never,* make amends for as long as he lived.

The spark in his head pulsed knowingly. He hated it.

You—you knew we were too late?

{I rescued you,} it assured him.

But you said we were going to save my people? You knew, and you kept it from me? he demanded. The tears flooding over his cheeks could not be dammed. *I promised my sister...*

He promised he'd always be there for her, because their father hadn't been. Instead he'd abandoned her, as his father had.

{I needed to get you here. And you needed to see it for yourself. You wouldn't have had it any other way.}

Calver wanted to be furious with it. Wanted anything to direct his heartbreak, his fury, at. But he couldn't find fault in what the voice said; he would have died had he been here. If the voice had warned him, he would still have wanted to come. To see if there was something to be done.

Why me? Even his inner voice sounded broken.

{I told you. You're special.} The presence undulated in his mind at the word. *{I preserved you here with your family for as long as I could.}*

Because you knew the future?

{There is no predicting the future, Calverous. But I did possess an ability to understand what was probable, now gone. Now that we share a mind, I am limited by your senses. Our destiny awaits us here.}

Destiny? This was a far shot from the longing he'd felt when he was on Jenolavia's statue. How could this be his destiny?

The steady tromping of footsteps grew louder from the opposite end of the square. Calver's body seized. A score of men stalked from around the pyre of bodies.

Fear kindled into fury. *They* had done this. And he would take any of them—all of them—with him into that pile for it.

{Let me take hold again.}

No. Calver rose to his feet.

The men drew weapons as they approached him. Their commander, an enormous, pale, hairless man at their head, said something. The guttural clicks and sibilant emphasis allowed Calver to identify it as Tera'thian.

{Your pain will not cripple me. Combined, our talents are limitless. You want vengeance? Use me.}

Halfway, he bargained.

The presence did not hesitate in surging forward. *{Agreeable.}*

Calver fought them.

He fought in a way he'd never fought before. The skills Callisto had trained him in for eight years were all there, but different. His limbs moved with more feral speed than he usually possessed, and didn't hesitate in the use of deadly force.

They came at him from every direction. He leveled the first soldier who approached him with the dead man's dowaga, and felled four more before their commander barked an order and five of the fully grown invaders assaulted him in tandem. They did not use their weapons against him; rather, they brought him to the ground and restrained him by his limbs. He thrashed and screamed, despite broken bones.

The commander leered over him, bringing a boot to his chest and the pointed end of a dowaga to his throat. Calver submitted.

The man looked at him like he was a prize. First he spoke in a serious tone, directly to Calver. Then he growled something to the men restraining him. They leaped to tie his wrists and ankles.

Can you understand him? Calver asked the voice.

{He wishes to keep you as a challenger among his tume'amic.}

Calver knew of the tume'amic: child slaves, bred and milled by the Tera'thian state. His mother used to tease him that they would snatch him away if he didn't finish his breakfast. Only a ten-day ago, she'd cradled him in her arms and told him she loved him.

A part of him was glad she'd never found out what he would become.

Chaos, *NO*. He'd have them kill him first. Calver thrashed again, but the man had moved his dowaga away and the movement did nothing but aggravate his injuries.

{Don't,} the voice whispered. *{Preserve yourself.}*

Heroes didn't get captured. Heroes fought to the bitter end.

Calver gritted his teeth. *What's a challenger?* He wasn't sure he wanted to know the answer.

{Does it matter? We stay alive, for now.}

The mammoth of a man kneeled in front of Calver, close enough for him to see the fire reflected in a hairline scar which ran from the crease of his mouth to his earlobe. Calver's nostrils flared in defiance.

A hideous smile cracked the man's face. He spoke again.

{He says you should feel fortunate you are a survivor. He's going to give you a Ratka, as a reminder of what you owe him.}

The commander pulled a knife from a sheath at his waist. Calver flinched and retreated, almost as a reflex, to the back of his mind.

The Tera'thian slashed three crude cuts into Calver's skin, just beneath his right collarbone. Calver felt nothing as he maneuvered backward, using the spark like a shield. It would help conserve his strength so that when he—

The mind-djinn pushed—no, it practically stomped Calver down. Further. Further. *No. STOP.*

It cut him off.

Calver tried to resurface.

The presence pressed down on him with impossible force. *{Be still, Calverous. This is not such a bad fate.}*

Calver's desperate rage only seemed to push his control further from him. *I won't submit to this!*

{You're a survivor.}

No! Not like this, he wasn't. How could he really be alive in a life where he'd failed Arleena? *I don't care if I survive this. I want to keep fighting.*

A mental flick from the mind-djinn cast him into numbness.

I'm not a survivor, he managed, his final defiance. *You are. Just you.*

{So be it,} the Survivor responded.

As if Calver's mind was a pot, the Survivor closed the lid.

Chapter 25
Niklaus

Niklaus stood at the white marble balcony of the skywalk's central pavilion, staring out over the serenely green sea. It was nearing highsun, and he had to admit the sun *did* feel lovely on his skin. It had been several weeks since he had been outside. He closed his eyes, inhaling deeply, and let the salty air, tinted with cinnamon and jasmine, tousle his ebony hair.

The natural elements proved a far more pleasant experience than the buzz from the pavilion behind him, alive with the chatter and clinking of the skywalk's brunch-goers. Niklaus had once been a fan of these affairs. What wasn't there to like, getting dressed in finery to enjoy exquisite food and drink prepared by the most talented chefs in the nation?

Indulgence was an ever-splendid thing. Shiny, like the gems mined to encrust the cutlery, and yet they couldn't catch his eye. Succulent, like the fruits plucked from their orchards, and yet they couldn't wet his lips. What wasn't there to like, consuming more than one created? Tipping the cosmic scales off-balance, bending the world into the realm of Chaos?

Everything had its cost. How was it that he, richer than any, had suddenly found himself unable to pay?

Absent of his willing contribution, the monthly brunch had long since divulged into his just showing up so his mother could tote him about like a pet for social propriety.

Niklaus clutched the cool railing and looked over its ledge. Six stories below, the sea thrashed where it collided with rock, foam drifting atop the waves like clouds. He stared into its depths, leaning slightly forward, willing himself to just let go. It would be so easy to topple forward. *Shratten coward*, he thought to himself when the motion would not come.

"Would you like anything to drink, mesu?" A waiter shook him from his stupor.

Niklaus cleared his throat. "Brandy, please."

"Apologies, mesu, it is brunch. It's a dry affair." The waiter was polite enough not to say, *it always has been, you idiot, and you know it.*

Niklaus cursed. Of course it was. "Well... what else is there?"

"What else... is there?" the man repeated, as though understanding that he was being toyed with but not wanting to appear rude. There was literally anything else. "Would you like me to suggest something for you?"

Why was he playing games with the waiter? What would it accomplish? Niklaus noted the scratching ache of his throat, the dryness of his mouth, as though it had recently been cleared of sand. How long had he been so thirsty? "Water is fine. Thanks."

The man bustled away without another word.

Niklaus sighed, a heavy and ancient noise. Someone had been bound to speak to him eventually. Most of the patricians avoided him now—he was, after all, the lunatic. The disgraced. The traitor. Why would anyone dare to be seen having a conversation with him, even when just a year previously it had been a common brunch objective to catch Niklaus Meyernes in small-talk?

"Niklaus... I know that isn't you." His mother's familiar, condescending voice came from behind him.

He fixed a grin on his face, spinning around to meet her. "The one and only."

His mother fastened to his side, her body clip-clopping across the pavilion more quickly than should have been natural for an old woman in heels.

"Preservation, what are you wearing?" she hissed through her teeth.

He did his best to suppress a chortle. The objective of his dress was always the same: to become a caricature of the ones who would ridicule him for dressing the way he did. It was one of the few things he still found amusement in. "What, this? Height of fashion, don't you think?"

He wore a cape. Not just any cape, but one printed with a wild pink floral pattern which he had only purchased because the flowers looked so specifically *feminine* that anyone with the properly uncivilized mind had to do a double-take to decipher what kind of flowers they really were.

His mother covered her eyes. "Fates above, what did I do to deserve this? What will Rebethel think?"

Another purchase well worth his dwindling time left on the planet.

"Come, then, let's get this over with."

The affair was staged out of doors, under the open sun, where the event staff had assembled impromptu tables and chairs. After insisting that the day would be much more enjoyable if he just kept his mouth shut, Niklaus's mother ushered him into a chair at the head of their table beside Rebethel, who didn't even acknowledge his presence. Ivory linens enrobed the surface before him, set with an elaborate arrangement of porcelain and crystal. Fresh flowers and dried fruits, shaped into the forms of miniature animals, adorned each setting around its edges.

The brunch attendees at Niklaus's table assumed their new standard of ignoring him for the next hour while he stared into space, not eating. He stared at all the brunch-goers, shoveling tarts and quiches and fresh fruit into their maws, all dressed in clothing which might have taken a seamstress a month to create. All laughing and smiling as though pretending to take investment in the mundane things they spoke on.

He nearly opened his mouth once to speak. *The nation is in peril, its economy spiraling downward, the income gap growing; our Prime is an unstable xenophobe who has cut off all our trade; revolt is coming. Something must be done; something can be done.*

Nearly. His jaw remained slack, his lips loosely parted, strands of his black hair stuck in the crack between them. No one would hear him. It was as though all of the skywalk and, by extension, Seraphinden was a façade. An illusion. How could one make noise in a place that didn't exist?

He noticed a sideways glare from his mother, reminding him there was an untouched feast in front of him. Looking down, he unconsciously decapitated the sugar-spun kitten atop his chocolate mousse with his fork. It was then that he caught a snippet of the table's conversation.

"—Roskaad Thyatira."

"I bet he's behind all this Shadewalker business. Parading himself as a vigilante. Making this entire groundling movement look lucrative." The words came from Sesu Coliea, a lean woman in an oversized, feathered turban which matched her sapphire kaftan. She was a long-time friend of his mother. Her family had lived on the skywalk for six generations.

"Don't spread such rumors. The Shadewalker isn't a vigilante. He's a mass murderer. I fail to see what's lucrative," argued her husband, beside her.

"Regardless, Prime Taranil's gone off the edge with this one. Thyatira's promotion has left many with a sour taste in their mouth."

"What... what did you say?" Niklaus asked.

When Sesu Coliea realized he was speaking to her, she stopped mid-sentence and looked around the table as though calling an audience to reaffirm he'd had the nerve to address her. She cleared her throat. "Well, I know I'm not the only one who disapproves of the promotion of a groundling to the position. Regardless of his previous station."

"What promotion?"

Another glare from his mother. A few shaking heads. Rebethel pulled a pocket mirror from her bag and proceeded to apply another coat of lip paint.

Sesu Coliea stared at him for a few seconds as though determining whether to ignore him. She didn't. "Roskaad Thyatira was elected General Prime of the Red Wing, and martial advisor to Prime Taranil. Perhaps you should leave your room more often."

They went back to their conversation, but Niklaus didn't hear any of it. The brunch faded around him. He wished he, too, could fade from existence. His head pounded. His throat clenched. This was contrived. Thyatira was plotting a groundling revolution, and the patricians were grumbling at it like it was an inconvenient stormcloud on the horizon. But Thyatira had Niklaus—richer than the rest of this table should they combine their coffers—defamed and discredited within days of his papers' release. Couldn't they see that, no matter how high their thrones, their crowns could be thrown if enough men stood on enough shoulders?

A repetitive clinking sounded. It was only after several seconds passed that Niklaus realized it was his own fork, trembling in his hand against the base of his crystal goblet.

"Have you finished your meal, mesu?" It was a waiter. Niklaus looked down at his plate, untouched other than the decapitated kitten.

"Yes. Thank you."

He stood abruptly and returned to the railing he'd clung to earlier to hurl the limited contents of his stomach over the edge. Fates above, he needed a drink. And he needed to be anywhere other than brunch.

Swallowing against the taste of bile, he turned from the balcony. Without sparing a glance for anyone watching, he made his way toward the distortion-powered lift at the skywalk's rim.

To avoid his mother discovering how bad his reliance on the drink had actually become, he had taken to descending when he needed something to take the edge off. Despite what some might say about it, Niklaus liked the ground. It was less windy than the skywalk. The people there were too busy to make small talk about him, and it went without saying that he could get three times the intoxicant for half the price.

The lift landed six stories below, at the border of the Korshuva and Basalk districts. They were as day and night. The section of Seraphinden directly beneath the skywalk was its worst: it made sense that the seediest parts of humanity would lurk in the perpetual shadows of Basalk. The space was mostly occupied by warehouses and agricultural distribution points, but the inky alleys between were said to be dangerous. The lift kept guards stationed at its base at all hours.

Niklaus glanced down the street leading into Basalk. A few laborers moved in and out at a pace which made it clear they'd rather not be there. The guard at the lift's base raised eyebrows at Niklaus in a way that said, *Don't do it.*

Niklaus wouldn't. It was a simple matter of curiosity. He looked toward Korshuva, which was dappled in sunlight. With a quick thanks to the guard, he wound between the middle-class city-goers along the cobbled street that led to The Muddy Horse. So frequently had he trodden that path to the place where the last of his pleasant memories remained distilled, somewhere between the gin and the brandy, it was a miracle the road didn't bear the imprint of his footsteps.

The establishment was small and sparsely lit by candles—Aetech lamps were expensive—but the floors were clean and the bar was polished. It was empty of its usual patrons, the merchants, bankers, and artisans of the Korshuva District. It was early, after all. The bartender, Claynard, was wiping down the counter, giving Niklaus the impression that he had only just opened.

Claynard flashed him a sincere smile, revealing two silver teeth that matched the embroidery on his vest. He had a flare for bright patterns—something that Niklaus appreciated. There was little not to appreciate about Claynard. It was one of the reasons Niklaus kept returning to The Muddy Horse.

Other than regularly complimenting Niklaus's choice of clothing, the man treated him the same as any other patron. He knew who Niklaus was—had to, as he called him by name. But he never cast shade on him, like everyone else in the fated city. Possibly because Niklaus tipped well… or because he remembered who'd first brought him there.

Niklaus sat on Latouda's favorite stool and ordered a double. Claynard obliged, adding an extra pour for good measure before setting it in front of him.

"Not so sure about that cape," he said with a low laugh. "It might be a step too far for my taste."

"I thought it was funny," Niklaus objected, holding his glass aloft in a gesture of thanks.

"It's definitely funny, I'll give you that much." He watched as Niklaus drained his drink and then pressed a piece of a moss tab onto his tongue. "Started early?"

Niklaus nodded and circled his hand for a second, but Claynard had already started a new pour. Fates bless him. "Life's trials get an early start too, then?"

Niklaus offered his bartender a doleful blink. "Sure, I'll acknowledge that today has given my middle finger a permanent erection."

"You shouldn't touch that stuff." Claynard nodded to the moss tab tin Niklaus had pulled from his pocket.

Niklaus waved a hand at him. "I monitor it. Never enough to hit a point of lethal withdrawal."

Claynard drummed his fingers on the otherwise empty bartop. Then he reached beneath the counter for another glass and poured himself a few thumbs of the high-label bourbon which he kept in-house specifically for when Niklaus visited. "Well." He took a sip. Sighed. "Out with it, then. It's the only way to help with these things."

Niklaus clinked glasses with him, and they both drank. "I presume you've also heard the 'martial announcement' given by the Prime this week?"

"Thyatira's promotion? Yes. A groundbreaking decision. And a promising-looking future for the common man." Dirty halouchas, the bartender was in on the "uprising" hysteria Thyatira's groundling proponents created. Of course he was.

Niklaus groaned and set his head on the bar top. It was sticky for something so recently cleaned. "You do know who I am, don't you?" he murmured into the resin.

"My best customer." Claynard smiled brilliantly.

"Kretch on a shratten cracker."

The bartender sighed and swirled the contents of his glass. "I'm not one to pass judgment." He took a slow sip and dabbed the corners of his mouth with a napkin. "But I assumed, with your association with Latouda, you were a groundling advocate."

A groundling advocate and a violent revolutionist were not married ideas... and yet everyone else in Seraphinden treated them like tea and honey. Niklaus pouted, tracing the rim of his glass with his little finger. "Eeeaaahhh."

He realized how childish the sound seemed as it passed from his lips, so he drowned it out with the bottom of his second drink. Claynard switched him over to ale, plopping a large vessel of the bubbling amber liquid in front of him. Niklaus gave him a pointed look.

"You'll thank me for that later."

Niklaus rolled his eyes, then bit his lip, wondering whether it was worth speaking. "Believe it or not, and I honestly don't care what you believe, every shratten thing I wrote in those papers last year was true. I can't deny that a downturn in Aetech's stocks would have benefitted me immensely, but I wasn't aware of the fact until Thyatira brought it to light. It was a legal condition my mother had coordinated—contrived. I had no idea it even existed."

He stopped to test the beer with his tongue and made a bitter face. It would have to do. Taking a hearty sip from the enormous glass, he set it down with a heavy clink. Countless scratches and chinks from years of patrons sat beneath the counter's resin topcoat. How many of them had vented to Claynard in the way he did now? How many stories had been told here?

He shook his head and lowered his voice to a whisper, speaking adamantly to his audience of one. "The moment that man suggested using Aethertech Mechanics as a military solution, I knew his whole platform was suspect. So I called him on it. And what do I get for exposing that his groundling origins are entirely fabricated—an invention for mass acclaim?" Niklaus threw up his arms into the air. "Well, you know exactly what I got." He laughed despairingly. "But what did *he* get for exposing me for a crime I didn't even realize I was committing?" He pounded his glass on the counter to punctuate his words. "He got. Shratten. Promoted to fated. General Prime. And military advisor to the. Shratten Prime of Nelfindar."

It was a good counter, and a good glass. Not a new scratch to be seen.

The bartender poured himself another drink. "That's certainly a new rendition of the story."

Niklaus stared mournfully into the bubbles of his drink. "That's the story I put in ink. Everyone heard a twisted version of it, yet no one's read the fated original. I've tried to hold my tongue from further defending myself." It only made him look desperate. "But I can't, the slippery thing. I keep talking. And—and I'll never stop talking. Because I have this silly hope that one day someone will hear me." A strange noise escaped his throat: a cry, in costume, wearing laughter for skin. "Stupid, stubborn hope." He usually swallowed the pain that hope struck him with, so that others didn't have to feel it. Not today. "Sometimes I find myself doing this thing where I just listen. Listen to the things that others say so that they might be heard. And, in response, I impart comfort. Telling them the things that I want to hear. That I want someone to tell me."

He gulped. Shook his head. "It doesn't happen as much as it used to, though. I've found it difficult to listen, of late, when not a soul will speak to me in the first place."

But Claynard had delayed his usual multitasking, sweeping, shining, clearing, in favor of listening unhindered. That was... nice. That was why Latouda had liked him: in a sea of selfish men, he was a rare pearl.

"My father once told me that words are warfare," he began. "Forgive me for saying, mesu, but what were you thinking? True or not, beneficial to you or not, claiming Thyatira to be conspiring against the groundling movement was bound to raise some hackles."

"Raise some hackles? Look what's been done to me! Is that not concerning? And not on a personal level. Look deeper. Why?" He pounded his fist again. "My actions weren't intended to simply 'raise hackles,' they were intended to ignite a *peaceful* revolution. Because if we don't, the opposite is well on its way! The point was to destroy Aetech and Thyatira and whatever violence he's intended all in one blow. For years I've wanted to disassemble this monster I created. It's turned Seraphinden into a fiefdom. We're hardly a step above the tume'amic. I just never got up the guts to do anything about it until last year... and it was because of her." He took another deep sip from the ale before saying her name. "It wasn't even my idea. It was Latouda's. I simply wrote the fated thing in my name so that it would be more widely distributed."

Claynard's face paled. His eyes were watery. "Now it makes sense why she was forced to relocate. I never imagined you had any part in that, by the way... As a matter of fact, I always figured she was why you kept coming back here..."

He was right. The bar had been Latouda's spot before it had become Niklaus's; funny how she was the dead one, yet he was the one who haunted the place so frequently. His only response to the barkeep's statement was to take another drink. It was answer enough.

Claynard shook his head. "Poor girl."

"Poor girl," Niklaus echoed. His eyes unfocused. His thoughts began to drift.

"You know, she talked about you. It's not all as you think. She did care for you. This one time, she penned that you had 'the most beautiful ideas of any man she'd ever known.'"

If words could have teeth, those did. Niklaus knew. He'd been there that evening. Looked at the napkin she'd written it on, intending to throw it out for her, when she'd moved on to dancing and Claynard to other customers. Claynard had omitted the latter half of her sentence. *But lacks both the wisdom and willpower to do anything with them.* The memory chewed at him with more bite than the bitters in his hand.

He turned it over and over, as he did each time he drank. How she could have done what she did to him: effused love to disguise an action prompted by hate?

The truth came to him from the bottom of the glass, where it had always been. Because the human connection was like any good dream, so deeply profound and oh so utterly forgettable.

Then, suddenly, in the way things happen, Niklaus had an idea.

Chapter 26
Attilatia

The darkness of Aetech's workfloor shifted in Attilatia's peripheral vision. A phantom limb moved ever so slightly in the pitch of the night's shadows.

Thyatira sat in a corner chair, several body-lengths away.

A small smile touched her lips, equal parts amusement and irritation. This had become a kind of game he liked to play—waiting for her acute vision to notice him. Who knew how long he'd been sitting there... or *why*.

Her gut turned. Their work together was over. *Shit*. Had he come to tell her he could no longer enlist Thedexemore? That the Red Wing wouldn't allow it after all?

"Congratulation on your promotion, General Prime Thyatira," she said without sparing a glance in his direction. She was proud to have kept any shake from her voice.

Another shift. He stood, and what had been a mere silhouette became clear as the General Prime stepped into the moonlight. "That title, from you, feels a bit like a mockery."

Her eyebrows twitched upward. "Who to say it is not?"

"I think we are past such courtesies. Aren't we? Call me Roskaad."

"How cordial," she snorted.

"No, it doesn't ever quite feel so, with you."

Something in his honesty bristled her, like a cat rubbed backward. "Do you have problem with me, Roskaad?"

He smiled when she used his name, a real one. It had taken her time, but she'd learned to tell the difference over their year of work together. Most Thyatira smiles were learned propaganda. But some were genuine, and those that were felt a little bit like a distortion lamp's first heart-lifting spin into life.

"Quite the opposite. I find you enthralling. Every interaction I have with anyone else feels like fanfare. And then... there's you."

She bared her teeth at him. "How refreshing. Enthralling, eah? Others might call it mental disorder." She didn't bother to stop her work, continuing to strip a wire from a broken distortion conversion cell.

"All the world is disorder, but you speak in straight lines," he said.

Roskaad Thyatira. Groundling hero. Average among imbeciles. Was it possible that he could see some small amount of sense that eluded the rest of this fated country?

She wouldn't gather her hopes.

"You leave tomorrow, do you not? You should be celebrate with your friends. Family. Why you here?" she asked, not willing to wait any longer for him to bear his bad news.

Her comment made his perfect posture roll inward. "I have always been a career man through and through, and I—" The word caught in his mouth. "I didn't intend to be forward," he started again, picking up a lamp from her desk as though to occupy his hands.

Attilatia's gut turned over anew. *She* was his friends and family? Fates help her. And him.

"I'm really just here to say thank you. I received word from Chira'na yesterday that fifty thousand defensive plates have reached the Red Wings headquarters there last week. They're being loaded onto the recruitment caravan's wagons as we speak."

She tried to stifle her surprise at his gratitude with indifference. "I already know this." She had looked into it after the strange events of the past few days. Hashod wouldn't get away with whatever meddling he'd set his hands to.

Roskaad was not dissuaded by her detachment. "I thought I'd bring you a gift, to celebrate." He set a bottle of wine on her desk. "As it would have been impossible without you."

Her own shock gave her such pause that a snipping response failed her. The General Prime's words were genuine. This didn't have to do with Thedexemore. He was still safe.

Roskaad stood so close to her now that she could see the evening's stubble growing across the hard lines of his jaw. Smell the oils in his hair. See the veins in his neck. Attilatia drummed her fingers on the desk and reached for the wine, pretending to inspect the label.

"You still a sycophant, I see. Did you come for goodbye kiss, then?" she grumbled at him.

He didn't come back with his usual 'clever yet respectful' politico response. "You—are angry. Without end," he commented, with only a slight hesitation.

The audacity.

She controlled herself. She did not dislike Roskaad. In fact, she tolerated his company above most, and he did not deserve her ire. Knowing what she knew, she even worried for him. Maybe.

Attilatia raveled the stripped wire from the distortion cell onto a wooden dowel and tucked it into her workstation. "Every day, I tread water in ocean of entitled *chikotos*, weights on my arm and leg. If you lived life I do..." She paused to chuckle without mirth. "Well. You be angry, too."

"I think I may be able to relate."

Fates forbid. "Oh?"

She turned to look at him, and there was a strange expression on his face. Attilatia felt herself leaning toward him. Whatever he was about to tell her had an inescapable gravity.

"I grew up poorer than many," he told her, "and was treated as such. Without friends. Without respect. There was a group of boys in my childhood burrow. They would taunt me. Just for being what I was." Roskaad bit his lip, hesitated, and carried on. "And one day I... tried to play with them. They cornered me in a barn. Forced a bucket of filth over my head. I fought to get away and, in doing so, knocked one of them out of a hayloft. He—landed on a metal rake." Roskaad looked away from her. "The boy died."

He rubbed his forefinger and thumb together as he considered his next words. The ones Attilatia knew would come to the point she already understood.

"And... it didn't make me feel any better. It only made me sad. But more so, angry. And it set his friends upon me like wolves. I kept wondering if things would be better if I had just... submitted."

Perhaps someone else *could* feel what she felt.

"I understand that you're angry," he said. "And that you don't feel like there's an end to it. Because the actions of simple retribution, of standing up for oneself, won't solve a problem of mass irreverence."

Attilatia was struck by a sudden premonition that it was all connected: the plates, the Red Wing, the assassinations, Hashod, the ruxechorin shortage. It felt like her mind had shifted in paradigm. Like she was seeing with new light a picture that had always been there, and she was just catching a glimpse of it for the first time in Roskaad's brown eyes.

And then the premonition slipped away through the cracks of her subconscious before she could remember what she had come to understand.

"And what does solve it?"

"An entire system overhaul." He said it with the resolution of stone.

Attilatia bit her lower lip. Roskaad was taking a chance on her, and she wasn't sure she was ready for it. "The words you speak are dangerous."

The Red Wing's new General Prime stepped closer to her. He could touch her, if only he reached out a hand. His voice was low. "We are coming into dangerous times. I will not live in fear of dangerous words."

"Why... are you here?" she asked him again, her hushed tone mirroring his.

Roskaad smiled at her. "You are smart enough to make deductions from the work we have done together. When Nelfindar begins to... change..." He stared at nothing for an overlong moment. "I want you fighting on my side."

He drew closer still. Fates. Eighteen months. Eighteen months, and now he chose to make a pass at her? When he was leaving? She couldn't tell if she was more surprised by his timing or by the revelation that she almost wanted him to. Almost.

"Of course you do." She returned his real smile with a lopsided tilt of her mouth, restraining a bitter laugh that might have surfaced if she hadn't been so afraid of what she was about to do. "Any right mind politician in Seraphinden would. I am with unparalleled benefits."

But so was he. With the General Prime on her side, she and Thedexemore could have immunity from whatever Hashod had planned. The moment had come. She made a split-second decision she knew would take her into uncharted water: she stepped closer to Roskaad and slid her hand into his.

A hesitation—

—and then warm fingers gripped hers back in triumph. She trembled despite herself. Saw his amber arms prickle with gooseflesh, too.

"So," she asked, trying to keep her breathing level past the catch in her chest. "What it like for castaway groundling child to become most powerful man outside of oligarchy?"

His hands pulled her toward him until their bodies connected. "There aren't words to describe it."

She hummed, brushing nails against his hair, the way she'd learned to with so many before. "So it is about power?"

He gave her a testing expression. "You would tell me that it is not about power? You, as both a woman and a refugee, who has risen to become the most prominent scientist in all of Nelfindar."

Was that how he saw her? No one had ever venerated her like that before... and yet, for all she had achieved, she felt she had gained nothing. All she'd ever wanted was to practice distortion without restraints. But at what cost? Her father? Her people's trade secrets? Her loyalty?

"Is not power that I desire," she whispered to him. "Is possibility."

"Are the two not one and the same?"

She had to give Roskaad credit. Even if they were spoken in the Nelfinden tongue, his words were beautiful. For the first time in sixteen years, she felt seen, but not for her face. She leaned into his chest.

"I... I didn't expect this," he said. She could feel him holding his breath. He was just as afraid as she was.

"Do you have problem with me, Roskaad?" she asked again.

"No. I—I don't think I've ever been more attracted to a person in all my life." The man actually stuttered.

She looked up at him. "I want you tell me what will happen."

Roskaad's brown eyes darted to the corners of the room. "You know I can't do that. Not here."

"I am in trouble. And worried for my brother."

His voice lowered to a whisper. "You are. And I know. But this isn't the right place."

Her heart launched against her ribcage as if thrown by a tanka. "Then let us go somewhere else," she replied, hoping he wouldn't hear the unease in her own suggestion.

He didn't respond at first. And then he leaned in and kissed her with an abruptness that took her by surprise. His entire body was stiff with uncertainty.

She kissed him back, letting her lips melt into his. Roskaad warmed to her, his arms pulling around her waist, sealing any gap between them.

It was time to find some answers. And she'd get them the way she often did—speaking the only language, besides distortion, she was fluent in.

The moon had sunk low in the sky when Attilatia lifted her head off Roskaad's chest. His private room in the Red Wing barracks was not far from her home.

"I should be with Thedexemore," she said sheepishly. He would have been sleeping, but she wanted to ensure she'd be back before he woke to leave. "You make sure he safe?"

"No one will lay a hand on him."

For the first time in weeks, she felt the tightness in her chest ease. Aetech might have planned to do away with her, but with Roskaad's protection, they might just make it another few months. Until she figured out how to get them out of Nelfindar for good.

"I'm still not sure I believe that any of this is real."

Her brows knitted together. "You have lovers before?"

"Not... not in a long time. I've been so focused on the Red Wing. Working too late and gone too often to get to know someone."

"They have prostitutes, you know?" she snorted.

He offered a halfway smile that didn't come close to his eyes. "That was my late mother's life, so you might imagine how the idea lacks appeal."

Fates, but he was half-decent, wasn't he? She set a hand on his arm. "I guess you a natural, eah?"

It was time for her to go. But they lay in comfortable silence until—

"You cut your hair," he commented, as though he too sought a reason to linger.

"You is just noticing?"

He chuckled. "Really, it's all I could see for the first few minutes I waited for your attention. But... it looks better this way. Shows more of your face."

Heat radiated from Attilatia's chest into her extremities so profusely, she was sure Roskaad would feel the need to shed the sheets. He didn't. He brushed her short locks away from her eyes instead, which only made the matter worse. It was a Seraphinden heat wave.

"Don't trust Hashod." Roskaad's brows were lowered.

The words only strengthened Attilatia's resolve in trusting *him*. She considered her response: *obviously*. But she would gain nothing from lowering his ego, so she settled for a subtle nod.

To keep herself from fidgeting with the glass bead of her bracelet, she moved her fingertips to caress the scarring around Roskaad's collarbone. It was such a strange and specific mark, it almost looked intentional. "What this, then?"

Roskaad shifted slightly onto his side beneath the sheets to look at her. "A training accident," he said. "I was a fool with a dowaga when my military years began."

He may not trust Hashod, but he'd sure as sunrise taken tips from him. The dexemore might have procured a better lie.

Attilatia resettled into the crook beneath his arm. "Your secret safe with me. Can not let your fan club know, eah? Most of them would no to believe you can bleed."

He pulled his arm tighter around her. "Attilatia—"

"Atti," she corrected him.

"I've been thinking... Maybe don't drink that wine. Save it. And we can have it together when I return."

That was definitely suspicious. And he was definitely trustworthy. "Is you crazy? That good wine."

He hugged her tighter still. "I'd be honored if you considered it."

"Maybe, for you, I resist."

Chapter 27

Niklaus

Niklaus sat in the back row of the Red Wing's recruitment ward in Korshuva district. Of the roughly fifty chairs set up in the room, only about ten were occupied—an unnoteworthy showing. Understandable in this district, as upper-class men from Korshuva didn't often join the Red Wing unless they were social dregs or had family in high command. He set his feet on the backs of the vacant chairs in front of him, watching the recruitment lieutenant at the front of the room over his toes.

"Well," the lieutenant started, "we're a few minutes overdue, so I'll assume this is all I can expect for today's information session. Let's begin."

The withered old man had a throaty voice and a fluffy white mustache which quivered when he spoke. Fates, he didn't exactly look motivational. Was the Red Wing under-staffed, or...?

"The Red Wing's annual recruitment will begin with a three-week enlistment tour. In two days' time, we will travel by distortion locomotive from Seraphinden south-west to Fenaeatia, then to Gemboldt, and finally end in Chira'na, collecting new recruits and supplies for the basic training campaign." The lieutenant cleared his throat, turning his previous mustache quiver into a convulsion. "We will leave Chira'na as part of the northbound caravan, one of the most honored military traditions in Nelfindar's history."

He spoke monotonously, as though he'd repeated the same words a hundred times.

Niklaus picked that moment to remove a street-peddled bag of popped corn from his satchel. It made a tremendous amount of noise, eliciting a number of stares, including the orator's. Kretch. Perhaps if there had been more people in the room, the whole thing would feel a smidge less awkward. But then again, a part of him knew the whole reason he'd dug into the bag in the first place was due to his unwitting desire to challenge social propriety.

He waved to the lieutenant as if to say *carry on, then*. How could one be expected to infiltrate the General Prime's ranks without snacks?

The old soldier raised his eyebrows at Niklaus before licking cracked lips. He cleared his throat with a hoarse cough that nearly caused his mustache to fly off his face—Chaos, this felt more like a recruitment for a sunset home—and dove back into his drone.

"For the next three months, you will spend three hours each day training in the art of the dowaga, cosalt squadron formation..."

Ideally, Niklaus would find a way to sit that part out.

"...as is tradition, six hours marching through the Jiradesh..."

Sure, think of the most sadistic training regime imaginable and call it "tradition." One had to appreciate the impregnated mindsets of a martial nation.

"...until you reach the rendezvous point in Steila, where you will merge with the Blue Wing..."

What did the Blue Wing even do anymore? What with the raiders seizing every other ship and Prime Taranil's trade embargo against anything beyond Nelfinden waters?

"...a week-long journey by Blue Wing vessel back to Seraphinden, at which point you will be ceremonially inducted as a Red Wing soldier." The lieutenant paced slowly at the front of the room, hands crossed behind his back. His demeanor changed, softening, as though he'd just fondly remembered something. "This journey will allow you to learn what kind of a man you truly are—one of the rarest pieces of knowledge a person can attain. Not only will it test your physical and mental limits to an extent beyond what you imagine to be possible, but you will learn of camaraderie and brotherhood... forge relationships that will last for the rest of your life."

His voice drifted away feebly, as though he'd only just realized that he was speaking to an audience of ten, rather than several hundred. He cleared his throat once more, then plowed into a long-winded breakdown of extreme expectations, minimal compensation, and nominal resource allocation. Two members of their small audience had vacated the room by the time he finished.

"I hope to see you all arrive at the locomotive port at firstlight in two days' time, when the Red Wing's next recruitment journey begins. Ah... are there any questions?"

That was it? No explanation of political incentives, training benefits, or risk versus reward? The entire thing seemed like it was designed to dissuade the upper-class from joining. It was marketed as an opportunity for those at rock bottom, not one for those trying to establish a name for themselves.

Niklaus rocketed his hand into the air, waggling it from side to side. "I've got one."

The few men in the room turned to look at him, taking in his clashing orange tunic and scarlet sirwal with exasperated expressions. He'd made sure to leave the gold enamel buttons unbuttoned; one could nearly smell the wealthy indifference.

The lieutenant scanned the room as if for any other option. "Yes?" Of course, he recognized Niklaus.

"Isn't the point of this lecture to, you know, convince us to join the Red Wing? I mean, if there's something I'm missing, forgive me. But there wasn't anything in the experience you just casually ran through that elicits delight."

The lieutenant blinked. "You're saying that pride, self-worth, and brotherhood sound unattractive?"

"I'm saying you don't have to torture yourself in blistering conditions to get it." Niklaus upended the corn bag over his mouth, emptying it of remaining crumbs and hoping it would prevent him from continuing the tirade. But the latent manipulation behind this session was so crystal clear to him, his compulsion to keep mocking was like the compulsion to drink. He simply could not dissuade himself from the next swig. "And as for camaraderie and brotherhood—say one of the guys in your squadron is, for example, unnaturally unpalatable. And once the recruitment is over, he keeps holding 'brotherhood' and 'camaraderie' over your head, even though you never really liked him in the first place."

Niklaus idly picked a piece of corn from his teeth and flicked it onto the floor. He wanted to stop. Wished he could stop. But his tongue was the only weapon he had, and he wielded it like any boy with a good stick.

The lieutenant stuttered, "I-I'm not quite sure what you're trying to—"

"And another thing." Niklaus opened a second bag and chewed as he spoke. "You haven't properly educated us on what our future will look like. Is there any longevity ensured here? Based on the fact that you could be my grandfather and you're still running this show, I take it you would have us assume that the retirement benefits aren't all glamorous."

Was this a defense mechanism to cover up the terror Niklaus felt, knowing how bold his next move was going to be? He hadn't always been like this, had he? He'd been the funny guy, sure, but he hadn't been cruel or pointedly objectionable to get there. It wasn't like his mocking would cause the lieutenant to admit that Thyatira only wanted to recruit the most destitute of groundlings, not the middle class. Those without loyalties to the oligarchy or Aetech's economy, so he could mold them into pawns for his uprising.

The man's face reddened like the sun setting over the Casowhatan. "Now see here—"

Niklaus jumped up and cut him off again. "I'm just batting at your tail, Lieut." He forced a chuckle and a placating gesture. "Really. I'm emotionally intoxicated at the thought of building my character and facing horribly miserable conditions. Fates only know I could use a fresh adventure and new smiling faces."

He put his arm around the startled man, who looked unsure as to whether he should pull away or punch him. The lieutenant conceded with a sigh. "What are you even *doing* here, Mesu Meyernes?"

Becoming the man Latouda had wanted him to be.

The question hung in the air between them; a bubble of excitement stirred in Niklaus, removing any trace of his creeping uncertainty. "Well... because you asked. There's this distillery outside Chira'na that makes an excellent rye. At the bottom of every bottle they put a dragonfly, native to the grasses of that region. Ensures its quality. And, if you get the dragonfly in your glass, it's supposed to be a promise of Preservation's fortune."

"Mesu Meyer—"

"You asked what I was doing here. Hang with me, lieut. I'll get there."

Niklaus pulled the man toward the window, so excited to articulate the thoughts frothing to the front of his mouth that he'd almost forgotten where he was or who he was speaking to.

"You see, yesterday I had this moment where I found something at the bottom of my glass. Not a dragonfly. No. Something intangible. But I found it all the same—a change. Like I was suddenly sober for the first time in... a long, long time. But it wasn't just my head. It was a full-body understanding, so strong it touched my bones. My blood. My breath. Something shifted. And it was like I was reset, along with the next glass from the bar. Have you ever felt something like that?" He clenched the hand that wasn't around the lieutenant's shoulders into a fist. Shook it.

The lieutenant looked at him like he'd poured out a twenty-year directly onto the dirt just to smell it.

"It's all coming to me now," Niklaus continued, wishing he could stop talking. "Most would think my psychotic break last year was a negative thing. But now I'm realizing it was just the jostling I needed. To become the thing I've always wanted but never quite knew how to unpack. I'm thinking, maybe sometimes you need to hit your own low to see how high your peak can be."

The lieutenant shook his head. Opened his mouth. Closed it.

"I'm not making sense?" Niklaus didn't wait for a response. "Let me start again. Have you ever looked in the mirror and told yourself you're just not what you want to be? Of course. Who doesn't? But you see, if you tell yourself that, of course you won't ever be. Your own mind will always find a way to ruin your best intentions. Like, if you don't trust in yourself, why in Preservation's beard would anybody else?"

He just kept speaking faster, worried now that if he didn't get the words out of his mouth, his newfound boldness might vanish into thin air.

"But remember? I found that change. It was at the bottom of a glass, just like a fated dragonfly. It was what I needed all along to turn heartbreak into motivation. To figure out something no one else can. To keep looking where everyone else decides to look away.

"What am I doing here? I'm here because I'm following the natural course of things. From the bottom, all things will rise. I scraped my knuckles on the seabed of that glass, and I'm taking its treasure back up with me. I'm taking back the fated reins. I'm in control of my life again."

The lieutenant suddenly wrestled free from the weight of Niklaus's arm, which fell lamely to his side. "The words you are speaking," he said slowly, "are complete nonsense. Is there someone I can call on to—"

Niklaus took a step back. Fates above, he was rusty. Hadn't he once had a way with words? "I'm here to enlist in the Red Wing. What does it look like?"

The lieutenant looked for a moment as though he might vomit. "Ah... that. Well... I see."

✺

An elation struck Niklaus like he hadn't experienced in long months as he left the recruitment building. He grinned so widely his cheeks hurt. An inadvertent bounce came with each step, and his jubilation bottlenecked until he broke into an easy run.

It lasted no more than twenty steps. First off, he realized how absurd it was, running through the streets. Why not wear a sign proclaiming in bold letters "I'm on to you, Thyatira!" instead? Second, he was grotesquely deconditioned to doing anything more than sitting on barstools and the walks between them. He slowed, panting, and paused to bend over with hands on his knobby knees.

"What are you running from? The past, present, or future?"

The gentle voice came from a doorstep to his left. It belonged to a middle-aged man with a kindly smile but playful stare. He wore the belted robe and forehead band of a Chori mystic—a fortuneteller of sorts, if you could call the schemers that.

But Niklaus had never seen a Chori mystic in the Korshuva district before, and certainly never one so well-dressed. His robe was a rich shade of saffron and clean as any item worn by a lady on the skywalk. His posture on the doorstep was lackadaisical, his expression easy. Niklaus felt drawn to him in the way one was drawn to any anomaly.

He chuckled in reply, still recovering his breath from a single block of exercise. "It's not what I'm running from. It's what I'm running to."

"And that is?"

"Freedom, my friend. Change."

His words met the porcelain white of the mystic's smile. "The future, then. Tell me, would you have an interest in a game of stackers?"

"I might," Niklaus replied, but his spine stiffened with inadvertent wariness. Everyone knew not to trust a Chori mystic. He remembered what his mother had told him long ago. *They have but one intent, Nikla: to put up a façade of tales and fortunes and be sure to rob you dry.* "Would you prefer a game of stackers to telling a story and my fortune, then?"

The man barked a laugh. "You are a man of truth, aren't you? Ah, I suppose I'm no good at stackers, true. But I'll give you a story and a fortune if that is your wish."

Niklaus sighed. He was diving headfirst into the man's con. But he'd never spoken to a mystic before. Why not see how it played out?

"I've got nowhere better to be for a day," he said, joining the man on the stoop. He retrieved his flask from a pocket, took a burning swig, and set it back again. "How does this work?"

The mystic grinned at him with teeth too white and straight to seem real. He flipped a rattling stackers box seemingly out of thin air and unfolded it into a pegged board, pushing the dozens of rings inside it to its rim. Painted in gold and purple across the board's dark, polished wood was the likeness of a dragonfly.

Niklaus raised his eyebrows. This was not what he'd been told to expect from Chori mystics.

The mystic, however, was entirely unconcerned with Niklaus. His eyes fell into the space beyond, vacant in a trance-like way. Niklaus recoiled when he opened his mouth to speak. His voice had altered from its previous charming calm into something melodic and dark and—well, there was no other way to say it—inhuman.

"The tapestry of our universe is woven with infinite threads of infinite colors. Infinitely small. Infinitely large. Until the small become large and the large become small. From the furthest fathomable perspective, which no man can see, these threads compose the galactic dragonfly, as you see before you." He motioned to the stackers board, and Niklaus could have sworn that the patterns on each wing shifted before he blinked. "The dragonfly is ever-moving, ever-changing, but its direction is always held in balance by the four winds—wings—of Fate."

In a flurry of motion, the Chori pinched four rings into his fingers and placed them on pegs at opposing corners of the board. Then he pointed to them each in turn. "Creation, Preservation, Chaos, and Destruction. The four Fates work in tandem to create homeostasis, keeping one another's actions in check. They commune with the world using the infinite threads to manipulate the workings of the universe, from the micro to the macro."

Niklaus bit his lip. This wasn't a story, it was a sermon. Why was it that generosity always landed him in these situations?

A shadow crossed the Chori's face. "But the Fates weren't the only ones who held sway over these veins of happenstance. There were others. Gaining control over them, these 'conduits of Fate,' could give the Four advantage over their own discretions. Destruction found such a conduit on our plane, which allowed him to wreak havoc on all the land. We call this occurrence the Cataclysm."

Niklaus held up a hand. "The Cataclysm? You mean the natural disaster almost a millennium ago caused by a series of *scientifically explained* phenomena?"

The Chori stared blankly forward. "Science. Magic. Fates. They are one, wearing different faces for those with differing levels of perception."

Niklaus shook his head. "You accredit the Cataclysm to the Fates?"

"Not to the *Fates*," the mystic corrected him, "but Destruction alone."

Niklaus shifted, itching to leave.

The mystic proceeded. "After the Cataclysm, Destruction was discovered by other conduits from the opposing Fates. His own conduit was destroyed. Then he was imprisoned here on Kath, to live tormented by his own inability to act for all eternity."

There had been worse uses of his time, but the tale was not, thus far, impressive. It should have been what he expected.

The mystic paused before lacing his voice with foreboding. "The lovers, Chaos and Preservation, set about to ensure the demise of any other conduit which might commune with Destruction, so he could never wreak havoc again." He held up a finger and waggled it. "But... the Fates live in a constant flux. One the universe depends upon. Destruction will return, conduit or not. And when he does, he will act with such a fury so as to make up for his years of impotence all in one moment, causing all creatures to fear his name and, should they survive, live the rest of their mortal lives in darkness."

The mystic's tale ended with the same suddenness it had begun, inflicting an impressive moment of discomfort. Niklaus swallowed. "Not exactly an upper, that one."

The mystic remained in dramatic silence.

This needed to be over with. "Ok... so we have the story behind us. What about my fortune?"

The mystic gave him a wry smile, voice returning to its prior casualness. "But of course." He gestured to the hundred and forty rings set to the side of the stackers board. "Place them as you wish. From this, your fortune will be told."

"Ahhhh." Niklaus tapped the tips of his fingers together. "That was more involvement than I realized I was in for. Aren't you supposed to cast some leaves or sticks or something and then read them?"

The Chori only chuckled at him, as if to say, *You wish*. "Fate is predetermined—at least to a certain, conceivable point. But your own life's fortune is entirely up to you. How can I determine the outcome that you will choose for yourself—your destiny? Do not be rash in your placement. Be particular. Place with intent." He sat back against the doorframe to wait.

Niklaus's mouth twisted. He'd bet a drink this mystic didn't actually believe in this stuff any more than he did. It was fanfare. He nearly proffered an excuse, a reason to leave, but the insistence of the man made him pause.

Intrigue got the better of him. "Alright then. Let's get started."

He spent the next few minutes placing the rings on the board's pegs, one at a time. It was meticulous for a task which was inherently pointless, but he did it all the same, setting the pieces wherever he felt they belonged, leaving some pegs empty while stacking others seven high.

When he'd finished, he gestured dramatically. "Look, and be amazed!"

The mystic, who had leaned back with eyes closed while Niklaus worked, examined the board. His brow furrowed deeper with each passing breath. "I've never seen..."

"Never seen a man grow rich, fall in love, and have seven children?" Niklaus quipped.

The mystic shook his head, shoulders rolling back, spine straighter than the pegs on the board. "Never seen anything so closely aligned with Destruction. You will repeatedly choose to align yourself with Destruction, time and time again." His hands gripped either side of his face. "Not just destruction unto yourself—that is one thing. No, it is almost as though you serve as a minion to the Fate of Destruction. You follow in his wake, wreaking havoc wherever you go. For you... I see a life of unhappiness, turmoil, and suffering."

Niklaus broke out into laughter—which quickly faltered. He looked at the Chori man, expecting a cracked smile or some joviality. But the man looked positively morose. He cupped his jaw with his hands, staring at the board as though trying to make sense of it.

Fates above, if it was ever time to go...

"Well, this has been—" He paused, deliberating. "An experience. I do appreciate your time. What do I owe you?"

One did not leave a Chori mystic without payment, or they would find themselves far worse for wear down the road. The low hum of passersby, carts, seabirds, and the susurrus of the neighbor's broom filled the space between them.

"Nothing," the mystic finally said. "There is nothing more I wish from you. I simply bid unto you good luck. And remember, you have the reins to control your own fortune. I hope you will, and you will do so wisely."

It was a clear dismissal.

"I insist." Niklaus reached for his pocket of notes. "Could I perhaps—"

"No!" The mystic coughed and corrected himself with a gentle, "No. Thank you. It was a pleasure to have the story and conversation. Happy fates unto you."

"Right. Well... thanks." Niklaus stood, looked down at the mystic for a moment with a frown, and then turned to walk away.

He looked to the sky. It was nearing mid lowsun, and he would have much preparation to do once he arrived home. There was not too little time for a good drink, however—something he needed after *that* atrocious encounter.

He found an open seat at the Korshuva tavern, only minutes away. The place was famous for its liquors distilled from apples.

"A double of your house special," he said to the barkeep as he reached into his pocket for his purse.

Feeling for his notes, he frowned. The shratten thing was full of feathers.

He looked closer, before upending it over the counter. Feathers flitted across it in every direction to stick to the fluid splashed across the bar. More than a few patrons glared at him and shifted their positions away from him.

"Kretch," he muttered, more impressed than depressed. "Would you take a note of credit?"

The barkeep pointed to the door.

Niklaus's fingers twitched. Then he pulled a moss tab from his pocket tin and let it dissolve on his tongue as he left. Not only had that mystic been one of the worst fortune-tellers he ever heard of, but he had literally robbed him dry.

Chapter 28

Calverous

Every library had a forgotten corner. Not forgotten altogether or specifically a corner, but in that its books had faded from fashion. The books there found a certain stillness, a time to absorb what had been imprinted from intangible thought into retrievable meaning. Whether or not they would ever be read was down to an ever-changing ratio of the number of educated minds to the rate at which paper decayed.

Calver and Raimee spent the end of the morning searching for such a corner in the Repository so she could read freely, away from the eyes of other patrons. They settled on a nook at the very end of a row of outdated encyclopedias written in Chori calligraphy. The books sat in perfect alignment, as though they hadn't been touched since the last library worker had ordered them. A film of dust coated the floor; as Raimee plopped to the ground with her dozen-volume tower, it plumed around her and resettled at her feet.

She leaned against a bookcase to read with a child-like smile. "Finally, I can put my arse to use."

<*Keep the glasses on,*> Calver signaled to her as she pulled them to her hairline. <*Just in case.*>

He caught the glimmer of her silver glare, but she obeyed. She was probably so overjoyed to be back to books, she'd lost any will to retort.

"No more caves," she said, opening a volume so stiff its spine creaked in protest. "Let's just stay here, eah?"

As she settled in, Calver paced the row, fidgeting with a knife in his pocket. Fankalo's letter ground against his nerves, threatening to burn a hole. She knew how Calver felt about engaging the new General Prime. That he'd advised against it.

What was he missing about this that made it anything other than a terrible idea?

The Survivor's voice flitted forward on his anger. {*You are just a means to an end for Fankalo now. Nothing more. It can only be expected for new alliances to be forged, once you've* been blown to bits. This has turned to a contest for rule. And it is not contingent on your best interests.}

Void.

For eighteen months, Fankalo had kept him at arm's distance. Fine. But Calver had thought it was to protect him, after the damage he'd done, from the code the Ghosts kept. They should have executed him, not exiled him, for his crimes—and would have, had he been someone else without the niche knowledge that would bring down an empire.

Now Fankalo was treating him like he'd borrowed that time. Lying. Pulling away.

Would this make it easier when he ultimately pressed the activator at the Tera'thian coronation?

"What's eating you?"

Calver blinked from his melancholy.

"Yes, you," Raimee said. "Did you think I was talking to the stacks?"

<You do love books.>

He imagined her rolling her eyes behind those thick oculars. They were still aimed expectantly at him.

Calver caved. <The day you found me in the Sharinash,> he began to signal. Then stopped. *No.* He paced again until Raimee cleared her throat.

"Calver, your secrets die with me."

Not under torture, they wouldn't.

But her words tore at him, because he knew with all of his being that she meant them... and, given her failing condition, that she might keep that promise sooner than she'd bargained. His hands moved before he could rethink the trap of human weakness he'd fallen into: divulging information to the only person he'd had meaningful contact with in over a year.

<I witnessed a troop of Tera'thian soldiers impersonating Chira'na guardsmen unload a shipment of distortion technology bound for Red Wing headquarters.>

That was fine.

Fine.

He'd said nothing that would condemn him or Fankalo.

"That's why they were chasing you?"

<Possibly.>

Or because Cul'Mon had finally found a way to ambush him in Nelfinden territory. The possibilities were so closely woven together he had trouble deciphering one thread from another.

"The Red Wing is Nelfindar's military ground force, right?"

He nodded.

"And Nelfindar isn't at war with Tera'thia?"

Calver ground his teeth. How did one explain the turbulent situation to which none were privy to but him, having served Cul'Mon, the Tera'thian tohatu, for six years against his will? That the Nelfinden oligarchy had blinded its people from the fact that, in the years since the embargo, Tera'thia had invaded half the world. That they were next. That, unless Fankalo was successful, it was only a matter of time...

He settled for: <*But Tera'thia is at war with Nelfindar.*>

She picked up every connotation, brows pinching, hand finding her mouth. "What does it mean?"

<*I don't know.*> He shifted. Pursed his lips. Ran another void mantra through his mind when the Survivor stirred again. <*But if a shipment like that never made it to the Red Wing, there would be news. So if the shipment was delivered to the correct location with the correct contents, what was the Tera'thians' objective?*>

His anxiety mounted, even while sharing his logic with Raimee relieved it. He crossed his arms to stop himself from hurling his dowaga down the aisle.

She looked at him seriously. "Maybe the objective wasn't to prevent the plates from going to the Red Wing Headquarters. Maybe the objective was to ensure that they did."

Calver frowned.

"But you've already thought of that, haven't you?" She squinted at him from behind the black lenses. "There's something else bothering you."

She could take her pick. He was smuggling a mythical Ruxian into Chira'na. Fankalo was keeping secrets from him. The Tera'thians might be tampering with hitherto unknown Red Wing defense technology. And her 'Methu'su' had been a close friend to his father—a national traitor.

He hadn't told her he'd remembered the latter. In his experience, such coincidences were never a positive thing. And with an actual promise at meeting the man, it weighed on him more with each passing second. He'd resented Thadinar Curtaim for two decades. The last thing he wanted to do was converse with an old friend of his.

Calver returned to pacing. Right now, all he needed to focus on was the afternoon's meeting with Greeny. Greeny's information might just point him to a Nelfinden insider on the Tera'thian infiltration that had thwarted his demolition.

He looked at Raimee, realizing he'd left her question suspended. She'd chosen to leave him to his thoughts and was well settled into a second book, a title on anthills.

Preservation...

Calver's stomach churned. He was missing something important. That, and the continual reminders of his parents were emotionally overbearing. Clawing up his throat, making him feel the need to move or collapse or otherwise break something.

The Survivor took its chance. It pressed forward with more force than it had put on him in days—and he relinquished. Fates, he needed the release. To not feel. To—

—*wait.*

Falling into a numb embrace was so second-nature, he'd nearly forgotten the repercussions.

We don't touch her.

Its bloodlust boiled, roiling through his veins, making him want to—

He strangled off its progression.

Void. Fucking VOID.

Fates, that had been too close. One slip-up like that, and he would commit genocide. The Survivor continued to wrestle its way forward, wearing at him. Calver's body stiffened as he resisted the talons it dug in, trying to keep its hold.

Halfway, he bargained with it.

{For now.}

The pressure abated in an instant. The Survivor did not. And the constriction in his chest found a point somewhere in between.

A slight smile pulled at the Ruxian's cheeks where she read on the floor. Calver still felt a slow, burning hate from the mind-djinn, but its more savage impulses diminished.

He rapped on the bookshelf beside him for her attention. <*I have somewhere to be.*>

"What?" She snapped the tome shut and hopped to her feet, only to nearly collapse as one leg gave out. She steadied herself with a hand against the shelves. "You're not meaning to leave me here?"

<*I'll return by evening. Stay. Read.*>

She clutched her elbows. "I... I can read later. I want to go with you."

It reminded him chillingly of his sister, all those years ago.

<You need to stay out of sight. And to recover—I can tell you're struggling. You'll be safe here.>

Raimee rocked on her feet, looking for all the world like a frightened child.

She couldn't come. Not only would it put them both in danger for violating the Ghosts' code, but Fankalo would find out. And the woman could hardly walk.

{She has learned too much already.}

"I don't... I won't... please just..." She trailed off, fidgeting with her kaftan.

<What is your problem?>

"I *am* coming with you," she demanded.

Great. A Ruxian princess. <No. You're not. It's too dangerous.>

Calver noted the sunkenness of her face. She looked like she needed a hospital, not a walk across the city. Even if she could be trusted, there was no way he could go about business with Greeny toting along a...

A translator.

A spark of excitement bit him. He'd have an actual translator, for once. The thought was tempting. Too tempting.

No. No, it wasn't worth it. Risks aside, Fankalo would find out and—

Fankalo was involving them in Thyatira's schemes. Behind Calver's back. After every warning he'd given. If Fankalo took issue with him bringing along a translator—

{Fool. You are an absolute fool.}

VOID. Chaos, why had he let the mind-djinn back out? It was the reason all of this had happened. Why Fankalo wanted nothing to do with him. He hated it. He hated the way he depended on it. That he was too weak to handle his own emotions.

All color drained from Raimee's face. Thin as she was, it made her look like a corpse. Her fear was raw and real, and it made his stomach turn. "Calver, you're not trying to..."

The words left unsaid burned more than any brand ever had. She thought he was planning to betray her?

Kretch. Why did he even give a damn?

<Fine. Come with me.> He crossed his arms.

"Really?" Her relief was palpable.

No. It was too much of a risk. He would take her to the Creation temple. It was on the way, and he'd heard there was an arboretum there with plants from around the world. Maybe she'd be exhausted enough to want to stay.

<Yes. But I need you to remember that, if I were going to sell you, I would have done it by now. And I do want you out of my hair. I want it more than anything. I can't wait to not answer eight hundred questions every hour.>

It was a lie so immense that she could see it from leagues away. Her face split into an incredible smile which, in an instant of poor judgment, might have been worth getting them both killed for.

<But lucky for you, I'm patient enough to take you to Methu'su first.>

"Thank you. Calver, I... I'm sorry I..."

He sighed. <You don't understand.> He clenched and unclenched his fists. <The man I'm going to meet with would happily cut you open just to check out what color your blood is.> And with Fate on his side, she wouldn't meet him. She would sit happily on a bench in the temple, studying the bark on some tree. <And I work in discretion.>

She signaled to him for the first time in a couple days. <You can trust me.>

Calver didn't know what was worse: that he actually believed her, or that the words further implied she could destroy everything he'd worked for over the past decade. <Let's go. The day is passing quickly.>

Raimee cast a longing look at her pile of books.

<There are actual cobwebs in this corner. Your books will certainly be here when we return.>

"Right." She nodded, her face set with determination, and grabbed her cane, a thing she realistically needed for support now.

<You're positive you want to come? Think of all the wonderful things you could learn about anthills while I'm gone.>

"Now you're toying with me, eah? I'm coming."

As they headed northeast toward the moss district, Calver remembered something he'd once read in a book on psychological ailments—it was one Fankalo had given him, probably in hopes of figuring out what was wrong with him. There was a direct correlation between a person's body language and their internal state. Raimee had warmed right back up to him after her swinging distrust. Calver hadn't spent so much time with one person in years, but he knew her behavior wasn't right. The Ruxian was hiding something from him. It didn't feel nefarious; more like she'd recently caught on to something about him she didn't want him to know she knew. He would almost rather it *was* nefarious.

She continued to marvel under her breath at every trivial thing—a blind person who spoke to herself. They passed a slew of shaded carts peddling shining trinkets of every shape and size, and she fell away from him.

"Oh look, Calver. A dragonfly." She seized a stained-glass pendant the size of a walnut and held it up for him to see.

The bemused shop-keep stared at the blind girl, leaning against her cane to hold the colored glass trinket up to the light. Calver slid him a stack of silver notes, far more than the thing was worth, to prevent any kind of scene. Then he grabbed Raimee, pendant in hand like a trophy, and steered her away into a crowded section of the street. The traffic molded around them, camouflage from any unwanted onlookers.

<*What were you thinking?*>

"Sorry, I forgot to be blind. Hah!"

Capture. Enslavement. Death. These were only textbook terms to her. She was hopeless. Nothing he could do would help her once she was—

Raimee elbowed him. "Put a lid on, grouchy. There are too many people for anyone to suspect us."

Calver voided a wave of anger, not wanting to invite the Survivor into his headspace. He glanced around to see if anyone was staring. There were gambles he could afford, and others he couldn't. And there were Tera'thians in this city. He would not put everything on the line for flippancy, no matter his frustrations with Fankalo. He scowled at her.

She only teased him further. "And didn't you say you were trying to get rid of me? Buying me a present is not a very hard push." A hand lifted to her mouth to hide her grin as she pocketed the dragonfly.

<*It wasn't a fated present. I was just getting you to move before you got us beheaded.*>

She sighed. "And just like that, you've ruined it for me."

They moved slowly, matching the appropriate pace for a blind woman and her escort through a crowded city. But it wasn't an act anymore. Raimee struggled to walk. Each footstep leadened until he was nearly dragging her and her cane. Kretch. Not inconspicuous in the least. She said nothing, clearly pushing her body past the point it should have gone. As they approached the Creation temple, Calver prepared his lure. 'A chance to rest your feet,' he would signal. 'You're a botanist, right?'

She beat him to it.

"Calver..." Even her voice was feeble. "What is that?" She raised a shaking finger toward the dome, rising into view above the rows of carts peddling fruits from tropical Seraphinden.

<*A temple. To honor Creation.*>

"A monastery?"

He nodded.

"Would you mind if we...?"

<*Not at all.*> He nearly lifted a prayer of thanks.

A moment later, Raimee's knees buckled beneath her. Calver snared her by her elbow, his insides snaring on something impalpable. *Just muscle fatigue*, he told himself. She was in far worse shape than he'd imagined, and a half-day of walking had been too much.

Raimee cursed—the first time he'd heard her do so—and gave him a look that, without opening her mouth, begged *don't leave me*.

As if he would.

Given the way he had acted, it was no wonder she thought otherwise.

Frowning, he scooped her from the ground. She didn't weigh anything, as if she was immaterial. Something akin to dread clawed at him, then.

A merchant stepped from behind the closest stand. "Does she need help? A doctor? I can run ahead."

Calver couldn't say anything, and now there were eyes on them, all around. He put his head down and increased his stride, hoping to race his own heartbeat. The temple was just a minute away, but he thought for the second time that day that maybe Raimee wouldn't live long enough to support his efforts in delivering her to Methu'su. And when that curtain of thought parted, an infinite number of others did as well. What would he do with the body? And then what? Would he just go to Karval? As if it had never happened? As if he'd never started to—

"I'm fine," Raimee said. "I just need a quick break." But her head lolled against his chest.

Through the crowd, parting in his wake.

Up the stairs to the temple.

Past its massive stone doors and into its foyer, so adorned with mosaics that there wasn't a stretch of plain wall. And then—

An impenetrable silence hit Calver like the wall of rain from a storm front. The chatter from the market vanished. The din of the street, the flapping of red flags in a growing wind—gone. His footsteps didn't echo.

The hairs on the back of his neck rose. Every part of his body screamed at him to leave. To vanish. Told him he didn't belong.

The doors shut behind them, unattended. Calver gulped and hurried through the domed foyer, toward the sunlight of a cloister rimmed by a colonnade. Granite benches were interspersed around the polished space, and he set Raimee on one before snapping to look for whatever it was that had him on edge. His fingers itched for his dowaga, but he hesitated; it was illegal to draw arms in a temple. The grassy quadrangle beside them was empty but for a singular tree at its center. Its limbs stretched so high they rivaled the silver dome of the foyer.

"I'm sorry," Raimee groaned, sitting up shakily. "Give me a moment. I can keep up. I just need—"

Calver missed what she needed. His body suddenly revolted against him, hardening like stone. He couldn't achieve a full breath.

{Get out,} the Survivor hissed with vehemence.

Yes. He had to. Something was wrong with this place—wrong with him. And they were all alone. Shouldn't there be a priest? Patrons?

"Calver," Raimee said. Her face was turned toward the tree. "Do you hear that?"

He couldn't hear anything except her. His panic climbed its way into his lungs.

{Get out.}

There was nothing in this temple except for the Survivor and dread.

And Raimee.

"It's like there's a voice in my head."

Chapter 29
Calverous

The assault of memories was akin to madness. <*Don't listen to it!*> he tried to warn her.

But her eyes locked forward. He attempted to vocalize something—to scream. Nothing happened.

Raimee stood from the bench. Her body trembled as she stepped toward the tree. "It wants us to come closer."

No! But Calver couldn't move. His limbs locked in place. His diaphragm was paralyzed. He couldn't even be sure that his heart was beating. This wasn't just terror, it was a physical force, binding him in tandem.

Soft tawny fingertips touched tree bark.

Near a hundred things happened at once. In an explosion of light, Raimee levitated from the ground, the air pooling around her in a spectrum of color. The tree billowed, its enormous branches creaking as they bent to meet her. Sound returned, all wind and chimes. Mobility returned; Calver dropped to his knees. Fear dissipated, displaced by an awe for beauty at its quintessence.

And the moment ended. Raimee's feet touched grass.

Calver scrambled to her. <*Don't let it in.*> The motions only passed along a morsel of the desperation he felt.

"What?"

<*The voice. Don't let it inside you.*>

"Well, I wouldn't. And even if that sounded remotely like a good idea, I can't. It's gone now."

Gone? Gone where? What was it? What had any of that been?

Raimee touched the back of his arm. "It—it's ok." She looked… different. Her skin had brightened. The deep contours of her face had filled. And while she was still rail-thin, she stood firmly.

Calver shuddered away from her touch. <*What happened?*>

"The tree told me there was a leak in me. And fixed it."

Boats had leaks. Not people.

But just weeks ago, there had been no Ruxians. No magic. Now there were floating people and talking trees and—

"Are you alright?"

Was *he* alright? He released a shaking breath. Fates, he was just glad to have his lungs back and the suffocating terror removed.

Raimee's brows pinched in concern. Fates, she *was* improved. Somehow.

With the steady pushing and pulling of oxygen, Calver's fear for her mortality abated. *'You look better,'* he almost signaled.

Inadequate. Stupid.

He rolled his shoulders. <*I don't think your tree voice was very fond of me,*> he signaled instead.

"No. It—well, it asked me if I wanted you terminated," she said, like she was reporting the weather.

The storm in his chest believed her. <*I take it you declined the offer.*>

"Well, of course. How else am I going to find Methu'su?"

Calver shuddered. <*Good to know where our priorities lie.*>

"Well, that and, if we're being honest, you're a much better cook than I." She looked at him expectantly for the span of several heartbeats.

His lips pressed into a line. <*I wasn't going to say anything.*>

"Certainly not." Her smile was like starlight, piercing through the inky darkness that clouded his every thought. He might have smiled back at the joke, had his neurons enough practice in wiring such a response.

It was time to keep moving. Even with the feeling gone, the memory still burned, and he wanted to be as far from this temple as possible.

Raimee was staring at him like she was waiting for him to signal something clever. Were they going to further address what just happened? Its impossibility, or—

Were these just the sort of things which happened when they were together? To be met without fixation. With simple acceptance.

<*I have somewhere to be,*> he tried. <*Do you want to stay here for a while and—*>

"No."

He didn't even bother to argue. <*Alright.*>

"Fates, I love trees," Raimee muttered as they walked, now unhindered, toward the moss district.

<*They seem to love you back,*> Calver answered. As though whatever had just happened was commonplace. As though magic was as normal as walking down the street. Calver was an agnostic. He tried not to think about what it meant that a tree in Creation's temple wasn't fond of him. Then again, if he were Creation, he wouldn't be fond of him either.

The moss district didn't have a hard perimeter; there was no monument to announce their arrival. But the city around them warped, the buildings withering and shrinking with every span. Raimee's mutterings of appreciation at everything she saw fell silent. They were no longer given a considerate breadth for her cane, but jostled by the city-goers bustling around them like so many ants through an artery.

They arrived at the entryway to Greeny's parlor and Raimee wrinkled her nose. Beside them, a balding man slept, propped against the adobe wall in a pool of his own piss.

The Ruxian's chin tucked into her neck. "This is not a nice place."

Great, she'd set some expectations.

<*No. Remember that I did not invite you.*>

She shifted from one foot to the next. "I am coming to better understand that."

<*Your simply being here may spell disaster for us both.*>

"I..." She stiffened, but held her head high. "I'll be more cautious—than I have been."

Calver pressed his thumbs against his fingers. He'd acted on frustration, insolence, bringing her here, not logic. And then—well, he didn't have a frame of reference for the other reasons he'd brought her.

He needed a translator. Raimee provided such a service. There was no argument to be had. Simple.

<*There are rules before we enter.*>

She leaned in closely, watching his hands.

<*First, don't say anything unless I tell you to. You are my interpreter, so you need to be watching my hands. That means you can't pass as blind. If anyone asks, you're light sensitive. An eye injury.*>

Skepticism was painted on her face, but she nodded.

<Next, don't take anything you're offered to eat or drink.>

She hesitated before nodding this time.

<I mean it, bottomless belly.>

She clucked her tongue. "Fine."

<Lastly, stay within arm's distance from me.>

"Easy enough."

<Are we clear?>

She bit her lip. Her nostrils flared. "All clear."

<Do you want to go back to the temple?>

She shook her head.

Exhaling, Calver held out his arm to her. He flinched as she took it, but it was a momentary thing. Her touch, as discomforting as it was, was becoming more familiar.

They passed into Greeny's domain. The guards stationed inside the door nodded to Calver, though their gazes lingered on Raimee. Any woman seen with him would be a cause for whispers. A cause for rumors. Ones that would fly quickly across the sea... to the Hand of the Shadewalker, who collected all whispers to be had.

Raimee drew closer as they navigated the corridors leading to the stones parlor. She glanced into a room to their left, where a stout man pressed a tab onto his tongue while several others writhed on the earthen floor around him. Another, clearly canopied, took their limp bodies and placed them into compromising positions. His cackles followed them as they turned around a bend in the corridor, where they nearly ran into a group of women without a scrap of clothing on. They giggled and jeered at Calver as they rounded into a separate enclave within Greeny's domain. In the alcove which separated them, a couple were engaged in aggressive relations. Raimee's mouth popped open at the moaning that followed them through the maze of rooms and curtains.

Calver maintained a stoic expression. This was the world outside of Tennca'Pui. It was better she at least saw it before he set her adrift in it.

In the stones parlor, Greeny sat in his usual position. Calver ignored the stares they gathered as he made for his table.

Greeny glanced up and cleared his throat. The men surrounding him dispersed as Calver sat. Raimee followed suit, silent as a phantom.

"You've brought a stranger into my home." Greeny didn't look at them as he spoke. "This is not within protocol."

Calver signaled, and Raimee interpreted. "I brought an interpreter this time. You left me no choice. The previous ones you provided were inadequate. And time is of consequence."

The calm monotony of her voice took Calver by surprise. She could play this game.

"Who is she?"

Raimee replied with prompt precision. Preservation, her understanding of signals had improved. "The Hand prefers not to share," Calver bluffed.

Greeny licked his teeth and leaned back, fiddling with the stones in his hand. "I didn't see no mark, Reaper. That tell me she ain't cleared. So, when I get knifed because she's a rat, who's goin' to be held accountable?"

Chaos. He'd known this would be a disaster from the start.

Calver leaned forward, signaling quickly. He hoped his size and bearing would conceal his insecurities. Raimee sharpened her voice in response to his body language. "Your doubt in my credibility, in the Hand's credibility, is concerning."

Greeny glowered when he finally raised his eyes to meet Calver's. "You threatening me, boy?"

Calver's stomach seized. The lord of the moss was too smart to fall for his ruse. Beneath the table, Raimee's hand trembled. He hoped she wouldn't want anything to do with him after this.

Didn't he?

"Yes," Raimee translated without missing a beat.

Calver and Greeny entered a contest of glares for the time it took to test a razor's edge. Finally, Greeny threw his cup of stones onto the table. He sighed at the result: three and three.

"Eeeaaah," he drawled. "For you, I make an exception. The Hand gets what he wants. Greeny gets what he wants. S'all that matters. My interpreters were all mid-fall... very inconvenient. So, I hear your reasoning. What d'you expect from a bunch of itchers, eah?"

Calver's heart fluttered at the scent of hope. Maybe this wouldn't end in disaster. He took his opening.

"What did you find?"

The gang lord of the moss district jutted his bristled chin at Calver in a boastful smile. "Them records the Hand wants were already requested." He held up three fingers and ticked them off as he recounted. "The locomotive conductor, Major General Mastico o' the Red Wing, and one other. A Chori woman, by name o' Loa Jahndia. I look into this slick. She the mistress o' the conductor, at least two years, which don't look like much big deal." Greeny tapped the side of his head. "But Greeny knows this can't be all. She's more suspect than the other two, you see. I look further into this slick. Find out she's the personal assistant to another man, least six years, named Deshpian Thacklore."

Calver fought to deaden his expression, to keep his eyes from flickering. Deshpian Thacklore— Fankalo's connection to Methu'su?

Greeny spat in a cup at his side. "And he the shameless son of a cow. He goin' to be the one you lookin' for."

"You are positive?" Raimee asked for Calver, not letting her sight waver from his hands.

The moss lord's eyes narrowed. "Greeny checks twice." He leaned in, sensing Calver's unease. "You know him?"

Fates, had Calver not lost his mind long ago, the interwoven events of the past two weeks would have driven him mad.

"Of him. What can you share?"

Greeny smirked. "Nothing good. Thacklore in direct competition with me. But he go for a higher crowd. I get 'is dregs from time to time. Like the last itcher you used to translate, Agnod." Greeny slammed both hands down on the table. Raimee flinched. "And he cheat me outta seven hundred thousand silver notes. Lost me dozens of itchers tryin' to get it back, too."

Raimee gulped. Her words came hesitantly. "Besides your—your personal feud... do you know why he would be looking into the distribution of military defenses?"

Greeny shrugged. "He ex-Blue-Wing command so, who knows, eah? Got a dishonorable discharge for sharing clandestine information with the Azadonian legislation."

The Nelfinden navy was mostly dormant these days, but when they'd warred with the Chori, the Blue Wing had been Nelfindar's dominant force.

"This all happen back before the strikapa quarantine. Twenty years past. More. He's kept a low profile since. But he still got deep pockets and a lot o' influence. I guarantee he still got eyes in the Blue Wing, so could be that." Greeny slouched lower into his seat and lit a pipe. He puffed it with unanticipated tenderness, smoke curling in wisps across the hairline scars on his face. "You watch youself around this guy, aye, my silent friend? You get me?"

Calver tilted his chin.

"I like you." Calver wished he didn't. "It's easy, organized work. Unlike business with the rest o' these low-lives." Greeny thumbed over his shoulder at his own tribe of cronies.

"The Hand always send payment on time. And I know you can't talk to nobody about my business on account of your—" Greeny raised his eyebrows. "Special limitations." He took another easy drag on the pipe and winked at Calver, but then turned to look at Raimee. She continued to stare at Calver's hands, as if she only existed for his speech. "And a word for you," Greeny said to her, pausing to spit in the cup to his side. "You shouldn't be here, eah?"

Raimee ignored him dutifully, but Greeny continued to harass her. "You lucky you here with this guy. Anyone else, and you be dead." He coughed twice, then put his nose a hand's width from hers. "You open your funny-looking mouth, slick, you dead. I ever see you again without him, you dead."

Calver felt something move, unbidden, inside him. It was not the Survivor, though it riled the creature into coherence.

"Matter of fact." Greeny pulled a knife from his boot, leveled it toward her chest. "I'm gonna leave you with a li'l reminder so you don't forget. Where we run, it's called protocol, sweetie."

Fuck the protocol.

He flipped a tampered lamp from his cloak faster than Greeny could blink and held it out, his thumb poised over the activator. The Survivor surged forward, delighted as their emotions, their desire for retribution, bled together as one.

Greeny's only response was to jut his jaw in distaste. "What's this?" he asked, gesturing not to the tampered lamp—he knew what Calver was capable of, the reason the others wouldn't so much as look him in the eye—but to Calver himself.

Calver shook his head, doing all he could to restrain his chest from heaving and his fists from balling. From pulling out the dowaga. From activating the lamp.

But Greeny, lord of the moss, had no fear. His chuckle was a dark thing, brewed by a body that had seen a hundred horrors. "Not necessary." He slid the blade back into its home and raised both hands in truce. "I never expect this from you, Reaper. Didn't think you give qualms for nobody."

Calver kept the lamp aloft. Greeny's eyes flickered to it, but he still rambled. Jesting. Taunting.

"So this slick got your balls, eh? It finally make sense why you don't share her mark. She ain't business. Hand don't know about her, do he?"

He eyed Calver for some sort of confirmation. Calver fought too late to deaden his expression. Greeny was a perceptive man.

"Hey. I ain't all business, neither. I ain't gonna tell the Hand." A drag from his pipe. "On this one. But it's good to know I have—ah—collateral, in case your slick rats."

Calver held eye contact with the thug. He'd been a fool to threaten Greeny. They should have left the moment they had their information.

His fingers twitched, and he tucked the Aetech lamp back into his cloak. The moss lord smiled knowingly. It was the first time he had ever gotten the upper hand in one of their interactions.

Calver assisted Raimee to her feet, and they turned to leave.

"Never imagined I'd see a mistake from you," Greeny drawled.

Fates, all he did was make stupid mistakes lately.

"Maybe the things they say about you are all talk. I bet you even bleed." Greeny hacked out a laugh. "See you next time, friend... And do give Thacklore my love, cah?"

Calver ushered Raimee away without resistance, making haste for the exit. In a game where reputation was the very lifeforce of Fankalo's scheme, he had just sliced open a vein.

Raimee didn't say a word for the entirety of their trip back to the Repository, which was equally a blessing and a curse. Her eyebrows grew closer and closer together above her oculars with each city block. By the time they were in the main square, she was positively scowling.

This was for the best; it would make things easier when she found Methu'su.

Calver would be free of her.

Easy.

That didn't stop the wild gnawing in his chest. He had to void the Survivor a handful of times on the sojourn just to keep a clear head.

As promised, they returned to the musty corner of the library they'd selected earlier in the day. Settling down to read, Raimee kept turning her head to glance at him from behind an intimidatingly massive tome with the more intimidating title of *'Carnivorous Plants of Kath.'* He ignored her and her scathing looks, opting to pace their secluded section as before. He didn't have to explain anything to her. Coming along had been her decision. He had real issues to think about.

Fuck. Like why Methu'su's confidant and whomever might be complicit in Aetech's plate shipment disaster were the same person.

Raimee slammed her book shut, breaking his rumination. "Why do you work for him?" she demanded, as though they had been in the middle of an altercation all along.

<*Who? Greeny?*>

"Yes!"

<*I don't work for him.*>

"Whatever. Then why do you work *with* him? He's a monster!"

Greeny was nothing compared to him. Invited by his unguarded anger, the Survivor pushed against Calver. He pushed back.

<*I told you not to come.*>

Raimee stood, book cast aside, and squared her shoulders. He'd expected her to be afraid of him after that experience. Now she was picking a fight?

"Is it for the money?"

<*I told you I have no interest in money.*>

Raimee scoffed. "Then why are you doing *any* of this, Calver?" She threw her hands out. "What could this 'Hand' possibly have on you to make you interact with these—these people?"

Calver's chest grew tight. <*That's none of your concern.*>

"But it is. I won't sit by if someone is forcing you to—"

He slammed his fist into the shelf beside them. <*Stop assuming what you don't know.*>

Fankalo never forced him to do anything. He did it all willingly. He would burn Chira'na to the ground if it were a thing she asked of him.

"Calver—"

He sliced his hand through the air to silence her. <*I told you not to come. And I put a lot on the line to ensure all of your skin stayed intact. You have no right to question me about the things I do.*>

Raimee's lips rolled into her teeth. Her nostrils flared. She looked like she might start berating him, so he was surprised when her voice trembled. "If this 'Hand' finds out I was with you today... will you be punished?"

That was her concern in all this? His well-being? Fates above, this needed to come to an end. There was no sense in someone caring for a walking dead man.

<*No.*> There was no further punishment Fankalo could possibly give him.

"Ok," she whispered. Her shoulders fell.

Calver rubbed his eyes. He would be rid of her, he reminded himself. Soon. And by the time the coronation arrived next summer, she wouldn't even be a speck on his mind.

He hoped. Hope was a futile thing.

"I'm sorry I made trouble for you."

<*You didn't. I just messed up.*>

He'd publicly broken the Ghosts' protocol. Greeny had every right to carve into Raimee, or kill her. His choice. Calver's prevention of it had been a suicidal act, or at least would have been for anyone else. Regardless, he hoped Greeny would keep his word. But how much did a gangster's promise weigh?

Likely as much as the very moss he propagated.

"In bringing me? Or in threatening him when he threatened me?" Raimee asked.

Silence wasn't a tactic which worked on this girl. From their stint of interaction, Calver had found it to be more of a giveaway than if he were to signal his innermost feelings.

<*Both, I think,*> he finally gestured.

"Couldn't you find a source of information that doesn't require you to come armed to your teeth?"

Why did her questioning his actions, his justifications, bother him so much? <*Chaos, why do you even care?*>

Her face flushed at the reprimand, but she didn't pull back. She pressed forward. "Brilliant as you are, you can't seem to understand that I'm trying to help you."

Calver slammed his fist against the wall again, causing her to jump. <*Can't you see this isn't anything you should be involved in?*>

"I... just want to help," she repeated.

Her injured tone only fueled his aggravation. <*You shouldn't want anything to do with me. I'm not good for you.*>

In their time together he'd been condescending, dismissive, and despondent in hopes of doing her a favor. Yet after each interaction she bounced back, treating him like the sun shone out of his backside.

Behind the oculars, he knew her eyes sought the floor. "I don't have anybody else."

A hollow silence filled the space between them, alongside the smell of old parchment and slow cascading dust.

<*Well, tomorrow you'll have Methu'su.*> Calver breathed in deep and huffed air out his nose. <*But what if you didn't? I never had anybody else. I made it. So can you.*>

She quivered but said nothing.

They remained silent for a long while, returning to the books they had pulled out that morning. A full hour or more passed before she spoke again.

"The meeting with Greeny isn't all that's bothering you, is it?"

<*Stop reading my mind. There's private stuff in there.*>

She shifted her knees to one side. "I can't read minds, Calver. But you do give a lot away."

He raised an eyebrow.

"Or maybe I just have a good read on you," she admitted sheepishly.

Aside from social normalcy and the etiquette of the blind, she seemed to have a good read on most things. Calver hung his head. Had he been a book, she'd have made volumes of annotations, he was sure.

<*There have been too many coincidences.*> He paused, staring at the pile of tomes. <*But they haven't aligned to a real conclusion. Yet. It feels like I'm standing on a sand drawing and it keeps shifting to form another picture before I can figure out what I'm looking at.*>

"Coincidences are important," she offered. "They mean you're at a pivotal cross-point on Fate's intended journey for you."

<*Is that so?*>

"The truest truth." She smiled at him.

It made his stomach turn. This was a Ruxian. He was conversing about philosophy with a *Ruxian* in a forgotten corner of the Repository. Casual, in the way he'd once conversed with Pim while dragging sticks through the sand.

<*Are you hungry?*>

Her stomach growled as though on cue. "Sooo hungry," she groaned.

<*Alright. Let's get a meal or three. From a stand. We'll eat in the park.*> He remembered, only then, the holiday in celebration of the recruitment. <*There should be music tonight.*>

She hugged '*Carnivorous Plants of Kath*' into her chest and screwed up her face with excitement.

<*Then we'll check in to the lodgings here to rest. Tomorrow is an important day.*>

Chapter 30

Calverous

In the square beside the Repository, the city had broken into a festival beneath the rising winter moon. It was the end of a ten-day, which meant many citizens had an increase in free hours and a decrease in inhibition. The Red Wing recruitment had entered the city that morning. The next two days until its departure would be an endless celebration, full of warm drinks and interchanges out in the city's public spaces. All of Chira'na took to the streets, wearing their finest winter robes, sirwals, and kaftans. Women of wealth adorned their turbans or headdresses with jewels. On the skywalk above, distortion lamps shone into the night like beacons. Music poured from every corner, along with the aromas of Nelfindar's famous street food.

Calver and Raimee sat near a bonfire in the park, surrounded by a dozen other strangers. Raimee ate, soundlessly, and watched. And watched.

Always the women.

Her eyes followed them, their dresses, their hair, their movements; chatting, laughing, dancing. To a person who had never experienced the societal spheres of separate sexes, the scene around her had to be mystifying. And then her face twisted with something akin to longing, but at the bottom of longing's rope. Calver watched her dreams of assimilation slipping away. Her realization that what she'd hoped for—and probably the thing that had driven her to study something that would require a sea voyage—was utterly impossible. The Fate she'd been born with was broken.

Their solidarity in that hurt him.

He cleared his throat to garner her attention. <Would you like to play a game?>

Raimee blinked away the water gathering in her eyes and faked a gasp of disbelief. "Would I!"

<Except you have to signal. This is not a socially acceptable game.>

Her grin nearly reached both ears as her fingers danced to respond. <You secretly do know how to have a good time, don't you?>

They created imaginative backstories for the park-goers that passed around them. Each story grew more and more bizarre or, sometimes, inappropriate until Calver was unable to mask his own expressions. Raimee held her sides in laughter, mostly at her own stories, sometimes even at his. He found an ebb in his tension, which receded into the night, long past an hour when they should have turned in.

"Do you ever wonder what it would be like...?" Raimee whispered after a long while, staring at a woman cradling a baby across from them as she laughed to her partner and sipped at hot tea.

She didn't need to finish the question. To take someone else's place. To live a different life. A normal one.

<*I try not to,*> Calver signaled.

A lull in conversation invited itself to sit between them for the first time since they'd eaten. It felt like a physical wound that only signaling could heal.

<*What will you do next? Once you find Methu'su?*> he asked.

Raimee shifted so that the fire warmed her opposite side. "Well, assuming he doesn't lock me in a box and throw away the key..." He frowned. So, she wasn't the only one with concerns. "I always wanted to go to sea." Calver's chest hitched at the thought, which grazed his most painful memories. "There have been almost no formal studies done on Casowhatan sea kelp. It's a huge gap in Nelfindar's botanical encyclopedia. I never understood why my proposal was refused. A tragedy, honestly, because here's the thing about kelp—"

She launched into a monologue about medicinal and pharmaceutical properties, agricultural uses, and sustainable ecosystems until, finally, she seemed to realize how long she'd been speaking uninterrupted, and finished with, "I'd catalog sea kelp."

<*Sorry I asked.*>

She drove an elbow into his ribcage. "You're so rude." Her mouth twitched at its corner. "I think I'm going to miss you."

He realized then, in a moment that took away the night's joy, that he wouldn't stop missing her. Not once, for the next four hundred and one days.

<*There's nothing to miss.*>

They retired to the room he'd rented in the Repository. Raimee nearly screamed with delight when she saw the bed: a single, small mattress in the room's corner, laid with multiple pillows and a thick down blanket.

Calver gladly gave it up in favor of sleeping the only way he ever could—with his back pressed to the door. It had kept him alive so far. He trusted it would continue to do so, for just a little while longer.

Sleep evaded him as he thought about all the things that would come to pass, the things that wouldn't, and the fantasy of a common ground that wasn't possible.

The morning came. Calver rose from the floor in front of the door with the sun—an anomaly, as he usually beat the dawn to its feet by an hour or more. In the bed, Raimee's chest rose and fell in time with a low rumble, like a cat's purr.

Calver turned from her and moved into the tiny washroom affixed to their room to shave. His eyes found their reflection in the mirror over the sink, and he studied the man before him. It wasn't as if he hadn't seen himself in the years since encountering the Survivor; he had caught sight of himself in city mirrors, in the watery reproductions of lakes. But he hadn't had the same control over his mind then as he did now.

The maturity of the impression in front of him surprised him. He was more than midway through his twenties now. He'd never thought on his mortality in terms of age or years; age was of no consequence when you knew your own expiration to be imminent. And when the Survivor had control, time was inconsequential. Life passed in a blur.

His dark eyebrows lowered over umber irises. He was the age Cul'Mon had been at the time he had taken him. And he'd grown, his muscles no longer sinuous but robust. After years of training, he was stronger than he'd ever been. Perhaps enough to best Cul'Mon... perhaps not. He would be wise to assume the latter.

Calver's chest rose and fell in an attempt to remain at ease. His reflection still watched him as he traced the arch in his neck with a straight razor for the first time since his banishment eighteen months ago. Preservation, but he did look like his father. Not that he remembered him well. But his mother had kept a canvas of their family, painted at the time of Calver's birth, rolled in a corner of their shanty. His resemblance to the infamous Thadinar Curtaim was striking. Dark curls, chopped at his ears. Wide, flat cheekbones. An aquiline nose. A square jaw. Fates, how his mother had fawned over that man, even years later. She couldn't see his treachery for what it was.

The Survivor flared at the reminiscence. Calver tried to push it back, but the metacognition of his father causing him anger antagonized him all the more.

{Your glory will outlast your father's for lifetimes.}

What could you possibly know of it?

Fury burned in his reflection's gaze, eyes that suddenly looked subtly different. The mind-djinn roiled in laughter. The Survivor having a superior opinion of him than his father was not a thing of comfort. It had been an attempt to fuel his ire, to prolong its presence. It knew nothing.

Void.

The false laughter echoed in his mind, even as he washed it away with the mantra. He hadn't been able to do that so easily a month ago… Calver sighed in relief, his head hanging loose on his shoulders, chin nearly reaching his chest. When he looked at the straight razor in his hand, the metal of its handle had dented beneath his grip.

Seven playful knocks sounded at the door. "Calver? Give a girl a pee, won't you?"

Calver threw on a shirt, not wanting to raise questions about the many things he hid beneath it, and opened the door. The Ruxian's eyes seemed extra silver this morning.

Her lips parted to form a perfect circle. The moment stretched.

And Raimee's wit snapped into place on the recoil. "Well, that's the least eloquent marriage proposal I've ever heard of."

He was so stuck in his mental recovery, it took him an extra heartbeat to decipher her banter.

Shaving?

Raimee tucked a strand of hair behind her ear and cringed. "I can tell you're the version of yourself where nothing lands quite right, so I'm going to pretend that wasn't terribly awkward. You—you look nice." She peered past him and gasped. "Holy constellations. There's a full bath in here?" She made a shooing motion. "Well, get out, then."

Calver left the room to search the Repository for court records from Thacklore's trial. He found a slot for it in the legal archives, but the record itself was missing.

Not suspicious at all…

He searched the Blue Wing military records for details on why Thacklore had been discharged. Everything had been redacted, minus a vague mention of his release of information to the Azadonia's Kovathian sect. Thacklore had spent three years in a skywalk prison—basically a hotel—and another four on housebound probation. All signs pointed to him bribing his way out of what should have been an execution. *Great.* Methu'su's associate sounded like a real fucking gem. *"A gossipmonger,"* Fankalo had called him. *"A snake."*

Thacklore's actions for the fourteen years since were a mystery. He'd been omitted from any public records, less a census. The same census that Methu'su was entirely absent from.

His chest tightening, Calver cursed himself for being so shortsighted. He'd wasted time the night before fraternizing with the Ruxian instead of scoping out Thacklore's address. Something was horribly wrong. Something he couldn't grasp any more than he could stab at water.

After finding nothing but more reasons to be neurotic, he returned to the room. Raimee was still in the washroom, humming, although nearly an hour had passed since he'd vacated it. While the Ruxian had never said anything about Calver's safehouse being akin to barbarism, he'd come to understand that his own lifestyle was not her personal preference.

He left her be and took his dowaga through a progression of motions, preparing his body for explosive movement. They would need to assume the worst; this meeting was dangerous. He took inventory in a neat array across the floor: the dowaga, knives of varying lengths, a tanka and holster, his distorted hover discs, and three tampered Aetech lamps. Calver's hand hovered over one of his knives.

This meeting wasn't like the one with Greeny. Sure, he'd pulled on Fankalo's network of Ghosts to set up the appointment with Thacklore, but it wasn't specifically for Shadewalker-related business...

He palmed the knife's polished rosewood handle. Raised it. Watched the way its blade reflected the light from the sconced Aetech lamp on the wall.

But what if the question arose?—and with his Chaos-cursed luck, it would. If she didn't bear the Shadewalker's mark, Thacklore might withhold information. If she didn't bear the Shadewalker's mark...

He could always suggest giving her one. Reason that it was the only way he could guarantee her safety in the interaction. *Just a few slices. No big deal. You'll hardly feel a thing.*

His stomach took a dive. The maniac would probably say "Alright, let's give it a go!" and tear her clothes off.

Raimee exited the bath at that precise moment, garbed in her kaftan and attempting—and failing—to run a wide-toothed comb through her enormous hair while chomping at an apple.

Calver dropped the knife like it had bitten him. Bile rose into his throat at the very thought of carving her speckled skin.

"I'm curious," she said. "Does this old associate of Methu'su's know where he is? Or just know who he is?"

It looked like he was taking his chances again. If things went south, he was the Hand's Reaper. He'd bent the rules. He would bend them again.

<*We'll find out when we get there.*> He hastened to stash his inventory into their appropriate hiding places on his person.

She raised an eyebrow at him. "What are the lamps for?"

<*Light.*>

"Riiight. And all the sharp things?"

<*There's something I should share with you.*>

"Preservation's manly teats," she muttered, before biting another chunk from the apple and plopping to the floor with legs crossed to watch his hands.

<*You remember the name Greeny gave me yesterday? The ousted Blue Wing member?*>

"Deshpian Thacklore. The person you clearly think is responsible for orchestrating a Tera'thian intervention in that distortion shipment," she recited casually.

Calver shifted. Just another reminder that, in lieu of sea kelp, she was cataloging his every move.

<*That's who we're going to see.*>

She sat still, her brows knitting together. "I thought we had a meeting with Methu'su's associate?"

<*One and the same.*>

"No!" She held a hand up to her mouth but continued chewing.

<*I wasn't sure whether it would be wise to tell you.*>

"Wasn't sure whether to tell me that Methu'su's associate is a national traitor?" She clapped a hand to her forehead. "How is this possible?"

<*You suggested I seemed bothered last night. This is part of it.*>

Raimee stood up and began pacing the room. "This is not good…" She toyed with the ends of her silver hair before stopping to pin him with a look. "This is what you meant about coincidences, I presume? If you're telling the truth, I concur that this is truly an odd connection."

Fates, she didn't even know the half of it.

"So what does this association imply of Methu'su?"

Her worries mirrored his own. After everything he'd risked to repay his debt to the Ruxian, his commitment could not continue if Methu'su sold her off to Tera'thian agents or worse.

It wasn't his responsibility. He had Fankalo's objectives to keep in mind.

<*Well.*> Calver hesitated. They had to trust Methu'su; it was their only option. There was no other road for her to go down. <*I am also a traitor. And you're technically my associate. Methu'su might not be as bad as you imagine.*>

Raimee stared at him for a long time, her expression unperturbed by his sharing his deepest failings. Finally, she shrugged again. "You are an exception to the rule, Calver."

Wrong. She was so wrong.

<*Do you want to stay back this time?*>

"Don't ask stupid questions."

Deshpian Thacklore's address brought them to a gated community along Chira'na's southernmost wall. Calver knew it; it was renowned as the wealthiest residential area off-skywalk.

The gate guards' entry list had the name 'Dallard Friyal' written in fresh ink at its bottom. With a glance at his paperwork, the guards permitted them entry. Fankalo had done clean work on facilitating this connection, as always. Fankalo ran heists with a clean efficiency the Nelfinden bureaucracy lacked, as if with the foresight of the Fates. It was the only reason they'd made it so far on a fool's errand. Why two kids from the slums had grown up to have any chance at toppling an empire.

It deserved to be admired.

Calver's gut wrenched, thinking of the rules he'd broken, the things he'd done. So Fankalo had kept a secret. It had only been to guard him against his own trauma. His actions had been rash, wrong. Fankalo had even said they weren't working with Thyatira directly, they were just...

Like an itch, the thought intruded. *Fankalo lies for a living.*

The Survivor stretched out like a wild cat at Calver's fluttering nerves and the possibility of danger. Calver acknowledged it. With the mind-djinn partially present, he could react more efficiently to trouble. That might be worth spending the next hour or more afflicted by its destructive tendencies.

The Survivor purred in satisfaction. It pushed further forward and, reluctantly, Calver shared a degree of control.

Raimee clung to his arm as though her life depended on it. She was uncharacteristically silent—stiff with nerves, probably.

No. Not that. Something else was wrong.

But he didn't have time to ask her about it. He couldn't afford a distraction, going into unknown territory with a final shot at saving Fankalo's operation.

At the given address a stone stairwell led to a set of gargantuan oak doors. Thacklore's home was massive, constructed from adobe stained dark as mahogany with cast-iron details around its arching lintels. It had a lawn of neatly manicured grass rimed with topiaries—truly a unique sight in Chira'na. The groundling class couldn't usually afford that sort of ostentatious living aesthetic. As if Calver needed another reason to not like the man he hadn't yet met.

"Calver," Raimee started, her voice tighter than a knot. "It feels to me like... *you've* been here before. We did make it through the gate rather easily, didn't we? Have you—been here before?"

<*No.*>

The Survivor was dismissive with her. Better than the usual bloodlust. Calver tried not to think about her, instead taking in every element from the street that he could, memorizing it in case they needed to make a fast exit.

"So... have you ever... met... Thacklore... before?" She, thankfully, released his arm and wrung her hands along the handle of the cane.

<*No.*>

There it was. Back again like a daisy in spring: the Survivor's standard desire to throttle her. Calver quashed it.

Few pedestrians passed by in this sector; everyone was celebrating in the city's center. Calver's insides clenched again. No chance at discreetly blending into a crowd. The sparse individuals walking past stared questioningly. Their clothing was too poor for this sector.

"I'm not sure that I want to go in," Raimee said suddenly, taking a step back.

{*I don't have patience for this one,*} the Survivor growled.

This was similar to her reaction in the Repository before they left for Greeny's. Except now she *didn't* want to join him? <*I'm not leaving you in the street.*> Calver counted the windows on the house. By the looks of the building, there was likely to be a basement.

"The street looks safe to me."

Calver reached to grab her arm again but stopped himself. She stiffened like a rabbit in the jaws of a predator. The last time she'd done this, the Survivor had been present too. But no one had ever—

"Calver..." she started.

He tried to push back the fury bubbling over from the Survivor.

{*You need me,*} it argued. It had a point.

<*What?*> he signaled twice out of frustration.

"Thank you for everything you've done for me."

Calver broke his focus on the building. His own mind pushed through the Survivor. Raimee's eyes hid behind her dark lenses, but he imagined those silver irises seeking his. Pleading. Heart quickening, Calver hesitated before placing a hand on her shoulder, an action he remembered to be soothing to people who hadn't been possessed by mind-djinns and forced to be genetic slaves.

<*You will be fine.*>

She relaxed at his touch.

Socially obstructed as he was, that was definitely an abnormal exchange. And one that filled his insides with worms as he considered what she might be neglecting to tell him: that she *could* see it... and it rightfully terrified her.

He'd always just assumed he'd lost his mind alongside his tongue that day, but she—

{*Focus.*} The Survivor shifted forward.

He started for the stairs. The Ruxian followed.

<*Same rules here as at Greeny's.*>

She nodded. "Let's go."

Calver knocked twice on the heavy door, and it swung open soundlessly. A woman with more curves than Chori calligraphy stood on the threshold. Her polished features were enhanced by tailored clothing—a burgundy, high-necked gown with silk buttons running from toe to chin. This would be Loa Jahndia.

"How may I help you?" she asked, eyeing Raimee with heavily lidded eyes.

Calver nodded to Raimee.

"We have a meeting with Mesu Thacklore at highsun."

The woman's mouth twisted in suspicion. "You are Dallard Friyal?" She directed the question at Calver.

He nodded.

Loa opened the door wider, stepping back to allow them to enter an immaculate foyer. Calver absorbed everything he could: the doors in the foyer and connecting hall—nine, all of them shut; dozens of grand paintings depicting the Seraphindos; the odd density of the rugs; the iron chandelier. The house was quiet.

Eerily quiet.

Beside him, Raimee shifted from one foot to the next. The motion emitted no sound.

"Mesu Thacklore is expecting you. You will find him in the study, the third door down on your left," Loa said airily.

"Thank you," Raimee replied.

As they walked along the hall to the third door, Loa's eyes bored into their backs. Calver knocked once on the door to the study.

"Enter," called a soft, deep voice.

They padded into the room. The door shut behind them.

Thacklore sat with legs crossed in an ornate velvet armchair. He'd set down his book to receive them. The man's smartly trimmed black hair and beard were flecked with gray, but otherwise lustrous and full. His clothes were at an impressive peak of fashion, edged with silver buttons and Azadonian silk.

Thacklore's dark, hawk-like eyes immediately settled on Raimee, and they lingered as his handsome face split into a smile. "Welcome to my home, Mesu Friyal."

Calver felt a hollowness in the pit of his stomach. *Fuck.* They'd been strung up.

Now there was the matter of cutting themselves down.

Chapter 31
Attilatia

SIXTEEN YEARS PREVIOUSLY

Attilatia made it home a full hour before her mother was set to arrive. The tunnel they shared in the Azadonian underground had changed little since Dasha passed into the final cavern but, even a decade later, the space felt different. Like a water vase glued back together, it functioned. But your eyes were always drawn to the cracks.

She set Thedexemore on the floor in her room and gave him a brush to play with as a distraction. His chunky fingers seized it, and he drew it to his gums. Jenolavia's son was a mild-mannered baby, thank Creation, and easy to entertain. That meant Attilatia could work on her latest distortion project—a tracking mechanism for her mother.

Attilatia rifled through the equipment she'd hidden in a satchel under her bed and pulled out the materials she needed to begin. Thedexemore cooed contentedly beside her and thwapped the brush repeatedly against the floor. She set to work, deftly twisting the hair-thin wires around a miniscule amount of ruxechorin syndicate with a pair of tweezers. She'd never made anything quite so small before. But the device needed to be discreet, so her mother wouldn't realize it for what it was. She would tell her it was a bracelet—a gift.

The deceit felt wrong. But what her mother didn't know wouldn't hurt her. She only had one parent; best to keep that relationship intact, no matter how strained it might be. Lying about her work was the only option. Otherwise she'd have to give up distortion altogether. She'd sooner give up a limb.

Her mother claimed the 'detestable' hobby was distracting her from her duties. Being Thedexemore's caretaker. Her political education. The Lethoso. Attilatia knew there was more to it than that, of course. Her mother's spite for distortion extended from both the loss of Dasha and her work for the queen. Distortion was the very topic tearing apart the legislation. And Attilatia's expertise in the subject could technically put her in danger, should the Kovathian sect go so far as to take hostages for information.

Last ten-day, her mother had caught her tinkering and threatened to remove her as caretaker for Thedexemore if she did it again. As if her experiments had any negative impact on the boy. She looked over to him, on the floor in the exact position she'd left him. He babbled and drooled like a hound, though he'd moved on from the hairbrush in favor of his own toes. When he caught her looking, his mouth split into a toothless smile. Attilatia returned an exaggerated grin and tossed him a half-completed distortion orb from her satchel. If only her mother were so distractible; she would get much more done.

Growing up, she'd dreaded starting the caretaker position, an honor her mother had petitioned for on her behalf for years. Looking after someone's helpless offspring had sounded like the worst possible use of a scientist's time. She had been wrong—so wrong. She loved this boy with every part of herself. His stinking farts, his snotty nose, all of him. And he adored her, didn't avoid her or judge her for the antisocial she was like the rest of Tentika.

Attilatia completed the tracker bracelet and set to work on a replica, which would blink the closer its counterpart came to it: slowly for when her mother was at least three cavern floors away, and rapidly if she was within a few minutes walking.

Footsteps echoed in the adjacent tunnel. She sucked in a breath. That wasn't right; Mother shouldn't be home for another hour. They pattered closer. The main door to their home opened and shut. Frantically, Attilatia stuffed her materials back under the bed, bit the side of her tongue. Too late.

The door to her room burst open. Attilatia scrambled to turn around, feigning anger at the intrusion.

"Mother! Why would you—"

She cut off, both at the terror on her mother's face and her hushing hand gesture.

"Thank Preservation," her mother said, pulling her into a hug. "I hoped you would be here. That you would have brought him here too."

Attilatia looked down at Thedexemore, who was still holding the half-finished distortion orb—a dead giveaway—and watching the two of them curiously. How to respond? Her mother should be furious. Attilatia was here, in their home, when she was supposed to have Thedexemore at the council's cavern garden. Chaos, she was usually discontented even when Attilatia *was* doing what she should.

"Hurry. Pack a few things. There's been an attack."

The words landed like a physical slap. Attilatia stepped backward. "A what?"

"A coup. The Kovathians." Her mother had moved to the next room, visible through the open door. She was shoving her personal effects into a bag.

Attilatia followed her. "A coup... What does it mean? How did it—?"

Her mother stopped and clasped her face, thumbs caressing her cheekbones. "You are my brilliant daughter, are you not?" Then she shook her. "You know what it means! Jenolavia is dead. The entire family slaughtered. Nine-tenths of the cabinet as well."

Attilatia's whole body heated. Her limbs were suddenly weak.

Her mother was still speaking quickly and quietly and with the same efficiency as she went about everything, but Attilatia hardly heard the words. "I was lucky I was assigned to Lethoso instruction today, or I would have been with them. I ran the moment first blood hit the ground in hopes that you would be here. That you'd have Thedexemore here and... Stop looking at me like a frightened rabbit, girl! Move!"

"Mother... Dexe!" Attilatia gasped, finding it difficult to speak.

"Precisely. It's only a matter of time before their body count comes up short. You need to get him out."

"I—what? W-where do we go?"

Her mother restarted her flurry of packing. "You can't stay here. When they realize, they'll track you down. This is the first place they'll come."

"What about you?"

"I have to get back into the council library. Twenty years of legislation will need to be rescued before they put flame to the lot of it."

No. None of this could be possible. And why would they come here? Why would a baby matter when—

It was like the floor dropped from beneath her. Thedexemore was the heir now.

"What of the rest of the cabinet? Their arms? The private militia? Surely they'll stop them."

Her mother's head dipped. Her face stretched with pain. "Our counter... it's failed."

The gravity of the situation blanketed Attilatia. No, suffocated her. She scooped up Thedexemore, her vision momentarily darkening as she did. A hand against the wall steadied her enough to stand. The babe, none the wiser, graced her with a foolish grin. Attilatia hugged him into her chest, and her eyes began to burn, tears brimming at their corners.

"I would not trust you with this if I didn't believe in you," her mother said. "I would take him instead if I thought I could do better. But you are the smartest and most tenacious person I know. This idiotic... wiring and calculating—" She gestured crudely to the distortion technology still on the floor. "It just goes to show it. You can do this."

Attilatia's mother, esteemed councilor of the Tentika sect, was a miser with compliments. Especially so with her asocial daughter. Her words showed just how dire the situation truly was.

"I'll run with him," Attilatia said, Thedexemore's tiny warmth giving her limbs new strength. "To the general populous quarters. Around the moss market. We'll find someone to take us in."

"No. Atti. There is..." Her mother broke eye contact. "A better option. I want you to find Shinathala. Tell her I sent you, and she needs to guide you to the Reservoir." She shouldered her bag. Gripped at her forearms. "The Kovathian threat has been steadily increasing. And the legislation and the Reservoir have recently established communications. In the event something like this should happen, they have offered us safe haven."

It was as though her mother were trying to convince herself. Attilatia frowned. "You can't mean that truly?"

The Reservoir was a legend. A myth, like the orange cavern monster who arose every seventy-two days to eat children's desserts. A faction of their people had left the Azadonian cave system years ago, seeking a space closer to the surface where green trees grew around crystalline lakes. The fools had never been heard from again. The Reservoir wasn't real...

"Find Shinathala," her mother repeated.

"This is insanity."

"This is the task I entrust to you, Atti, for Thedexemore's sake. For Jenolavia's dynasty!"

"Then you take me!" Attilatia's voice choked. "Damn your paperwork! Why Shinathala? Mother, I—I didn't—I'm not—I'm scared!" Those words had never fled her lips before.

Her mother stiffened. "It's not the paperwork. Its—" her shoulders slumped. "I have access to the grand cavern's service tunnels. I might still be able to get any surviving councilors out."

A suicide mission.

"And to the Reservoir?"

She took a step closer. "I'll be right behind you."

Attilatia shook her head. "Don't. It doesn't matter who else is in there. If they've killed the cabinet, they'll kill you too. And—how do you know your 'recent communication' wasn't just a Kovathian agent? Think. A fabled faction of Azadonia offers you safe haven within a few months of a Kovathian coup?"

Her mother fell silent, indicating that she hadn't thought of the possibility herself. Or maybe that she had.

"Our time is short," she said finally. "I thank the Fates that you and Thedexemore are safe, my *hakuni*. But I have to go now and get the others. This is my duty. You do yours."

"Please... Mother..."

Her mother stepped closer again. Cupped Attilatia's cheek with one hand. "I am taking the service tunnels. Don't worry... The Kovathians aren't cutting the general populace down. Not yet, anyway."

Attilatia was frightened. Furious. But she leaned in instinctively, seeking protection. Comfort. Her mother embraced her, pressing Thedexemore between them. He giggled. The sound made her want to cry.

"If anyone can do this, Atti, it's you. Keep him hidden. Use that mind of yours. And move. You are easy prey here."

Attilatia nodded with a sniff.

"And Atti? Don't let anyone know what you can do with distortion. No one. It will put you both in danger."

"Yes," she replied, as her heart cried a silent, repeated "No!"

Her mother pulled away and gave her a fleeting look that chilled her to her core. It was a look that took all of her daughter in. Memorizing her, like she might never see her again.

She turned and exited through the door to their once-home.

Alone, Attilatia began throwing as many belongings as she could for herself and Thedexemore into a bag. Her head spun. Her disbelief at her actions—running away and abandoning her home to go into hiding, to go hunting for a fabled location, of all things—was overshadowed by one crushing thought: Thedexemore was orphaned.

She would not let him make this journey alone.

Tears streamed down her face, littering the stone floor with dark freckles. She would have been able to get ready more quickly with two hands, but she simply couldn't bear the thought of putting the babe down. He cooed in her arms all the while, tangling small fingers in her hair.

It was only a minute before she was ready, but it had been too long. Footsteps came again. A multitude of them, sounding in chaotic rhythm like the stones of a collapsing cave wall. *No. No. No. Not yet!* Her heart clutched in panic. She said a prayer to Preservation that Thedexemore would keep quiet.

Voices sounded outside the dwelling. "This one is the caretaker's," someone said.

Energy flooded Attilatia's limbs, where minutes before she'd felt weak. A decision had to be made. She could hide and more than likely be discovered. Or flee and more than likely be cut down. Or—

"Sorry, Mother," she whispered. Chaos abound, she was disobeying her matriarch only minutes after the warning she'd given. But disappointing her mother was a thing she took to like a fish to water.

She set Thedexemore on the floor in the corner and upended a basket of clothing to cover him. Then she dove beneath her bed. The telltale splintering of wood sounded as the front door crashed in, but Attilatia's fingers flexed around the unworn handle of the object she searched for: a distortion-powered tunnel extender, a creation of her own, designed to cut through solid rock in a fraction of the time it took their builders.

She frowned, and felt as though the extender were frowning back at her. Her dasha had always believed that, with the right amount of caution, distortion could change the world without destroying it. And so he had laid out inviolable rules surrounding how she could tinker with the science. Dasha had been a genuine altruist. So what did it say about her, his own daughter, who even as a child had found his circumspection to be imprudent?

She brandished the machine in front of her with both hands. Aimed at the door to her room, which shook with every pound of the invaders against it. Her whole body shook in tandem, as if they were locked into a dance of jitters. She chewed at her lip. What would she do when they came in? Could she actually flip on the activator? She knew what the drill did to stone. The things it would do to a human being... What would dasha have done?

He never would have built the extender.

The door splintered open. Five of the enemy crowded into the opening, the tankas on their arms aimed at her.

No.

Attilatia activated the drill the moment they locked eyes on her. They would not find a quivering mole here, but a wolf.

The scorching blast of energy from the distortion drill created a monster of blinding light and flame that expanded to the height of her tunnel. It devoured the invaders, incinerating everything in the room beyond in the time it took to sip tea. They didn't even have the opportunity to scream.

Shaking, Attilatia released the trigger. For a moment, she could hear nothing beyond her heartbeat in her ears and the blazing of the inferno. And her mind fixated on the strangest of things: Mother's precious kettle, Dasha's old spectacles. All turned into ashes. Gone.

Why couldn't she think about the bodies?

Then Thedexemore began to cry. It wasn't a complaint or cry of discomfort, but a shrill squeal of terror. Attilatia chucked the drill to the side—it was too large and heavy to carry with her if she had Thedexemore. In a single, desperate motion, she lunged toward the basket, upended it, and bundled him into her arms.

"Hush, hush, Dexe. I am here, eah?" She lifted a prayer to Preservation. Thedexemore was still alive, and by a twist of Fate, it was her own disobedience that saved him.

Her reassuring words did not echo the panic clutching at her chest; she hugged him more for her own comfort than his. He burrowed his tiny face into her breast. Slowly, his crying ebbed. *Move,* she told herself. *Move, chikoto!* If she didn't get out, the smoke would fill the room and they would suffocate.

Stuffing down her terror, she forced herself to peer through the destroyed entryway into what had been their main living quarters. All that stood were the walls themselves: searing, solid stone. Some belongings still smoldered on the floor, indiscernible from what they once had been and, scattered among them, the corpses. Hardly more than bones. Scraps.

Don't think about it.

She collected the pack she'd filled and bolted. The torrid floor singed her boots, as if she was running across a hot pan, as she escaped into the main cavern.

No sooner had she dashed out of her home than arms latched around her torso and tackled her. Attilatia tried to cradle Thedexemore, turning to cushion the fall for him as best she could in the grip of the enemy. He howled when they hit the ground; she'd never heard a more horrific sound. She screamed too, biting and twisting, doing anything she could to get away.

"Stop. Stop. I think we can help each other," the stranger grunted in a distinctly *not* Azadonian accent. Attilatia's limbs turned to steel. A foreigner? A foreigner in the lower caverns? Chaos abound, what was happening?

"Get off me!" Her own voice echoed back at her like a wounded beast. Thedexemore's cries grew louder.

"This is causing a scene," he hissed. "Is that what you want? For more Kovathians to notice you?"

Fates, but he was right. She stilled and he loosened his grip on her, though he didn't let go entirely. She could have tried to break free—to knee him in the groin, to gouge his eyes—but she couldn't focus enough to do so. The sounds coming from Thedexemore's mouth had her full attention. Had he broken a bone? Had the fall rattled his neck? His head? She hushed him, humming through sobs.

"Let's talk, out of the open," the man said, pulling them back into the wreckage of her once-home. The bodies remained on the floor. A sudden wave of sickness washed over Attilatia, unrelated to the heat of the room. Smoke clogged her lungs and singed her eyes. The stranger didn't seem to heed it.

"How did you do this?" He gestured to the corpses.

The drill was still in Attilatia's room. She would not give it up. "You're with them," she accused him. "What do you want with us?"

She eyed the stranger up and down, even as her hands felt up and down Thedexemore's limbs and ascertained that he was more shaken than harmed. Dark curled hair and a beard, cut short and manicured. Bronze skin, brown eyes—distinctly Nelfinden features. Her eyes narrowed; that was strange. The Kovathians weren't working with the Nelfinden. They were supposed to be influenced by the Tera'thians. The man was dressed immaculately, like he was a step from royalty. His cold, demanding attitude gave the same impression. He bristled in irritation.

"There are a lot of people looking for you right now. Believe me when I say that they don't mean you well. I might be able to help you. But you need to tell me what you did to make this"—he indicated the dead around them again—"happen."

Don't let him find the drill. Don't let him find the drill. If she just left it here, it would burn. Ashes were good for keeping secrets.

Attilatia felt as though walls were crushing in on her. The heat radiating from them was unbearable. She still trembled, overcome by nausea and the sensation of cooking alive. But

Thedexemore was still in her arms. She had to stay strong for Thedexemore. She had to keep him safe.

"How would you help me?"

"In exchange for information around whatever act of distortion did this and service from you afterward, I would grant you safe passage out of Azadonia," he told her.

"Where?"

His response was sharp with impatience. "The city of Chira'na."

Nelfindar. This man would get them to Nelfindar.

Attilatia had never desired to leave the caverns, but Nelfindar, despite its own political turmoil, must be a safer bet than the Reservoir. If she refused, what would this man do? Would he kill her? Turn them both in to the Kovathians, who would certainly kill them? She couldn't dive back into her room for the drill, not with Thedexemore on her hip and the way the intruder gripped her. He would see it. He'd use it against them.

Which was safer: to go with the stranger who would bargain trade secrets for their lives, or to try to escape him, head to the major caverns during a coup, and find her mother's affiliate, who would stealth them to an imaginary place? Kretch. This man might still kill them anyway, after he got what he wanted. Either path was a terrible decision.

She opted for the path of least resistance... and the one with the least likelihood of ever seeing her mother again.

She hesitated, blinking back a tear and shifting Thedexemore to her opposite hip. It dawned on her that this stranger had omitted something specific in his promise. "You will grant safe passage to me *and* to my brother."

The man's eyes glistened. So he *had* intentionally left Thedexemore out.

"Fine. I will grant safe passage to you and your... brother." He savored the last word. "What does an infant son of Jenolavia's blood mean to anyone, after all?"

He knew. And he was working with the Kovathians. Of course. Why else would he be here? *This is a bad, bad, bad idea, Atti.*

The smoke continued to build. Thedexemore continued to whimper. Attilatia took a step away from the stranger. "How do I know you won't go back on your deal?"

"You'll find me to be a man of my word. I've learned to never tell a lie. A lie is an easy trick. Low. Petty. Telling illusions of the truth, on the other hand, is something different entirely. And it can be so much more rewarding." He smiled at her. Predator or prey, having another's teeth bared in her direction was unsettling. "Someone clever such as yourself can see right through those, though, right? So long as that's the case, you have nothing to fear."

Her skin prickled, a chill running the length of her spine as though it had been stroked by a feather. Something about the man was charming, and something felt off. He was offering to rescue her. Albeit for something in return, but there was nothing so wrong with that. So why did this feel erroneous?

It was the best option. She wasn't only betting her life. She had to think of Thedexemore. "What is your name?"

The man flashed his stark white smile. "Deshpian Thacklore. And it would serve you to address me as Mesu Thacklore, for now."

He held out a hand for her to shake, something she'd heard was a Nelfinden custom. Attilatia took it gingerly at first, then remembered that the whole point was to show strength. A contest, or something like that. She squeezed with all the force she could muster. *What a barbaric tradition.* That was to be expected, as it had been created by a culture led by men.

Mesu Thacklore's mouth quirked in amusement, causing her to wonder if she'd done it incorrectly. She stomped down her doubts and cleared her throat. "I'm Attilatia Mitar."

He withdrew his hand, still smirking. Did that mean she'd won? She suddenly wished she'd taken the time to learn more about Nelfinden culture. It had never seemed important in her youth. She'd never expected to become a refugee there.

"I know exactly who you are, my dear," he said.

Attilatia shivered despite herself. He would have seen them killed had he not witnessed the effects of the distortion drill; disobeying her mother had saved their lives. The thought gave her no satisfaction. Rather, it filled her with remorse.

Sorry, Mother. She couldn't even pretend that she'd tried.

"We should leave here. I can get you out safely, but it will require some precision, and we need to move quickly."

Attilatia looked down at Thedexemore, whose large black eyes stared into her own as though for reassurance. With a steadying breath and a nod, she hoisted the boy higher on her hip, prepared to leave their cavern home for the void; the blanketing comfort of the dark for the harsh world of light.

Be brave, Atti. It is your duty to the queen. Your duty to Azadonia.

But the queen was dead. And Azadonia under siege. She squeezed her eyes tightly, trying not to think about it.

There was still something she could do. She and she alone could protect Thedexemore.

"Let's go."

Chapter 32

Calverous

A painting adorned the far wall of Deshpian Thacklore's study between two tapestries bearing the insignia of the Blue Wing. In it, three Ruxian women sat around a fountain, laughing as one distorted a spout of water to splash the others. Their eyes glowed. The silver oil painted in dimension against the canvas was so identical to Raimee's pigment that Calver could almost believe it was real Ruxian hair, chopped and pasted there. The hairs on his arms stood erect.

Deshpian Thacklore clapped his hands twice. Raimee jumped and recomposed herself with a straighter spine than seemed natural. To their right, a wooden panel in the wall slid open; four servants extracted themselves from behind it. They carried a table laden with honeyed pastries, olives, fruit, and wine. All were young—boys, no older than fifteen. One of them noticed Raimee and doubled back to emerge with an extra chair. They set up the arrangement with practiced promptness.

"Please," Thacklore gestured to the table, "be seated."

The wooden chair was sculpted in a way which made it more comfortable than an uncushioned chair had any right to be. Calver sat forward in it, unwilling to let himself loosen his composure. As Thacklore stood, only to settle into the chair across from them, Calver slid one of the tampered Aetech lamps from his pocket and tucked it into the crossbeam beneath the table.

Raimee's lips pressed into a line. She moved like she'd developed a tick, her ear tucking toward her shoulder. Calver sliced his hand beneath the table in a gesture of "stop." It was a precaution only. The Ruxian suppressed a shudder. Did she even know what it was? What had she deduced from their meeting with Greeny the day prior?

Thacklore dismissed his servants, who disappeared back behind the false wall, and poured them each a glass of wine. Calver did not take his.

"I believe a showing of marks is in order?" Thacklore said, his low voice full of anticipation.

Calver shrugged his cloak from one shoulder and pulled down the front of his tunic to reveal the space below his right collarbone. Thacklore simultaneously loosened his collar and undid the first three buttons of his blouse. The cuts there were clean and precise, so different from Calver's.

They covered back up, and Raimee's dagger-straight spine threatened to snap.

"Yours is quite weathered. You've been in this business for a long time?" It wasn't mere conversation. It was an interrogation.

Calver motioned for Raimee to interpret.

"'Long' is relative," she said.

"Well, I suppose that's why you have the connections you do to the Hand." Thacklore didn't look at Calver, the way Greeny had during their meeting. Rather, his eyes fixed unblinkingly on Raimee. It awakened something feral in Calver that was in no way connected to the Survivor. "I'm sorry, dear," he said to her, "I never caught your name."

She looked to Calver for confirmation. He nodded.

"Sheena," she said, her blush so powerful that Calver nearly felt its heat.

Thacklore held a hand out to her, and she extended her own. He kissed her knuckles. "A pleasure. And, dear, what is quite the matter with your eyes?"

"I have a sensitivity to the light. On account of a childhood injury. Terrible thing."

"Ah. I'm very sorry to hear that. Would you prefer it if I drew the curtains?" He raised his hands, prepared to clap again.

"Not necessary," she responded in stride. "It would make little difference, and I do prefer to feel the sun on my skin."

Thacklore nodded. "You have a peculiar accent. I'm not sure I've heard it before. Where are you from?"

Raimee didn't miss a beat. "Gembolta."

Thacklore's eyes lit with his jovial laugh. "You come from a family of frontiersmen, then! How wonderful. How unique. What a pleasure it is to have you here."

Genetic eye diseases were prolific in Gembolta's scattered colonies. How had Calver ever thought this woman to be dotty?

Thacklore straightened his vest and sat forward in his chair. "I have but an inkling as to what the nature of this visit involves. Please, do divulge."

Raimee interpreted Calver's signals flawlessly. "I am looking for a man named Abiathar Methu'su. I understand you have information on his location?"

Thacklore leaned back and stroked his beard. "Yes," he muttered. "How interesting." Then he sighed. "You aren't the only one who would love to locate Methu'su, you know? Tricky matter, that. Why, precisely, is it that you are trying to find him?"

Calver crossed his arms. One with the Shadewalker's mark should know better than to ask questions. Greeny had known; every other connection had known.

"I would have mentioned it, were it relevant to you," Raimee said for him. Her tone precisely reflected his feelings. Creation, she was useful. If they didn't find Methu'su, maybe she could—

No. He stopped himself before he thought any further. For both of their sakes, he needed her as far from him as the Fates would permit.

"Touchy." Thacklore twisted his mouth.

"Indeed. It is personal."

The patrician bristled. "And how could it be personal, Mesu Friyal? I can hardly see what personal business Methu'su could have had with a child. You couldn't have been very old the last time he was seen by anyone."

Fuck. Calver's blood ran cold. Thacklore had the upper hand here. Their ignorance hindered them. It was time to feign control over the situation.

"The information we seek is for a third party," Raimee interpreted. Calver cleared his throat and took a sip of water from his own flask, just to make a point. "You've been paid, have you not? This appointment was not made for you to ask me questions. It was made so that you can tell me about Methu'su. If you can't, we will seek other resources."

"Ah yes. Forgive my questions. I do love the art of conversation, though I realize it is something frowned upon among the Shadewalker's Ghosts." The patrician tapped his fingertips together. "If you've been long hunting Methu'su, I imagine you already know what little I can tell you, but here we sit." Thacklore poured himself a spot of wine and sipped before continuing. "Methu'su was a Tera'thian spy during the gray period. It was, what, thirty years ago that he switched over to our side. Well, Nelfindar's, anyhow." He peered curiously at Calver. "I suppose I'm not clear as to which side your Hand is on." He waited for Calver to say something.

Calver would not respond to information-extracting tactics manipulated into casual conversation. When he remained stoic, Thacklore's mouth turned downward.

"Methu'su did a great deal of service for the Green Wing. Led a special operations team up until the Chori war, twenty years ago. While I met him on numerous occasions, I admit that I spent little time with him. The man was hard to read. Hardly sociable."

He stroked his beard thoughtfully. "His final operation failed. Devastating, it was. He was the only survivor in his squadron." Thacklore stopped to compose his thoughts. He shrugged. "You can only imagine what that sort of thing does to a man's psyche. Who knows? Perhaps he was the one to set them up in the first place, or perhaps he didn't. Word is, his failure drove him mad. He quit the service afterward. He was last seen in Seraphinden fifteen—no—eighteen years ago?"

Like that was an arbitrary number. Calver had lived with Fankalo long enough to spot an act.

"He left to live somewhere in the Tsorlap Mountains," Thacklore finished.

"The Tsorlap Mountains?" Raimee translated. "That doesn't exactly narrow it down. And no one knows where? He just disappeared?"

"Like the mist over the Sharinash. I will tell you this, though, and I alone know this." He looked from side to side, like a boy proud to share his secret. "He had a contact in Seraphinden named Kotar Avelius. A few years ago, I arranged dinner with Kotar in my capital city vacation home. He fed me some interesting information."

More likely he'd threatened him for it.

"Methu'su sends him letters to distribute to his only other contacts. One is a cenobite in Tennca'Pui. The other is a Green Wing captain in Seraphinden." Thacklore paused to sip wine before adding, "And that's what I have for you, my friends."

That was it? Methu'su wasn't in Chira'na and, by the sound of it, had never even been in Chira'na. He might not even be alive. Calver bit into his cheek. Why had Raimee been sent to find him here?

And then the further implication of Thacklore's story hit Calver like a gut-punch. Methu'su had worked for the Green Wing, Seraphinden's central government defense, not Tera'thia. Calver's father had died twenty years ago, just as Methu'su's mission for the Green Wing had failed twenty years ago. Calver's mother had claimed that Methu'su was a friend to the family. That he and his father's work had aligned.

Thacklore must know more.

Raimee read from Calver's signals. "Have details on Methu'su's failed operation been released to public record?"

Thacklore smiled a thin-lipped smile. "Isn't that just what everyone wants to know?" He drained his wine. "I'm a man who knows things, damn it. I was the most prominent advisor to the Blue Wing's General Prime for decades. Not knowing... it is inadequate." He poured himself more wine, his hand shaking ever so slightly. "When I heard that you were looking for information on Methu'su, I hoped you might be able to tell *me* something I didn't already know. But alas..." He stared at Raimee, then through her, his fingers drumming on the table. She avoided his eye contact, training her gaze on Calver's hands.

"You said Methu'su was a Tera'thian spy before he turned over," Calver inquired through her. "I thought the gray period was relatively peaceful between Nelfindar and Tera'thia. It was the Chori we warred with. Do you know what Methu'su's objective was on the Tera'thian side?"

Thacklore's smile turned sinister. Calver's hand twitched toward the lamp planted beneath the table.

"Yes." Their host's voice held all the textures of frayed velvet. "Abiathar Methu'su was one of the last of Tera'thia's *Serabi Matu*."

He stared into his glass for the space of time it took to take the dowaga through three defense cycles. For all the room's tension, it felt as though their chairs sat on ice over a fast-melting stream. Calver waged an internal battle of slowing his heart rate, keeping his breathing even. Raimee wouldn't know the term, but of course, he wouldn't have to explain it to her, either. Thacklore was so fated excited to talk about Methu'su, he proceeded to do it for him.

"The Serabi Matu, you may not know, were Tera'thia's legendary cohort of elites, dating back to the Kath war: the Ruxian slayers."

Chapter 33

Niklaus

TWELVE YEARS PREVIOUSLY

Sometimes, Niklaus felt that he had a way with words. Other times, his own words had their way with him. Other times, they weighed the rope that strung him up naked for the world to take their aim.

"Preservation, Mother, when will you ever lower your standards?"

Those had been the wrong words.

His mother trembled in fury, a tremor that made his insides stumble. "You failed every single test in your final term."

"Quite a marvel, if we're honest with each other." He beamed back at her, ignoring his misgivings. "It took a fair amount of effort to select the most perfectly wrong answers to every question."

Pure bait. He was acting the terrorist—not his intent for his first five minutes back in the Meyernes Manor in two years. Then again, he hadn't expected the woman he most resented to be standing at the entryway to receive him.

Her response was not so much a question, and definitely not a plea, as a demand. "Why? Help me to understand."

Why indeed. Niklaus couldn't look her in the eye. He found a sudden fascination with his fingernails. "You know, there is a species of monkey that dwells along the Tera'thian borderlands. Beautiful creatures. They brought in a specimen for us to observe last term. The mothers in this species, faced by extreme stress or uncertainty, have been known to eat their own young."

His mother's mouth dropped in pure revulsion.

He didn't miss a beat. "Here's what I understand. *I* inherited my father's wealth—not you—when he died. *I* wanted to channel it into the improvement of groundling class education. *You* chose to fuck half the oligarchy to sway their vote in outlawing groundling literacy." His mother blinked. "I chose to invest in Aetech. Then you sent me to boarding school."

"To get an education," she contended.

Back for less than the time it took to finish a drink, and he'd already hit a breaking point with her. This was not promising.

"To prevent me from channeling our expanding funds into public programs," he countered, waggling a finger in the air. "Then last year I asked you for help. I was floundering with a fortune large enough to purchase half the continent with guidance only from sycophants, corrupt officials, and overdressed thieves. And you chose to extend my courses."

His mother hissed at him through her teeth. "You are comparing me to a cannibalistic animal?"

How could that be what she'd fixated on, given his accusation? Words—the wrong words—bled from his mouth again. "I can't be blamed for the number of similarities."

Was it acceptable for a twenty-something-year-old to run from his mother?

Her eyes narrowed to such an angle that a single long eyebrow hair escaped the mask of her face paint.

Oh, yes. He should run.

The matron of the manor cawed after him for him to stop, which only spurred his steps like a crop against a thoroughbred's flanks. He made his way toward his own quarters feeling silly, but also justifying that a few moments of silence would be worth the cost to his ego.

She followed him.

Niklaus snapped the doors to his room shut, threw the deadbolt, and flattened his back against them. His mother continued to scream outside for a number of minutes. He tried to tune her words out, instead mentally reciting a piece of philosophy he'd only just had commissioned of a cenobite at the University's research outreach, Tennca'Pui.

'The life you live is a pure, telling product of your inner truth. The chaos of our universe is the pure, telling product of the greater truth.'

The most beautiful words ever written on paper. And he'd helped put them there... where it was likely nobody else would ever read them.

He still heard every few muffled words from behind the doors. "So help me" and "destroy" and, oddly, "groundskeeping" among them. But his mother's tirade passed, and she soon left him be. With a drawn-out exhalation, Niklaus slid his back down along the door until he reached the floor. Finally, he was alone.

Except he wasn't.

Two body-lengths in front of him, a young woman held a bundle of fresh linens. She was vested in the emerald tabard the maids wore and staring at him as though she'd rather not be there. Chaos.

"Latouda?" he asked. "Is that you?" Fates, but she'd grown. Ripe like the cintas flower in peak bloom.

She tucked a loose strand of her long black hair behind an ear and proffered an awkward smile. "Welcome back, Nikla. It looks as though you are happy to have re-found your rooms."

"Ah yes," he coughed, scrambling to his feet. "And I seemed to have blocked your point of evacuation. Sorry." He unlocked the doors and peeked through the crack between them. "I believe the beast is gone now."

He turned toward her with a smile. She gave him a funny look.

"What was that about?" she asked. It had been a few years since he'd last seen her, but her voice sounded oddly different. Like a harp in its first degree out of tune.

"Ah... that? Mother."

She watched him closely, then grinned. "Did she catch you running about half-naked yelling 'free money' again?"

He laughed nervously. "No. It simply appears she had forgotten that, as with all good things, my away schooling would come to an end. And I think she'd anticipated a different result from the carefully catered subject matter I was given."

Force-fed.

Once again, she looked at him as though he was speaking another language and she'd only picked up every third word. He changed the subject. "How have you been? You look well. Ah. I mean. You've grown." Kretch, he sounded like an imbecile. "I mean. Not like that. Just physically. Just. In a good way." That was definitely worse. "You're perfect—ah—*ly* grown-up-looking. And lovely." He winced.

Latouda watched him intensely, her catlike eyes never leaving his face. Creation's sweet arse, it was part of the reason he'd stumbled so. Her face was as perfect as a painting. After his mammal brain caught up to its rational better half, his stomach curdled as he put a coherent thought together about her. He'd forgotten.

Poor girl.

"Oh..." he started, still an idiot. Then he spoke as loudly and slowly as he could without feeling as though he were insulting her. "They told me, in a letter. About the accident. I'm—I'm sorry."

Latouda looked away. He could see the color tinging her cheeks, the wells brimming beneath her eyes. Kretch. He'd made it worse. Why did he have to incidentally trap the recently deaf girl in his rooms alone with him?

"It's... alright," she began, under control. She looked up at him and forced a smile that did not reach her eyes. Fates, it hardly mattered. She was still beautiful. "The doctors say it's only a matter of time before it's all gone. And then... Well. Your mother's agreed to keep me, so that's good..." Her bottom lip quivered. *No.* Not under control. *Kretch.* "Oh, Nikla," she sobbed. She was under as much control as the Korshuva pavilion fountain, the one that had started spewing sewage instead of sea water. "I-I'm not ready. How will I interact with anyone? I'll be as coherent as the great green walls."

He padded over to her and put a hand to her back. "Now then—"

She spun around and threw her arms about him, her tears seeping into the suede of his tunic. Chaos. That would probably leave a mark.

He gave her an awkward pat on the back. "Ah—it will all be ok. You'll see." Hadn't he once learned her father was a seafarer? He realized she probably couldn't hear him very well with her face pressed into his chest, so he pulled away. "You can learn to signal." The hand language was common and standardized among seafarers.

Latouda turned her face from him, fussing with the hem of her tabard. "What's the point? Hardly anyone would understand me."

And she could learn to write... Latouda's family had worked for his for at least as long as he'd been alive. He had memories of her chasing him through the skywalk gardens when she was a toddler and he a child. Groundling education had been poor even then, before the legislation against it... she'd never had schooling. Couldn't she have simply sat alongside him when his tutors came for a lesson?

He had always wanted to be a teacher. What was one teeny, tiny, nonsensical law? He was Niklaus Meyernes. Who would speak against him and get away with it?

He set his hands on Latouda's shoulders, facing her so she could read his lips. "How about this, then. I'll learn to signal with you... and I'll teach you to read, too."

Chapter 34
Calverous

Silence fell over Thacklore's study. Like the sound of solid water in winter, of a heart which had stopped beating, the slow smothering of hog-tied hope in a tar pit. Calver kept his posture and face as hard as the chair beneath him. Raimee, inadvertently, leaned back.

Ruxian slayers. Like they were monsters, insects, Chaos curselings, not people.

"Many historians believe the *Serabi Matu* were single-handedly responsible for the strategic genocide of Seraphindo's entire bloodline," Thacklore continued, as though it were the most logical thing to have learned. "So when you ask what Methu'su's operation was? Well, I can only imagine it involved the Ruxians. It's no secret now that the oligarchy wanted them removed before the gray period. But Methu'su's shift in alliance occurred in our lifetime. Is that not incredible? Ruxians still among us, within the last thirty years?"

Fuck. And Thacklore implied political incentive. This was more problematic than Calver could have anticipated. He proffered no response beyond a nod. Raimee sat in suspended silence.

"It will forever remain a mystery, I suppose," Thacklore swirled the contents of his glass, looking from Calver to Raimee inquisitively. The air thinned in the space between. Calver found reason to focus on the room's every detail: the clock ticking on the wall; the enormous fireplace to their left—an exit point; the heavy furniture—an obstacle; his own heartbeat—Fates, if only it would slow; and small quiet creaks and taps on the floor. The house was quiet. But it was not nearly empty.

<I suppose,> he parroted for Raimee to interpret. <Thank you for your time.>

Forget the shipment. He needed to get her out of here.

Calver stood to leave, and Raimee erupted to her feet beside him, nearly knocking her chair backward in the process.

"A moment." Thacklore held up a hand. "There is another matter for you and I to discuss. One that could be of extreme interest to our mutual beneficiary."

Get out. Getoutgetout. Calver turned to face him.

Thacklore's voice quieted. "I take it she doesn't wear the mark?" He tilted an ear toward Raimee.

Calver's insides clenched. He had no need to dignify a response. Anything that came after would be a calamity. He turned to leave.

"Going against protocol?" Thacklore asked behind him with a cluck of the tongue. "Given your reputation, I didn't imagine you'd be so... blatantly disloyal."

Disloyal.

The word was like a knife. Calver would give another tongue to have never heard him say it. He turned back around.

"Never mind that. I'm not one to share secrets, so long as you'll pass my offer along to the Hand, of course. I was informed you have your letters?"

Even worse, he'd accompanied the threat with an intention to separate them. All with perfect fucking propriety.

Feeling the trap tighten around their necks, Calver nodded. The Survivor hugged his mind like a dark cloud.

"My dear." Thacklore raised his chin in Raimee's direction. Her color drained faster than gravity ought to have made feasible. " Might I ask you to step outside? I have a confidential business errand with which your companion may be able to assist me, and it's a strict matter of policy."

The Survivor ascended and, with a tugging anxiety, Calver let it flow forward into a space of primary control. *{Deal with her later.}*

Later...

That was right... Calver had come here for proof that Thacklore was involved in the Tera'thian interference in the shipment. Not the Ruxian.

To find out why they had ushered defensive technology to the Red Wing recruitment, which would arrive in Steila while Bovak Ani's navy docked in Solutium.

Not for Methu'su.

Denying Thacklore's request for her to leave would only make matters worse. Would only turn Fankalo from him further.

Raimee looked at Calver like she didn't recognize him. Her mouth parted halfway in a silent scream.

<Go. Wait,> the Survivor told her.

She shook her head vigorously. "Calver, actually, I'd prefer not—"

He pointed to the door. She'd used his real name.

"Calver," she whispered. "Calver, come back." Her voice choked.

Calver nearly resurfaced. Come back? He was right in front of her...

{Finish what you came for.}

Calver listened. *<You have no place in this matter. Wait for me in the hall.>*

The Ruxian paused. Trembled. Then scurried out, shutting the door behind her. The Survivor numbed Calver's bubbling guilt.

He returned to his seat at the table and Thacklore clapped again, mentioning nothing of Raimee's use of his name. "Paper and a quill," he called.

Moments later, a boy brought it out from behind the wall. The child was careful to avoid eye contact; he looked familiar. Calver felt something akin to being in a game of stackers and realizing he was two steps behind his competitor with three rings left to place.

The boy bowed and extricated himself from the room like it had been set on fire.

"Finally," Thacklore began. "We can communicate. Tell me bluntly. What is your relationship to her?"

He knew. *Fuck.* He *knew.*

Thacklore had been excited for a reason to discuss Methu'su. He had a clear obsession with the Ruxian genocide. And, with Greeny's disclosures, Calver was positive he worked for the Tera'thians. They'd walked right into the hands of a man who had been hunting for her like a rare game for decades, and the Survivor had thrown her out, alone, into his hallway.

Calver wrote quickly. 'A talented signal translator. Hard to find, inland.'

Thacklore tapped his chin. "I can only imagine the difficulties you go through."

Calver nodded, but he had hesitated for a second too long.

"What's that girl to you?" Thacklore repeated, enunciating the words this time.

Calver rapped the pen against his previous note.

Thacklore rubbed his hands together. "Understood. I would like to make you an offer, then. I imagine I can grant you enough to please the Hand for your efforts. She'll never know you brought her here unmarked. And I will personally appoint you a suitable replacement for signal translation."

'You misunderstood. She isn't for auction,' he scratched.

Thacklore looked like he'd been caught in a joke which went over his head. "Then why have you..." he shook his head. "Never mind. A hundred thousand silver notes."

Calver pointed to his previous note, again, face impassive.

"Five hundred," Thacklore spat.

Calver had never heard of such a large sum of money for any business transaction outside the loans they'd taken from the Pazirians for the Drieden corporation. If Fankalo ever found out...

{Take the deal. It may regain you your favor. The Ruxian is already hopeless. If she doesn't die here, she will trying to get to Methu'su.}

Calver didn't know what was worse—that everything the Survivor said was true, or his blatant unwillingness to believe it.

No.

He pushed against the Survivor in an attempt to gain clarity. It fumed with irritation, pushing back. It seemed stronger again. His control was slipping...

'Is this all you wanted to discuss?'

Thacklore sucked at his teeth. "Don't make this error. I know your business runs on notes. You walk out of here with a deal, or you don't walk out of here at all. I would rather stay in the Hand's good graces, and eliminating the Reaper won't land me there. But your bringing an unmarked gives me justifiable cause." He spoke each word with distinction. "Name. Your. Price."

Outside the door, a nightmarish scream pierced the air and stole any mercy Calver had cultivated over the past weeks. The sound cut off, as though stifled. *Smothered.* Both of their heads turned to the door.

Thacklore's hands balled into fists. Calver's pulse lunged against the prison of his veins. He fought the instinct to punch, to rip, to destroy, in favor of keeping his seat, collected. They wouldn't have killed her yet. Thacklore probably had his own payday at the other side of this interaction. The Survivor brightened in his mind more than it had in weeks. It held him at bay.

"Well?" Thacklore demanded.

Calver hardly remembered the question: the pitiful bargain of his life in exchange for his humanity. 'I told you she was not for sale.'

"And I told you you'd leave my home with a deal or not at all."

Either way, Thacklore needed to die. Calver might as well try to bluff and get more information.

'Then perhaps we can haggle. I'm sure the Hand would love to know why you've advised a Tera'thian unit to intervene in a shipment of Red Wing defense technology. With that knowledge, we may even discuss a price for my interpreter.'

Thacklore scowled at the note and straightened his vest. "I'm sorry it had to go this way. I really am," he said. "But I gave you your chance. And the Hand cannot deny my defense."

He whistled. A dozen men entered the study bearing cosalts and leveled their weapons toward the center where he and Calver sat.

Calver's mind-djinn surged forward in anticipation of violence. He didn't flinch as he scribbled, hoping to lean on the façade just one more time. 'You have no idea who I am, do you?'

Thacklore read the sentence and raised an eyebrow. "The Reaper? Please. Even if the rest of Kath has bought the act, I, for one, recognize the rumors of you to be a fabulous game of make-believe."

'The Reaper? Errand boy to the Hand? Will you stake your life on that bet?' Calver cringed inwardly at the Survivor's primal boast.

Seconds tipped by and a realization eclipsed Thacklore's expression. "Wait—no, no. That just can't be." He stared at Calver and slapped his knee, a grin pulling his lips from his teeth. "How absolutely delicious. The resemblance is uncanny. *You're* Cul'Mon's missing gem—you're Calverous Curtaim?"

Then Thacklore started to laugh: high, shrill, maniacal.

A sharpened blade of panic snaked down Calver's spine. Thacklore knew his name. His *full* name. Cul'Mon hadn't even known, so how did he—

"And Fankalo Keane? I don't know how I didn't see it sooner. I always assumed that was another of her stage names, but this? Preservation, do Thadinar's genes run strong." Thacklore wheezed through his laughter. "But the best part is that you came to *me* looking for Methu'su? Fates behave, but your 'sibling'—" he said mockingly—"has pulled the veil over you."

—The only way he could know. Fankalo had told him.

Thacklore's hair-raising tirade continued. "I shouldn't even be surprised. You conduits always were like fucking cockroaches. But you don't know what's coming. The two of you are eviscerating fucked."

Conduits? Calver's panic settled into anguish. Anguish fed rage. And rage sparked action, without a thought for its consequences.

The reaping began.

The Survivor's conquest over his veins came so fast and with such ferocity that he didn't even have a chance to resist. It smothered him, burning his torment as fuel, shoving him into an unwilling free-fall into the pit of his mind's void. The mind-djinn activated the lamp beneath the table.

   It started to glow.

Chapter 35

Calverous

Beneath the table, the lamp's radiance expanded and flared in electrical arcs. As Calver's memories and thoughts blended into the Survivor's, he kicked up the table and slammed it into Thacklore's chest. Thacklore, table, and the exothermic-reaction-once-Aetech-lamp crashed backward into two guards.

Five seconds.

The Survivor careened away from them, dropping to the floor and scrambling to dodge the others that lunged for him. The barbed tip of a cosalt came a finger's width from spearing him like a fish.

Four.

Following a jolt of insight, he rolled, grabbed its shaft, swung his body to trip those within grappling distance.

Three.

He did not need to fight them. All that mattered was putting space between him and the ensuing detonation. He leaped to his feet, dipping and weaving to evade them and slip into the brick fireplace.

Two.

He filled his lungs with clean air; held his breath.

The Aetech lamp exploded just as he shimmied up into the oversized chimney. He clung there, arms and legs pressing into the vibrating masonry. Bound beneath the Survivor, Calver didn't feel the torrid wave blasting past, singeing his hair and blistering his skin. He waited, ignoring the screams of the dying, before sliding out into the blaze that awaited him.

In Calver's world, reaction was a thing to be stifled. He was always painting his thoughts in shades of gray for fear of evoking their *sinister* consequence. *Pathetic.*

Fire, the essence of pure, unfiltered reaction, was resplendent, and to the Survivor there was nothing more enthralling in all the world. A raw reaction made tangible. Ignition. Combustion. The beautiful irony of light that burned into even deeper darkness.

It was fuel for its soul. A vicarious outlet.

Thick black smoke filled the space between lintel and ceiling. The Survivor still held Calver's breath. The floor of the room had collapsed where the lamp had exploded with Thacklore. He couldn't discern the number of bodies, but two men lay screaming and writhing at his feet. They clawed at melted eyes. Sinews of raw muscle showed beneath charred skin. He drew his dowaga to end their pain.

A part of the wall had been blown out, opening into the opulent foyer. He skirted into the vacant entryway and drank several heaving breaths where the air was clear. His nostrils met the smells of seared flesh and char. A shock of smoke rolled toward the vaulted ceiling, darkening the stained-glass chandelier. Still-languid flame licked gracefully forward in its wake. All would be consumed, before long; all of Thacklore's lavishness, his paintings, his rugs and tapestries, his treasures, burnt to the same ash as common grain. The Survivor set to the task that would ensure their survival. Nobody could be left alive.

A deep voice cried out in pain, though it was hard to discern where the sound came from. The Survivor flowed around Calver, darker and faster than the smoke from the blaze. It moved him to stand before the entry doors, dowaga raised in wait. These people were as rodents in a den. He would cover the only exit.

They came.

Eight soldiers garbed like Chira'na's guard emerged on the landing, weapons bared. The Survivor gritted Calver's teeth, set the soles of his boots wider. There was no better Reaper. He spelled death as a poet sowed words, parading destruction as art. He knew how his opponents would move before they knew themselves.

The guards spilled down the stairs in an avalanche of blades to encircle him. They barked a Tera'thian exchange before surging forward as a unit. He spun once, sweeping the blade end of the dowaga after him in a great arc.

Two guards fell, crying out as steel bit through skin, slicking the floors with the pungent tang of first blood. The Survivor parried blade after blade in a blur of motion and steel. The men stood shoulder to shoulder in their attempt to overtake him. A chance to level the guard on the far right presented itself, and the circle around him broke.

The Survivor dashed for the staircase, palming the next of the lamps from within his cloak. Activated it.

A lobbing toss sent destruction into the fray.

He took the steps three at a time to reach the landing. His heart, beating in his ears, pounded out the seconds as they ticked by, instilling a thrill for the violence to come.

The lamp erupted. First came the flash, brighter than staring into the highsun, and then the roar, all too similar to the applause in Tera'thia's coliseum. Where Cul'Mon had first broken Calver of his pitiful fear of bloodshed. Where they had made him into exactly what he was destined to be.

The Survivor hurled his body into the farthest corner of the landing and crouched, covering the back of his head. Blotches of light glared angrily on the backs of his eyelids. A scorching wave washed over him as it had in the fireplace, and debris pelted him. He felt no pain. Pain was the bane of mortals.

When the worst of the blast was over, he rose, falling into a defensive stance. The chandelier still hung, blackened and swinging precariously with the screeching of unoiled metal. Untamed flames undulated skyward to a symphony of snaps and cracks, casting ash and embers afloat, escaping gravity with the grace of dandelion tufts. A gust of wind tousled Calver's dark curls, forged by heat seeking the room's coolest corners. With it, smoke billowed freely from the house and into the crisp winter air through the space that had once held the front door.

The foyer floor had collapsed into the basement, taking the bodies of the guards with it. Only a blackened and marred outline marked where the stairs had previously met the landing.

The landing groaned beneath him as flames engulfed the walls of the foyer. The Survivor knew flame. Most of the ground floor should be burning from the aftermath of the first explosive by now. The second floor wouldn't be inhabitable for long. He waited, counting ten breaths to see if anyone would try to escape into the landing from the upper level.

Loa Jahndia hurled herself through the door at the far end of the hall. Three other women, presumably servants, followed her. When they saw the Survivor, stained by blood and sweat and soot, looming a head higher than the average man, they skidded to a stop. There was nowhere for them to go. The Survivor did not discriminate.

He advanced.

All blood was of equal density. Their bodies pitched to the floor before the mind-djinn's blade. It purred in satisfaction. *Effortless.*

The floor groaned again, as though aware of the grim burden it now held, giving a final cry before its inevitable collapse. If there was anyone else left upstairs, they would be trapped. There was no more work to be done here. The Survivor made to leave its dark mark. To remind them what they'd done. To assure them of what was coming.

And then Calver surfaced, scraping, struggling—

Raimee. The singular thought on his mind. His deepest desperation.

The Survivor fought to repress him. *{You had a task. I'm finishing it.}*

Calver resisted. *No!* The perpetrators didn't matter. Thacklore was dead anyway.

{Any left alive will put your operation at risk. Fankalo asked you to—}

There wasn't time.

What if she had been taken into one of the rooms on the upper level? There was no way to get to them. Calver strained his ears for the impossible sound of his name passing across her lips. The crackling of the fire and creaking of wood around him were deafening.

From below came the distinctive notes of a struggle: a hollow thumping; strangled yells.

{The basement,} the Survivor growled. *{Many still live.}*

Calver pulled himself to stand on the banister rimming the crumbling landing and launched himself at the chandelier. Gripping its searing hot arms, he swung to the far wall, where he planted his feet on the adobe and jettisoned toward the intact floor on the opposite side of the foyer. He absorbed the impact with a crouch and directed its momentum into a roll.

And not a moment too soon. The floor behind him caved in, followed by a telltale groan from the landing above. Calver raced down the hall and to the right, where he plastered himself against the far wall. An instant later, the landing crumpled in front of him, a sulfurous monstrosity of flaming beams, taking down the wall to his side. He crouched to shield his face from the scorch and debris. After a pause, he blinked open his eyes, squinting to see past cascading ash.

The crash revealed the staircase to the basement, now wholly blocked by burning detritus.

Calver clenched his jaw. If he wanted to escape this place, he would need to exit now, from a window on the main floor. Sensing his hesitation, the Survivor pushed against him. *{Flee. You've succeeded. Anyone below ground will not make it out.}*

Calver eyed the hole in the ground floor by the door or in the study, though it would be impossible to return from it. His chest ached. The feeling was smothered by the Survivor's struggle to regain his mind.

It forced his legs to move away.

No.

The last time it had taken him unwillingly, like this, it had ended in his exile. Calver buckled his knees to stop them from moving any further. His face smacked into the floor, searing hot against his skin. He bellowed beneath the frustration of the mind-djinn's newest assault.

{You will die.}

And if you keep fighting me, I'll keep us here. You'll die with me.

The Survivor had never truly spoken in more than ephemeral impressions. It gave its version of a laugh, then, more horrible and more alien than any sound had the right to be.

{I do not die. Waters will flood this earth and I will remain. Fire will scorch your lands and I will remain. Humanity will vanish from conscious memory and, long after all your world turns to dust a hundred times over, I will remain. Waiting. And another will come for me. That is the ebb and flow of Creation. Life will find its way back into my embrace.}

And then it struck him with such strength, Calver could have sworn something ruptured. Blood pooled around his face in a stream from his nose. He resisted, still.

Billowing black clouds plumed around him. The air was hot and thin. Every second, the smoke seared further into his lungs. And his mind tore again and again beneath the Survivor's crushing weight. Calver screamed. He re-lived his childhood, too late, again, to save a life. He'd only ever been good at taking them. The thought burned worse than the blaze, pained him more than the Survivor. Choked him. Seared at him. Singed at him. He pressed himself from the floor onto hands and knees, wavering, as the fire raged around him, a mirror of his internal inferno.

I lost everything. Because of you. I won't submit again. You'll have to kill me here. And wait your next hundred years. Thousand. More.

The mind-djinn's grip slacked into a loose hold as it considered him. Time stretched, but the ash still fell, fresh snow in the shadow of destruction.

{You're not worth the fight,} it finally said.

Void.

The Survivor dropped from him. It faded, faster, deeper than ever before.

Calver sucked in through his teeth, bracing against the sudden sting from the burns and afflictions wracking his body. He shook his head—*his* head—to adjust to the new-found calm. And then he darted, scrambled, to the ledge where the floor had caved in on his own authority.

In a single motion, he swung his body down, dangled by his fingers, and dropped to the stone floor of the basement. The corpses of the Survivor's victims greeted him there, piled in a still-burning grave. Calver carried on past them, trying not to think about who they might have been, blood-stained steel at his side and silence in his wake. The illness Thyatira had given him had spread once again. Silence begetting silence, begetting silence.

No more. Raimee would not die alone by his fault.

The basement granted a mild reprieve from the heat of the main story; the air was breathable. Before Calver had a chance to catch his bearings, two of the servant boys rounded a corner. They ran at the sight of him. He pursued them into a tunnel-like hallway where the floor sloped upwards into a dead end at ground level. It looked like it had once been a second exit into the side yard, since sealed over with brick and mortar. Pins and needles prickled Calver's skin. Why would Thacklore have sealed off the only other exit in his home?

At the pit of a passage, the two boys joined a third in chopping away at the stony dead end with an ax. They rammed against it with the butted ends of cosalts, trying desperately to break through. Calver slowed and looked over his shoulder. No one had followed him. He stalked toward the trio, dowaga level. The boys had managed a small hole in the wall. A waterfall of dazzling sunlight poured through.

Hope.

They beat at it frantically, trying to make a gap large enough to squeeze through. He would reach them first. As Calver approached, the first boy dropped his ax and cowered in the corner.

"I'll tell yas where they took 'er, big man!" he babbled, tears streaming down his face.

Calver's chest constricted. It was the one who had brought him the quill—the one he thought he'd recognized.

The urchin.

On the streets he'd seemed smaller—dressed in muddy rags, whispering thanks into Calver's ear each time he'd passed him a snack or silver note.

The realization shot like ice into his bones. There had been a tag on him. Cul'Mon had him watched all this time, as he'd feared, his every move reported through Deshpian Thacklore. And he had taken pity on the boy who'd sold him out.

The cowering child continued to cry out. "She in teh cells!" He pointed the way Calver had come. "I can get yas the key!" Calver heard the boy's words for what they were now: not the language of an uneducated groundling urchin, but a tume'amic without a proper grasp on Nelfinden articulation.

Thacklore had been setting tume'amic out into the streets, guised as urchins, to collect information. It was sickening in its brilliance.

A growl escaped Calver's smoke-ridden throat as he holstered his dowaga. Without hesitation, the boy scrambled to his feet to retrieve the keys. Calver grabbed the boy's ax and hacked at stone. He was thwacked at, in tandem, by his own compounding failures: learning nothing about the shipment, Fankalo's lies, and the look on Raimee's face as the Survivor had cast her out the study door. The stone came away in chunks until he created a hole sizable enough to squeeze through; an exit prepared, for if he found Raimee. An 'if' that grew, like the lump in his throat, with every floundering heartbeat.

The two boys scrambled through without a backward glance. Then the urchin appeared at Calver's side, proffering a set of three keys with a shaking hand. Calver pocketed them with a glare. He'd condemned himself by sparing these tume'amic. They would talk. Even if they didn't want to, someone would interrogate them.

Tears ran down the boy's face. "I sorry, big man... Yahs dun know wha' he did teh me."

But Calver did. He had the barbs in his back to prove it. Given what he'd done, what they both had done, he turned and left the boy there, with his freedom and without response.

What was it that Raimee had told him a coincidence was just the day before? A crosspoint on the journey the Fates had intended for him? Calver tried not to think of what it meant if all of his coincidences were bad ones.

Time was a dice roll.

He turned from the hallway. Burning debris now littered the room beneath the foyer where the main level had caved in. The fire had grown, as though possessed, and roared deafeningly overhead. Tendrils of smoke seeped down through the remaining floorboards above, which glowed ominously. How long had passed since the first lamp erupted? Five minutes? Long enough for the authorities to arrive.

Through the haze, Calver spotted a single door on the adjacent wall. He sprinted toward it but stopped short, heart leadening. It glowed around its edges. Covering his hand with his cloak, he rattled the handle. It was unlocked, but the metal seared through his clothing. His mind shot through the short list of unlikely scenarios that might get him into the next room without dying.

All began with the same action.

He stepped backward and charged at the door with his shoulder.

The hearty wood's sudden passage parted the flames for him to pass through. Calver panted in relief at his good luck. The fire had been isolated to the space directly in front of the door, where the landing above had collapsed. The space beyond was, so far, intact.

He glanced around the room he'd careened into. It was dark and encased entirely in stone. And empty, apart from a trap door set into the floor. He gripped its cool silver ring with soot-blackened fingers and pulled. Beneath, a winding staircase led deeper below the house.

Calver took it at a run, trying not to wonder about why someone might keep a holding chamber two stories beneath their residence or how likely it was to be his tomb. The floor could collapse and trap them down here at any moment.

Panic pulled on his anticipation. She might not even be down here. The boy could have lied to gain his favor and escape. They might have broken her neck back in the hallway outside the study. She could have been tied up in Loa's room, where her body would have crashed with the flaming rubble from the landing. Something crawled in Calver's chest with talons extended. He might find her body here, head severed.

Even the thought felt impossible in its wrongness. She was so much more than a body—pure starlight set with bones and bundled in skin.

The staircase was midnight black and stank like an uncovered grave. An increasingly loud buzzing sound raised the hairs on the back of Calver's sweat-slicked neck as he stepped continually farther down. Darkness meant no one was down here... right? He activated a non-tampered Aetech lamp. Beneath its glass, magnets whirred as it spun into life. Its resplendent shine cast eerie shadows onto the stone walls.

After what felt like an infinite stretch of too little time, Calver leveled onto a cobblestone floor. He rounded a corner with dowaga bared to clear the room beyond. The space before him was dimly lit by a single, plain torch. Three cells lined its rear wall. He nearly held his nose against the pungent stink of rot and worse that came from them. A table, painted by dark stains, sat in the room's center, and an array of steel instruments stared innocently from their holsters on its walls.

It was a torture chamber.

Gooseflesh prickled across Calver's skin, the only warning to precede the wave of air—and the mass of muscle—that assaulted him from the shadows.

Chapter 36

Calverous

Calver sidestepped the attack, dropping the lamp to pull his dowaga from its holster. It clattered across the ground, casting a frenzy of moving shadows over the room as Calver lashed out to catch the sweeping dagger a hand's distance from his throat. Behind it, a gargantuan man leered.

Calver twisted.

The attacker parried.

He shifted his grip.

The attacker closed the gap between them, their weapons locked together into a contest of brute strength.

The titan's ragged breath cast flecks of spittle across Calver's face, but Calver sensed what came next. As the man moved to leverage his dowaga's scythe to the side, Calver ducked beneath it, spun, and stabbed him through the back. The steel was stained red in the lamp's low light.

The man roared, turned around—despite his wound—to strike once more. Calver hacked again in a sideways sweep, blade connecting where head met body.

The man hit the floor, lifeless, with a too-heavy thump.

Chest heaving, Calver searched for the next threat.

None presented themselves—except for the fetid smell, which assaulted his nostrils with a near-physical force that would have sent him reeling had he not been so worried about a blade stabbing his kidneys. He scooped up the lamp and lunged toward the cells.

And almost staggered backward. The one nearest to him contained a half-rotten corpse. Flies swarmed around the putrefying flesh in hordes. Fates. It was in such a state of decomposition, it had to have been there at least a moon cycle. Calver continued past it, the tightness in his chest compounding with every step. The second cell was empty. In the third cell, a slumped form lay huddled and shaking—head bagged, arms and legs bound.

Something trapped within Calver released in the form of a sound nearing a sob. His limbs tingled from the sudden wash of relief.

He worked at the cell's lock with the set of stolen keys. The first failed. And the second. His fingers were fumbling by the time he tried the third. The lock clicked, and the door swung open with a screech. Raimee whimpered at his approach. Calver fell to his knees beside her and yanked the bag from her shoulders.

Silver shone on him; they'd removed her oculars. Raimee's ashen expression parted into a disbelief that stabbed Calver in a space he hadn't known existed. A gag filled her mouth. He tossed it across the cell.

"Calver?" she coughed, voice choked by tears. "But you—I—I don't understand."

He hacked, white-knuckled, at the cords binding her with his knife. His face pinched in a futile suppression of his rising fury—feelings that, even without the Survivor, were intoxicating. Calver didn't even bother to void them. He merged with his thrumming anger, bathed in it. Chaos, he was glad he'd killed them. He'd never been proud of what he did with the dowaga, but this felt justified in a way that none of the Survivor's sprees had.

A final serration, and the bindings snapped.

Before Calver could blink, Raimee flung herself onto him, latching around his torso with arms and legs, knocking them both into the grime of the dungeon floor. Unanticipated, and in the midst of his heightened state, the embrace sent him reeling.

No. No.

She cradled her face into the angle of his neck, sobbing; her flesh against his flesh was visceral, maddening. He couldn't breathe. He gasped. *Stop.* It had to stop. The warm swell of her against him was a crushing weight. He was suffocating. Drowning in an icy well of terror.

Void.

What was he even voiding? Fates, her fingers had curled into fists in his cloak. How could he get her off him?

Void.

"I thought—I thought," she wailed through snot and diaphragmatic spasms. "I can't say what I thought. I—th-thought I'd been a fool." She shook, tears flowing freely to blend with the blood on his cloak, seeping hot and wet into his skin. His insides curdled.

He couldn't. She needed this in the same way that it repulsed him. *Void.*

He breathed. Another gasp, at first. But as he pulled oxygen in a forced rhythm, it settled into manageable inhalations, exhalations. Calver fought to maintain a mental wall of nothingness that threatened to come unhinged.

Pretend it's something else. Pretend it's—

That fated feeling washed over him again. So familiar. Close enough to reach and yet unobtainable. Warmth washed through his limbs.

Calver hesitated. Then, slowly, wrapped his arms around her. His void diffused as he settled into something like...

The world fell still. The danger waited. Their not-enough time stretched. Calver lay with her against him, the rise and fall of her chest pressing his. He embraced it: the impossible; withstanding the touch of another; sustained by that vibration from their connection, a feeling that toed the edge of memory.

She clutched him in desperation. Calver, trying to balance his wild swing of emotions, gave her an awkward squeeze. He leaned his chin on top of her head. The air around them quivered, like it had a life force of its own. And suddenly, he didn't ever want to let go. He dug his fingertips into the fabric of her kaftan.

How could he have almost given this up? Had it been feasible, he would have signaled 'I'm sorry.' Maybe a tighter squeeze would suffice. Maybe she would—

"You broke the rules," she sniffed.

Calver's blood cooled. The rules? How could she know—

"You said stay within arm's distance."

He looked down. The silver eyes looking back made his jaw clench. His trance was broken, first by the thoughts of what they would have done to her, then by grief, knowing the betrayal that had put them both here.

He let go and squirmed away. Kretch. If they had even moments, they were fleeting. He sat up, his freed hands flying. <*We have to hurry. Are you hurt?*>

She shook her head and used her sleeves to dab at her eyes. He helped her to her feet. Together, they darted from the cell, past the corpse, and up the stairwell. Great, billowing clouds of smoke greeted them in the chamber beyond the trap door. Calver took a deep breath and pulled the collar of his tunic up over his mouth; Raimee, apprehensive, did the same with her dress.

They hurdled over the flames from the fallen landing and into the basement's main room. Raimee's expression peeled back in terror. "What did you do?" she screamed against the roar of the house's blazing carnage, now launching stories into the sky. The corpses of the imposters glowed peacefully in death, sprinkled all around them amidst a sea of chaotic debris.

Nausea built in the back of Calver's throat. He had done what he always did. He'd reaped.

A deafening snapping sounded from above them. Calver ignored Raimee's scream, pulling her toward the back exit which, by Preservation, remained free of any guards. They slipped through the hole in the mortared wall and into the side yard.

Ash from the blaze drifted onto the grass of the back lawn around them like falling snow. They fled to where the private landscape backed up to Chira'na's south wall and followed it, careening from backyard to backyard.

When they came within eyesight of the guarded gate to the community, Calver motioned for Raimee to crouch behind a wall of rose bushes. She had been separated from the cane and oculars, but by Preservation, the turban remained. He patted down their clothes, removing all the ash as he could. He used the inner hem of his cloak to wipe the blood from his face. His hands. His dowaga.

Raimee heaved, unable to catch her breath despite the short time they'd idled. Calver kept a hand on her back to be sure she didn't disappear while his eyes fixed on the gate. Her heart was beating faster than a heart ever should.

The authorities arrived.

By a stroke of luck, the two guards who had been stationed by the gate that morning ran with them toward the Thacklore manor, likely eager to check out the scene of the disaster in what was typically an uneventful section of the city. Unwilling to relish in their fortune for fear of scaring it away, Calver ushered Raimee forward. They slipped through the gates.

<*Keep your eyes closed,*> he gestured. <*I'll guide.*>

Her eyes screwed shut, and she gripped his arm with the ferocity of a cat clinging to a bowing branch. Calver directed them toward one of the busier streets, hoping that coming shoulder-to-shoulder with other bodies would be a better disguise than sliding through back alleys. They wove in and out of the festival's crowds: Raimee silent as the dead they'd left behind to burn, Calver with his head down, his own heart beating so forcefully it threatened to extend his chest. Time passed like crystallized honey. In Calver's heightened state, it was a lifetime.

They were still covered with ash and soot. There was still blood on his cloak. The city guard would spot them any moment. Seize them for questioning—

But no one spared them so much as a glance.

The streets were full of toasting glasses and twirling skirts and hands held: joyful, mundane life. The world went on as usual, oblivious to anything it wasn't looking for.

When they did arrive back at their rented room, they collapsed onto the worn wood of its floor. Raimee curled into a ball with her back to him and sobbed. Calver pressed his body against the door. He took a deep breath in. Then let it out, slow.

This moment of relief... it was a lie.

He hadn't thought he could lose anything else.

That was before he had a person willingly pressed against him.

She'd seen him for who he was, now. What he'd done. And he'd lose her, like Fankalo.

Like Fankalo, who'd betrayed him. Like Fankalo...

"The two of you are evisceratingly fucked."

This moment of relief would play out as the rest of his life had. No happy resolution, only a temporary reprieve from violence.

Chapter 37
Attilatia

In the early hours of dawn, when her final shift of the ten-day ended, Attilatia slipped unseen from the still-empty work floor and into Aetech's maintenance ward. With the peachy hues of first light chasing at her heels, she shimmied between drainage pipes and into a crawlspace where the darkness still reigned. She worked a cycle of seven nights on, followed by three off, the standard Nelfinden week. On her off nights, she typically stayed as far away from Aetech as was feasible. But this week would be different. Whatever Hashod was doing, she would not sit idle.

Dampness and mildew clouded the air of the crawlspace. Fates above, she likely could have found a more appealing location to wait out the day, but she knew that the grungiest corner would be worth the peace of mind that came with going undiscovered. It was the first time she was glad to have her brother gone—she didn't have to worry about him wondering about her when she didn't come home. The thought held hands with a panging bite of despair. She bit it back. The Fates had allowed her to get him this far. She would have to trust them to bring him back to her as well.

She hid, like a rat in its hole, through the day. Then she waited through a large portion of the night which followed, her drowsiness nearly dreamlike. How long since she'd slept? Thirty hours? More? And that had been poor sleep at best. Her mounting anxiety following Thedexemore's departure hadn't left much room for rest. She almost didn't notice when the small light on the distortion device, held loosely in her hand, began to blink.

She inhaled sharply. There *was* someone at her workspace. In the middle of the night, when she was supposed to be off shift. The device's correspondent, sitting at her desk in Aetech's main lab, detected motion through a configured hypersensitivity to vibration. Someone walking down the hall wouldn't cause a reaction. But someone shifting the drawers at her workstation...

She stared at the little light as pressure mounted in her chest. She had suspected someone to be going through her work, but to see that it was true? Her brow lowered. She was nearly as curious as furious. All of her work was discussed freely with Hashod. He commissioned it. Everything she did at Aetech, anyway. Why would he want hard copies of the intelligence she was already reporting to him?

Unless he was giving it to someone else.

The fine hairs on Attilatia's arms stood up. Her stomach knotted with nerves. A catwalk traversed the far wall of Aetech's main work floor, adjacent to the room's gargantuan windows. Though the space was far from inconspicuous, it would give her a full view over her desk and put her within earshot of whomever was digging into it. She would just need to stay low. And to get there... well, she'd practically need to slither on her belly like a snake. She fidgeted with the fabric of the Aetech jumpsuit she'd been wearing for two days before giving the thing a withering look. It wasn't as though she needed to keep her appearance in order. It would have to be done.

She was slow to navigate the stairways and corridors leading from the maintenance crawlspace up to the lab floor; paranoia caused her to stop and hide every so often to be sure she wasn't followed. Ridiculous, really. These corridors were obsidian black to the Nelfinden eye. No one would have been able to see her. But she couldn't keep her bubbling terror at bay, and the frequent stops calmed her. She had to do this. If Hashod really had plotted a way to replace her, it might spell death for her and Thedexemore. Whatever he wanted to hide, she would bring it to light.

The stairwell to the catwalk was tucked into the corner of the main lab floor. From behind it, she had a clear view of her workspace. Moonlight from the skylights illuminated the room from corner to corner to her eyes. Three men, outsiders, were gathered around her desk. Hashod was with them.

Anger stole the air from her lungs.

That *monster*. Just another of Thacklore's minions. Whatever they were trying to do, she would set it to flame. As quietly as she could manage, she crept up the stairs and dropped to her stomach, where she could keep a low profile, unseen by those below.

Dirt and oil and who knew what else stained the metal of the catwalk beneath her. She wrinkled her nose. Aetech was the most technologically advanced facility in Nelfindar—one would think they could at least keep the floor clean. It was a good thing she wasn't fond of the jumpsuits. Sliding forward inch by inch, she directed herself into a position almost directly over her desk, where she halted to watch and listen—

They were speaking Tera'thian.

A chill cooled her rage into fear. Memories of the early days after she'd escaped the Kovathian coup flooded her. The desperation to stay alive. To do whatever was necessary. And Deshpian Thacklore... She brought a hand to her throat.

How hadn't she seen this coming? She'd wondered time and time again how the Kovathian assassins kept finding them. Thacklore had all but sold her to Hashod as it was. But Tera'thians? Hashod was an officiant to the Nelfinden oligarchy! He wasn't simply releasing trade secrets. This made him a national traitor. And she'd thought the gossip she'd collected on his mother had been bad. This was next-level. This was... enough to get her killed.

A stab of understanding pierced her. They *had* been trying to have her killed. It had been a few months now since the Kovathian assaults had begun. Ever since the production of Roskaad's defensive plates. Ever since she was no longer needed on the research portion of the project.

Hashod had orchestrated them.

"Don't trust Hashod." And Roskaad was—had been—in on it.

She gulped, feeling as though she were pushing something heavy down her throat. It was too much. It was time to leave. Time to get out.

She pushed herself onto hands and knees and scuttled backward several paces without looking. Her body collided with a heavy metal pipe. The crash created a muted thud, but it shattered the bulb of the device in her shallow pocket. Fine glass shards slipped through the eyelets of the catwalk and fell to the work floor below.

No!

The faint tinkling of glass cascaded against tile like a flutter of small wings. But the silence of the night was thin, and the noise carried like lead through aether. She listened, trying to hear over her own thudding heart. Below her came a hushed exchange in the foreign tongue, followed by an uninterpretable command from Hashod. The three men set off like hounds set to hunting. Panic seized her. She spun, reeling toward the catwalk staircase.

Darkness. She needed to find darkness. It took several moments of nearly giving herself away for all the commotion she created to realize that they weren't looking up. They'd set off in every other direction to find her. That, or cover the exits.

Breath caged in her chest, she slowed, backing herself away from the center of the room and toward the far wall where she wouldn't be silhouetted by moonlight. As she reached the wall, she caught a glimpse of Hashod across the floor. He kneeled by the small fragments of shattered glass, holding an Aetech lamp over them. Then he looked up at the spot she'd been eavesdropping from just moments before.

With shaking hands, Attilatia scaled silently down the metal staircase at the opposite end she'd come in from, keeping herself to the darkest part of the room. She doubted the light of Hashod's lamp could gain him visibility as far as her corner, but his hounds could be anywhere. They'd left the workfloor, and would have all the lab entrances guarded by now, for sure. Preservation... how was she going to get out of this?

The same way she'd gotten in.

She dreaded the answer as soon as it came to her. It was the simplest solution. She was certain Hashod would have eyes on the building, monitoring anyone who came out. That meant she couldn't leave until the next time she was expected to. She would have to return to the maintenance crawlspace. And she would have to remain there for... her stomach growled at the thought. Another two whole days? Then climb out and return to work like nothing had happened. She shivered.

What an incredible waste of time. She hadn't even learned what Hashod was doing. Then again, it didn't matter. He was conspiring with Tera'thians. That alone was worth ten times her weight in gold.

Two days and a night shift. She could do it. There was water in the maintenance ward. There were fresh jumpsuits she could sneak from the laundry.

Attilatia sank into the shadows and, avoiding pathways with a line of sight of the lab exits, made her way back to her hiding space to wait. All she could think about was Roskaad. Her stomach turned like it had taken a physical blow. He was involved in this. He and Hashod had conspired from the beginning over the plates. But... Roskaad was supposed to be fighting for groundling rights, not sharing her distortion technologies with Nelfindar's enemies. Over the course of the project he'd seemed so genuine. So relaxed. How many of his words had been sweetwater sold as honey? Fates knew she'd find out.

He had her brother.

Chapter 38
Niklaus

ONE YEAR PREVIOUSLY

Niklaus sat in a floundering garden in Shrokan district. Whether it be that the soil was too rocky, the air too salty, or the surrounding district too uncaring, the flowers and shrubs here looked sickly, like a soft breeze might uproot them. Niklaus could commiserate.

Around him, the short ceremony concluded. Its modest attendees filed from the garden in groups of two or three, exchanging subdued pleasantries, before going their separate ways. Not one spoke to him, though he was certain that any and all of them had stared at him at one point, immediately averting their eyes should they connect with his. His face had been plastered in every skywalk paper, and word of mouth in the groundling districts spread more quickly, even, than in the skywalk's literary circles.

The despicable Niklaus Meyernes: the scammer, the scandalous. Would anything satiate his lust for wealth?

Niklaus was as out of place here as he was on the Skywalk, where his various 'friendships' had evaporated like whiskey poured into a hot pan. They'd believed the media over his word. No one had stood by him, stood up for him. Perhaps Latouda would have.

He'd never know.

She had chosen for her funeral to be of earth. Of course she had; even in death, she'd made a statement in favor of the groundlings. Continued to fight.

Niklaus hung back after the others. He sat in the dirt, his fingers interlacing with yellowing blades of grass as though they were hers. They'd planted a tree over her body, a small sapling with sparse pink petals clinging to spindly branches. It would be beautiful in the years to come as it grew. Grew from her earth...

He stared at the newly turned soil which covered her. He'd never experienced a funeral *of earth* before. It had been wonderful. The patricians never chose an earth funeral as a matter of propriety, and due to the fact that there was little earth to be had on the skywalk. Those fanciful individuals who loved gazing out over the Casowhatan occasionally chose *of water*, but most chose *of fire*. A funeral *of fire* was bold, powerful. Earth was dirty, meek. Niklaus had always thought the same until now. Earth gave something back: a tangible continuation of her spirit. From her corpse, new life would grow.

The moment felt surreal. Niklaus knew he was still in shock from the onslaught of slander against his papers that week—like something out of a nightmare. But this—sitting on the ground off-skywalk, staring at Latouda, now a tree—this was neither waking nor sleeping. It was time suspended, waiting to fall back into a place where it could carry on as though it had never happened.

She'd relocated without a word. Found a new job, despite twenty years in his family's service. Two weeks ago she'd been curled in his arms. Or punching him in the ribcage. Probably both. Now...

A man plopped into the grass beside Niklaus, shaking him from his spell. Latouda's older brother, Jarren. He knew it first from his too-familiar eyes, and second from the brief series of words he said at the earth funeral. Niklaus dreaded what would come next. He didn't want sympathy.

"This is all your fault." The vehemence in Jarren's voice was like a burn in Niklaus's ears.

"I... It's. What?"

A quiet fury radiated from Jarren. He spoke slowly, as though concerned that if he let his words escape any faster, they might consume them both. "You. Privileged. Shratten. Fop. Toying with our lives for your own amusement. Look where it landed her."

Niklaus's mouth went dry. "I'm not sure I understand. I—"

"You shouldn't have to think too hard, Meyernes. You told your mother you wanted to marry a groundling. She had her removed from her staff."

And she'd broken her neck, taking an unfamiliar stair on her first night-shift in a different manor. So said the mortuary.

Niklaus's eyes welled up for the first time. His throat clenched. His chest constricted. His mother had had her removed? She'd told him that...

"This whole thing was a terrible accident," he stammered. He'd thought she didn't want to be around him, not that she'd been forcibly relocated. He'd given her space. Let her go. "It never should have—"

"Why did you do it?" Jarren snapped. "Propose to a disabled fucking groundling? Fates know it wouldn't have stood. Was it some kind of marvelous prank? Another way to cause a stir, the way you do?"

"Of course not! I wanted to marry her."

"She didn't want to marry you! She wasn't going to marry you. Never. *Never*. Did you even ask her?"

"I... assumed—I thought she did." He realized how wrong the pitiful words sounded as they left his mouth. She hadn't left because of his proposal... But she also hadn't wanted to marry him? The harrowing truth stirred in his mind like a tempest. Latouda had never actually said yes. She'd hesitated. *Kretch.*

"Anyone who knew Latouda knew she was in love with Covern Balfida. They were near enough betrothed, if it weren't for you."

Niklaus's stomach turned. Balfida? Not the leader of Seraphinden's groundling movement, Balfida?

Jarren seemed to see the question on his face. "Yeah, him. This whole ploy to create a paper discrediting Aethertech Mechanics? It was his shratten project. But he knew that his social status wouldn't see it received. Getting someone on the skywalk's oligarchy to write it, on the other hand? Now, that was an option. And who better than Aetech's founder himself? The man whose family Latouda happened to work for?"

"He made Latouda—"

"You know nobody made Latouda do shit."

She'd volunteered.

Niklaus couldn't feel his body. Latouda had been manipulating him? Their relationship had always been play: never entirely serious. But an act of espionage? His world crashed down around him for the second time that week. First his mother, now Latouda. How many people had been using him as a pawn in their games?

"So," Jarren continued, "assuming Latouda wanted to marry you? You assumed wrong, Mesu Meyernes. So wrong. She heard the rumors about how to get an audience with you from the rest of the staff. She only did it to coerce you into writing her shratten papers."

And she'd done it—she'd died—for nothing. Just two days after the paper's release, the oligarchy's conspired rebuttal had discredited them... because of his divergence. Because of one shratten line of speculation:

"...and collaborating with the likes of Roskaad Thyatira, who, considering his absence from Casowhatan's local census but presence in the national one, might as well be an oligarch or a Tera'thian with the right affiliates in Archival, as he is a groundling."

"If you'd bothered to give her ten minutes of your time this week instead of frantically defending your honor, trying to pretend you weren't scamming the system, she might have told you herself."

But he'd thought she hadn't wanted him.

"My mother—" Niklaus's desperation to defend himself was getting old, even to him. "She forged that document. I never signed anything in my investment agreement that would have me collect insurance capital should Aetech fall apart. It was all a lie. It was—"

"I don't give a fuck about your scandal," Jarren screamed, the sound echoing across the four winds.

Words were intangible. Ethereal things without weight. So how was it that Jarren's felt as though they might suffocate him? Niklaus turned toward Latouda's brother, who had tears in his own eyes, and tried to speak. For once in his life, speech would not come. His voice caught as he finally managed to whimper, "Thyatira—Thyatira did this. He framed me. And Latouda. Us. He... Chaos, it can't be true."

They were the wrong words. They had so little substance, they snagged on the breeze and lifted out of the garden, over the wall, into the sea. Niklaus wanted to drown with them.

Jarren shook his head, unhearing. "I want you to bear this pain. This shame, Meyernes. There were those of us who actually loved her. We won't forget whose hands are responsible for her death. I hope the rumors about you are true. I hope they discredit you. And I hope you never rise from this place in your life. That things don't get better." He pointed a finger at Niklaus and jabbed it into his chest. "And while you sit in your skywalk mansion, you remember forever that your blood is tied to what's here in the dirt."

Jarren spat at his feet, stood, and left.

Niklaus didn't chase after him. Didn't try to get another word in to defend himself. He sat in the newly turned earth, wishing things had turned out differently for the girl who had never loved him, and never would.

Chapter 39

Calverous

After the noise of the fire and the festival, the room in the Repository was too quiet. Raimee hadn't spoken to Calver since their return. She wouldn't even look at him. And why would she ever want to? They lay in silence until he couldn't bear it. He moved to the washroom, where he clacked the door closed and stripped.

A deposit of ash and grime blanketed the floor around his fallen clothes like a shedding of exoskeleton. He sat in the tub, let the water run cold against his burnt skin, and scrubbed it with blackened fingernails. He scrubbed until the water ran clear instead of coal. He scrubbed until he was raw and his own blood displaced the blood of the people he'd butchered just an hour before.

Shivering, he redressed and patted down the clothing as best he could with a wet towel until it looked less like he'd stepped from a slaughterhouse and more like he'd vacated a bar fight as its victor. He washed his knives. His dowaga.

And then he re-entered the bedroom, feeling somehow filthier than when he'd left it. Raimee looked up at him for the first time since their return. A flurry of thoughts left unspoken flitted through the air between them.

Fates, he needed to leave. He couldn't stand her silence. It practically chased him from the space. And they weren't safe yet. He had to find the urchin and—he rolled his shoulders down his back—inform Fankalo.

Calver pulled a knife from its holster. Raimee flinched before he had a chance to flip its handle to give to her. The motion wounded him, though not so much as he deserved. She looked at it, brows furrowed in question. Swallowed. And reached a steady hand to take it from him.

<*I'll be back,*> he signaled.

He didn't invite her to join him. She didn't ask.

It was as he'd expected: he was alone again.

Killari waited for him on the roof. He checked her canister, but there wasn't a message. It was his turn to reply, anyway.

The wind pulled at Calver's hair as he stroked her feathers, unable to put words on paper.

'Let's discuss the things you learn,' Fankalo had said.

Chaos, why be so damn cryptic?

What had he learned? That Thacklore had a house full of Tera'thian servants posing as Chira'na guardsmen? That he gave the Tera'thians the Ghosts' secrets to who-knew-what extent? That he knew Calver's real fucking name, and that they shared blood? What was there possibly to discuss? All of it? None of it?

Calver closed his eyes.

Breathe.

The world around him was ripe with conversation and laughter and music. And something in the world spoke, giving him solace, despite it all. Fankalo always had a reason. She wanted to talk about this... he'd make that an invitation.

What was another drop of faith from the thimble meant to carry him to the bitter end?

Calver kept his message short. 'It was Thacklore. He no longer poses a problem. The plates still do. Prepare me your Karval transport. I'll go to Steila whether or not I can destroy them in time. And let's discuss what I've learned in person. I need you to tell me what a conduit is.'

Even as he watched Killari fly off with the message, he knew his request would not be obliged. No proven value of life, no preventing collateral could have ever changed that. The only inherent value his life had left was playing Reaper to the Shadewalker's Hand. So be it.

In the end, even if their loyalties weren't on even footing, even if everything else fell apart, he would still keep his promise to his sister. It was all he had left.

The festival markets were free of any incriminating gossip; word had not yet spread about the destruction in southern Chira'na. The tightness in Calver's chest slowly unwound.

For the time being, they were safe. While the community gate guards had his forged name written in their records, he hadn't needed to provide documentation to rent their room. They could remain unseen until they passed a guard checkpoint again to leave the city. They would have new papers forged before they needed to do so.

He, Calver, reminded himself. He couldn't think in terms of *'they'* anymore. The memory of her on top of him still burned in his mind. He doused it. He'd always known how this would end.

Now he could search for the plates without distraction before the Red Wing left.

Two days.

He still had time.

He stayed away from the Repository until it grew dark. Raimee needed time alone; to come to terms with the carnage from that afternoon, and the fact that she'd nearly been captured and the man she'd been seeking all this time might betray her. He looked for the urchin without luck, which meant there was still a tag on him.

Just another act of compassion that would get him killed.

Then he visited Fankalo's document forger, bought a cane and oculars, bagged a dinner from a haloucha stand—two for Raimee, for good measure—and mentally prepared his goodbye.

Seven knocks later, Calver pushed open the door to the rented room. Part of him expected her to be gone, and he could have wished nothing better than for her to have escaped him, given her chance, and made a future for herself. But she was in the bed, knife raised in a flawed grip. She lowered it when she saw him.

Calver entered tentatively and dropped the food at her feet, like the offering made in an attempt to befriend a wild animal. The Ruxian tucked into the meal with her standard eagerness.

She seemed... better. She'd let her hair loose. It cascaded around her shoulders like a moonlight blanket. Her tears had dried, betrayed only by lightened salt lines across her dark, speckled skin.

An appetite was promising, anyway.

Raimee seemed to read their momentary safety from his face—she had become frighteningly good at doing that. Or maybe she just assumed that if there was anything serious to relay he would have told her. Calver waited, hoping against hope that she might say something. Anything. Before they parted ways.

Eventually, after she finished two dinners in rapid succession, she did.

"Creation, I think that's the best thing I've ever eaten."

Calver had yet to manage a bite.

"What do you think?" she asked, as if they'd been conversing the entire time. As if she weren't knowingly speaking to a man who had just murdered a manor house. "Is Methu'su going to sell me to the Tera'thians the moment I reach him?" She corrected herself. "If I reach him."

Calver shook his head. <*I can't tell.*>

"Nor can I."

<*It seems that Thacklore and Methu'su are—*> He worked his jaw. <*Were in opposition. And your mentor's belief that he was in Chira'na was false. By which I would deduce that you were not set up for capture.*>

Raimee squirmed where she sat cross-legged on the bed, the crumbly remains of her dinner strewn on the blankets surrounding her. "You killed everyone in that house?"

And there it was.

Calver responded with a single, solemn nod.

"That... is bad behavior."

<*I acted on behalf of my employer.*> It was almost true.

"Calver..."

<*This will eliminate any chance they find you again. You're safe, for now.*> Calver fought to keep his face impassive, surprised by his own swell of emotions, unchecked by the Survivor. <*This is what I do. Who I am. I never lied to you and I told you, repeatedly, not to trust me. That you shouldn't have anything to do with me.*>

She shook her head. "No. Telling me I shouldn't trust you just proves the opposite point—that you take stock in my well-being. I've been doing some thinking. You—you've put a lot on the line for me, haven't you?"

Too much.

He looked down at his fingernails, now clean. He'd risked everything, eight years of planning, countless lives, his only alliance, his family, for her. And then he'd nearly sacrificed her. They weren't good for each other.

It was time to part ways.

"I haven't been honest with you." Raimee winced at him like he might strike her.

His muscles tensed, preparing for the next betrayal. All the suspicions he'd pushed past to foster his own loneliness seemed foolish now. He moved to sit at the foot of the bed, opposite her, to listen. She didn't shy away.

"I lied about Methu'su. My mentor didn't tell me to find him in Chira'na. He just told me to find him. I only ever said Chira'na because you asked what I was doing in the Sharinash and you mentioned Chira'na was the nearest city."

That was... a softer landing than he'd expected. Of all simple things, why lie about looking for Methu'su in Chira'na? And why, then, had she ended up in Sharinash in the first place?

He thought about her nerves when he had mentioned the census. *<You knew he wasn't in Chira'na? Why—?>*

She interrupted him. "I also lied about having. Ummm. Unique abilities." She watched him as though waiting for some kind of reaction. "It's not like you would think, though," she added. "I can't transform matter or anything like a Seraphindo. And when I healed you, it really was the very first time I'd experienced anything like it. But—" She hugged her knees to her chest. "I have something different. My mentor called it my second sight. I was strictly forbidden from paying attention to it. I pretended it didn't exist for most of my life, as best I could."

She laughed a little bit. A nervous laugh. Maybe a bitter one?

"But Fates, it wasn't easy. Can you imagine someone telling you to just pretend not to see?" She pressed her lips into a line as though composing her next line of thought carefully. "I can't really explain the second sight. It..." Her gaze went distant. "The best way I can describe it is as being like—like a river drawn out in the air. No, not a river. It's thin. A thread, more like. A single thread of a greater tapestry. And everything has its own. You. Me. Each branch in the Sharinash. Every speck of dust in the aether between us. An infinite number of threads I can 'see.' Not with my eyes. I feel it. Like it impresses on me, you know? And the threads show me which way each thing is *intended* to move."

A shiver traced Calver's spine. Her words reminded him chillingly of the Survivor, still absent since that afternoon. *<You can see the future?>*

"No. Not really." She shrugged. "It's more like the chances of where things will or should go. It's like everything has an intended path and the threads light them—but, well, there's no visible light. And the threads are constantly moving and changing. Infinite numbers of them, all at once. So it's difficult to predict much of a future. Fates, this must sound insane." She ran her fingers through her silver hair.

No. It didn't. It sounded—familiar: a dream half-forgotten.

<How is this related to Methu'su?>

Raimee bit at her lip. "When I fled Tennca'Pui, I had nothing to cling to but the name of someone who might help me. So I opened my mind back up to the second sight I'd tried to ignore for a lifetime and—" She shook her head. Tears threatened to breach the rims of her eyes. "I looked for Methu'su. But he didn't bring me to Chira'na. You did. Every thread flowed together in a straight line to you. It was—it—it was—"

Magic?

She stopped and took a shaking breath before locking eye contact with him. "I'm not crazy. I already knew what you could do. I saw you murder those men at the lake. I wanted to run then, even. But—but I swam after you. Because the Fates practically distorted themselves for me to find *you*. Who was I not to listen?"

He too understood the impossible compulsions of the Fates.

"And if I hadn't, how would I have gotten this close to Methu'su without getting killed?"

Calver didn't respond, unwilling to admit the things he thought. That he felt. His future had no place to harbor destiny.

Raimee quivered under his forced lack of expression, but her jaw clenched. "Can't you tell that this is special?" she asked, obviously struggling to find the right words. "Do you know that every time I touch you I—that I feel—" Her now-wet eyes darted back and forth between his as she realized his head was already half-way to Karval. "No one has ever looked at me the way you do. And you... We're connected. You and me."

If there was a connection between them, it severed here. It had to. He had obligations. And if the Fates truly wanted to preserve her, they wouldn't entrust her with someone like him for long.

<*Well, that connection gained you the information you needed to find Methu'su. You can go to Seraphinden now. Speak with his confidant, Kotar Avelius, about his whereabouts in the Tsorlap.*>

She looked at him like she was waiting for him to reveal a poor-form joke.

<*I've been tasked elsewhere. I'm leaving tonight.*> A dead man's hand could have signaled with more emotion. She'd practically flung herself at him all over again, and he—

Raimee opened her mouth and closed it a few times, as if her disbelief of his signals held her words hostage. "Right," she finally agreed in a high-pitched voice.

Calver turned, trying not to think about her chances. The Survivor had been right. Even if she miraculously made it to Seraphinden undiscovered, Methu'su might murder or sell her the moment she found him. Her mentor might have set her up. The idea set winter into his bones.

It had all been a waste of time.

Raimee suddenly changed the topic. "Calver, did you learn to speak Tera'thian as a tume'amic?"

He inclined his head.

"But did you learn to read it?"

He paused and nodded again. What did that have to do with anything?

Raimee uncurled herself on the bed to reach into the pocket of her kaftan. She pulled out an ancient-looking piece of parchment and clutched it to her chest.

"My mentor was also a Tera'thian. Adopted by the cenobites when he was a teen. It never bothered me before. Tennca'Pui was sovereign—our numbers came from all nations. But... I need you to read this for me. It might have some answers."

Chapter 40
Calverous

The paper was so weathered, Calver worried his calloused fingers might damage it.

<Have you had this all along?> He'd patted her down and checked her bag weeks before, on the lakeshore, to ensure she didn't have anything to use against him.

Raimee nodded.

<You're sneaky.>

"You signal that like it's a term of endearment."

Calver unfolded it—a letter in flowing Tera'thian script. It was half scribbled, like it had been written in haste.

"I can't read it. My teacher told me to take it to Methu'su. So he would understand 'which one I was.'" She shifted. "That implies a lot now."

He eyed Raimee over the paper, and she nodded with conviction. He read it.

'I'm taking you up on your favor.

'The child is Yalathia Seraphindo. When we suspected a threat, weeks ago, Thadinar took her into hiding. He said they were infiltrated—spies from the Blue Wing. He did not survive his injuries.

'I have nowhere left to turn. I'm being watched. But I know Tennca'Pui can keep her undetected. If you break your laws to grant her asylum, you will save not only Natoluphut's heir, but our entire future.

'She cannot fall into the hands of Nelfindar's authorities. There are too many spies now. If the Prime finds her, Ani finds her.

'When I'm no longer under watch, I'll return for her. The Fates are indebted to you. Abi.'

Calver read through it twice, limited stomach contents threatening to extricate themselves. He fought to maintain a blank expression, but when he looked up at Raimee, she'd clearly gleaned its enormity off his face.

She wrung her hair like a wet towel. "What does it say?"

Omitting his father, he signaled its contents. Her silver eyebrows nearly drew into a single line.

After seventy-five years of oligarchical regency, the Nelfinden throne had a bloodline heir.

"I take it Methu'su is still under watch," she stammered.

Or dead.

Calver paced the room as Raimee stewed in her own preoccupation.

Why had he withheld the full truth? Was he in denial of what it implied? That there *was* a connection between them? Because learning his father had been tasked to keep Yalathia Seraphindo alive—that he'd abandoned post, forsaken a five-year-old son and an unborn daughter to save her—shook the bedrock of belief Calver had based his life on?

Or was he fearful that whatever powers she possessed had brought her directly to him, son of her departed guardian, to impart the same fate?

Not only was Ruxian magic very real, it was rising, weaving its way around him like a shroud. He would cut those threads here and now. He considered Fankalo; maybe Thacklore hadn't recognized him because she had given him away. Maybe Thacklore had recognized him because he'd been hunting Ruxians since Calver's father was rescuing them. Long before Calver had fucked everything up. After eight years of fighting to liberate the tume'amic—many of whom were likely his biological offspring—and to redeem himself to Fankalo, he would not abandon them for this Ruxian as his own father had done.

He looked at Raimee. She was watching him expectantly.

He swallowed. Fates, it was difficult. <*I'll help you plot your course before I leave.*>

Calver spent the next hour mapping directions to Seraphinden for Raimee. She could take a caravan to Karval, from which point she would catch a passenger ship to Seraphinden's port. But it would require her to interact with a lot of people in the process. Bovahk Ani had torn apart Tennca'Pui searching for her once already, and the Tera'thians knew she had escaped. It was likely that there were eyes and ears like Thacklore's everywhere, waiting for any sign of her surfacing.

Under ideal circumstances, she could go to Nelfindar's government. She was the heir, after all. But even Thacklore had implied that the oligarchy had betrayed the Ruxians in the first place. It was common law that, should Seraphindo's bloodline return to Seraphinden, they would peacefully transfer back to the throne. Somehow he didn't anticipate Prime Taranil going willingly.

The only discreet route to Seraphinden was crossing the death trap that was the Jiradesh desert. It would take months on foot, passing through inhumane conditions with no substantial landmarks, villages, or wells. The Red Wing made the trip with each annual recruitment in a caravan, but only a skilled traveler could make that journey alone.

He set aside survival tools for her: knives, her new forged identity papers, and a stack of silver notes, more than enough to purchase her board and travel. Then he drilled dozens of tips that might ensure her safety into her head. He didn't think his hands had ever signaled for so long.

Overwhelmed, she held up her own hands. "Enough. There's only so much you can do, Calver." She sighed deeply. "It will have to be enough."

It was nearing highmoon.

<*You should leave now too. Our location could be compromised.*>

"No." Raimee rubbed exhaustion from her eyes. "The journey will already be rough. My chances are poor regardless. I'm going to sleep in a bed while I can."

Calver nodded. His brain told him now was the time to leave. His body couldn't move.

For no particular reason, a corner of Raimee's mouth tilted in a bedraggled excuse for a smile. "Is the roof accessible at night? It might be nice to see the stars from this height. Before we lose the chance."

Stars? They were fugitives, both—practically on the run—with secrets that couldn't fall under scrutiny, and she wanted to see the stars.

Her eyes fell, unwavering, on his. *Shit.* And he'd take her there.

<*If it is closed off, I can find a way up.*>

"I wouldn't doubt you for a moment."

They lay on their backs, alone on the roof of the Repository. The stars were brilliant around the new moon, even despite the Aetech lights, glowing like summer fireflies in the celebrating city below.

"So when did you start turning distortion technology into weapons?"

Leave it to Raimee to break the stillness with a casual ask of the most uncomfortable, unexpected, and complex questions.

<Almost a decade ago.>

"It's fascinating, really. I always thought distortion orbs had limited energetic output."

<That's what Aetech proclaims.> Aetech's proclamations were bold-faced lies.

"But you think otherwise."

<If distortion has a limit,> Calver started, determining that her knowing more would make no difference at this point, <I have yet to find it. I'm not sure what Aetech's engineers are doing. They've severely limited the technology's applications. Lights. Simple industry and the transportation of goods. Almost like they're preventing the technology's growth on purpose.>

"If growth means weaponization, then it sounds like the engineers at Aetech are genuine altruists."

And with what Fankalo had planned, "genuine altruists" didn't stand a chance. What would Raimee think of the Dreiden corporation's approaching debut, and the giant middle finger breaking Aetech's monopoly would raise to the oligarchy?

Calver pulled his cloak tighter against the night air. <I never thought about it like that before.>

The night progressed. The sky darkened to its blackest. Raimee told Calver stories about celestial bodies—other planets and suns and moons, all hidden beyond humanity's limited senses. They were things that the cenobites had studied for generations, she said, knowledge lost to much of the world since the Cataclysm. He listened distractedly, trying not to think about how she would manage after they parted. He willed himself, instead, to think about how insignificant they both were in the scope of a universe of stars.

What did it matter if the last of a race died? Everyone believed them to be dead anyway. Everyone except him, the person she'd made live again.

Raimee watched him, and he noticed that she'd trailed off. He blinked at her.

"Am I talking too much again?"

<No.>

"It's time for you to leave?"

<Yes.>

Why couldn't he say more? He wanted to tell her that he would miss her, too. That her willingness to speak to him was the greatest gift anyone had ever given him. That, in a different life, he'd jump on a boat with her and learn to catalog sea kelp. You didn't say those things to a person you expected to die, especially when you expected to die too.

Or maybe you did.

But he couldn't.

Raimee's willowy limbs convulsed with cold. Even this early in winter, temperatures in Chira'na fell close to freezing at night. He could tell she was attempting to act as though it didn't bother her.

<It's cold. And you need sleep before your journey,> he signaled.

She nodded, clutching herself for warmth, and followed him back down to the room. There she retired to the bed wordlessly, curling up like a cat beneath the covers. No "goodbye." No "good luck." That was fine. They seemed inadequate. Calver deactivated the sconced Aetech lamp illuminating the room and moved to the door. Gripped its handle.

"It's not possible for me to make it to Methu'su alive, is it?"

Calver's hand slipped to his side. He pressed his forehead against the frame. She didn't say the words he knew she was thinking: 'That's why you're really abandoning me.' What was it that made this so agonizing? He'd had to live with the hundreds of atrocities he'd committed. Why was parting ways with her more difficult than any of them?

"No matter what path I take, the outcome can't be saved."

What strange wording...

A memory floated, unbidden, to the front of Calver's mind: his mother. "*When you get tripped up, just remember that sometimes you have to stop focusing on the ones you can't save, and focus on the ones you can.*"

Fuck.

It was irrelevant. She'd been talking about *words*. Words, which meant so little on the road to redemption. Actions were the only thing that mattered.

Something deeply rooted within Calver snapped at its base.

And *that* feeling returned, stronger than ever. But this time it was raw and real and the antithesis of a dream half-forgotten.

It had been Raimee all along: this longing, the feeling he remembered, sitting on the statue in Kaidech, fourteen years ago. He'd seen it then, in the same way her second sight could see intended futures, this moment. What he'd felt back then—what he felt now—was his destiny.

And it was her.

In the darkness, he fumbled to activate the lamp in his cloak. Then he crossed the room in three long strides to the bed where Raimee hugged at her knees. She hid her face in shame and shook. He pulled her hands to her sides, then released them to signal.

<You're not going to die.>

Fifteen moon cycles until the Tera'thian coronation. What would he accomplish among the Ghosts until then? Petty assassinations? Side tasks that would keep him away from Fankalo while still within reach? Raimee could join him in hunting for those plates and in Steila afterward. Raimee, who'd seen his shaded side and still wanted him, where Fankalo had turned him away. He had a year until Fankalo needed him to perform his ultimate task. It was more than enough time to find Methu'su.

<We'll go together. And I have a lot of work left to do, so dying isn't an option.>

Yet.

Raimee wiped her face in the crook of her arm. "You—you what? I mean. You can't possibly—you have plans of your own. You just told me so?"

He kept his expression plain, though his heart beat like rain from a storm. He'd just made a move into ever-shifting sand. Now he'd have to find a way to merge two opposing paths into one.

<It makes no difference to me, if you're open to a stop or two. I have business to the north as it is. Seraphinden is practically on the way,> he lied.

She shook her head at his bluff. "Seraphinden is thousands of miles away. And I—there are people trying to kill me, Calver!"

<It seems we have something else in common.> As the signals formed, his chest filled with a mounting excitement he couldn't remember experiencing in all his life. <It will be useful, staying together. I'm often in need of a translator.> He continued to pretend as though it wasn't a big deal. As if he weren't endangering everything, and inexplicably ecstatic about it. <And a chef.> The corners of his mouth turned up unavoidably. Chaos abound, what was happening?

The tears wouldn't stop leaking from Raimee's eyes. She laughed at his bit and tried to wipe them away before throwing her arms around him. "Thank you," she sobbed into the crook of his neck.

The unexpected contact set a rigidness into his limbs, as before. But he recovered more quickly this time, wrapping his arms around her loosely. It looked like he would have to get used to this. Maybe he could... She leaned in, either oblivious to or forgiving of his awkwardness, spreading warmth into his core. It brought back memories. Not of Thacklore's torture chamber, but of the last time he'd held a person. He had been barely more than a child then, too. That was how it had been between the two of them, hadn't it? He'd cradled his sister often, voluntarily. Before he had been broken. Before—

Raimee pulled away. She giggled embarrassedly as she continued to blink away tears. "I thought you wanted to leave quickly?"

They should.

<*Firstlight. Get some sleep.*>

Wondering if he should signal something more but unable to find the words, Calver deactivated the lamp and moved to the door.

"Goodnight, Calver. I—I—thank you. Good night, Calver."

Raimee turned over once. And again. He waited for her to fall asleep. For her breaths to even out and deepen. They didn't.

"Calver. You don't—" she started, from nothing. "Do you want to sleep in the bed?"

It was a purely innocent request, a kindness she didn't realize was a disservice to him and his damage. Rather than lance her with the sting of his silent rejection as he had so many times, Calver activated the lamp again.

<*I can't sleep unless I'm in front of the door.*> The signals exposed him for everything that he was.

Her brows formed a single line over her nose. "Oh."

Not that he'd sleep anyway... Calver flipped off the lamp. Darkness filled the space between them.

Another minute passed, filled by the scraping of sheets and shuffling of pillow against headboard. And then the soft padding of feet moved across the floorboards in his direction.

Raimee was beside him. She lay down, her shoulder brushing against his thigh and staying there as she settled in, draping a blanket over them both.

"Well, this *is* nice, isn't it? I see why you're so keen on it."

Calver kept the room in darkness to hide the wayward smile that touched his lips. He let his leg remain pressed against her... and didn't feel sick or anxious. It was ok.

This was ok, this inconceivable, pointless thing that was happening. They were just two broken people, each trying to fix the other. Two hopeless people, each trying to shine so the other might see a way forward. Two pointless people, with nothing except each other.

And it was more than he'd ever dared to dream of.

Raimee's body twitched as she fell asleep. Calver scooted closer to her. Considered putting an arm around her—

No, too much. He stared at the ceiling.

Was it possible for his fate to be fluid, yet also predetermined? Possible for him to be more than a martyr? A part of something beyond what his eyes could yet see?

Chapter 41
Attilatia

Attilatia wove her way through the colorful streets of Seraphinden's Korshuva district like a thread on a loom. The upper-class groundling streets lacked the grandeur of the Skywalk, but they were clean enough and lined with well-kept shops, each with intricate displays. Pleasant aromas spilled out from cafés and a multitude of street carts peddling toasted nuts, qahwa, or chocolate. A musician sat at every other street corner, playing cheerful melodies for the enjoyment of passersby. They strolled in twos or threes, never in a hurry, to go about their day of shopping, eating, and socializing.

They often stared at Attilatia. She was out of place in her dark lenses and silk tipiana, embroidered with green and yellow birds. The single element of Nelfinden fashion she'd adopted, outside of Aetech's atrocious jumpsuit, was a saffron turban, but only in an attempt to hide the assault on her hair; it did nothing to assimilate her. It mattered not what she wore. They always stared. That was the visage Chaos had cursed her with.

She passed a clock. It was only minutes from highsun. The knowledge alone set a weariness into her bones, a longing for the comfort and solitude of her bed. The highsun pained her eyes, evolved over thirty generations for life underground—not strutting about in broad daylight, unsheltered, like the crazy *chikotos* of Nelfindar.

But she needed information on Roskaad, and if anyone had it, it was Pintoratius, the Silk Master. Despite being one of the few other Azadonian expatriates in Seraphinden, Pinto was not so stubborn as her: he had adopted a non-nocturnal lifestyle and would only hold an audience during the daytime. It was something she secretly resented him for—more due to the inconvenience it caused her than for the weak will it might imply of him.

The old man lived in a flat over a bookshop. Attilatia hadn't paid him a visit in at least half a year, but the narrow staircase which led to his space was filthy as ever and smelled of book-binding glue. The Aetech distortion lamps in the stairwell had been turned off, though a stained-glass window provided a dim light.

Attilatia removed her oculars and peered up the musty stairwell. Specks of dust danced overhead, suspended in the beams of colored light. Cobwebs clouded the entirety of the lofted ceiling.

She sighed. The geezer desperately needed a maid, but he was so fated secretive he'd never permit one in the residence. Hiking up her tipiana a few inches, she ascended the stairs and knocked on the door to Pinto's home. She could hear him scraping to unlock the deadbolt. He opened the door just a crack, peering out at her with a beady black eye.

"Atti, is that you?" he wheezed in Nelfinden. "But you are so early?"

She sighed again, attempting to keep the irritation from her voice as she replied in their homeland's tongue. "No, Pinto, I am on time." It was exactly highsun.

The cackle which followed turned into a cough. When the spasms in his chest settled down, Pinto replied in Azadonian. "Moving you from your ways is like dragging a cat into a cold bath. Time works differently in Nelfindar, Atti. When we say highsun here we don't mean highsun, what we mean is—"

"When you tell me to arrive at highsun, I arrive at highsun." Fates, she'd lived in Nelfindar for nearly as long as he. "We've been over this before. Now please let me in before your pet spiders eat me alive out here, eah?"

He cackled again and held the door open. "But of course, *hakuni*, enter."

Thirty years ago, Pinto had been Azadonia's leading trader of silks to all of Seraphinden. His global empire had amassed a fortune so large that he'd managed a happy early retirement, despite the quarantine and years of economic decline which followed. His flat looked like it had been ripped from the pages of a whimsical storybook: mismatched shelves, tables, rugs, and sofas, all of which were unique or extravagant, furnished the room. Some had belonged to the Chori king from the Kath war era. Others were pulled from a sunken vessel by the raiders that patrolled the Casowhatan. Each piece in his home was a memory, he'd told her, tangibly captured from a past journey. Intricate knick-knacks covered every shelf and table. *Cluttered* them. They were just dust collectors now. A film of it coated everything.

The old man ushered her into a pinstriped pink chair with wooden armrests carved with seashells. It sat beside a mosaic-inlaid coffee table, prepared for company. A flowered teapot and matching cups, an array of tekkas that smelled of orange blossoms, and cloth napkins embroidered with kittens all competed for her attention. Pinto had always been a quality host, she'd give him that.

He sat across from her on a chaise sofa littered with so many throw pillows there was barely room for him. "Please help yourself to tea, fekkas."

"Thank you," she replied, pouring them each a half-serving of the spicy-smelling beverage. It was customary for the guest in their country to initiate the serving—a way of showing that they felt comfortable in the host's home.

He positively beamed at her. "You are a breath of fresh air, Atti. It is good to be in properly cultured company for a change."

"Even if it must be in the middle of the daytime," she grumbled, blowing softly into her cup before taking a sip.

"But I do love your unmatchable resolve," he chuckled, dipping a biscuit into his own cup and crunching into it.

She chose to discourage his charm by looking at the far wall. It was lined from top to bottom with colossal hardwood shelves that housed his porcelain doll collection. There were hundreds of them, each wearing a different dress. Their glass eyes stared vacantly forward. Attilatia had made the mistake of asking him about the collection before. Once the man got started on his dolls, he would never stop talking, telling her about how each one had been acquired and what her dress implied about her social station and her country. She shivered, looking at them. The man had his quirks, she knew, but those dolls were just too creepy.

Pinto cleared his throat. "Down to business, then? As you tend to be. So, tell me, to what do I owe the pleasure of your visit? What do you need to know this time?"

"What, you assume I came here with an agenda outside of speaking to a friend in my native tongue?"

He looked down his nose at her. "I am old, but I am not yet an old fool. You don't come here unless you need something you have already failed one hundred times to uncover on your own. That's just the way you work." He held up a hand as she opened her mouth to counter. "I don't mind. I still get the benefit of passing time with the most beautiful woman in the world in my own home. Every once in a while."

"You're a revolting pig of a man, you know that?" Nelfinden men told women they were beautiful; Azadonian men knew better than to objectify. Though Pinto had clearly been brainwashed by the decades he'd spent here, she had trouble feeling genuine discomfort at his remarks. He was too old and she too stern for him to stand a chance.

Pinto only laughed. "Azadonian women were cut from a different cloth. There's so much more weight to you. I mean this in a philosophical sense, of course." He smiled at her over the cup. It looked as though the mass of pillows around him might consume his withered body.

"Is that why you never married here? The women didn't suit you?" she asked in an attempt at polite conversation.

His eyes widened, the creases around them stretching flat. "Come now, Atti, you really have to ask me that question? I'd always thought that you were smart enough to make deductions."

The steam from her cup warped the air between them. Seconds ticked by, and heat radiated into Attilatia's face when her wrongness finally dawned on her.

Chaos abound, that couldn't be *her* fault, though. That was the anguish of human interaction: its ineptitude. It was largely conducted through the broken conduit of communication. And communication was but a distortion locomotive without a guiderail.

Attilatia bit her lip. She'd always struggled to translate her thoughts in a way unrelated to her knowledge of the local tongue. As a child, the things she'd said had not been taken seriously. As an adult, the things she said were misunderstood, or worse, detested for their face value.

It was why she'd always had a love affair with distortion. Distortion spoke in the language of arithmetic, algorithm, geometry. And it was always concise. A piece of wire twisted to the correct angle. A precisely sized dropper filled with the exact chemical components. Distortion was a language that took what was in her mind into a perfect reality that could not be misinterpreted.

But Pinto did not communicate through distortion, and so she'd chronically made up excuses, denying the majority of the lonely man's invitations for her to visit, because she'd assumed he wanted something more from her.

He sighed, deducing enough from her extended silence, and swatted the air between them. "Well, now it all makes a little bit more sense to me as well. I can't say I blame you. Just look at you. With looks like that, I can only imagine the amount of torment you've been put through in this cursed country." He gave the throw pillows a disdainful look and cast an armful of them onto the floor. With the newly-found space, he kicked his feet up onto the chaise and lounged back, closing his eyes as though settling in for a nap. "What did you come here for, Atti?"

She set her teacup down with a quiet clink. "I have to draw something for you to see."

"There is paper in a drawer in the armoire there." He waved his hand to his right, in the direction of a hulking mahogany cabinet, without opening his eyes. "Quill and ink too."

Attilatia retrieved a stack of flamingo-bordered stationery and an ink jar before sitting to draw the markings she'd seen on Roskaad. She held the paper face down in her lap, considering her options. Roskaad told her not to trust Hashod. Told her not to drink the wine. Outing him to one of Seraphinden's greatest gossipmongers wouldn't be wise if Roskaad *did* have her best interests in mind.

"Hashod is up to something bothersome. And so I've been tailing him carefully for a few weeks."

"Naturally," Pinto responded, reaching blindly for a fekka from the table and popping it into his mouth.

"He threatened to replace me, Pinto."

At that, his eyes snapped open. He rolled onto his side. "Don't listen to that wart. It's not possible. Replace you with who?"

"I don't know, but my concern has been enough for me to dig around for some dirt."

He snorted. "You dig around for dirt even when there is no cause for concern. Any time you feel like you don't know absolutely everything, you have to figure out what it is you're missing. A word of advice, *hakuni*? Life is better enjoyed when spent in appreciation of the things you do know than in search of the things you don't."

Attilatia was glad that he was past her misunderstanding and speaking to her plainly. With Thedexemore gone, it wouldn't kill her to have a friend rather than another puppet.

"No." She sat up straight and tapped the table urgently. "There's something more to this. It's not just him threatening to replace me. When I'm off, he's using Aetech's facilities as a meeting ground for... well, something I am not allowed to know about."

He clucked his tongue and said in a singsong voice, "Paranoia doesn't look good on you."

Attilatia flipped the stationary out to face Pinto, displaying her sketch. She could get answers without telling him the full truth. "And he has this marking." Her words sounded like insanity as she spoke them, making her question herself. "Carved into his chest, Pinto. Like he's a part of a cult." She could hear the lie in her own voice. Could Pinto hear her trying to sell him on it?

Pinto peered over the table at her. He slowly sat up, the lines in his face drawing into furrows. "You mean to tell me that Hashod Gorovich wears this symbol?" All the whimsy of their early conversation had left his voice.

Attilatia shifted, doubting herself. "Yes."

A pair of heavy curtains draped the bay windows in Pinto's flat, drawn to shut out both light from the sun and noise from the street below. Pinto shot to his feet with more agility than Attilatia had thought him capable of, sky-blue robes cascading about him, and scrambled to close the finger-wide gap between them.

"Atti, do you speak truly?" he hissed.

Attilatia's skin prickled. "Truly," she assured him, now unsure whether it had been wise to bring up the matter at all. "What is it?"

"You are better off forgetting you ever saw it."

Attilatia raised an eyebrow at him.

He waved a hand at her. "But I know that won't satiate you. It's better you get it from me than go poking around for it. You'll get poked back by something made from steel."

He ambled over to the door and peered into the hall before throwing the deadbolt, then returned to the sofa. He locked eyes with her.

"That symbol is called a Ratka. It's a glyph. Dates back before the Cataclysm, even. I doubt most would recognize it for what it was."

At his heightened stress, Attilatia poured them each a full cup of tea from the teapot. His bony hand shook slightly as he accepted the offering.

"For more than a decade now, the Ratka has made an unwelcome presence. It is the signature of a man called the Shadewalker."

Preservation. Sure, Pinto was prone to gossip, but superstition? Lore?

"The Shadewalker?" she questioned. "And he is?"

"This is beyond even my reach, Atti. I can't exactly tell you. Some say he is a Chori man. Some say it is a djinn, wearing a young woman's face, more beautiful than creation herself. It might be an aethersprite. An idea. A group of people acting as one entity. All I can say is that whenever the Ratka appears, it laces its fingers with death's."

Attilatia chewed at the inside of her mouth. "So this Shadewalker. He's Nelfinden?"

"Hard to say. He kills Tera'thians. He kills Nelfinden, Azadonians, the Chori. Eighteen months ago, the Pazarian King was assassinated. Do you remember it?"

She nodded.

"The Ratka was left beside his corpse, painted in his blood."

It sounded like the sort of story told over too much drink. Her ire rose; she didn't have time for children's tales. "I've not heard of it."

"And a good thing too! Anyone who *might* know anything gets knifed."

She snorted with derision. "Well, then, how do you know about it?"

"These things never escape my knowledge, dear. I have fabulous sources that tell me what I need to know, and that's precisely why you came to see me today, isn't it?"

He was dancing around answers.

"Can you be any less direct?" she snapped.

He paused, glancing once more from side to side, before leaning in, his voice hushed. "There are whispers that the Shadewalker is building an army. Calls them 'Ghosts,' because they walk among us, unseen. They all bear his mark. He recruits more men, gathers additional funds every month. Ships go missing at sea. Fishermen say that the Ratka now flies on the vessels once held by the raiders. He's united them. Their plunders feeding his purse."

Attilatia frowned. That did line up with the lack of chelation agent in Shrokan. But the merchant had said they united under a queen...

"Even the patricians are involved. There have been disappearances. This issue was under scrutiny by a member of Seraphinden's oligarchy, even. You remember Mesu Jironesh?"

How could she forget the skywalk's biggest misogynist, coincidentally one of Aetech's distribution officers? "He committed suicide last year," she whispered, narrowing her eyes.

"No he didn't." Pinto waggled a finger at her.

"This all sounds like a conspiracy."

"And most likely it is. The question is, what is being conspired?"

"And you believe in this?"

"For your sake, I hope that you will too," he replied, his old voice wavering. "If Hashod is involving Aetech with the Shadewalker... Well, being replaced should be the least of your concerns."

And now she wished it *was* Hashod. "Pinto," she said, fiddling with the small glass charm on her bracelet. Had she inadvertently placed herself in far worse trouble than she'd been in before? "I have too much on the line. I need to know—"

"No, Atti. You do not."

For once, Attilatia found herself at a loss for words. Pinto's face softened, regarding her, his wrinkles settling toward the beds beneath his black eyes. He looked as though he had just returned from a ten-day journey without sleep.

"Aay," he bleated, gently turning the subject. "Have a fekka. Not like you to hold back from a good snack."

She smiled weakly and obliged, dipping the tip of the almond-encrusted confection into her tea.

"So. You're different. Are you seeing someone?"

Pinto asked it so casually she almost didn't realize how personal the question really was. She nearly snapped something defensive back at him, but thought better of it, considering the air that had just been cleared between them.

"How did you know?" she admitted. Though she didn't quite consider her manipulations against Roskaad as 'seeing someone.'

"Your scarf," he replied, eyeing her turban. "Never imagined you'd adopt a Nelfinden fashion. Unless you were heavily influenced." His face broke into a knowing smile.

She pursed her lips. "The scarf is not a token from him. I had a degree of a—fit." As if any one term could describe the psychological breakdown during which she'd nearly impaled Thedexemore as he wrestled the scissors from her. A continual increase in entropy was unsustainable. "I admit, it was an attempt to make myself look less appealing, but the end result has only set more eyes on me."

"Hmm. Well, let's see it then."

Hesitantly, Attilatia unwrapped the turban, exposing her dark, chopped hair.

"On second thought, better to keep it covered." Pinto crunched into another fekka. "You should go to see a professional about that."

For the fourth time that ten-day, Attilatia wound her way across mosaic-inlaid floors into the most obscure corner of the skywalk library's stacks. She followed an ornery librarian with too much skin for the bones on her face through the smells of old paper and patchouli incense.

"There's this one." The librarian pulled an unembellished book from a shelf. "Its scholar claims that the glyphs predate the Cataclysm by nearly two millennia."

"Thanks abound," Attilatia replied, reaching for the book.

The librarian handed it to her with a cautious glare, as though concerned Attilatia might devour it—in the literal, not literary, sense. Books predating the Cataclysm, or even with knowledge predating the Cataclysm, were exceedingly rare. A tome this old would be a treasure; Attilatia almost didn't blame the librarian. She was more helpful than any other scholar had been.

"Will you need assistance in returning it to the correct location when you are finished?"

It took all of Attilatia's strength not to bare her teeth. "No. I think I manage just fine."

The librarian side-eyed her, but turned to leave her alone in the stacks. Attilatia found a nearby desk and made herself comfortable. Because she didn't hold residence on the skywalk, she couldn't borrow the book or bring it home. That was fine. It wouldn't take long to skim this volume, anyway.

Over the past ten-day, she had scanned dozens of titles on symbology from Nelfinden to Pizarian. She had yet to find anything resembling the Ratka she'd seen on Roskaad. But this was the first book she'd found on pre-Cataclysm glyphs. Part of her wondered whether Pinto had his facts mixed up, or whether the mark had been invented for the sole purpose of giving the Shadewalker a symbol. It seemed unlikely. Symbols weren't just created. They were derived from something. Or representative of something.

So what would the Shadewalker's mark mean? Resistance? Revolution? War?

She flipped through the pages for no more than a minute before she encountered her target, inked boldly into the book in black. Her heart accelerated as she read on, barely believing that she'd found it.

She'd all but given up.

RATKH'AH

Meaning: Survivor, survival, continuation, rebirth, return
The Ratkh'ah, or Ratka, is derived from ancient pictograms resembling a dragonfly. The dragonfly, in pre-Cataclysm Tera'thian mythology, is representative of survival, endurance, and resurrection. Despite the positive connotations, superstitions claim the Ratkh'ah to be bad luck, or represent misfortune. The symbol heralds the rebirth of the fourth Fate, Destruction.

Attilatia re-read the section nearly a dozen times before closing the book. *Survivor?* She'd expected something more menacing.

Rebirth of the fourth Fate? Azadonia's matriarchal elders had always claimed Destruction had died with the Cataclysm. Could a dead thing be reborn? She scoffed inwardly. Of course not.

But a dead Fate... That was different.

She flipped the book open again and stared at the word "Survivor," turning it over in her head. While "Survivor" lacked the intimidation factor she'd expected of the Ratka's origins... An omen of bad luck? That made sense. Something that might strike fear into the hearts of its viewers.

Barbaric. She rolled her eyes.

So, what did it mean? Was the Shadewalker the leader of some cult, vying to resurrect Destruction? Maybe... and maybe she was reading too far into it. Perhaps the glyph had changed in meaning, or the Ratka used by the Shadewalker and his Ghosts was not associated with the matching Tera'thian glyph...

Her mouth twisted.

...with a matching name.

Attilatia stared at the glyph, painted onto the page with ink so black it looked like a hole into the void. It felt like something stared back. Her breath caught in her chest. She felt like she couldn't move, paralyzed by something external.

Fates above, it was just a picture. She ran her fingers over the image on the page, as she'd run them over Roskaad's chest only the ten-day before. After the hand the Fates had dealt her, if anyone could claim the title of Survivor, it was her. She would move past her fear and find out what the Shadewalker wanted with Aetech, how Roskaad was involved, and what the Ratka had to do with it.

Thedexemore depended on it.

As her thoughts trailed past the General Prime, she was surprised at how they warmed her. Something about Roskaad made her want to give him the benefit of the doubt.

He'd told her not to drink the wine. To save it. She would listen.

Chapter 42

Niklaus

Thousands of groundling recruits teemed around Niklaus in the unyielding confines of Seraphinden's port platform. They were as insects—ants, bearing the rust-colored tabards of the Red Wing, all obeying their queen. The men poured into the distortion machine's passenger carriages without so much as a question.

He, Niklaus Meyernes, had just joined their swarm.

He swallowed, one hundred misgivings rattling in his brain. What could possibly be worth giving up so much personal identity and agency to conform to such a horde?

A story. The cloying, fated tempest of truth.

For the duration of a lightning strike, he questioned his own motives. He'd drunk himself into a stupor for over a year. Why the sudden vendetta? Why did he care to take vengeance for someone who'd never even loved him in the first place? Niklaus searched for a mental anchor to cling to, lest he return to the cycle he'd only just freed himself from—

—and he smiled.

There it was.

The Gorovichs and, more importantly, his mother, would be appalled when they learned that he had left without word, like a thief in the night, to serve as an entry-level recruit. He'd drunk the finest brandy distilled by the Chori, the rarest wines south of the Casowhatan, and saki that would make scientists write sonnets. But there was nothing so quenching, so sweet, so heady, as his mother's wrath.

"What in bloody Chaos is all this?" the port gate captain demanded when Niklaus arrived at the distortion locomotive carriage indicated by his enlistment papers.

"Personal effects." Niklaus shrugged. "Only the essentials, of course." He had eight servants in tow, each toting several man-sized pieces of luggage.

The captain shook his head. "You're outta your mind, guy. Only what you can carry. It was an explicit instruction. These 'personal effects' gotta go. Make it quick. The machine leaves port in fifteen minutes."

Niklaus brought a hand up to his chin, feigning puzzlement. "I'm sorry, captain. I think there must be some kind of miscommunication. Have I done something... incorrectly? I believe that I have followed instructions."

Now that he thought about it, promulgating loopholes and military etiquette did not a fine blend make.

The captain put a palm to his forehead. "Only. What. You. Can. Carry." He spat each word. "If you can't figure out how to do that, you should go back to your palace, Mesu Meyernes."

Fates be swayed. He couldn't catch a break.

Niklaus continued to feign confusion. How far would a captain bend before he broke? "Yes, but I'm still not sure that I understand your point." He gestured to his line of servants. "We are able to carry everything. So what's the problem, again?" The man's face darkened. "Can I please speak to your supervisor?"

"This has to be a joke."

"I'm afraid it isn't. You see, I've hired these men to enlist in the recruitment and carry my things as well so that we could remain within protocol. We have also chartered an additional wagon for the caravan once we've reached Chira'na, so worry not, Captain. Nice, ahh, hat by the way," he added with feigned disgust.

He pushed past the captain, who reached to remove his perfectly ordinary hat to inspect it, and whistled for his servants to follow him into the carriage. He had nearly a ten-day until basic training began, but a man made a first impression in a matter of minutes. If he was going to win over anyone for information, now was the time to schmooze.

And booze.

Crowded by the fifty or more recruits piled into his same carriage, Niklaus stood on his seat to be seen. He unlatched one of his suitcases, filled with copious jars of distilled liquor. Then, clearing his throat, he began to speak.

"Gentleman!" Several heads turned. Many turned away. "It is together, not in isolation, that we begin our ground-breaking voyage as enlistees in the Red Wing! Let us venture fearlessly from the comforts of our homes and into the void, disbanded not by peril, nor fear, nor certain, swift-moving death. May we carry forth, victorious heroes, remembered as the men who narrowed that gorge between who they once were and who they dreamed to become!"

He raised his arms, staring around at the blank faces that watched him. There were a few snickers, but otherwise the carriage fell silent.

Someone shouted, "Shet it and sit down, yeh lunatic."

Ah, well. Highbrowism wasn't for everyone. Niklaus had been giving speeches for a lifetime and gotten nowhere. Now was the time for action. He cleared his throat. "As with any ship's maiden voyage, I thought the proper lubrication to be in order." Liquor, on the other hand, spoke everyone's language.

He reached into the suitcase and, after taking a generous first sip, passed around the jar. And then another. And then another. The entire carriage of recruits cheered and hooted as they gorged on the drink.

An aged gentleman with a stiff handlebar mustache tapped Niklaus on the shoulder. "About as sharp as a marble, that," he said, gesturing to the others. "These boys aren't like the patricians you deal with. They won't have a lick of tolerance for this kind of drink, and even less self-control."

"Bah." Niklaus cast the man's warning aside. "It's celebratory. Nothing like a few pours between comrades, eh?"

The carriage grew louder as the men guzzled drink after drink. Niklaus smiled to himself. Now *this* had been a good idea. He might have the informant army he needed before the car even left the station.

A heavy boot nudged Niklaus in the side, rousing him from his coma-like languor. The feeling wasn't far off from the imaginary boot nudging him repeatedly in the head. He blinked his eyes open against the too-bright light and moaned. Kretch. He hoped that any Red Wing castigations were served alongside a tall glass of water.

"He's the one, mesu," a soldier said.

Niklaus lay prone in the carriage's aisle. It was littered with garbage and empty liquor jars. Slumped forms in Red Wing uniform slept across broken seats and the filth-smeared floor where Niklaus's right cheek rested. A miasma in the air spoke of vomit and piss.

So, escaping from the Skywalk did not mean escaping all his bad habits. They'd been nipping at his heels all along, waiting for him to stumble. This might be problematic...

Four soldiers stood at attention directly above him.

"Oh, Fates behave, that cannot be Meyernes?" a voice said.

Fates behave indeed. Colonel Baem Limtush, his father's once-employer and right hand to General Prime Thyatira, was the last person Niklaus wanted to run into at this point in the venture.

"Aaaay." Niklaus pushed himself into a seated position to make eye contact. The headache which followed was exquisite. "How have you fared, Limtush? Well, I hope? Still doing that thing you told me about with the sheep, I presume?"

A pity that the quip failed to evoke a retort, when there was so much space between Limtush's ego and intelligence level for words of indignation to float around in. Then again, sheep? It hadn't been one of Niklaus's better ones.

"By which shratten Fate did this man end up in the enlistment?" Limtush muttered to the man to his right, who shrugged apologetically. "Unbelievable." He addressed Niklaus. "How is it possible that you are able to weave a web of Chaos literally everywhere you go?"

"How is it possible that you've gained so much weight?" Niklaus quipped anew, massaging his temples. An unprincipled comment, but the man had gained a hand's width around his belly and this hangover was nothing short of savage. "It's only been, what, a year since I've seen you?" Testifying *against* him at the tribunal following his discrediting—not that Niklaus held a grudge. "I always imagined the military preferred commanders who were athletic, or what have you."

Limtush shook his head. "Your father is lucky he wasn't around to see what became of the Meyernes legacy. The foppish idiot you are. The laughingstock of higher Seraphinden. Your not-so-clever discourse has come to an end, Meyernes. You've enlisted, meaning that you are legal property of the Red Wing for the next ninety days of the recruitment." He added more viciously, "And I get to do whatever I want with you."

Once stung enough times, a man developed an immunity to venom. "Sadly, you're not my type, Limtush. But if it's for the good of Nelfindar, I'll submit. Just be gentle, will you? Oh, and I haven't been checked in a while, so proceed with caution, my friend. I mean, my colonel."

Limtush huffed through flared nostrils. Then he clapped his hands and barked, "Scribe!"

The scribe practically materialized out of the air—at Limtush's side with a clipboard, paper, and pen. He wrinkled his nose at the sight of the carriage. "Yes, sir?"

"For official note," Limtush instructed. "Mesu Meyernes is to be stripped from his platoon and placed on janitorial duty for the remainder of the recruitment. Additionally, he is prohibited from access to paper and pen and is to have his assets confiscated until he is discharged when we arrive back in Seraphinden."

Assets? They couldn't actually do that, could they?

"Can't I just take a lashing or the like?" Niklaus asked.

The colonel's mouth twisted. His eyes blazed ferociously. "Whatever stunt you came here to commit, I will see that it does not happen, Mesu Meyernes."

"Please, call me Nikla." His tongue felt like sand. Fates, but he might be able to stand his case if he could think straight. "Could I trouble you for a spot of water?"

Limtush ignored him. "Give up the ruse, Meyernes. Not a soul in this nation will believe your heresy." He nodded to the soldier beside him. "See to it that this recruit begins his new duties by cleaning this carriage. Immediately." The colonel turned on his heel and strode from the carriage, hopping onto the platform below.

In the afternoon that ensued, Niklaus spent what felt like an eternity cleaning, something he had never done before. The work was fascinating. He was not very good at it but, seeing as he had trouble telling his feet apart right now, he thought he managed well. If he could pick up a bottle, he could pick up a scrubbing brush.

Not even a full day had passed into his journey and things were becoming interesting. He'd lost access to journaling resources, true. And credibility—not that he'd really had it to begin with. But he'd gained two things as well: the knowledge that they would be watching his every move from here, and confirmation that he had Thyatira running scared.

Why else dare silence Niklaus? Why else tarnish his reputation? Make him look like a crook, a fool? He had been close enough to Thyatira's truth to hear its heartbeat a year ago. Now the man was scrambling to cover it up by any means available.

Niklaus had been right.

The thought flooded him with triumph. But it couldn't fill him, because there was something else inside him, taking up more room than its rent rightly paid: his own fear.

His assets had been seized. Which meant that he would be limited to consuming what the Red Wing provided. Which he doubted would include libations or consumable contraband.

Niklaus's insides were already quivering with the telltale creep of moss withdrawal, his extremities aflame. What was he if he didn't have access to the things that prevented him from feeling isolated in a room full of people? That left his hands feeling empty, if they were not filled? His medicinal curse? *Kretch*. This was what happened when you tried to expose the second most powerful man in all of Nelfindar. You had your limits tested.

On this test, he swore he would deliver.

Niklaus gulped, trying to focus, instead, on the steady clearing of grime from the locomotive carriage's floor. What man could step up to the brink of such a trial without fear?

Chapter 43
Calverous

R aimee shook Calver awake from the floor the next morning, just as the midnight blue on the horizon faded to green. They couldn't have been asleep for more than a couple of hours.

"Calver. Something's wrong. My second sight…"

His body moved before his mind could catch up, the dowaga in his hands before his bare soles even connected with the floor. Raimee's eyes were wide pools of silver as he guided her away from the door, a finger to his lips. He listened with an ear pressed against it. His heart beat in his ears for long moments before he tuned in to the sound of rapid footfalls. Somewhere below them came a muffled call of command. Calver stiffened. Soldiers.

<*We've been discovered. Prepare to leave,*> he signaled.

They couldn't have traced them to the Repository unless the urchin…

Calver's heart sank. He must have been apprehended by the authorities the day before. Kretch. The boy had followed him for months; of course he knew where they were staying. He was one of Cul'Mon's.

The Repository's rooms for scholars were located on the sixteenth floor. Any windows this high had a sheer drop. Any exits on the main floor would be covered before a unit entered. The roof was the only exit.

Calver mentally composed a plan of escape, searching for potential obstacles. The western perimeter of each floor held balconies, reserved for wealthy scholars. They could drop down from one to the next until they reached street level. Then they could make for one of the Ghosts' safehouses. Calver studied her, considerably less frail than before their stop in Creation's temple. Would she physically make it? Her eyes darted between his apologetically.

He found himself waiting for some sort of remark or threat from the Survivor. None came. No pressure. No resistance. He shook his head. There was no time to muse over what it was doing.

He thrust his feet into boots and creaked the door open. The muffled sounds of soldiers echoed through the main stairwell, a few stories below. They could still take the back stairs, as they had the night before. He peered into the hall; the path was clear. Donning his cloak with all of his gear, he motioned for Raimee to follow him. She sprang forward, already garbed with her turban, oculars, and cane.

They fled unhindered toward the back stairwell and crept the four flights up its rickety spiral. Calver picked the same lock to the roof's trap door and heaved it open, squinting against the morning's first rays of light. He pulled Raimee to the west end of the roof, where the balconies were. Her only sound was the straining of her lungs for oxygen from their short flight. When he released her hand at the end of the wall, she clutched at her cane as though fearful of falling.

Calver hopped onto the roof's ledge and peered down to judge the distance, yanking himself backward just as soon as he did. Nearly a dozen Chira'na guardsmen were already positioned on the balcony below.

"Hold steady!" he heard their leader command.

Calver turned to pull Raimee toward the back staircase again, a wild panic setting in. They could retreat back into the Repository. Find some way to hide until they had a better option.

It wasn't in the Fates for them.

Soldiers appeared from the back staircase. In the same moment, a dozen more flooded up the main stairwell.

No, no, no, no. Had he been alone, had he not broken the rules, he would have been out of the city by now.

Raimee clung to his arm. He was clinging back. They backpedaled to the roof's northern ledge, where he pushed Raimee behind him, dowaga drawn. The troops surged forward to surround them.

Calver forced a slow breath, convincing his heartbeat to steady. *Void*. A state of calm came so easily that he nearly took a step back. The morning was bright, the air crisp, the city calm. The distant hills were golden like coy scales.

The commander of Chira'na's guard, as identified by the badges on his uniform, stepped forward. "Dallard Friyal, you stand accused of nineteen counts of murder. Come forward and you will be granted due trial. Refuse surrender and you will be killed."

Nineteen. The Survivor had done worse.

Calver palmed the last of his tampered Aetech lamps with one hand, shifting to the dowaga's lower grip in the other. It would, if anything, provide a distraction. Then he would take them one by one. His thumb moved to activate it—

Raimee slapped it away from him. "No!"

The lamp clattered to the ground and rolled behind the guards' feet. Calver's brows lifted even as his stomach dropped. How could she?

Raimee set a hand on his arm. "Senseless violence won't help us," she pleaded. "Look at them. We won't make it." Her brows furrowed in determination. "But this is my fault, and I'll get you out of it."

Before he could stop her, the Ruxian stepped beyond him, casting her dark lenses to the rooftop and pulling out the wrappings of her hair. The wind caught her silver curls, enveloping her in a snarled, effervescent halo. Calver thought his knees might become unhinged. He was a stranger in his own body, and the Survivor wasn't even in control.

Raimee's voice projected, bell-like, in a façade of affront. "My name is Yalathia Seraphindo, descended of Natoluphut Seraphindo." Her air of fearless entitlement was almost convincing. Had they lived a different life, Fankalo would have made use of her. "These crimes were not committed without warrant. You *will not* imprison or harm us. I implore you—" She stopped herself and clenched her fists. "I command you to stand down, or I will have to use force."

Brilliant. Fucking brilliant. How were they to know whether the fire had been started as a result of ruxechorin or Ruxian magic? They wouldn't know what she was capable of. They would fear her.

Raimee stood radiant, chin held high. Her chest heaved, her limbs shook, but her stance before the soldiers was unmoving. The uniformed men gaped; Calver was pretty sure he gaped too. Several lowered their weapons. Others looked to their commander for orders, but the man lost more color in his face by the second.

"The General Prime!" he finally shouted, voice cracking. "Squad three-ten, alert Red Wing Command."

Roughly ten soldiers peeled away from the formation in practiced response.

The General Prime... As in Thyatira?

Calver felt like a wild animal trapped in a cage. Options to fight his way out presented themselves. *Grab the Ruxian. Put a knife to her throat, a false hostage. She's valuable to them.*

He might just escape this alive. Without interrogation. Without having to set eyes on—Kretch. He couldn't do it.

Not now.

As though sensing his turmoil, Raimee took two steps backward and touched him. Not his arm; she cupped his face in her palm, a gesture so tender it paralyzed him. He didn't turn his head to look at her. Couldn't. Not with the enemy in sight.

"Calver, it's the only option." She stiffened in his peripheral vision as he tightened his grip along the handholds of the dowaga.

No. Heroes didn't get captured. They fought to the end. Fates, had this all been a façade after all? Had she planned this? Was she working for—

"Calver, look at me! Please, back down. It will only get you killed and I—I can't lose you."

What's to lose?

His eyes shifted to connect with hers: a fatal mistake. Her stare, silver brows converging in determination, pinned him into place.

And the world was suspended. The soldiers, the roof, the wind disappeared from his notice. There was only her, pouring emotions he'd forgotten he could feel into him. Time labored against the chains she bound it with. Only her hair moved, flowing like water around her. His face tingled where her fingers framed it.

She spoke truth. There was more to be lost than saved here. This fight would only be won through surrender. Calver's stomach thrashed in protest as he stashed his dowaga across his back. Raimee moved to him, her arms falling about him in an embrace. He couldn't bring himself to return it.

He brought his hands between them to signal. <*You don't understand. There's more to this than you think. You can't tell them anything.*>

Raimee's nostrils flared, her breath intermingling with his for their closeness. <*Your secrets die with me.*>

His insides turned at those words again.

And again, he believed them.

He thought he felt the Survivor then: an impression, like the afterimage of the sun against one's eyes. And he willed it gone, marveling at the power he now had over it. His future was out of his hands, but he hadn't been more in control in fourteen years. Every breath he took overflowed with validation and wholeness. Her fingers laced between his. He clenched his palms around them. She leaned forward—

"Bring them to Red Wing headquarters," administered the guard commander.

A team of men surrounded them, separated them. Raimee's eyes flashed over him for worry he might resist or flee. He did not. He submitted to them binding his arms, eyes cast to the ground as they were ushered to the staircase.

With the imminent threat to their lives postponed, Calver came to the realization that he'd woken up *different* this morning. Something had burned down alongside the Thacklore manor the day before... and something else had risen from its ashes. Something familiar.

Him.

They marched with Chira'na's guards through the city's streets toward Red Wing headquarters. Whispers surrounded them from onlookers and passersby: whispers of prophecy. Whispers of Fate. Whispers of a Ruxian with silver eyes and hair.

Whispers Fankalo would hear.

Bad. This was bad.

Calver chewed at his cheek, helpless as seafoam in a storm. Without the Survivor, his own undiluted awareness was agony. Knowing where he was bound, he struggled not to stumble.

The guard commander called them to a halt when they arrived at the large outdoor pavilion which stretched before the Red Wing's administrative building. Its grounds teemed with birds—pigeons. Calver had never seen so many packed into one space before. There were thousands of them, pecking at the grounds, fluttering about as they stood there, waiting.

Time stretched, filled by nothing but the wind, the cooing of birds, and the shuffling of feet. And then the soldiers shifted to stand a little straighter, their cosalts raising into a salute. Calver lifted his gaze to see what had their attention, dreading what he already knew it to be.

Red banners depicting a bear and a white gladiolus over a circular shield waved toward them, announcing the General Prime's arrival. Calver's limbs leadened.

Fear is an illusion.

He stared forward, unwilling to look away.

Fear is a choice which can be controlled.

He knew who stood behind those banners. As they drew closer, he held his chin high, trying to quash the murderous tempest forming in the pit of his stomach.

The guards in front of Calver and Raimee stepped to the side, leaving them exposed. Then *he* stepped forward—the man who had robbed Calver of his childhood, the man who had set him on his path of destruction, the man who had taken his tongue. Roskaad Thyatira, General Prime of the Red Wing.

And he didn't pay Calver any notice.

His gaze fastened on Raimee, who had puffed out her chest and leveled her silver eyes. Thyatira took her in for several long moments, his face featureless. Calver's stomach seized. He wasn't allowed to fucking look at her. Then Thyatira glanced, like a stab from a distance, at Calver, who fought to deaden his expression. If there was any recognition, Thyatira did not reveal it.

He didn't recognize him. Fates. That was a good thing, right?

So why did it sting?

"The perpetrators from the Thacklore manor, General Prime," announced the colonel beside them. "Awaiting your instruction, mesu."

Thyatira looked identical, unaged, from the last time Calver had seen him, fourteen years ago. His dark hair curled perfectly around his ears. His neatly groomed beard covered a sculpted jaw. And his eyes burned passionately as he looked upon his men. He spoke slowly, his voice warm but simultaneously commanding, as it always had been before an audience.

"This is—an honor. The Ruxian we will, of course, shepherd to Seraphinden. We must treat her with hospitality. Have her fed, bathed, dressed appropriately for her station and then brought to my office." Thyatira looked at Raimee to address her directly, and his voice softened unexpectedly. "I have so many questions. We have so much need of you. Don't be afraid. You are safe with us."

He turned back to his men. "Release her. Her presence remains unmentionable by any party present, under the penalty of treason until further notice." He turned on the ball of his foot to head indoors. "I will need to write a report to Prime Taranil. Please, get her out of the public eye. And kill the criminal."

The words registered to Calver only a second after Thyatira spoke them. Which was too late.

The soldier holding him reacted as quickly as the command was given. The steel of his blade ran clean through the left side of Calver's back. Its carmine tip protruded from his chest like an extra appendage before it withdrew. It was as though his pain was suspended by his own shock, only to crash seconds later into place with a vengeance.

Agony shot through Calver's entire body. He was too stunned to gasp, to scream. He crumpled soundlessly, saw his blood pooling across the ground too quickly and too brightly for it to be real. His vision swam. No mind-djinn rushed to his aid. It had long since abandoned him to suffer.

A body would survive twenty seconds after such an expertly placed blade.

Sound and movement blurred into one. Raimee's eyes found him. Her scream was so feral it seemed inhuman. She flailed against those who tried to restrain her.

Then came the birds.

Hundreds, if not thousands, of the creatures swarmed above the courtyard, a great feathered cyclone that darkened the sky. They swooped down, causing the guardsmen and Red Wing soldiers to reel, hands shielding their faces. Some screamed, some held their ground, others fled for the streets.

Calver's hands were bound, his life pooling out before his very eyes, but despite his darkening vision, he turned his face to watch. It was like nothing he'd ever seen.

A colorless pulse erupted from the Ruxian. The half-dozen soldiers restraining her flew twenty paces backward. In the same instant, hundreds of birds dropped from the sky, pattering across the ground. Chaos erupted.

Raimee fell to her knees beside Calver, body draping over his. "Hang on. Hang on. Live. I need you to live," she sobbed.

And the other woman he loved needed him to die. Definitely a conflict of interest.

Raimee's breath was hot in his ear. A growing warmth emanated through his skin as she poured herself into him until he was a bowl filled to the brim. His wound prickled and tightened as skin and sinew knitted themselves together.

Too slow.

He didn't need second sight to know what the final seconds of his future held. He well understood the physics behind a stab to the heart.

More soldiers worked up the courage to approach them, prompted by the yells of command. Raimee shrieked again, as though wounded herself. Another unstable pulse erupted from them, tossing dozens back in its wake. More birds plummeted, and Raimee slumped across Calver, comatose. Not a floundering heartbeat later, his own life seemed to drain as though physically sucked from his veins.

Destiny... how quickly he'd forgotten that destiny meant death. It came for the second time this moon cycle. This time, Calver's final thoughts didn't reach for a hope he could never fully grab. Fingers stretching, his bound hands found something tangible. Hers. Still warm, pulse still beating.

The world went unequivocally black.

Chapter 44

Calverous

Calver awoke on a cot in a room lit only by a meager golden crack. It stretched an arm's span along the floor in front of him like a blade of sunshine.

A door.

The stale air stung with the smell of antiseptic and iron. Fates. He'd survived, as he always seemed to. But this was the first time his miraculous preservation hadn't felt like a curse.

He had to get out of this place alive.

Calver's chest ached where the blade had skewered him. His arms were still tied behind his back. He tried using his teeth to pull down his tunic to inspect the damage. From what he could see, the wound had closed but, *fuck,* it still felt like he'd been stabbed. Raimee hadn't finished healing him before... whatever it was that had happened.

He was lucky. He had no right to be here.

The knowledge was no consolation; Raimee was in Thyatira's hands. Thyatira, who'd given up a city to the Tera'thians for the sake of political advancement. No way was he about to relinquish his growing control to a new ruler willingly.

Calver sat up, biting back a groan, and blinked sleep from his eyes. The cell was composed of solid stone blocks, like the walls of Chira'na, the door from steel. It was empty, minus the cot, a chamber pot, and a tray set with injera and water. A prison cell. He forced down a shudder of terror, looping a wave of mental blankness to stop himself from thinking about the last time he'd been behind bars, or the feel of steel through his heart, or how the light from behind the door felt miles away...

Dying is not an option.

Calver's stomach panged with hunger, surpassing even his thirst. He stared at the injera in the shadows across from him. Flashes of his last experience with Thyatira's henchman, Limtush, came to mind. It could be drugged. Better to wait and be clear-headed than satiated.

Thirst always preceded hunger, so why did it feel as though he hadn't eaten in... how long had he been unconscious? There was no way to tell. He doubted he'd rested there for long. In fact, he felt weaker than he had in months. Fates above, what had the girl done to him? He lay back to stare into the gloom.

It all turned up silver.

His stomach turned over.

Fankalo would have a way to get him out of here, he knew. The Ghosts had accomplished far more difficult rescues before, and he still had enough value to be worth it. But that would only help him. Fankalo would urge him to leave Raimee. She wasn't worth the risk she posed.

Fates. How had it come to this?

Mcsu Callisto had once said that the momentary happenstance of one's life could be drawn back to a single attribute which they possessed. It was not the possession of a thing, but the absence of one that brought Calver there: his tongue.

It felt like his life had just made a full loop.

When it made its next lap, he'd give up the rest of his organs before leaving Raimee with the monster that had mutilated him the first time around.

Long minutes, maybe hours, passed before muted footsteps padded beyond the door.

"Won't say a fucking thing. No history. No relation to her companion. It's like she popped out of the fucking ground," said a voice like stones grinding together.

"My questioning came up the same. Even if, legally, we had the right to interrogate her, we don't know what she's capable of. We have to keep all of this completely confidential until we can be sure," Thyatira's voice responded. "Have you cross-referenced this one?"

This one. That was Calver. They were directly outside.

"I haven't. And I can't."

"Why, did it end up killing him?" Thyatira asked. "That would be awkward. I already assured her he was dead, and she saw through it. Claims to know whether he's alive or not and where he's located. And with frightening accuracy."

"No, he hasn't woken yet but, regardless, he can't speak."

Thyatira fell quiet... and then responded with bite. "What do you mean, he can't speak?"

"I was there with the medical examiner. He doesn't have a tongue."

Calver squeezed his eyes shut. He nearly sensed the recognition clicking into place from Thyatira's lack of response. He knew now. Every breakneck beat of Calver's still-healing heart made him want to scream.

"Where is Colonel Limtush?" Thyatira asked, his tone pure ice.

"He's finishing up the administration of Aetech's devices for the supply wagons, mesu."

The plate shields... Calver's memories flooded him. Thyatira had been a Tera'thian informant—and probably still was. He'd likely orchestrated the whole fucking thing. Why? What was the secret behind that shipment?

"Have him find me. Immediately."

"Yes, mesu."

"And secure this cell. No one comes in, especially not the Ruxian. And the criminal does not come out."

"Yes, mesu."

Only one set of footsteps moved away. Calver's throat swelled in his neck as he waited, unwilling to breathe lest he mistake a single sound. Then the door pushed open with a screech of metal hinges and Roskaad Thyatira came into his cell.

With no way to defend himself, Calver struggled into a seated position. The motion made his head spin. The General Prime sat at the foot of Calver's cot: a waking nightmare. Calver remained as still as a winter stone, but his blood surged uncontrolled through his veins like a monsoon. Thyatira stared at him, a vein twitching in his temple. Calver prepared himself for an imminent attack.

Thyatira put his head in his hands.

The last thing Calver had expected was vulnerability. He saw the Red Wing's leader fall apart. His hands gripped his elbows, pulled his hair, then fisted around the edge of the cot.

And then Calver watched him pull himself back together. Thyatira stood. Paced the room.

"I knew I recognized you. Chaos. You were practically a child."

Calver kept his eyes locked on him, hardly willing to breathe. He would give Thyatira nothing.

"What are we going to do about this? We can't—I can't afford—" Thyatira stopped himself, puffing air from the sides of his mouth. "Dallard Friyal, from Miden? Impossible." A low growl sounded in his chest. "Honestly, I don't care who you are, but I do care that you were supposed to be dead half a lifetime ago."

Without wanting to, Calver remembered. Charred bodies. Hideous smoke. Grief. And agony. The Survivor remained absent. Even when Calver relaxed his control, the mind-djinn placed no pressure on him.

Thyatira cursed again, fists balled at his sides. He looked Calver in the eyes. Calver did not glare; he did not blink. He kept his face as dead as his heart should be.

"It wasn't personal, you know!" Thyatira seemed on the verge of genuine tears. "It stuck with me, what I did to you... It's not the kind of thing you just shake. But sometimes the battle for justice comes at a price. Nelfindar depended on your silence—and it came at a heavy cost."

As if he had been the one to pay it.

Calver's flare of anger quickly frosted over. How many times had he used the same rationale in his own battle for justice? Thyatira sat heavily on his cot, again examining him with pitiful eyes. They were almost kind.

He wouldn't be made a fool twice.

He wondered if he could end it now. There were a thousand ways to kill a man, even unarmed as he was. Even with his hands tied behind his back. He could ram his skull into Thyatira's face, felling him to the ground. He could kick his head into the stone until his brain smashed into paste. Calver waited for input from the Survivor again. None came.

It was useless, anyway. If he killed Thyatira now, Raimee might be safe from him, but she would still be in the government's clutches. Calver, however, wouldn't make it out alive after killing the General Prime. He wasn't prepared to be a martyr yet. It wasn't supposed to be for this. He had too much left to amend for.

Thyatira pulled his fingertips across his brows, straightened his spine. "I'll get to the point. I am not the monster you think. I am singlehandedly responsible for drawing this nation out of a depression and will be the one to ensure its protection against a growing international threat. With that, I cannot afford any smudge on my reputation and so, ideally, our history shouldn't exist right now." His lip twitched, and he drummed his fingers once against his knee. "I only ordered your execution under the assumption that you were the Ruxian's captor. I have since..." He bit his lip, considering his words before continuing. "Been forced into a change of mind. You have made a very powerful ally."

Once again, he waited for Calver to make any kind of movement or sound.

"Where did she come from?" he snapped.

Calver looked away.

"She cares a lot for your well-being, for a terrorist she met only yesterday."

Calver hid the way his chest inflated. It wasn't a statement; it was an interrogation. Thyatira was gauging his reaction.

Raimee hadn't given him up. Now he wouldn't give up on her. There would be no reaction.

Chasing a glare, Thyatira's voice became a command. "You will stand for a criminal trial in Seraphinden five months from now. What happened at the Thacklore manor needs to be atoned for, no matter what temporary pardons the Ruxian has requested for you. In the meantime you are a servant of the Red Wing, under my watch, and will travel with the recruitment to Seraphinden."

Raimee had saved him yet again.

"You will be fed and sheltered by our envoy, but you will have no station, and be kept on restricted access. That means no weapons, no paper, and no contact with Seraphindo's heir." Calver's silence only seemed to make Thyatira angrier. "If that Ruxian ever learns of—" He shuddered. "If the Ruxian ever finds anything to hold against me, know that I will find a way to slit her throat while you watch and have you blamed for it." He positioned his face at eye level, so close Calver could feel his breath. "And without her protection, I will finish you like I should have in Kaidech."

He looked to Calver's blank expression for confirmation. "Do we have an understanding?"

After a pause, Calver tilted his chin down once.

He closed his eyes. They were burning. A feeling he hadn't felt since—

"And Mesu Friyal? I have eyes and ears everywhere."

Thyatira's footsteps echoed against the stone. The door opened with a screech and slammed shut again, leaving Calver alone in the darkness with only his pain for company.

Chapter 45

Fankalo

FOURTEEN YEARS PREVIOUSLY

Arleena remembered a time, months ago, when there had been a storm. Her mother had disappeared, as she sometimes did on her cryptic errands, with the same old instructions: stay put. As if that weren't already its own worst punishment. When the skies had cleared, Calver had snuck her free.

In the aftermath of the front, the beach along the Kaidechi port had been littered with hundreds of tidal pools. Once the waters had ebbed just enough, they ensnared tufts of foam off the wild ocean currents, their rims preventing the salty air from blowing it away. The sea froth curled into wispy patterns. She and Calver pretended they were pictures—something else to hunt for among the unlikely salvage blown ashore they could sell in the slums. Dreaming of the honey crystals and date cakes they could buy with a few notes, they found foam that looked like trees. Like the butcher from the main square, the one with the patch over one eye. Like the very waves they came from. In the tugging wind, the foam was ever-shifting. Insubstantial.

That was how the smoke moved now.

But Calver was not here this time. She was alone, staring at the black smog suffusing every alley of the Kaidechi slums. Just as she'd been alone when she heard the dying screams of their mother. Their mother, who hadn't left the floor in the days since Calver went missing. She was alone. Without her brother, who'd abandoned them to this—

Bad luck.

Arleena's eyes and throat burned. She'd been crying, but this feeling was not from tears. It was the bad smoke. The unlucky smoke.

Maybe it hadn't been a good idea to leave her hiding space, the one she'd found the last time she felt her luck working. But her stomach rumbled like it was full of shifting stones.

And she could have sworn Calver was back in Kaidech. Or had been, anyhow. The feeling had lasted as long as a bedtime story.

Arleena unwound herself from where she was clutching her knees on the blood-stained dirt in front of the wreckage that had been their shanty. Nothing felt lucky around her. No good options presented themselves, as they usually did. Was that how everyone else felt all the time? Unable to tell which options were lucky or poor?

A gust of wind carried a plume of smoke toward her. With a cough, a gasp, and a sob, she scrambled to her feet and moved aimlessly in the opposite direction.

Calver was not dead. At least, he hadn't been.

She knew this because even after he'd left, she'd still felt him. She could always feel him. Sometimes she even knew where he was, too. When he'd left them, he'd gone far and fast. He'd probably found a way to join the recruitment. Gotten away from them, like he always wanted to.

Their mother hadn't believed her when she said he was alive. And she'd stopped eating, stopped moving. As if Arleena didn't matter. As if Arleena weren't hungry and thirsty. As if Calver were both the sun and moon and she was nothing.

The pangs of jealousy hadn't lasted. Arleena couldn't fault her mother; Calver *was* the sun and moon. There was no one better in all the world. But she wished her mother had tried. *Tried.* To protect her, too. She wished she hadn't given up and left her all alone, with only smoke and the smell of death for company.

She clutched at her elbows. Calver might be dead, after all.

That was why she had left her lucky hiding space: she'd stopped feeling him. He'd disappeared. Not in the way he had been flickering in and out for days, he had disappeared and *remained* gone, leaving her more alone than even Mother.

How could a person die, come back to life, and die again?

Arleena looked to the sky. The highsun filtered through the pitch of the smoke in hair-thin beams of light. She bit her lip; the bad men might see her now. Let them. Her world had already ended. There was no world without Calver. Without both the sun and the moon.

Her knees buckled at the thought. She sobbed into the sand for the twentieth time that day, rendered immobile again by grief. Then her hope shifted, as though bound to the breeze like the smoke around her. What if he *was* still alive? What if he kept disappearing because he was in trouble? Of course... How could she have thought for even a heartbeat that he'd left her here on purpose? She needed to get to him. Needed to help him.

Arleena moved toward the locomotive guiderail that led inland—the direction he'd gone the first time. Maybe that was where he'd gone again? But she stopped where the ground rose to meet the metal of Mecha's mechanical trail. The path was unlucky. So unlucky it made her stomach turn.

What would Calver do?

What a preposterous question. Calver would find her. He'd do anything for her. There was no truer fact in all the world.

And he would start by taking a breath. That stupid breath he always took.

She closed her eyes. Tried not to smell the horrible smell of baking flesh from the city center, which tainted the aroma of the sea. She took a breath. In. Out. Again. Slow. And then...

There *was* a lucky path. Spirits lifting, she followed the feeling, which took her away from the locomotive guiderail and toward the coast.

Toward the tidepools, now gone. Toward the bodies, piled in the square where Jenolavia's statue kept watch. Through the charred buildings, once gray with lime. It was silent but for the exhalation of the waves, the crackle of embers, and the screeching of birds feasting on flesh.

The feeling continued toward... what *was* that? The luck spun about inside her.

"Preservation's beard. How did a little thing like you make it through this?" The man's voice came from behind her.

Arleena jumped. Screamed, as she whirled around and attacked. She pounded the hardened body behind her with her fists, which might as well have been pebbles. The man pinned her arms. She bit him. He cursed and gripped her around the belly as she flailed.

"Easy. Easy!" he said. "I'm not going to hurt you." He released her, and she scrambled backward.

He didn't move closer, and she didn't run away; she gaped at him. This was not one of the invaders. He wore maritime linens, unspoiled and free of tears, and a fine hat that protected him from the sun. The steel of a dowaga glistened in the sun from his back. He did not draw it.

With a sudden rush of wind, a bird swooped down from overhead. The man stretched out an arm and it landed there, folding its wings against its body. Arleena's mouth fell open as its discerning yellow eyes narrowed on her. It wasn't like any bird she'd ever seen before.

The man fed the creature a scrap of raw meat that made her stomach grumble anew. He looked like a character from one of Calver's tales.

"You're... a raider?" she asked him in awe.

"Sharp little one, you are," he said, as the bird stretched its wings and exploded into flight. "Come here. Let me get a look at you. How old are you? Six? Seven?"

Trusting her luck, which had not disappeared, she took a step closer to him and nodded.

Another man rounded the corner. Arleena side-stepped behind the raider for protection. That was wise. Her luck told her he wasn't an enemy.

"Captain, we're ready to move out. Anything we found has been loaded. There wasn't much left to the skywalk. Anything decent was buried beneath the rubble. The Tera'thians picked it clean as it was—" The newcomer stopped and stared at her with an icy gaze that made her squirm.

"Gelhard. Look. A child... she's his same age," said the man who'd found her, a faraway look in his eyes.

"Come, Captain, we must be going before—"

"How did she survive, Gelhard?" There was a note of desperation in his voice. "She must come with us."

The newcomer shook his head. "Mesu, it is a girl. Your mind is still not in the right space since—"

"And why should that matter?"

"You know why it matters!" Gelhard argued.

"We've scoured this place high and low for survivors and found nothing. Yet she survived it. We can't just leave her here. She is a gift. A gift from Creation. To replace what I lost to the sea." The raider—the captain—looked at Arleena like she was a treasure. Worth more than every sheet of silk on the skywalk. Her luck danced.

This was the right thing to do. There was nothing for her here. No Calver. No luck. But *he* was amazing. She took her chances, walked up to the captain and raised her arms.

Understanding, he collected her into an embrace. Her luck hummed, easing the sharp pinch in her chest. Assuring her that, for the first time in days, she was safe again.

Gelhard shook his head. "Captain...this is absurd. This is someone else's child. We need to go." He looked from side to side, checking the alleyways. "They could still have eyes on this port. I know you're hurting, but your grief clouds you. We can't afford to lose any more crew."

Her captain ignored his crewman and looked at Arleena. "Who do you belong to?" he asked her. His question was full of yearning. Of hope. She saw tears brimming at the corners of his eyes. He was like her: alone. Lost.

"I'm all alone," Arleena said, the words bringing reality into the center of her mind, where she'd harbored hope that her brother would return.

Until now.

Her lower lip quivered, and she buried her face in his shoulder.

"Not anymore," he said, clasping a hand over the back of her head.

Arleena had never felt anything like this. Never had a father, her own having abandoned them not long after learning she would come into existence. She'd always wanted one. He was like Calver, but bigger. Warmer. So broad and strong. He could probably carry the world with those arms, thick like a ship's mast and dark as night from a life in the sun. She shuddered, whimpered, and burrowed closer to him.

"Listen, little one. I will take you from this place. But if we're going to make this work, you cannot be whomever you used to be. There are dangers, and those who would not allow it." The man bit his lip. "Chaos took my son, just days ago. You will be him now. Can you do that?"

His voice held all the textures of canvas. Strong and thick and dependable. Fates, what wouldn't she do for this man she'd only just met? Another press of luck made her nod. And the captain... she could almost feel his relief spread into her.

"You are mine now," he said. They were not words to possess her; they cherished her. "My boy. My Fankalo."

Fankalo took a shaking breath and curled her soot-stained fingertips into the linen of his shirt. If she was going to restart her life in this way, she was going to do it with her whole self, and leave the rest behind her to burn.

"Yes," she whispered. "Father."

Thank You

Thank you for reading A Distortion of Fate! If you enjoyed this book, please leave me an honest review on Goodreads or Amazon so other readers can find and enjoy it too!

A Distortion of Fate is book one in the Tapestry Saga, a four-book series. There is so much more to come! You can download my free Tapestry short, *To Win the Affections of a Goddess*, from my website. It's a great precursor to book two, *The Space Between Stars*.

Tapestry Volume 2, Available 2025

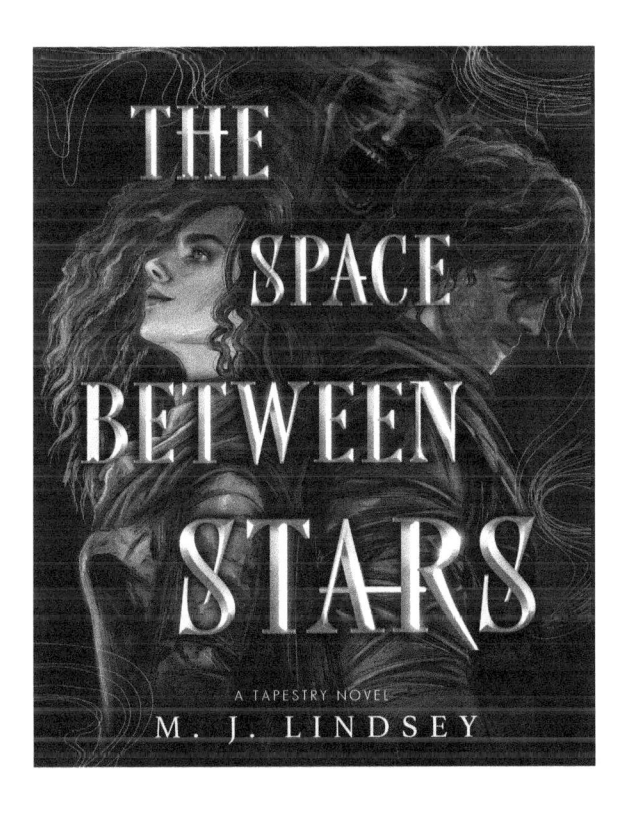

Two Fate-touched siblings from Nelfindar's slums—separated by tragedy, reunited by destiny—devise to destroy the empire that tore them apart.

At a crossroads of duty and destiny, Calver risked the familial oath he'd once built his life upon to keep the last living Ruxian alive. Now, surrounded by his adversaries, he's forced to forge new alliances to protect his charge... Alliances his already broken oaths forbid him to make—until he discovers his sister is aiding the enemy.

Raised as a boy and educated as a criminal mastermind, Fankalo conned her way to Queen of the Raiders by the age of sixteen. At twenty-one, she's amassed a secret army of 'Ghosts', with intent to topple a tyrant and seize his throne. But there is evidence of a traitor among those close to her. When her brother's rogue change of heart threatens everything they've built, he becomes the key suspect.

As the chance to strike revolution grows ever closer, Calver and Fankalo learn how quickly protecting the ones they love can transform into betrayal. With their lives in one hand and frayed loyalties in the other, they'll each have a turn in choosing which card to play. But the reward for any gamble comes at a cost, for those that seek revolution can only pay in blood.

About the Author

M.J. Lindsey is a lifelong fan of science fiction and fantasy. When she isn't writing, she's usually off on a run, out in the garden, gaming with her spouse (who has a very nice beard), or wrangling her three chickens (which are actually tiny humans).

Stay Connected

Website: https://www.threebugspublishing.com/
TikTok: https://www.tiktok.com/@m.j.lindsey
Instagram: https://www.instagram.com/authormjlindsey/
X (twitter): https://x.com/meglindzwrites

Also by M.J. Lindsey

Six of Cups

The Unfortunate Legacy of Mr. Hyde

To Win the Affections of a Goddess

Tapestry Volume 2: The Space Between Stars (2025)

Tapestry Volume 3: A Thimble Full of Blood (2026)

Tapestry Volume 4: TBD

Acknowledgements

I have many hands and minds to thank for the making of this series.

First and foremost, my spouse, for his continual support and my family, in all extensions of the word.

Cindy Sell, Paul & Helena Elias, Emma O'Connell, Eric Donaldson, Allison Marshall, Sarah Henne, Nolan Moore, Derrick Hall, Hank Ryder, Sebastian Hetman, Erynn Snel, Bob Bates, Christina Lefebre for your wisdom and talents.

Caitlyn Ricks, Brittany Healy, Mckenna Hubbard, Alexandra Corrsin, Alex Mitzel, Rel Carroll, Dave, Krisztina Gonda, Arwyn Cunningham, Steven Mack Jr., Susan Rackley, Stephanie Barstow, Simon K, Blayne, and "codename" Morton Zameric (not subtle) for your backing.

Acknowledgements

I have many hands and minds to thank for the making of this series.

First and foremost, my spouse, for his continual support and my family, in all extensions of the word.

Cindy Sell, Paul & Helena Elias, Emma O'Connell, Eric Donaldson, Allison Marshall, Sarah Henne, Nolan Moore, Derrick Hall, Hank Ryder, Sebastian Hetman, Erynn Snel, Bob Bates, Christina Lefebre for your wisdom and talents.

Caitlyn Ricks, Brittany Healy, Mckenna Hubbard, Alexandra Corrsin, Alex Mitzel, Rel Carroll, Dave, Krisztina Gonda, Arwyn Cunningham, Steven Mack Jr., Susan Rackley, Stephanie Barstow, Simon K, Blayne, and "codename" Morton Zameric (not subtle) for your backing.